ABOUT THE AUTHOR

Wendy Lewis was born in West Sussex and grew up enjoying the freedom of the countryside, and the neighbouring farm. Educated at Chichester High School for girls, she went on to a varied career as a Post Office Clerk, Pub Landlady, Dog Breeder, Farmer, Freelance Journalist and mildly successful poet.

She has had many magazine articles published, and five short stories read on local radio.

Her first book *THE RELUCTANT FARMER* has proved very popular.

Rustic Vendetta is her second book.

GW00586911

Cover detail of a wild boar, reproduced from a stained glass window in the Church of St. Martin cum Gregory, York. By kind permission of the Archdeacon of York.

RUSTIC VENDETTA

RUSTIC VENDETTA

by

WENDY LEWIS

MAZARD
West Sussex

Paperback ISBN 0-9545022-1-3

**Published
by
Mazard
5 Heathfield Gardens
Midhurst
West Sussex
GU29 9HG**

My thanks to Mick
for constant help and encouragement.
And love to Tim, who knows about pubs.

Rustic Vendetta

The thin screams of swifts, wheeling and diving on the summer midges above the thatched roofs, were the only sounds to break the silence of the drowsing village square. Heather turned her head slightly as she thought she heard the echo of another scream. But no - it was only the birds. The stone walls of the cottages surrounding the square glowed honey-coloured in the mellow afternoon sunlight which cast a metallic sheen onto the coat of the square's only other occupant, a grey cat, sleeping, bonelessly, astride the wall of the garden beside the pub, paws dangling.

She glanced at her watch as the clock on the square church tower chimed the quarter, rousing a muted 'chack' from a jackdaw which was preening itself on the castellated wall above the clock. From her seat on the bench outside the pub, she could feel herself relaxing into the same state as the cat. A sudden eddy of air wafted the drifting scent of drying hay around her, mixing it with the delicate perfume of roses from the garden behind the cat.

It was for this that she and Alan had deserted the stressful uproar of the city and bought the Shepherd and Dog pub, whose sun-warmed wall now supported her back. She was finding it odd not being able to hear the sound of traffic. She strained her ears for a moment; then, just faintly in the distance, managed to pick up the noise of a tractor engine. The buzz didn't seem to be coming closer, but was continuous, and she remembered driving past a field on the edge of the village where the farmer was turning hay.

A movement from across the square, on the road leading into the village, caught her eye. She idly watched the figure trudging up the hill towards her. The woman's body was bent forward at a sharp angle against the weight of the man in the wheelchair she was pushing. Heather was wondering whether to rouse herself and offer to help the woman up the steepest part of the hill, when raised voices from the couple reached her. They appeared to be having a row. They would have known that she had heard them and might, she thought, be embarrassed if she approached them now.

She would soon learn that embarrassment was not an emotion upon which the residents of North Tegridge wasted much energy. Vindictive violence was more their line.

The man sitting in the wheelchair shouted again. Although they were too far away for her to make out what he was saying, he sounded angry. Life was so different out here in the country that, in the two days she and Alan had been in the village since taking over the pub, she had realised that it might take a little while for them to be accepted. Best not to interfere.

She leaned back against the wall and lowered her eyes to her hands - rather than be seen to be watching the small drama across the square - then froze. Her hands were covered in blood, as was the knife she was holding. She blinked furiously, heart racing, and glanced up at the approaching pair to see if they had noticed. She seemed to be gripped in a cloud of black despair. Looking down again she saw that they were...just her hands...no knife...no blood...nothing unusual. The dark, claustrophobic feeling vanished as swiftly as it had come.

'What the hell was that?' she said quietly.

The woman steered the wheelchair onto the pavement

and stopped beside the spiked iron railings surrounding the churchyard. She straightened up, struggling for breath. Her passenger must have weighed at least fifteen stone.

'Come on,' he complained.

'Just a minute…while I do catch…me breath.' She brushed straggling wisps of greying dark hair off her forehead.

'You can do that at 'ome. I want me tea.'

Heather thought that if Alan ever spoke to her like that, she would give his wheelchair a push and send him back down the hill, on his own. But Alan didn't have, or need, a wheelchair. And could you also stab someone? her mind asked. She looked back at her hands, which were shaking slightly. 'Why am I sitting here in this idyllic place with my mind full of thoughts of violence,' she muttered.

The man looked up at the church clock.

'I'm going to miss me programme. Get a move on, woman.'

'Just a minute,' the woman repeated.

'I'll give you 'just a minute,' he shouted, his voice echoing round the empty square. The jackdaw took off, sweeping across the treetops down to the bottom of the valley. The cat opened one, yellow eye.

Heather was horrified to see the man turn awkwardly in the chair and give the woman a resounding, back-handed crack across her shoulders with a heavy walking stick. She made no sound; just tightened her grip on the chair, lowered her head, and began to push again. As they drew level with her, Heather couldn't stop herself from asking the woman, quietly, if she was all right? She stared at Heather for a second with impenetrable black eyes, before lowering her head and mumbling something in which Heather caught the words 'dance' and 'grave'. Then continued with her burden towards the housing estate on the outskirts of the village.

'You mind your own business,' the man shouted, peering round the woman and waving his stick at Heather.

The latch rattled and the pub door creaked as Alan came out.

'Oh, there you are,' he said. 'I thought you were upstairs doing some more unpacking. I fancied a cup of tea. Isn't it quiet out here.'

'There's too much happening, for my liking,' she said.

Alan stared round the empty square.

'Where, exactly?'

Heather pointed to the couple in the distance.

'He just hit her...with a bloody great stick.' She shuddered and wished she hadn't said 'bloody'. She clenched her dry, empty hands.

'He what?'

'He hit her. As if she was a donkey, or something. If she had been a donkey, the RSPCA would have had something to say about it.'

'Why?'

'Why what?' said Heather

'Why did he hit her?'

'She wasn't moving fast enough for him. I'm not sure I'm going to like it here.'

'There's probably more to it than we know about,' said Alan, trying to sound comforting, but not succeeding. 'I'll go and put the kettle on.'

'That poor woman didn't even complain,' said Heather, staring after the couple who were just turning the corner into the estate. 'We seem to have stepped back into an earlier, more brutal, age.'

'I thought that was what you liked about North Tegridge. Not the brutal bit, but the slower pace of life, the lack of traffic, the fact that we don't have to lock our cars. Come on. We'll be open soon. Our first night as publicans.'

4

'I think I had a sort of premonition,' said Heather, still sitting and gazing unseeingly across the square. 'It was a bit creepy.'

'Oh…er…what d'you mean, exactly?' Alan had always been very dismissive at any hint of there being a supernatural, but he could see something had disturbed her.

'I don't really know…there was a knife, and blood on my hands,' she said, glancing down at them again.

'Well, I wouldn't brood on it. Just be careful when you're cutting stuff in the kitchen,' said Alan, making light of it to try and lift her out of her sombre mood.

Half an hour later, Heather walked across the polished wooden floor of the bar and pulled back the old iron bolts on the heavy oak door which opened onto the village square. She swung the door back and faced their first customer, a puzzled looking ewe with her black tongue lolling out, panting heavily from some recent exertion. As Heather backed away, out of range of the ewe's smelly breath, she realised the square was full of sheep which were being efficiently penned against the front of the pub by a pair of lean, filthy collies. A man in his late fifties rose from the bench against the wall and pushed his way in, past the ewe. He walked over to the bar where Alan stood, hand suspended over the beer pumps, transfixed by the scene framed in the doorway.

Heather regained her composure first. She grinned at Alan.

'Well, you can't say the pub isn't well named.'

'Pint of bitter,' said the man, finding no need to explain the presence of his flock.

Alan, though, couldn't ignore them.

'Nice looking sheep,' he said, trying not to sound like a 'townie' and managing to do just that, as he passed the man his pint.

The man gave him a funny look.

'Just moving 'em,' he said, lowering the level in his glass considerably with one swallow. 'Warm,' he explained, seeing Heather's glance at his glass. He wiped the back of his hand across his mouth. Heather winced as the greying stubble on his chin rasped against the flesh.

A woman came into the bar, the sun behind her picking out red tones in her long black hair. She could have been attractive, but the effect was spoiled by the fact that she obviously didn't care about her appearance. The hair could have done with a wash, and her grubby crimplene trousers and shapeless jumper were covered in hay seeds. On her feet she wore men's boots, which clattered on the bar floor. She frowned as she adjusted her eyes to the gloom of the bar after the sunlight, then she saw the bar's other occupant.

'Your bloody sheep are crappin' all over the square, Dave,' she said. 'People 'ave to walk through there. You wants to 'ave more consideration.'

'That's rich, looking at where you come from; muckiest bloody farm in Devon.'

Alan's eyes locked with Heather's, their glances a mixture of suppressed hysterical laughter and panic. Heather quickly stepped behind the bar.

'What can I get you? Please... both of you have your drinks on the house. You are our first customers.'

'Oh. Right,' the woman looked thoughtful. 'I'll 'ave a Dubonnet and lemonade.'

'Dubonnet and lemonade!' scoffed Dave. 'She usually drinks pints, like the rest of us.'

'Shut up! You rude old bugger.' The woman held out a large square hand and Heather went to put the glass in it before she realised the woman wanted to shake hands. The hand which gripped hers was unsettling in it's ugliness. It was coarse and clumsy, with short thick fingers and square nails. It reminded her of a photograph she had once seen in a book on palmistry - the hand of a murderer.

'Peggy,' the woman introduced herself. 'Peggy Ashley. I used to do the cleanin' 'ere. I come round this evenin' to see if you would want to keep me on. I do a good job, an' I knows where everythin' is.' She raked her fingers through the mass of black hair, dislodging more of the countryside onto the bar floor as she studied Alan with eyes as dark as those of the woman Heather had seen earlier.

'Good lookin' bloke, your 'usband,' she said to Heather, her eyes following Alan as he lifted the bar flap and walked across the room to the window.

'Er, yes.' Heather watched him, too, as he pushed up the heavy sash window, caught the pungent smell of hot sheep, and closed it again.

'Well?' Peggy was leaning across the bar looking questioningly at her.

'What do you think, Alan?' Heather asked.

'Think?' He re-joined her behind the bar.

'Peggy used to be the pub cleaner. She would like to work for us.'

'Yes, fine. If that suits you, darling.'

'Good,' said Peggy, leaving no room for manoeuvre. 'I'll come tomorrow mornin' at eight o'clock. I'll 'ave a pint now… thirsty day…been 'aymakin'.'

'Where's Luke, then?' asked Dave.

'Mendin' the baler. Keeps tanglin' up the twine. 'E's good and mad. Thought I'd get out the way for a bit before 'e decides it's my fault.'

'When you two going to get married, then?'

'None o' your business. Anyway, when they can't find no body you 'ave to wait seven years before they can assume she's dead.'

There was a commotion outside in the square and two sheep

banged against the door as they dived into the bar. Over their heads Heather could see the cause of the problem was a little red dachshund who, thinking he had caught his supper, was gamely hanging onto the hind leg of a struggling sheep while his elderly owner tried to drag him off.

Peggy and Dave caught the two ewes and pushed them out of the bar. And Dave shouted to the woman that he would be round later, to shoot her dog. A swift kick from Dave loosened the dachshund's hold. The farmer whistled to his dogs and began to move the sheep down the road out of the village.

Peggy came back into the bar and finished Dave's pint for him. ''E won't be back now. 'E's takin' them down Small Profits.'

'Small Profits?' said Alan.

''Is farm.'

'Will he really shoot her dog?' asked Heather, who quite liked dachshunds.

'Won't be the first,' said Peggy.

The dachshund's owner came into the bar.

'You don't mind dogs, do you?' she asked, taking the answer for granted as she tied his lead to the leg of a chair. He lay down and proceeded to try to dislodge a piece of wool which had stuck between his teeth, by clawing at it with a front paw. His mistress didn't seem unduly perturbed by the encounter.

'Gin and tonic, please. May as well make it a large one… Anne,' she introduced herself and held out a hand.

'Heather and Alan,' said Heather, shaking the hand, as Alan poured the drink.

'Silly old fool should know better than to leave his sheep unattended in the square, like that. Dreadful temptation to any dog. Can't blame Rudi for succumbing.' Rudi looked up at the mention of his name then went back to picking his teeth.

'How's your father, Peggy?' asked Anne.

''Bout the same. Miserable old bugger. 'E makes out 'e's worse than 'e is, you know. I don't know why Mum puts up with it. 'E can walk better than 'e lets on, but 'e still makes 'er push him about.'

Heather made the link with the dark eyes. It was Peggy's mother who had taken the beating that afternoon. She rather wished they hadn't been so quick to employ Peggy. It would be very hard to be civil to her father, if she ever had to meet him.

As it happened, she was spared this problem. Peggy turned up the following morning and announced that she couldn't start work that day, as she had to take her mother to the undertakers' in town.

'Dad's dead,' she said, with no emotion. 'We've got to sort out the funeral.'

'I'm so sorry. I didn't realise he was that ill,' Heather said.

''E wasn't. Silly old bugger tripped over his walkin' stick and fell down the stairs. 'It 'is 'ead a couple of times on the bannisters, on the way down, and that was that. Blood all over the new stair carpet. Didn't show too much on the bannisters 'cause they'm red anyway.'

'How's your mother?' Heather asked, with genuine sympathy, tinged with horror at Peggy's callous attitude to the death of her father.

'Not too bad. Shocked, you understand; but 'er's a tough old bird. Between you and me, I reckon it's a blessed release - and I don't mean for Dad. He was rotten to 'er. Right. I'll be in tomorrow mornin', then. Anythin' you want in town, while I'm there?'

'No, no thanks.' Heather couldn't consider anything as mundane as shopping at that moment. She was remembering the muttered comment from Peggy's mother in the square the previous afternoon, about dancing on a grave.

CHAPTER TWO

'How're you getting on with Peggy, then?' Anne handed Heather a cup of coffee and pushed a plate of biscuits across the coffee table towards her. Rudi sat at her feet with his head on one side, eyes switching between Heather and the biscuits. Sunlight streamed into the small conservatory at the back of Anne's house, and Heather moved the plastic bag containing her groceries, out of it's defrosting rays. She had met Anne in the village shop and been invited for coffee.

'Peggy? Oh, quite well, really...I think. She's a good worker.'

'She's that, all right. Works like a man down on that farm. Does the milking most mornings before she comes up to you.'

'What's her...what's Luke like?' Heather tried to avoid Rudi's hypnotic glare as she raised a piece of shortbread to her mouth.

'Bit of a brute, really. Handsome, in a coarse sort of way. I heard he bullied his first wife unmercifully. I never met her. She died a year before I came to the village.'

'Yes. What was that about? Peggy was saying something to Dave, the other night, about there not being a body. Talking of Dave and bodies, Rudi's looking remarkably well for a dog that's been shot.'

'Oh, you don't want to take much notice of Dave Fordesh. He's not a bad old boy. Well, not that old, really...he scrubs up quite well. He wasn't looking his best the other night. If you get in with him he may let you go down to Small Profits and pick mushrooms, later on. Best wild mushrooms I've ever tasted. They grow in that field down by the river, just over the bridge. He makes some very good cider, too. Yes, a good person to keep in with,

Dave. Quite a lad in his youth, I'm told.'

'So what happened to Luke's wife?'

'Bit of a mystery, really. I gather it wasn't a happy marriage. When she disappeared the postman said they'd been rowing that morning. Said he'd heard Luke telling her to get out before he killed her. That didn't go down too well at the inquest. Luke had had the digger out that morning, working in the little wood near the farmhouse. Burying a dead sheep, he said, and a dead sheep was all they found. But the police had him in for questioning, several times. Then they found this half-empty bottle of vodka by the river, where she used to go and sit sometimes. She'd been depressed for a while. They found more bottles hidden in the bottom of her wardrobe. Everyone reckoned she'd committed suicide by drowning herself, but they haven't found her body yet. Don't think they will. That was four years ago.'

'How come he and Peggy are together, now?'

'She went down there to cook and clean for him. Wasn't long before she was doing a bit more than that. Then she moved in. They're a match for each other, those two. She can be as fiery as him. Another cup of coffee?'

While Anne went into the kitchen, Heather admired the immaculate walled garden which was filled to bursting with healthy flowers and shrubs set around a small lawn, its perfection marred by a pile of earth and uprooted pansies scattered over the neatly trimmed edge. Through the open window she listened to the stunningly clear song of a thrush, repeating each glorious phrase from its perch on top of the greenhouse in the corner. Apart from the bird, and the crunching of Rudi's teeth on the half biscuit she had just slipped him, she was surrounded by a comfortable silence.

'You seem to have a mole,' she said, indicating the garden as Anne re-appeared with the coffee.

'No. It was him.' She nudged Rudi with her foot. 'He thought he could hear a mouse.'

'You don't know how blissful this silence is,' Heather sighed. 'Where we lived before we were only two miles from the airport. The sound of planes was constant, but this…'

The ear-splitting bang, from what seemed like two inches above her head, sent her instinctively ducking over the coffee table. Her hand caught the edge of the plate of biscuits and the resulting bounty strewn across the carpet exceeded Rudi's wildest dreams. As she straightened up she recognised the roar of an aero-engine disappearing into the distance.

'I'm so sorry,' she said, trying to retrieve the biscuits without losing any fingers to Rudi's busy teeth. 'That plane was much too low, surely?'

'You'll get used to it,' said Anne. 'The air force use the church tower as a navigation point for their Tornado pilots to practice low level flying. You can't hear the damn things coming. First you know is that terrifying blast of sound that has been known to send strong men to their knees. Leave the rest of those for Rudi. I'll get some more.'

'No, really. I must get back. We'll be open soon and I have sandwiches to make for the lunch-time trade. Thank you very much for the coffee.'

'I may be over later for a noggin, if there's nothing on the 'telly' tonight.'

Heather looked round to say goodbye to Rudi, but he had retired to his bed and was guarding a chocolate biscuit with an expression which said 'Keep Off'. She smiled at the steely glint in his eyes.

Back in the pub, she found Peggy sitting at the bar with an almost empty pint glass in front of her. Alan smiled at Heather, looking relieved to see her.

12

'Just a little somethin' to give me strength,' said Peggy, nodding at the glass. 'Got to muck out the boar, this afternoon. We've got some visiting sows comin' to 'im. I 'ate that bloody boar. It's a vicious bugger. But Luke thinks the sun shines out of its 'you know what'. 'E won a first prize with it at the Devon County, last year. Won't 'ave a word said against it. Well, I'd best get on.' She slid off the bar stool and picked up a shopping basket. 'See you tomorrow.'

'Where have you been?' Alan asked Heather.

'Anne asked me in for a coffee.'

'Peggy makes me nervous,' said Alan, watching the tall dark woman stride across the square towards the shop. 'She stands too close to me. Don't smile. It's not funny.'

'Sorry. I'll get some sandwiches on the go for lunch-time. It's such a lovely day we may catch some trade from tourists on their way through to Exmoor.'

CHAPTER THREE

Mr Ashley's funeral was held two weeks later, after a coroner's verdict of accidental death. It was another glorious sunny day, and it seemed it was all Peggy could do to attend the service which, apparently, was interfering dreadfully with the hay-making.

'Could've got the whole of Longacre done, this afternoon,' she muttered to Luke, as they shuffled sideways into the front pew.

Heather heard her from the row behind. She and Alan had felt that they should attend the funeral as some kind of support for Peggy. She was glad they had as there were only a few other people there, and the church looked embarrassingly empty. Not that Peggy or her mother seemed worried by this. Mrs Ashley had had her hair cut and re-styled, and her lightweight black coat looked new. She also looked taller, Heather thought…and happier.

After the service, during which the vicar struggled to find something nice to say about Josiah Ashley, they all trooped out to the newly dug grave in front of the church.

'I wanted it to be round the side,' Mrs Ashley muttered obscurely to Heather, as they skirted other graves beside the path.

As the coffin was being lowered into the ground, Heather looked up to find Mrs Ashley watching her, across the grave, from under the brim of a black straw hat, incongruously decorated with a blood red rose. Their eyes met, and the woman gave Heather a secret, complicit smile that sent a chill skittering across her shoulders. She dropped her eyes instantly to the coffin again, her mind racing with a suspicion to which she knew she could never give voice.

The mourners were leaving the churchyard when Mrs. Ashley caught up with Heather and Alan at the lych gate.

'Thank you for coming,' she said. 'Would you both like to come back to the house for some tea? My name's Mercy, by the way.' She held out her hand to Alan.

'That's very kind of you. I'm sure Heather would like to; but if you'll excuse me I have to change a barrel and get the pub ready to open this evening.'

'I'll kill you later,' Heather muttered to him, as Mercy Ashley turned to extend her invitation to Dave. Shaved, scrubbed up, and out of his working overalls, he was looking very presentable in a, slightly old-fashioned, blue pin-striped suit. He must have been quite a 'looker', in his day, Heather thought.

They all walked up through the village towards the council estate.

'This is Luke.' Peggy introduced her companion to Heather.

His hand was rough and his eyes swept down and up her body, missing nothing. His smile was sardonic and over-confident. Did this man murder his wife? Another chill snaked it's way across her shoulders in spite of the warm sun on her back. Again she mentally cursed Alan for landing her with this unwanted tea-party. Then, shaking off the feeling, she decided to make the best of it. After all, they were all potential customers for the pub. She pulled her hand free of Luke's grasp and turned her attention to Dave, who was walking on her other side. She marvelled at the fact that, because there was so little traffic, they could all spread out across the road: and found herself marching in time to the rhythmic squeaks coming from Dave's highly polished brown shoes.

'Us'll get a good tea,' he said. 'That Mercy's a dab hand at cakes. You wants to get to the cake stall early come féte day.'

'I'll make a note of that,' said Heather, as they filed through Mercy's garden gate and walked up the path to the front door.

The first thing she saw, as they entered the sitting room, was Josiah Ashley's stick, hanging on the wall above the fireplace. The stick with which he'd beaten his wife. The stick which had eventually killed him. The words 'murder weapon' flicked through Heather's mind before she hurriedly suppressed them. What was it doing displayed like that? Peggy followed her eyes.

'It's Dad's stick. Mum 'ung it there. A sort of memento.'

'How er…' the word 'macabre' sprang into her mind, … 'nice,' Heather finished weakly.

'How d'you like North Tegridge, then?' Luke asked her.

'After where we lived before it's so quiet and…'

'Well, we'll have to liven it up a bit for you, won't we?' His raised eyebrow and leer promised all manner of horrors, and she blessed Mercy Ashley's timely intervention carrying a plate of ham sandwiches.

Two ladies came over to Heather and introduced themselves as Jennifer and Josephine. She placed them as probably being in their middle fifties.

'But call us Jenny and Josie; everyone does,' said Jenny.

Heather stifled a wave of hysteria as she faced these two and found she didn't know where to look. There was a strong family likeness between them, which extended to matching squints. Well not so much squints, she thought, but compensatory wandering eyes. Josie's right eye looked away to the right; and Jenny's left eye seemed to be studying Luke on her left hand side. Heather coped by keeping her gaze midway between the two.

'Welcome to the village, my dear,' said Josie. 'We're Mercy's neighbours. So shocking about poor Josiah, wasn't it?'

'Yes. A dreadful thing to have happened,' said Heather. Again she caught the merest lip-twitch of a smile from Mercy, who was listening as she offered Dave the plate of sandwiches. He took three.

'Sixth funeral I've been to this year, and it's only June,' he said cheerfully, stuffing a whole sandwich into his mouth and eyeing a plate of chocolate cake. He reminded Heather of Rudi.

'Pardon?' said Heather. She had missed what Jenny had just said to her.

'The church, my dear. Will you be coming to the church? We could do with a hand at the jumble sales.'

'Ah…I'll have to see how much time I have. We're quite busy at the moment…getting settled in, and so forth.'

'Don't forget we've got a match with the River Inn, next Saturday,' said Luke.

'Match? What sort of a match?' Heather was puzzled.

'Darts, gal. We're going to wipe the floor with them this time. It's an away match. You coming?'

'Shut up! Luke. I don't expect 'Eather's interested in darts.' The sudden intimacy of Peggy using her Christian name - almost - was not entirely welcome. Until that moment she had called her Mrs Pearce, although Alan had been Alan from day two.

'Go on, Heather. You want to watch your own team play, don't you?' said Luke.

'My team?'

'Well, yes…the Shepherd and Dog team.'

'Oh, I see. Perhaps Alan will come. It's more of a man's thing really, isn't it? Darts?'

'If you ask me it's an excuse for a good booze-up,' said Peggy.

'Josiah was a good player before his accident,' said Luke.

17

'Oh. What happened to him? Was that what put him in the wheelchair?' asked Heather.

Jenny and Josie gave up trying to compete with Luke for Heather's attention, and drifted off towards the table and the chocolate cake.

'Him and Mercy had come over to help with the hay-making, years ago now, when my Dad had the farm. The tedder got fouled up with some old wire.'

'Tedder?'

'Hay turner,' Luke explained. 'Anyway, Josiah put Mercy up on the tractor, so's she could pull the tedder forward while he held the wire back, but she couldn't hear his instructions properly over the tractor engine. She thought he'd said to go. He was still bent under the spikes when she started to move forward. He got dragged in under the machinery and all mangled up. It took ages for the ambulance to come out. Nowadays, of course, it would have been the air ambulance helicopter, and they might just have saved some of the damage to his legs.'

Heather wondered if that was Mercy's first attempt at getting rid of her husband. She glanced across at her, and watched as she cut a large slice of chocolate cake for Dave.

'Think I'll have some of that,' said Luke, leaving her in favour of the cake.

'How do you like the village, then? A bit quiet after London, I should think,' said Josie, taking Luke's place, and handing Heather a plate with a piece of cake on it. Not as large a slice as Dave's, she noted.

'Oh, North Tegridge is wonderful. It's so quiet, and everyone is so friendly. Not like where we've come from, where mostly you didn't even know your neighbours. It was getting rough around our area, too. Not really safe for a woman alone at night. Lots of muggings and some murders.' Bit like here, really, she thought, her eyes sliding to the walking stick.

Peggy came across and offered them both some more cake. Heather glanced at her watch.

'No, thank you. It's lovely, but I think I had better be going now. We'll be open soon and I have a few things to do.'

She thanked Mercy and Peggy for the tea. Expressed her condolences again, and said a general goodbye to the others.

'See you later,' Luke called.

Alan was sitting on the bench outside the pub, with a half pint of lager. He indicated a glass of white wine on the bench beside him.

'Thought you might need this. It's still cold,' he said.

Heather plonked herself down on the bench and emptied half the glass in one long swallow.

'I can see I was right,' he said, looking at her glass. 'How did it go?'

'Well, apart from the fact that I have just had tea with a group of murderers in a room littered with their trophies… well, not exactly littered, perhaps. Do you know, Peggy's mother has the walking stick which killed her husband, displayed above the mantelpiece.'

'Bit macabre, that.'

'Exactly what I thought.'

'Who else was there…who are the murderers?'

'A couple called Jennifer and Josephine - they live next door to Mercy. And Dave, and Luke and Peggy,' she swallowed the rest of the wine. 'Can you get me another one of those please,' she said, holding out her glass.

'Who did Jennifer and Josephine murder?' asked Alan.

'Nobody, as far as I know.' Heather looked puzzled for a moment. 'No…you're asking me two questions at once. They were just there. The murderers are Mercy and Luke.'

'Right,' said Alan, nodding his head slowly. 'And they have murdered?'

'Their spouses, of course,' she said.

'Right…I'll just go and fetch the rest of the wine.'

Alan returned with the bottle, and a packet of crisps.

'You eat those,' she said. 'I'm full of ham sandwiches and chocolate cake. Oh, by the way, you did know that you are expected to escort the darts team when they play the River Inn on Saturday, didn't you?'

'No! They don't want me to play, do they?'

'Luke didn't say. He just seemed to think that one of us would be supporting the team, and I think it would be better if it was you. Luke makes me nervous.'

'Yes, Peggy has the same effect on me. She won't be going, will she?'

'How about if I ask her to stay here and help me in the bar for the evening.'

'Brilliant idea.'

Later that evening, feeling pleasantly relaxed from the afternoon wine, Heather was leaning on the bar chatting to a couple of tourists as they studied the bar snacks menu at the table near the door. A small thud and a cheer from one of the two village youths playing darts at the end of the bar, indicated a winning double. Heather suspected that they might be slightly under the legal age for the pints of cider they were drinking, and mentioned this quietly to Dave who was sitting at the bar. He seemed surprised that she was bothered.

'They be all right. They were weaned on cider. Drink it in their high chairs around here, they do. Don't worry. The police never get as far as North Tegridge.'

Alan, who had been fiddling with one of the beer pumps, pulled up the trap door in the floor behind the bar and switched on the cellar light.

'Just going to change that barrel. I think there's something wrong with it. The beer won't clear. Don't fall down the hole.' He disappeared down the steps.

The tourists were just ordering their sandwiches, when there was a sudden scuffling sound in the doorway as a heavily built, elderly man, tripped on the step and stumbled into the bar.

'Right!' he shouted hoarsely, steadying himself with one hand on the back of a chair. 'Nobody move. Get down on the floor.' He followed up these conflicting instructions by swinging round to face Heather. 'Put the money in the bag,' he snarled, making a 'gun' of his hand and pointing two fingers at her.

As she got a good look at the 'gun', Heather began to lower the hands she had started to raise above her head, contrary to instructions. He didn't say 'hands up,' she thought, as the shock began to wear off.

'What bag?' she asked, stamping on the floor to attract Alan's attention.

The old man looked down at his empty hands with a puzzled expression.

'Hello, Colin. What'll you have?' asked Dave.

Colin relaxed his 'gun' hand, and scratched the back of his bristly grey head.

'Pint please,' he hauled himself onto the bar stool next to Dave.

A woman, around the same age as the 'robber', stuck her head round the bar door.

'Is he in here?' she asked, then caught sight of Colin at the bar. She came in. 'There you are! Why didn't you say you were coming in here?'

'Problem?' asked Alan, coming up the cellar steps.

'No. Not now. You just missed an armed robbery - with a hand gun,' she turned a nervous giggle into a cough.

'And you're laughing?'

'Sorry. It's all right now. It was him,' she nodded at the man next to Dave.

'Oh, Colin! Have you been and done it again?' the woman asked. She turned to Heather and Alan.

'He gets a bit confused. Used to be a 'minder' for the Kray twins, years ago, before we retired down here. Sometimes he goes back to the old times in his mind. I'll have a gin and tonic, please. I'm Audrey.'

'I'll get that,' said Dave.

The two youths, after a snigger at Heather's initial reaction, and a mime of raised hands and shooting, had gone back to their darts. The tourists, who had half risen to their feet, measuring the distance between their table and the door, sank down again laughing.

'The Krays! has he ever ki…?' Alan's voice tailed off.

'He's done his time, love. He doesn't like to talk about it. It's all behind us now,' said Audrey, reaching for the glass Heather had put on the bar in front of her.

'I'll just do this snack order,' said Heather, trying to keep a straight face as she pushed past Alan and went into the kitchen. He followed her and found her bent, helpless with laughter, over the sink.

'Quiet country village!' she choked. 'It's filled with murderers and gangsters and mad people.'

'Shhh!' said Alan. 'They'll hear you.'

Heather was still giggling when they went to bed, but slightly less hysterically.

CHAPTER FOUR

'What was wrong with Peggy today?' asked Alan, as he pushed home the top and bottom bolts on the pub door. It was three o'clock and they had just finished a satisfyingly busy lunch-time session.

'She was angry with Luke. He didn't get home from the darts match until after four o'clock this morning. Do you know where he went?' Heather dried the last of the glasses and hung the cloth over the pumps.

'Three of them said something about going on into Exeter, to a club. There was a mention of 'pole-dancing', but you'd better not say anything to Peggy.'

'Don't worry. There's no way I want to get involved with any problems she and Luke may have. Whew!...I could do with a breath of fresh air, love. How about a walk? We could go down the hill and along the river path for a while. It'll be cool near the water.'

'We're almost out of crisps. I think I'd better go to the Cash and Carry. We need mixers, as well. Do you want to come?'

'Not really. I think I'd rather walk than sit in a hot car. Oh! We could do with some butter, too. You don't mind if I don't come, do you? I want to get the smell of tobacco smoke out of my nostrils.'

'Course not. I'll see you later. We should get a dog to take for walks. A big one. I'm not sure I'm happy about you roaming the countryside alone.'

'Oh, Alan. What on earth could happen down here? You hardly ever see a soul outside the village.'

Heather changed into some walking shoes. She waved through the kitchen window to Alan as he backed their estate car out of the small cobbled yard behind the pub, and then watched as Peggy, who'd been walking along the pavement, stooped down beside the car to speak to Alan. After a word or two she went round and climbed into the passenger seat. He threw Heather an agonised look through the window as he raised a hand and drove away. She grinned, wondering whether Peggy had cadged a lift home or persuaded Alan to take her to the Cash and Carry with him. She had certainly been dropping hints in that direction. It seemed she had always done most of her shopping on the last landlord's card.

Heather locked the door behind her and set off across the square and down the hill leading out of the village. Anne and Rudi were coming towards her.

'You should get yourself a dog,' Anne called, advancing up the steep hill as if it wasn't there.

'Alan just suggested the same thing. Hello, Rudi.'

Rudi wagged his tail at her, then spoiled the friendly greeting by diving into the bushes beside the road, in full cry. The grey cat with the yellow eyes shot out and streaked across the square, hurdling the wall into it's own garden, while Rudi tried to strangle himself on his collar.

'You must come round for coffee again soon,' Anne called as Rudi dragged her into the square after the cat.

'Thank you,' Heather waved and carried on down the hill. She stopped at the bridge and leaned on the parapet, looking down into the clear water as it swirled through under the moss-covered stone archway. Long strands of green weed streamed out from the shallow side, where the river curved, but on the inner side of the curve the water was deep and ominously dark. The bank jutted out above this area and was covered with brambles, stinging nettles and stunted willows. Was Luke's wife's skeleton lurking under there, trapped in the tree roots and weeds? She shivered. A large trout swam lazily through the weed on

24

the shallow side. She wondered if trout ate people, dead people. If there had been another path to walk on at that point, she would have taken it; but to reach the next footpath she would have to walk half mile along the narrow road, braving the traffic, such as it was.

Telling herself not to be so silly, she climbed over the stile at the end of the bridge and down onto the footpath by a series of crumbling stone steps with a rickety wooden handrail. She let go of this after a splintering sound came from one of the posts when she put her weight on it. Turning sideways, she descended one step at a time, hoping no-one was watching her clumsiness, and set off along the path on the shallow side of the river.

The land along this bank was part of Small Profits farm, belonging to Dave. There was very little vegetation on this side as Dave's sheep and cows drank from the river and the banks had mostly been trodden down, leaving an attractive little shingle beach between the close grazed grass and the water. It all looked very neat, but natural.

What didn't look natural was a ewe, halfway up the field, lying on her back with her legs pointing to the sky. Heather looked around to see if Dave was in sight anywhere, but she couldn't see anyone. She walked up the field to the ewe, which struggled feebly as she approached.

'You poor old thing. Are you stuck?' Stupid question, she told herself. She walked round it, trying to work out the best way to turn it over. Then taking hold of the front and back legs from the other side of the beast, she pulled. It rocked, then rolled back into the hollow which was trapping it. She tried from the other side, and as it began to come over she grabbed a handful of wool and pulled it upright. It just lay there with its forelegs stuck out in front of it, looking vague.

'Get up!' she said, making 'shooshing' movements with

her hands. It blinked.

'What d'you think you're doing trying to frighten my sheep?'

'Hello, Dave. I wasn't trying to frighten it. I was just re-arranging it. I've always understood that sheep are supposed to have their legs pointing downwards; only she won't get up.'

'On her back, was she? They get like that sometimes. She's probably a bit dizzy,' he said, tucking the ewe's front feet underneath her and kicking her rear end.

The ewe grunted and struggled to her feet, then pitched down onto her nose. Dave pulled her up again and supported her for a few minutes until she looked as if she might be able to stand for herself. Soon, she dropped her head and began to graze ravenously. Heather wondered how long she had been trapped like that? When she asked Dave, he said: 'Not long, I checked them this morning,' but the grass where she'd been lying was very flattened and yellowing.

'What are you doing down here, then?' he asked.

'I just came out to get a breath of fresh air. We've had a busy lunch time.'

'Oh - well, I've got to get on. You can walk where you like on the farm, long as you close the gates...only not if you're with that Anne and her dog,' he added as an afterthought. 'Little bugger puts all my farm cats up trees when they're supposed to be killing vermin.'

'Thank you, Dave. See you this evening?'

'No, not this evening. Tuesdays I go up to Mercy's.' He didn't elaborate on this bald statement.

''Bye, then,' she said, making her way down the field to the footpath. She carried on following the river upstream through two fields, then climbed another stile through an unkempt hedge into a field of sheep. The hedge was so untidy it made her look back to the others on Dave's farm. They were neatly cut and laid, the hawthorn pleached into a sheep proof barrier, and set on tidy banks. Here the banks had been worn away and the hedge was so full of gaps that an orange mesh electric fence had been erected to keep the sheep from straying. She knew instinctively that she was no longer on Small Profits land, and wondered who owned this farm.

She looked up the steep, sloping field, searching for a farmhouse; and caught her breath. Halfway up, its silver grey coat standing out against the dark green background of the hill, was the most elegant horse she had ever seen. It was watching her, ears pricked on the small, neat head; neck arched and silver mane lifting gently in the breeze. It raised its head slightly, sniffing the air and trying to catch her scent; then snorted, tossed its head, and started down the hill towards her, weaving its way through a flock of sheep as it followed a narrow, sheep-trodden path which led to the river. It wasn't until the horse moved that she realised there was something wrong with it. Its journey down the hill was slow and painful as it seemed reluctant to put any weight on its front legs, but its determination to investigate this human further, drove it on.

She waited, suffering every awkward step with it, until it stopped a few yards away from her, and 'whickered' from deep in its throat, nostrils fluttering. She walked up to it and held out a hand towards the velvety nose. It investigated the hand, but was disappointed by its emptiness and dropped its nose down towards her jacket pocket.

'Oh, you beauty! I haven't got anything for you. I've only got a packet of peppermints.'

The horse kept nudging her pocket until it had managed to get across the message that peppermints are what horses like best in the world. She offered it one, which it took carefully from her hand. Obviously it was more practised in peppermint taking than she was in giving. It crunched blissfully and came back for more.

Someone whistled from the top of the hill, and a black shadow streaked across Heather's vision, curling the flock of sheep up into a white ball and sending the ball scudding up across the field towards a figure standing by the gate at the top. She had not realised just how fast a fit border collie could move when working sheep. The man at the top of the hill shaded his eyes as he picked her out, standing by the horse. She gave it the last two sweets and continued along the footpath, but the horse wasn't going to let her go that easily; she still smelled of peppermints. It limped painfully after her.

'Is that Heather?' Her stomach shrank slightly as she recognised the voice shouting her name. It was Luke. She found his earthy machismo and supreme confidence disturbing, and would have preferred to walk on, but that would have been rude; and he had already started down the hill towards her.

'I didn't know you had a horse,' she called.

'Oh, he's not mine. He belongs to a chap who lived over at East Tegridge. Used to race him over hurdles, but he's buggered his legs up. He won't race again. In fact he won't do anything again. The owner has just gone to live abroad, and he left him here for me to find a home for him. But he's no good. Nobody will want a horse with tendons damaged that bad - so he's going to the abattoir with some pigs I'm sending next Thursday.

'You can't!' Heather was appalled.

'They'll give me two hundred 'quid' for him. He's no good to anybody. Nobody's going to keep a horse like that just to look at. He's a thoroughbred. Needs stabling in the

28

winter. It's not cheap to keep a horse you can't ride.'

'Wouldn't he ever get better?'

'Oh, he'd probably mend well enough for light hacking, eventually. Or he may not. We'll never know.'

The horse nudged her pocket where she had pushed the empty sweet packet.

'I'll give you two hundred and fifty pounds for him, Luke. And I will pay you whatever the going rate is for grazing...and stabling in the winter.' Alan was not going to like this, she thought, and wondered if she would be able to keep the horse a secret; realising, just as quickly, that this would be impossible.

Luke's eyes lit up, and it occurred to her that she had committed herself to more visits to Hawkridge Farm than she would have liked.

'Done!' he said, spitting on his palm and holding out his hand to her. As he saw her expression he apologised, and wiped his hand down his trouser leg before offering it again. 'Sorry - habit,' he grinned. She took the hand, gingerly, and quickly dropped it as it began to tighten round hers. 'I'll bring his papers up the pub this evening, and we'll do the deal. What's your old man going to say?'

'I hate to think,' said Heather, turning and running a hand down the horse's smooth neck and wondering if she had just gone mad. 'Does he have a name?'

'He raced as Silver Wolf, but everyone at the trainer's yard called him Jimmy.'

'Jimmy it is then. It suits him. Right, I'd better get back. Alan will be back from Cash and Carry soon.'

'Oh...that might explain something. Peggy didn't come home. Has she gone shopping with him?'

'Erm, I did see her getting into the car. I thought he might be giving her a lift home.'

'No, she didn't come back. That must be where she's

gone. Just hope he behaves himself.'

The thought of Alan 'misbehaving' with Peggy, who terrified him, made Heather smile.

'I'm sure he will,' she said.

She retraced her steps to the stile, as Luke went back up the hill to rescue his sheep from the collie who had been holding them in a tight bunch with excessive enthusiasm. She paused on the top step of the stile, holding back a wayward branch of hawthorn which bore barbs capable of taking the eye out of an unwary walker, and looked back at her new acquisition. He had given up on her and was limping slowly up the field, towards the sheep. Taking a deep breath, and hoping Alan was in a good mood, she swung her leg over the top rail and jumped down onto the footpath.

He was just unloading the last of the boxes of crisps from the car as she arrived in the yard.

'Have a good walk, darling?'

'Lovely thanks. Successful shop?' she smiled with a raised eyebrow.

'Nerve-wracking. I thought she was only after a lift home, but when she found out where I was going she said she'd come too. There wasn't anything I could do about it.'

'I met Luke. He hopes you weren't misbehaving. And, of course, so do I,' she said, with her tongue firmly in her cheek.

'With Peggy! Are you mad ?'

'Well, now you come to mention it, I think I might be. I'll put the kettle on and tell you about it.'

'I know. You've got yourself a dog. Luke's sold you a sheep-dog.'

'Horse.'

'I knew it would be a good id....what?' he exclaimed,

catching the corner of the box of crisps he was carrying on the door jamb, and dropping it.

Heather picked up the box and carried it into the kitchen. She switched on the kettle.

Alan was still standing in the doorway.

'Did you say 'horse'?'

'Oh, Alan. He's so beautiful, and Luke was going to kill him.'

'No…wait a minute…how was Luke going to kill him?…No, I don't want to know. He looks capable of strangling a horse with his bare hands. Why am I joking? Where is this horse? Have you ever ridden a horse?'

'Once or twice when I was younger. I had a friend who had a pony.'

'When you say 'horse', what exactly do you mean?'

'A grey thoroughbred racehorse called Silver Wolf - but you can call him Jimmy.'

'It gets worse…a racehorse! What do we want with a racehorse? Racehorses cost millions of pounds. Why was Luke going to kill it? I know - it's ancient and due for the knacker's yard and you've gone all soft-hearted.'

'He's lame, but he'll get better. It's just that no-one wants to keep him for the months, maybe a year, that it will take to get him sound again.'

'Nor do we.'

'Yes we do.'

'No we don't, Heather.'

'Alan, I can't let him die. Luke was going to send him to the butcher with a load of his pigs. He says I can keep him at the farm. Please, darling. Wait till you see him. He really is beautiful, and he has these soft brown eyes….'

'Forget the tea. I need a drink.' Alan went through to the bar and Heather heard the clink of a glass as he put it under the optic. She heaved a sigh of relief. It was going to be all right. She picked up the local paper, ran a finger down the classified section until she came to the heading 'Horses', and began to study the advertisements for saddles, bridles, rugs and halters. She'd better ask Luke if the previous owner had left any of these things with the horse. He must have a halter at least, or how was he going to catch the horse ready for the butcher. She wondered whether all farmers had this callous streak. Perhaps it was necessary when you had to constantly send animals off to the abattoir.

CHAPTER FIVE

Peggy was swinging the electric polisher around on the parquet floor of the bar, seeming quite happy to complete this task in semi-darkness. The sun didn't reach the windows on that side of the pub until mid-day. Not that she wasn't doing a good job, but Heather switched on the little red-shaded wall lamps, anyway, and for the first time paid proper attention to the small framed sampler which hung in the far corner. She lifted it down and carried it over to the window to study the detail. It was an exquisitely worked piece depicting what looked like a coat of arms. A boars head with prominent tusks, above which floated two crossed daggers. Under this picture was an odd couplet. 'Twixt wielded steel and razor tooth. Be only one who knows the truth.' Down in the right hand corner the sewer had worked the initials RB.

Peggy switched off the rattling polisher and rubbed a slight smear off the floor with a yellow duster. The dark wood gleamed with years of polishing.

'Do you know what this means, Peggy? I hadn't noticed it before. It must always have been hung out of the light; the silks have hardly faded at all.'

'Well, it's not that old, really. Luke's wife what killed 'erself made it. She was good at sewin', Rose was. You should see some of the kneelers she did for the church.'

'What does the rhyme mean?'

'Oh, don't ask me. She was a bit strange in the 'ead some times. Reckoned she could see the future. Must have been the gypsy in 'er. She used to tell fortunes at the féte. Come to think of it she once told me I'd be having a lot to do with animals. Strange that. D'you think she knew I'd be doing the milking most mornings?' Then Peggy laughed.

33

'Mind you, she might have meant Luke. He can be a bit of an animal at times.'

Heather didn't think she wanted to know how Luke's animal nature manifested itself, and tried to take the conversation back to the subject of Rose.

'She was a gypsy?'

'Well, story was she was some kind of foundling. She worked some roses on the design, like they have in the gypsy caravans. See?' Peggy pointed a stubby finger at the picture.

'So there are.' Heather gazed at the tiny yellow roses. 'What's it doing hanging up in the pub? Shouldn't Luke have it?'

''E didn't want it. After she died, 'e sent it to the jumble sale and the last landlord, Bill, bought it. I guess 'e forgot to take it with him. Keep it if you want it. 'E's forgotten it by now.'

Heather replaced the sampler on its hook, noticing the evil gleam that Rose Butler had managed to work into the boar's slanting eyes. It really was a very accomplished piece of needlework.

She was showing the sampler to Alan at breakfast next morning, when an uncomfortable thought struck her.

'Peggy said Rose Butler could see into the future. D'you think she left this as a sort of clue as to what happened to her?'

'What d'you mean? What have pigs and daggers got to do with filling yourself with vodka and jumping in the river?' Alan asked.

Heather's train of thought was momentarily deflected as she visualised Rose taking a flying leap off the bank into the swirling water.

'I don't think you'd jump…you'd sort of fall if you were drunk,' she said thoughtfully.

'Does it really matter?'

'No. What I mean is, perhaps she didn't fall into the river. Perhaps she didn't drown. What if Luke stabbed her with a dagger and then fed her to the pigs?'

'Pardon!'

'I saw it in the newspaper once; where somebody fed a murder victim to the pigs. Pigs'll eat anything. That bacon you're eating could have some of Rose going into it's make-up.'

Alan moved a rasher of bacon to the side of his plate and cut into a sausage. Heather smiled.

'Those are made out of pigs, as well.'

'Why don't you start thinking about how you are going to look after a racehorse? And are we going to have any toast this morning?' Alan pushed his plate away, his breakfast half eaten, muttering something about eating alone in future.

Luke came in at lunch-time carrying an old halter which would have fitted a brewery dray-horse.

'I'll throw this in as well,' he said. An obvious hint that he had come for his money.

'Will you take a cheque?' Heather asked.

'Cash'd be better,' said Luke.

'In that case you'll have to wait until I've spoken to Alan,' said Heather, finding a crack in the leather of the halter he had handed her, which went most of the way through the strap and could break any moment.

'Do you want to pay for the grazing by the week or the month?' he asked.

Alan sighed and went out to the kitchen to fetch some more sandwiches for the refrigerated display cabinet on the bar.

'Heather! Are we out of prawn sandwiches?' he called from the kitchen.

'Just coming,' she said. 'Luke, I'll come down to the farm and sort this out with you this afternoon. Alan isn't so keen on the idea of me owning a horse.'

'Well, it doesn't matter to me if you want to change your mind. I can still send him off with the pigs.'

Alan, coming back into the bar at that moment, heard the word 'pigs' and gave Luke a speculative look, which in turn made Luke frown in puzzlement. Heather stepped in hurriedly.

'I do want him. I'll be down with the money later.'

'Hurry up, darling. I've got two prawn sandwiches ordered,' said Alan.

Heather dashed into the kitchen and hurriedly made the sandwiches. As she was cutting off the crusts, the knife slipped and sliced a sliver off the side of her left index finger which began to bleed profusely. She stuffed the finger in her mouth whilst she plated and garnished the sandwiches, one-handed, then called Alan to fetch them.

'Good God!' What have you done?' he said. Blood was now covering both her hands and dripping on the floor as she carried the knife to the sink and turned on the cold tap.

'Cut myself rushing those sandwiches. It'll stop in a minute.' She dropped the bloody knife into the sink and held her hands under the tap.

It was more like twenty minutes before she had the bleeding under control, and Alan was beginning to suggest a visit to the surgery.

'Well,' he said. 'There's your premonition come true.'

'So it has!' she said, with relief. She hadn't wanted to admit to herself that the strange vision in the square, the day before Josiah had died, had been troubling her.

After closing time that afternoon, Heather, her finger well bandaged, snatched a quick sandwich and persuaded Alan to give her some cash out of the till to pay to Luke for the horse.

'I won't be long,' she said.

She drove down the hill and over the bridge. Halfway up the hill the other side she passed the track leading to Small Profits farm, belonging to Dave. The next turning on the left was signed 'Hawkridge', in cracked, almost illegible, lettering on a tatty board nailed to an oak tree. The remains of a five barred gate drooped from its hinges onto the grass verge, embracing nettles and a small hawthorn tree which had grown through it since anyone had last tried to close it.

The car bumped slowly along the pot-holed track as Heather steered from side to side to try to get the smoothest ride. Rounding a slight bend she snatched in her breath and stood hard on the brakes, the car slid sideways and stopped.

In the middle of the track, lying in the sunshine, was a ewe with a long tatty coat and a cauliflower ear. Standing beside her was a lamb. Heather unclenched a hand from the steering wheel and tooted the horn. Neither of the sheep moved. She straightened the car up and edged towards them. The ewe got up and stamped a front hoof threateningly, then lowered her head and ran at the car, hitting the offside wing with a thump that Heather felt sure would have left a dent. She opened her door and swung it backwards and forwards, hoping to frighten the ewe, who promptly charged the offending door with the enthusiasm of a Spanish fighting bull. Heather slammed the door shut just in time, with the skill of a matador snatching away the cape.

The ewe's momentum carried her beyond the car, and her lamb, losing sight of its mother, 'baa-ed' and trotted after her. The two wandered on along the track towards the road. Assuming that the locals would be quite used to finding stock loose on the roads, Heather decided against getting out of the car to try to herd them back. She could still feel the jarring thump the ewe had given the car. Luke could use his dog to retrieve them.

Another curve and a few more potholes took her past the end of a long stone and cob barn and into the farmyard, where her car was once more attacked; this time by a cock pheasant who seemed determined to drive off his reflection in the car's newly-polished body-work.

Luke came out of the house and laughed at the bird, who was now totally enraged at the sight of a rival pheasant threatening him with lowered head and a ruff of raised neck feathers.

'He lives here,' he said. 'Came in when they was shooting, last winter, and decided to stay. Feels it's his duty to attack everything that comes into the yard. Postman won't get out of his van any more. I've had to make a letter box so that he can drive by and drop the mail in through the van window.' He pointed to a red wooden box nailed to the door of the barn.

Heather began to laugh.

'Is everything on your farm this dangerous?' she asked, and immediately wished she hadn't as Luke arched an eyebrow.

'Depends what you'm looking for?'

She ignored this remark and climbed carefully out of the car, glancing round for any more psychopathic livestock.

'You've got a ewe and lamb out on the road,' she said.

'I don't think so...whereabouts?'

'She was up on the drive when I came in.' Heather ran her hand over the bumper. There was a small dent, but it should push out all right.

'Ugly old ewe...thick ear?' he said.

'Yes.'

'She belongs to Moor Farm, down the road. He can't keep her in. Doesn't bother any more. Reckon she gets tupped by somebody else's ram every year, and never at the right time. She's been away from her own flock so long they don't recognise her, and when she gets in with another farm's ewes, they soon see her off.'

Heather began to feel a bit sorry for the friendless, wandering ewe, but not sorry enough to offer her a home - like Jimmy.

'I've brought the money for the horse,' she said.

'Come in. Peggy's doing some baking. She'll make us a cup of tea.'

He led her into the largest kitchen Heather had ever seen. Stretching along part of one wall was an eight foot long dresser carrying china of various shapes and sizes. On the opposite side of the room was a huge solid fuel range which was pushing out a steady warmth and a wonderful smell of baking cakes. The centre of the kitchen was taken up by a twelve foot long refectory table, with benches running along either side. There were only two small windows, one at either end of the room, set into the two foot thick cob walls, and Heather had to adjust her eyes to the gloom after the sunlight outside.

'My goodness! What a huge kitchen, and a wonderful old table.'

'Yes. Back in grandfather's day we needed a table that big to feed the workmen. The place was much busier then. Didn't have today's machinery. Needed more people to work the farm. Come hay-making, with the men and their wives and families helping, this table used to be full,' said Luke. 'Sit down. I'll get the papers for the horse.'

Heather sat at the end of the long table, watching Peggy take a tray of perfect rock cakes out of the oven, and set them out on a wire rack on the table to cool.

'Cup of tea?' Peggy asked, dumping the baking tray into an enormous butler's sink, where it sizzled as the hot metal touched the water.

'Yes, please.'

'Give you a bun, in a minute - when they've cooled down, a bit.'

Luke was searching through some dog-eared envelopes in a small desk in the corner.

'Ah! Here it is.' He put the rest of the envelopes back in a pigeon-hole, lifted up the flap of the desk and locked it. Peggy put a mug of tea down in front of Heather.

'D'you want one, Luke?' Peggy asked.

'Yes.' He handed the envelope to Heather. It appeared to contain Jimmy's pedigree.

She opened her handbag and took out the money, while Luke wrote something on a pad he had brought over from the desk. He tore off the sheet and pushed it across to her. She read ' One seven year old, grey thoroughbred gelding. Silver Wolf. Sold as seen. £250.'

'You don't want the vet to look at him, do you?' he asked.

It hadn't occurred to Heather to get the horse vetted. I haven't a clue what I am doing, she thought, as she said: 'No,' and handed the money to Luke. He signed the paper and gave it back to her.

'You sign mine,' he said, pushing an identical copy across to her.

They agreed a price for grazing, and stabling in the winter.

'I'll show you the stable,' Luke said, picking up two rock cakes and handing one to Heather as they got up from the table. 'Oh, I'll be going out tonight,' he said to Peggy as they left the kitchen.

Heather saw Peggy's mouth tighten, but she didn't say anything.

''Bye, 'Eather. See you tomorrow.'

''Bye. Thanks for the tea - and this,' she held up the warm rock cake and smiled her thanks as she followed Luke out into the yard.

'Bit mucky. Mind where you walk,' he said.

Heather picked her way round the steaming dung heap, where the pheasant and several chickens were now scratching the dirty straw out across the yard and chortling quietly to each other. The pheasant ignored her. Luke led her around the end of the barn where there were two lean-to stables. Also, along the back wall of the barn, were a row of pig sties which, judging by the snuffling grunts and squeals, all seemed to be occupied. Heather had stopped in front of the stables, but Luke turned and beckoned her on. He pointed to a single stable in the far corner of the field beyond the barn. It looked very dilapidated.

'It'll have to be that one,' he said. 'The horse hates pigs. You'll never get him past them into one of these. It's quite snug over there. The wood keeps most of the wind off.'

There were tractor tyre marks running across the field and into the wood. Heather wondered if that was where they had suspected Luke of burying his wife. The lonely stable across the field looked a bit creepy against the solid backdrop of dark trees.

At that moment a huge pig, in the sty next to Heather, reared up and hooked its front feet over the low wooden gate. She jumped and spun round. Luke laughed. The pig sniffed the air, trying to get her scent, its mouth slightly open exposing unpleasantly sharp teeth. She decided Jimmy wasn't so stupid after all.

'Isn't he something?' said Luke, scratching the beast behind the ears. 'Best Large White at the Devon County this year. Could even make Champion next year; he's come on a treat.'

'Oh, yes. I heard about him. Peggy told me.

Congratulations.'

'He likes you. Give him a scratch.'

'Erm, maybe not just now,' said Heather, backing away.

'You'll need straw and hay. It's all in the barn. Help yourself. We'll sort out the money for that later. The horse is still in the river meadow. He seems quite happy with the sheep. If it's all right with you I'll move him round with them as they change fields.'

'Yes. That's fine. I'll just go down and introduce myself to him as his new owner.'

'I'd better get back. Got to go and buy some more pig nuts,' said Luke.

Heather had a short conversation with Jimmy, during which he consumed an entire packet of mints. When he finally gave up willing her to magic some more and wandered off across the field, she made her way back up to the yard, keeping a wary eye out for the pheasant. She spotted him watching her from the top of the dung heap, but he held off the attack until her car began to move. Her last sight of him was in the rear view mirror as his talons, dripping dung sodden straw, just missed tearing off the rear windscreen wiper.

'What on earth have you been doing?' Alan asked, as she got out of the car in the pub yard.

'I've been down to Hawkridge - to pay Luke. I told you.'

'No, the car...look at the car. I'd just cleaned it. It's covered in mud, and there's filthy straw all over the back.' He walked round the car. 'There's a scratch on that door. Looks like claw marks, and...look...there's a dent in the wing. Have you had an accident?'

Heather began to giggle. 'I don't know where to start.' She put a hand over her mouth as she looked at the car, and tried to control herself. 'I'll clean it. And it's only a small dent. There's a ewe somewhere with a headache.

And Luke's farmyard is home to a sort of Don Quixote of pheasants.'

'You're going to enjoy living here, aren't you? This place is just daft enough to suit you,' Alan said, shaking his head.

CHAPTER SIX

Something woke Heather, although she couldn't quite pin down what it was. Footsteps? She listened. The only sound was Alan's quiet breathing beside her. Moonlight was streaming into the bedroom through a gap in the curtains. The bedside clock showed two a.m. She slid quietly out of bed, so as not to disturb Alan, and went along the landing towards the bathroom. It was such a bright night that there was no need to switch on the light. She paused for a moment to gaze out of the landing window which overlooked the silent village square, starkly lit by the cold white light from a full moon, and slashed across with inky shadows thrown by the houses and the yew trees in the churchyard.

The front of the church was plainly illuminated. Heather's gaze dropped from the solid square tower, to the pathway leading to the great studded oak doors. Mist was rising from the ground and swirling to a height of about three feet.

A movement on the left of the path caught her attention. She watched in cold horror as Josiah Ashley rose, naked, from his grave, stretched out his arms and slowly began to circle on top of the mounded earth. His macabre dance became faster and faster as he stamped his feet in a wild tarantella. As he began to slow down again, Heather got the strangest impression that Josiah had grown breasts. Her hands were gripping the window ledge and she was frozen to the spot. Then, to add to the horror, another ghost arose from behind a large tomb on the other side of the path, and attacked the first. They sank, struggling, into the mist above Josiah's grave, and disappeared.

I'm dreaming. I have to be dreaming. This is a nightmare, thought Heather, blinking hard as she looked

44

down at her hands and willed them to let go of the window ledge. She looked again at the churchyard and, as the mist cleared for a moment, realised that the ghosts had not vanished back into the grave. They were still there, lying on top of it. Two white arms were raised towards the moon. No, not arms, her sluggish brain told her. There were feet on the end of them.

She released the grip of one of her hands and pushed the window open slightly, catching a series of soft grunts on the still air, followed by a quavering moan of 'graaave'.

She rushed back to the bedroom.

'Alan! I've just seen Josiah Ashley rise from his grave and...and...Alan, wake up!'

'Mmmm?'

'I've just seen two ghosts copulating in the churchyard!'

'Mmmm', Alan turned away from her and pushed his face into the pillow.

'Alan!'

'Go back to sleep, darling. You've been dreaming,' he muttered.

'I haven't. I...' she gave up. Alan was snoring gently.

Shivering, she drew on her dressing gown and went back to the landing window. The churchyard was quiet and so was the square, but through the curtain of mist she thought she could make out a figure hurrying up the road towards the council estate.

As she looked the other way, along the road leading out of the village, there was another form striding away through the mist, thicker here as it rose from the river. Were these her ghosts? She was rather glad Alan hadn't woken up. But who on earth would choose the churchyard, in full view of the village, to hold their tryst.

She ran the scene through her mind again; and as she did so, Mercy's words came back to her. The muttered words

Heather had caught as Mercy pushed Josiah's wheelchair past her in the square, the day before he died. 'Dance' and 'Grave'. It was Mercy! Fulfilling her promise. With a vengeance.

'Some dance!' Heather muttered, as she got back into bed, trying to control a smile which didn't feel quite appropriate. But who was the man? 'Tuesday,' her mind said. 'Tuesdays I go to Mercy's,' Dave had told her.

'No,' she said. But she knew it *was* him. That figure walking away down the hill had been on his way home to Small Profits. It wasn't 'graaave' that the ghostly Mercy had moaned. It had been 'Daaave!'

At this Heather began to giggle. Alan reached out in a semi-conscious state and tried to turn off the alarm clock.

'It can't be morning yet, it's pitch dark,' he said. 'Was that the clock? What time is it? Were you laughing? You woke me up.'

'It's about half past one.'

'Oh God! Why don't you take a sleeping pill, or something?'

'It was Mercy and Dave,' she said.

'What was Mercy and Dave?'

'In the churchyard…doing 'it' on Josiah's grave.'

'Doing what?'

'Making love.'

'Don't be disgusting. They're old!' He propped himself on one elbow to look at her.

'That's unkind, Alan. They're not that old. I think people their age have been known to still have a sex life.'

'Not in the churchyard at half past one in the morning,' he said.

'How do we know? How often have we kept watch on the local churchyards in the dead of night?'

'You're mad. Tell me about it in the morning.'

....

Peggy turned up to work, the next morning, with two boxes of large brown free range eggs.

'I've brought you some eggs. I've got Mum's, too. I just rang 'er to say I was bringin' them up, but she said not to bother as she was 'avin' a lie-in. Said she'd meet me 'ere at lunch-time for a drink. What you grinnin' at?'

'Nothing,' Heather dragged her face into a serious expression. 'Just something Alan said at breakfast...about the government,' she floundered.

'Oh,' said Peggy. 'Could 'ave done with a lie-in myself, this mornin'. Was awake half the night waitin' for Luke to come back. Said 'ed been to an NFU meetin' in Exeter, then some of them 'ad gone on to a club, after. Don't know 'ow 'e got back without bein' arrested. 'E bloody weren't sober.'

She picked up the box of polish and dusters and went off into the bar, muttering to herself.

'Seems half the village were out on the 'toot', last night,' Heather said to Alan, as he passed her. He was carrying a crate of tonics into the bar.

'Well, they weren't in here. Yesterday's takings were pretty dismal.'

'No, I mean *after* closing time. Luke was getting legless in Exeter until the wee small hours, and then Mercy...'

Alan interrupted her. 'You dreamt that. And even if you didn't I think we'd better drop the subject. Don't forget all these people are our customers. It's best we ignore their private lives - however bizarre,' he added with a grimace.

'You're a bit grumpy, this morning.'

'Is it any wonder? I hardly got any sleep with you rampaging about all night.'

'I'll get on with making some sandwiches,' said Heather,

burying all the other answers to this statement which were struggling to leave her lips.

Mercy came in at lunch-time.

'Where's Peggy? Out the back? Tell her I'm here…two halves please, Heather.' She yawned hugely. 'I'm so tired today…must be the weather.'

Heather struggled with her expression, while Mercy suddenly narrowed her eyes, studying Heather's face closely. She seemed to come to a conclusion. The corners of her mouth twitched.

'Told you they should have put it round the side,' she said.

Heather choked back a giggle, and suddenly they were both laughing. Mercy put a hand on Heather's.

'Our little secret,' she said.

'Cross my heart,' said Heather. 'Those drinks are on me.'

CHAPTER SEVEN

Heather came out of the shop a few days later, and bumped into Anne.

'Come and have a coffee. Alan and I were just about to stop for one. Bring Rudi, we might find the odd biscuit for him,' Heather bent down to pat Rudi, whose eyes were flicking round the square in search of the grey cat. He glanced up at her and gave a quick wag of his tail. Heather could see the cat. It was sitting on the roof of a garden shed, well out of reach, glaring at Rudi with it's tail twitching angrily.

'I was coming to see you, anyway,' said Anne. 'I'm collecting for the jumble sale.'

The milk tanker rumbled through the village and Anne nodded towards the driver.

'That's the bloke who ran off with Dave's wife.'

'Dave doesn't seem too heartbroken about it,' said Heather.

'No, well, he's always had several other women on the go. He was quite a handsome lad in his youth. He's in that photo of the cricket team, hanging up in the bar.'

They crossed the yard and went into the pub kitchen which was full of the rich smell of the lasagne Heather was cooking for bar meals.

'Hear you've bought a horse,' said Anne, as she sat at the kitchen table and accepted a mug of coffee from Alan.

'Not me. This loony mare,' he said, smiling at Heather.

'Thank you, darling…I suppose that's a shade better than being called a stupid cow.'

'Have you done much riding?' Anne asked.

'Virtually none. I just couldn't let Luke kill him. He was going to send the horse off with some pigs, to the butcher. He's a cruel so and so, that Luke. Jimmy's terrified of pigs.'

'Jimmy?'

'The horse. That's his pet name,' said Heather.

'A racehorse, no less,' said Alan.

'You're going to race him?' Anne asked, her eyebrows raised.

'No...it's a pet name for a pet horse, at the moment. I may ride him when his legs get better - if I can pluck up the courage. He's very lame. Luke said he bowed the tendons when he was racing,' said Heather.

'I used to ride, in my youth,' said Anne.

'Oh, that's good. Now I know where to come to for advice,' said Heather.

There was a bang and the sound of breaking glass from the bar, accompanied by some very unladylike language from Peggy. The door from the bar to the kitchen crashed open as she stormed through.

'Bloody dustpan and brush,' she was muttering, making for the cupboard where the cleaning materials were kept. 'Oh, sorry! Sorry, Anne! Didn't know you was all in 'ere. I've broke an ash tray.' She took the pan and brush and went back into the bar.

'What's the matter with Peggy? She seems a bit flustered,' said Anne.

'She's not a happy bunny, today,' said Alan.

'I think maybe Luke is staying out too late, too often,' said Heather quietly.

'That wouldn't surprise me. Now - have you got anything you can let me have for the jumble sale?' said Anne

'Come upstairs and I'll have a look,' said Heather.

'Not my tweed jacket,' said Alan, rinsing his coffee cup and standing it upside-down on the wooden draining board. 'See you later, Anne.' He pushed open the door to the bar, then stood back to allow Peggy through with a dustpan full of glass.

'You running a stall at the jumble on Saturday, Anne?' Peggy asked.

'Yes.'

'You see any nice warm winter coats, stick one under the table till I gets there. Doesn't have to be the 'eight of fashion. The cows don't mind what I wear. And I'm sick of dressin' up for a bloke what don't notice.'

'All right.'

'Thanks,' said Peggy, as she went out of the back door and shot the contents of the dustpan vigorously into the metal dustbin, banging the lid back on with unnecessary force.

'If I were Luke, I would think twice before upsetting Peggy,' said Heather quietly. 'Come on. We'll go upstairs.'

Anne tucked Rudi under her arm and followed her up onto the landing, stopping to look out of the window.

'You've got a good look-out position here. You can see what everybody round the square's doing.'

'Yes,' said Heather, biting her lip, horribly tempted to confide in Anne about the graveyard romp. But she had promised Mercy. She put the picture of that night out of her mind.

At that moment Rudi spotted the cat on the roof, and began to bark furiously. The cat's head shot up with horror at the sound of a dog coming from above it. It pinpointed the noise, then jumped from the shed onto the cottage roof, shot up the tiles and crouched by the chimney. Anne put Rudi down, where he proceeded to demolish the landing wallpaper whilst trying to jump back onto the window ledge. She put his lead on and pulled him away.

'Will the cat be all right? D'you think they'll have to get the fire brigade to get it down?' asked Heather.

'Hope not. The cat could die of exposure before they

arrive. Years ago, and I mean years ago, there were three cottages up at the end of the village - where the council estate is now. They were thatched, and they caught fire. The only fire engine was in town, ten miles away, and it was horse-drawn. By the time they had collected the third horse, who was out pulling the roller on the cricket pitch, and galloped the ten miles, the cottages were burned to the ground.'

Heather laughed, and was relieved to see the cat gingerly making its way back down the roof, towards the shed. She opened the wardrobe, and hesitated before pulling out a pin-stripe suit she had bought three years before, in the days when 'power dressing' for women was all the rage. She had only worn it once and Alan had laughed at the concept; rather nervously, she thought. There wasn't going to be much call for it down here. The powerful women down here wore thorn-proof trousers and wellingtons bought at the farmers' co-operative shop.

'I'm sorry, Anne. I don't seem to have much. I had a good clear-out before we moved.'

'That'll be fine. Every little bit helps,' said Anne.

They went back downstairs and Heather put the suit into a bin liner for Anne, who left dragging a reluctant Rudi. He had grown roots by the cooker and was trying to tell Heather that dachshunds are extremely fond of lasagne.

Peggy came through from the bar into the kitchen, and began to put the cleaning materials away in the cupboard.

'Would you like a coffee before you go, Peggy?' Heather asked.

'Wouldn't mind.' Peggy sat down at the table with a sigh that said: 'ask me what's wrong.' So Heather did.

'It's Luke. We used to get on really well, but somehow 'e...oh, I don't know...'e treats me as if I were a nuisance. 'E don't tell me where 'e's going, or when 'e'll be back.

It's as if I don't really matter no more. Still expects me to keep 'ouse and do the mornin' milking…for nothin'. But 'e don't seem to want, well, you know, the bed bit, any more…and I misses that. Main reason I moved in in the first place.'

'Have you asked him what's wrong?'

''E just says, 'nothin', and tells me to stop naggin'.'

She was distracted by the sound of bolts being drawn back in the bar as Alan opened the pub door to let in the lunch-time customers. There was a buzz of chatter and Heather glanced through the open kitchen door to see Dave, Audrey and Colin enter together.

'I better go.' Peggy got up and rinsed her mug.

'Any time you want to talk, you know where I am,' said Heather. She was to regret that remark over the coming months.

She turned off the oven and opened the door slightly, leaving the lasagne inside to keep warm, and put some plates on the rack above the cooker before joining Alan in the bar.

There was quite a jolly party in progress, with Dave, Audrey and Colin looking very flushed, and laughing uproariously at a 'not very funny' joke Alan had just told. Even he looked slightly surprised at the result of his tale.

'Was that one of the old elephant ones?' Heather asked quietly.

'Yes. Perhaps they never reached down here in the wilds,' he said.

'Oh yes they did,' roared Dave.

'Oh no they didn't,' shouted Colin.

'Don't mind them,' Audrey giggled. 'Dave's just tapped the first barrel of last year's cider, and we've been having a tasting session. Blimmin good stuff - even better than last year, Dave…and that was good.'

'Yes. It's that same secret blend of apples my father and grandfather used. Though I says it, as shouldn't, it's bloody good stuff. Fordesh Tanglefeet Cider - famous round these parts. You two'll have to come down and sample a glass or two,' he nodded at Heather and Alan. 'In fact, why don't we all go back there this afternoon, after you've closed? I don't think I'd better get on the tractor after this morning's session. Don't want to go the same way as Dad.' There was a moment's thoughtful silence from the three customers.

'What happened to your father?' Heather eventually asked. Visions of another horrific village death colouring her thoughts.

'Silly old bugger got smashed...'

'Oh, how awful,' said Heather.

'No! Not smashed,' Dave said. 'Smashed...drunk...out of his skull he was, with Luke's dad. Spent most of the afternoon cider tasting. Then they decided to have a competition to see who could get the little old Ferguson round that steep sheep meadow, the quickest. Dad went first. Got halfway along the top of the hill; hit a rut too fast and rolled it. Killed two of them on the way down.'

'Killed both of them?' Heather gasped. 'Does anyone die a natural death in this village?'

'Pardon?' said Dave.

'You said they both died.'

'No! Not Dad...two of the ewes. Dad was all right. Tractor was never much good after that though.'

At two thirty, Alan closed the pub, and Heather cleared away the plates from the bar table used by Dave, Colin and Audrey, who had decided to have lunch there as a foundation for the afternoon's cider sampling. Then they all set off towards Small Profits. The road was so quiet they were able to spread out and walk abreast down the hill.

They paused on the bridge and leaned on the parapet to stare at the river. Alan thought he could see a trout, and Dave told him he was welcome to fish from his bank, if he wanted. Alan grinned at Heather.

'If you are going to start riding, and possibly hunting, maybe I should take up fishing.'

'I wonder if she *is* still hereabouts,' said Audrey thoughtfully, gazing at the dark, overgrown, deep stretch of the river which had made Heather shiver the first time she saw it.

'Who?' asked Alan.

'Rose, Rose Butler,' said Audrey. 'Poor thing.'

'No. We've had some very wet winters since then,' said Dave. ' She'm probably washed right out to sea. I liked Rose. Went out with her for a bit when we was young. Terrible shame for her to end like that.'

The stone cider barn at Small Profits was comfortably cool after the warmth outside. The tiny window and high beams were draped with centuries old, filthy cobwebs. Sunlight shafted through the window into the gloom, struggling to penetrate the haze of dust motes, and dimly lighting the huge shadowed casks standing on their wooden cradles.

'These barrels once brought sherry in from Spain,' said Dave. 'That's what helps to give the cider its flavour.'

Just inside the door stood two great oak presses, at least eight feet high, waiting quietly for the autumn harvest. Next to them, bolted to the floor, Dave pointed out the apple crusher. A long wooden chute down which the apples tumbled to be crushed by a fearsome, nail-studded drum with its drive wheel linked by a canvas belt to a small petrol engine. The belt was stained orange by years of apple juice, as was a nearby pile of sacking into which the crushed apple was folded before being stacked under the press.

In the comfortable summer silence of the barn, the only sound was the chittering of hunting swallows, and an occasional flutter of wings as one swooped through the wide barn door and up into the rafters, where they had a nest.

Dave took some half pint mugs out of a low cupboard that stood just inside the door, and turned the wooden tap on the nearest barrel. The twisting golden stream flowing from it, into the mug, was lit by a beam of sunlight which had fought its way through the small, dirty window.

'That looks good, Dave,' said Alan. Then, sweeping a hand round the barrels lined against the walls on all sides: 'How much have you got here, altogether?'

''Bout three thousand gallons.'

'What do you do with it all?' Alan asked.

'You can have some if you like. I supply the 'Black Dog' and the 'Smugglers Inn'. Used to do your pub as well until I had a bit of an argument with Bill. He reckoned it was my sheep wrecked his flower tubs, out the front of the pub. Wouldn't have it that I hadn't taken them through the village that day. I saw the mess the tubs were in, but it wasn't till the day after that I took mine through.'

'Perhaps it was the ewe with the cauliflower ear,' said Heather.

'What, from Moor Farm? Yes. I never thought of her. She wanders about at night sometimes. Still, Bill's gone now. Would you like some cider, Alan? It sells well.'

'I'm not surprised,' said Alan, taking a deep draught from his mug. 'It's superb.'

'That's nothing...you want to try some of the stuff I bottled earlier this year.'

As if on cue, there was an explosion from the other end of the barn, followed by the clatter and tinkle of falling glass. Something hit Heather's foot and she looked down to find a piece of broken bottle near her shoe.

'They're in! They've got the safe open,' said Colin, starting forward. 'Get the car, Audrey!'

'No, Colin…it's all right…we're in Devon…we're retired, remember?' she put a restraining hand on his arm.

'Sorry about that,' said Dave. 'I think we'd better start on that bottled stuff before it all explodes. That's the third one this week. Nobody hurt is there? I'll get a bottle.' He walked off towards a dark corner at the far end.'

'I think I'm going to drink mine in the sunshine,' said Heather.

'Good idea,' the others chorused.

The bottled cider, they all agreed, was better than champagne, and of course they had to open several bottles to save them from exploding. Heather and Alan had a hazy memory of them all sitting in a row on the wall of Dave's farm yard, getting uproariously inebriated. Followed by the four of them staggering home. A journey broken by an argument on the bridge, when Alan and Audrey decided a nice cooling swim in the river would be a good idea, and were only stopped from trying to put this plan into action by the arrival of a passing police car, an unusual sight on these quiet country roads, and enough to sober Colin and Audrey up, slightly.

The pub had stayed closed that evening, until hammering on the door from an irate 'would-be' customer had finally roused Alan - who had collapsed into a chair in the sitting room and fallen instantly asleep, the moment they had staggered in. He couldn't get any sense out of Heather, who had passed out on the bed in the act of changing her clothes. He just managed to crawl through the evening single-handed until, with the pub empty at nine o'clock, he closed and bolted the doors, and joined her.

CHAPTER EIGHT

Peggy seemed to be getting more morose and taciturn as the days progressed. Heather tried to speak to her in their coffee breaks, but after the initial conversation about her relationship with Luke, she now refused to talk about it. Even when she came to work with a hand-shaped bruise on the side of her face, she wouldn't admit that they were still rowing. Then, one morning she turned up at her normal working time and dragged a huge suitcase through the back door, into the kitchen.

''Ello, 'Eather. I just looked in to say I can't work today. Got to take this up to Mum's,' she nodded down at the suitcase.

'That looks heavy. I'll run you up in the car, if you like,' said Heather.

Peggy's bottom lip quivered and Alan, sensing trouble, found an excuse to be doing something in the cellar.

'Thank you,' said Peggy. 'It's just…' Suddenly she burst into muffled, then not so muffled, sobs, whilst scrabbling for a handkerchief in her anorak pocket. Heather gave her a handful of tissues out of a box on the work-top. Then she placed the box on the kitchen table. It looked like being a rather damp morning.

Peggy closed the back door and pulled a chair up to the table. Heather reached down another mug from the dresser.

'What's happened?' Heather asked, pouring some milk into the mug.

'Luke's told me to get out.' Peggy sniffed hugely.

'What?' Heather had somehow assumed that Peggy had had enough of his brutality, and was leaving Luke.

''E's told me to get out. We're not married, so what can I do?'

Heather put three spoons of sugar in the tea she had just poured for Peggy, dimly remembering that sweet tea was recommended for shock.

'Are you sure he really means it? After all, you've been together a long time,' she said.

'Oh, 'e means it, all right.' Peggy blew her nose. 'Found 'isself another woman. 'E says she's movin' in.'

There was a pause which Peggy probably hadn't intended to be dramatic, but it was exquisitely timed.

'Stripper from the local night club,' she said.

It was a few seconds before Heather could collect herself. Fortunately, Peggy was too busy taking a huge gulp of tea to notice the conflicting emotions which Heather could feel wrenching at her face muscles.

'More'n three years I been at that farm, workin' my fingers to the bone for 'im. 'Elpin' 'im build up the 'erd. Milkin', muckin' out, lambin', cookin' and cleanin' for 'im...now 'e says, get out. Just like that. Does 'e think she's goin' to do all that? Bloody stripper? What do she know about farmin'?'

Heather was beginning to find this conversation hard to handle, and she was very glad that Alan had made himself scarce. She turned her struggling face away from Peggy and fetched the biscuit barrel from the dresser, removing the lid as she placed it on the table beside the box of tissues.

'I don't know, Peggy. But somehow I can't see it lasting. As you say, what would this woman know about farming?'

'Mandy Letts,' said Peggy.

'Pardon?'

'Mandy Letts. That's the cow's name. Used to live in East Tegridge before 'er family moved to Exeter. When we was at school she were known as 'Mandy lets everyone'.'

They were at school together? Heather's curiosity got

the better of her.

'How old is this woman?' She pushed the barrel towards Peggy, who took a handful of chocolate biscuits.

'Dunno. Must be about forty.'

Heather found a picture creeping, unbidden, into her mind; of a night club that employed forty year old strippers. A seedy place. Probably in a back street somewhere on the outskirts of the city…and with very poor lighting.

'How did Luke meet her?' she asked.

'Them bloody darts matches, wasn't it.'

Peggy pushed back her chair with a scrape on the kitchen floor.

'I'd best get this case up to Mum's. I'm movin' back there for a bit while I sort myself out. Thanks for the tea. I expect I'll be in tomorrow mornin'. Really need the money now. I'll 'ave to give Mum something for my keep. All right if I takes these and eats them on the way?' she held up the biscuits. 'Only I didn't get no breakfast.'

Mercy invited Heather in for a cup of tea, when they arrived, but she made her excuses and went back to the pub.

'What was all that about?' asked Alan, as she walked into the kitchen.

'Luke has replaced Peggy in his bed.'

'Oh! Who with?' asked Alan. 'Somebody younger, I assume.'

'No, about Peggy's age,' said Heather nonchalantly.

'From the village?' Alan asked, beginning to lose interest as he studied the calendar to see when the next brewery delivery was due.

'No. She's a stripper from an Exeter night club.'

Alan was suddenly all attention. 'No! Really? What's she like?'

'Dressed or undressed?' asked Heather, now

60

unreasonably annoyed by this prurient interest she had deliberately aroused.

'I didn't mean…well, I don't really know what I meant. Bloody Hell! That'll set the village alight with gossip. We'll have to be careful. Can't take sides.'

By the following morning, the sad Peggy was turning into an angry one. She said that, after a long talk with Mercy, her thoughts were turning to revenge.

Mercy was good at 'revenge', Heather thought, trying not to smile at a mental picture of a misty churchyard.

'Wait till the cow moves in. She's goin' to wish she'd never met Luke,' Peggy said.

'Why? Is he really that difficult to live with?' asked Heather.

'No. It's not 'im she's goin' to 'ave to worry about. It's me. I'm making plans,' Peggy said darkly, tapping the side of her nose with a forefinger, before collecting the vacuum cleaner and disappearing into the bar.

Heather's fertile imagination went into overdrive. Thoughts of another unnatural village death filling her mind. She blinked hard and pulled herself up straight. This was ridiculous. Peggy would probably realise, in a little while, that she was better off without Luke. He certainly hadn't made her happy lately. Why would she want him back? What was it about Luke that seemed to attract all these women? She pondered on Luke and his apparent sex appeal.

Alan came into the kitchen, and slight guilt at the way her thoughts had strayed made her blush.

'You look hot,' he said. 'You want to open a window in here.'

'You're more than usually observant, this morning,' she said.

'I've had some practise. I've been observing Peggy.

She's in a strange mood today. Muttering to herself and giving what I can only describe as an evil grin, from time to time. She's making me nervous. Is there anything you want from the shop? I think I'll 'bottle up' later, when she's gone.'

CHAPTER NINE

Heather walked quickly down the hill towards the bridge; the hood of her storm-proof jacket pulled up against the rain. It had turned colder and had been raining heavily all night, and she was worried about Jimmy. If he seemed very cold she intended to start putting him in the stable at night. She could have driven to Hawkridge Farm, but the combined deterrent of the mad pheasant and a possibly angry Luke had made her decide to walk across the fields from the river, thus avoiding the farmhouse and yard.

She went carefully down the steps onto the river path, through Dave's fields, and climbed onto the stile between Small Profits' land and Hawkridge, pausing on the top step to look for Jimmy. The sheep were still in the field, but the horse was missing. Her heart sank. How had he got out? And where should she start looking for him? Now she would *have* to go up to the farm and enlist Luke's help.

A gust of wind blew heavy raindrops in her face. She pulled the strings of the hood tighter under her chin, and climbed the steep hill to the farm. The pheasant was sheltering in the cart-shed with the chickens, all of them looking bedraggled and dispirited. She kept a wary eye on the bird who watched every step she took across the yard to the house, but he didn't venture out into the rain. She knocked on the door. After a minute it was opened by Luke.

'I've just been trying to ring you,' he said. 'Come in.'

She walked into the kitchen warmed by the solid fuel range, untying her hood, aware that it was not the most flattering piece of headgear.

'Jimmy's got out,' she said.

'No. That's why I was ringing you. He was getting a bit cold, so I've put him in the stable.'

'Oh, Luke, that was kind of you. That's really what I had come down to try to do.'

'I haven't had time to bed it down properly,' he said. 'There's a bit of straw in there, but you'll need another couple of bales. I'd give you a hand, only I've got to go into Exeter. I've left some bales on a barrow just inside the cart-shed.'

'With the pheasant,' said Heather.

'He won't bother you. He doesn't like this weather. He'll be thinking about perching up for the night soon. With all this rain it's going to be dark early tonight. Where's Alan, then? Doesn't seem to be anybody at the pub.'

'Oh, he's gone to see the accountant. Well, I won't hold you up. Thanks again for getting Jimmy in. I'll tuck him up for the night and be down tomorrow morning to let him out, if it stops raining.'

'Lucky Jimmy.'

'What?'

'Being tucked in for the night. Wouldn't mind a bit of that myself,' he took a step towards her

Heather just stopped herself from remarking that she'd heard he was fixed up in that department, as she edged round, putting the table between them. She settled for a non-committal laugh; then pulled up her hood and moved towards the door. A quick glance around the kitchen had not shown any sign that Mandy Letts had moved in yet.

'There's a bale of hay with the straw,' he said. 'Give him a couple of sections to keep him going through the night. He's got some water. Don't really know how much you know about horses, so tell me to shut up if I'm teaching my grandmother to suck eggs.'

'Not much. All suggestions gratefully received. Thanks again, Luke.'

She unlatched the door and let herself out, as he pulled on his jacket and picked up the keys to the Land-Rover.

She was at the cart-shed entrance as he climbed into the vehicle. He waved and backed into the dung heap to turn round. She waved back, a small gesture for fear of enraging the pheasant with any sudden movement. She couldn't see the bird, but was sensing a malevolent presence watching her. She traced the source of these unpleasant vibes very quickly. It was sitting on top of the bales of straw which Luke had put ready on the wheelbarrow, for her. She turned back to the yard, but he had already pulled away up the track.

'You're only a pheasant. I have eaten some of your relatives. 'You don't scare me,' she lied, to it's lowered head and the glistening eyes which seemed to be fixed on hers. She moved her arm out to the side and it followed the movement with menacing attention, the feathers on its neck beginning to rise.

Heather backed out of the shed slowly and walked over to the back door of the farmhouse, beside which an outside tap was dripping gently into a half full bucket. Carrying this back to the shed, she took a deep breath, and flung the contents at the pheasant. The effect was dramatic. Screeching an alarm call he shot into the rafters under the cart-shed roof dislodging several hens who were already beginning to settle for the night, in spite of the fact that it was only mid-afternoon. A brown feather floated down and settled on the straw bales, which were now soaking wet. Heather swore.

Lifting the bales off the wheelbarrow - they were surprisingly heavy - she pushed the barrow across the yard and round past the pig sties, which were thankfully quiet apart from the odd subdued grunt from the occupants, who had decided to sleep until it stopped raining.

She collected two fresh straw bales from the barn. By the time she got back to the yard her arms were aching, and by the time she had pushed her load across the muddy field to the stable, they felt as if they were being wrenched from their sockets.

Jimmy saw her coming and neighed a welcome. She opened the door and he barged past her, jumping the wheelbarrow, and galloped off, bucking his way round the field. She spent a fruitless twenty minutes chasing him. Then decided to bed down the stable before catching him. As she struggled to get the string off the bales, she made a mental note to bring a knife with her next time.

By the time she was ready for him, Jimmy was getting cold again and finding that running away was no fun when no-one was chasing you. One rattle of his feed bucket soon brought him back into the stable. As she waited for him to finish his meal, she looked at her watch and was surprised to find she had been at the farm for over an hour. Jimmy knocked over his empty bucket and began happily tucking into his hay, his damp coat steaming as he warmed up. She leaned against the wall beside the door watching him for a few minutes.

As she was about to leave the stable she saw a movement by the hedge, two fields away. She worked out that this hedge must be the one which ran alongside the farm track to the road. Perhaps it was the Land-Rover returning that she had glimpsed through a gap in the hawthorn. She listened, but couldn't separate the sound of a vehicle engine from the steady drumming of the rain on the galvanised iron roof of the stable.

Jimmy left his hay and drank deeply from the water bucket placed by the door. It would need re-filling. She picked it up and set off back to the tap in the yard, hoping that it wasn't the Land-Rover she had seen. She didn't really want to meet Luke again. Not that it mattered, but she felt scruffy. The legs of her trousers were covered in mud and her jacket was liberally sprinkled with hayseeds.

She glanced back as she placed the bucket under the tap. There was that movement again, in the same place. She began to run water into the bucket, watching the far hedge. She made out a figure, wearing a blue hooded jacket, standing just inside the field by the track. She could also hear the Land-Rover engine in the distance. She'd better tell Luke someone was lurking on his farm.

She turned off the tap and picked up the full bucket, her foot slipped in a muddy patch and she had to concentrate on staying upright. When she looked again, the figure had gone. There was a squeal of tyres from up the track, and she pictured Luke having a near miss with the wandering ewe and her lamb.

The Land-Rover pulled into the yard as she opened the field gate. There were two people in it. Luke and a woman with long blonde hair, who was holding her head. The windscreen of the Land-Rover was smashed. Heather paused as she latched the gate. They hadn't seen her. This must be Mandy Letts. As Luke helped her out of the car, Heather could see she had blood on her face, which seemed to be coming from a cut on her head.

'I'll kill the bloody bitch, when I get hold of her,' Luke's voice was raised. Picking up something from the floor of the vehicle, he flung it towards the barn wall. As it landed, Heather saw it was a brick. He took Mandy into the house with his arm round her.

Heather decided to keep well out of the way. She delivered the bucket back to Jimmy; and left the farm by her cross country route, without being seen from the house.

'You're looking lovely this evening, darling,' said Alan,

as she closed the kitchen door behind her. 'No, don't come any further. Let me admire you from here. I suggest you get most of that mess off on the doormat. Can't have Peggy moaning about the mud and whatever that other stuff is...looks like grass seed!'

'It is.'

'Not been rolling in the hay with Luke, have you?'

'Not funny, Alan. Let me get cleaned up and I'll tell you about my exciting afternoon. Can you make me a cup of coffee? I'm freezing.'

'Take the car next time. I'm sorry I needed it today.'

....

The following morning Peggy arrived for work in a foul temper.

''E's moved the cow in,' she said viciously to Heather, hanging her blue, hooded anorak, roughly, on the hook behind the back door. 'She'll regret goin' to live up there, you mark my words.'

Heather didn't really know what to say, and found her eyes irresistibly drawn to Peggy's blue anorak, and a small tear in the sleeve.

'Gotta mend that. Got torn on a bush,' said Peggy, following Heather's gaze.

She collected the vacuum cleaner and disappeared into the bar.

CHAPTER TEN

A few days later, Heather drew back the bolts on the door and opened the pub for the evening session. The two youths who she'd been sure were under age, and three slightly older friends, came in. They took their drinks and retired to the far corner of the bar, where they became engrossed in serious conversation and began piling up the butts of 'roll-ups' in the ash trays.

Peggy and Mercy arrived.

'Thought I'd bring Mum up 'ere for supper; that steak and mushroom pie you was cookin' this morning, smelled good.'

'I'll set you up a table. Where would you like to sit?' Heather asked.

Peggy looked round the bar.

'That lot are bein' surprisingly quiet. Wonder what they're plottin'?' she said.

'I hope that, whatever it is, it isn't going to take place in here,' said Alan.

'You don't want to worry about them; they're 'armless, really,' said Peggy. 'We'll sit over there. That all right, Mum?' she pointed to a table next to the lads.

'I don't mind where I sits, long as there's room in case Dave comes in.' Mercy went over to the table and sat down.

''E wont be in tonight,' Peggy muttered to Heather. 'I 'eard 'im outside the shop, this mornin', arrangin' to meet that woman from East Tegridge. What's 'er name, now? Big woman,' she shook her head. 'Oh, I can't remember. 'Ope Mum isn't gettin' too keen on 'im. 'E always was a bit of a bugger with women, that Dave.'

Peggy carried the drinks across to the table and sat

down. Heather went into the kitchen to put their vegetables on to cook. When she came out again she saw Peggy was leaning across to the lads at the next table, deep in conversation with them. All Heather could hear was the occasional cry of 'yeah, wicked'. She carried some cutlery and napkins over, and set up Peggy and Mercy's table.

'Your meal won't be long. Selection of vegetables okay?'

'Yes, lovely,' said Mercy.

Peggy turned back to her own table. One of the youths rose to his feet and bent towards her.

'Great! Thanks. See ya,' he said, and raised a thumb, his wide grin separating the sparse hairs on his top lip which were struggling to turn themselves into a moustache.

The rest of his mates pushed back their chairs and trooped out of the pub. The roar of a disintegrating car exhaust system erupted into the peaceful square as they drove out of the village towards Exeter, in search of something more exciting in the way of night life.

'What was that all about, then?' asked Mercy.

'Never you mind, Mum,' Peggy tapped the side of her nose.

'You be careful,' said Mercy.

Heather decided she didn't want to know what was going on. Alan smiled at her as she returned to the bar.

'That's good. Peggy seems to have cleared out the under-age element. It worries me a bit having them in here, though, come to think of it, I've hardly seen a policeman since we moved down here. She seemed very friendly with them, didn't she? I wonder what they were talking about?' he said.

'I don't think we want to know. Mercy told her to 'be careful'. Oh! Could you put another chair at their table, just in case Dave does arrive.'

'It's Thursday,' said Alan. 'I heard he visited a lady in East Tegridge on Thursdays.'

'Who told you that?'

'Well, he did, actually.'

'Good grief!'

The rich smell of steak and mushroom pie drifted into the bar, reminding Heather of her duty. As she got back to Peggy and Mercy's table with their meal, she overheard the tail end of something Mercy had just said: 'if he goes to the police?'

''E won't,' Peggy scoffed. ''E's got no time for the police.'

'Oh, well…Oh, here's our supper. Doesn't that look nice?'

'Told you it smelled good, Mum. She's a good cook is our 'Eather.'

'Have you got enough left if Dave comes in?' Mercy asked.

'Yes, plenty,' said Heather. 'Enjoy your meal.'

Colin came into the bar and raised a hand in greeting to Peggy. Mercy looked round, then, disappointed, returned to her meal. Colin pulled himself onto a stool at the bar.

'Pint please, Alan,' he looked round the bar. 'No Dave? Oh no, it's Thursday, isn't it?'

Poor Mercy, Heather thought, as she walked over to take the order of two people who had been lured into the pub by the smell of cooking drifting across the square. Anne came in and sat on a bar stool next to Colin.

'Gin and tonic please, Alan,' she said, hanging the loop of Rudi's lead on one of the hooks Alan had screwed under the lip of the bar to accommodate handbags. Rudi sat down and leant against the brass foot-rail, looking bored.

'Hello, Anne,' said Colin. 'Hey! You know about dogs, don't you?'

'Well, a bit. What did you want to know?' she asked.

'It's our old dog; she keeps shaking her head. Why do you think that is?'

'I don't know, perhaps it's her ears. You should go to the vet and ask him.'

'Oh, right, then. I'll have a word with him about it,' said Colin.

'Where's Audrey this evening?' Alan asked him.

'She may be in later. They're showing a double episode of East Enders on the telly, tonight. Makes her go all nostalgic for London and the old days.'

'Doesn't it have that effect on you?' Anne asked.

'It was all right for her…she was on the outside with the money. I was 'doing time' to pay for it. No, I'd rather forget it, really. We've only been back once since we moved down here. That was for Violet's funeral.'

'Violet?' asked Anne.

'Their mum. The Kray's. Violet Kray. That was some 'do' that was. Black horses with black plumes pulling this beautiful old hearse. Huge turnout.'

Two more people came into the bar and began to study the food menu. Heather went into the kitchen and put some more vegetables on to cook. As she was replacing the knife she had been using, in the block with the others, she remembered she would need something to cut the twine binding the straw bales at the farm. She had been going to buy a penknife; but there was a knife in the set which she hardly ever used. She removed it, wrapped some newspaper round the blade, and put it in the pocket of her jacket hanging on the back of the kitchen door.

She mused on Jimmy, as she worked. He didn't seem quite so lame as he had been. Maybe she would start leading him out for walks, to get him used to the area. It might make him easier for her to handle if she ever did start to ride him. She realised that eventually it would be expected of her - by Alan and Luke anyway - and the idea made her very nervous. After all, she really had no idea how Jimmy re-acted to being ridden. Did he have some violent and dangerous habits? Would he bolt when faced with a tractor in a narrow lane? Would he turn into a racehorse the moment they reached some open ground? Had she bitten off far more than she could chew? She comforted herself with the thought that, once he was sound, she could always sell him if she lost her nerve.

'One prawn cocktail, one paté and two more steak and mushroom.' Alan called through the door. 'And Colin would like a toasted bacon and mushroom sandwich.'

Heather was suddenly too busy to worry about Jimmy...anyway, there was plenty of time for that.

CHAPTER ELEVEN

It had come on to rain heavily during the morning, and Heather decided, as they closed the pub after lunch, that she had better go to the farm and get Jimmy into the stable before he got too cold..

She parked the car on the side of the track, just outside the farm yard, to avoid any possible damage to it from the pheasant. She needn't have worried; he was sheltering from the downpour inside the cart-shed with the chickens. She walked across the yard with her head down to avoid the stinging rain, and bumped into Luke as he came round the corner from the pig sties.

'Whoops! Didn't hear your car come in, with all this wind,' he said, taking hold of her shoulders to steady her.

She quickly stepped back out of reach. 'I thought I'd get Jimmy in. Looks like being a dirty night.'

'Yes, this rain's set in for a few hours. You going to the darts match tonight? At 'The Bull', over East Tegridge?' he asked.

'No. One of us has to stay with the pub. Alan's going, though. He's getting quite keen.'

'He's not a bad player,' said Luke. 'We should beat them. Their best bloke got kicked by a cow, last week, and landed up in hospital with a ruptured spleen.'

That was some kick, thought Heather, allowing her mind to visualise this Devon farmer flying through the air from his farm dairy, straight into accident and emergency at Exeter hospital. She dragged herself away from this cartoon picture.

'Poor thing. That sounds nasty.' She studied Luke's cows, who were beginning to congregate by the field gate ready for afternoon milking. 'Cows always look so relaxed. You don't sort of think about them kicking people.'

'Oh, some of them can be tricky buggers...they're females, aren't they? Depends how you handle them.'

Luke's conversations always seemed to turn in this direction, Heather thought, as she began to walk on towards Jimmy's field.

'Anyway, best of luck this evening,' she said, opening the gate.

'See you,' said Luke.

She gave a whistle and the little grey horse looked up. She whistled again and he began to trot towards the gate, but halfway up the field he stumbled and dropped back to a walk, still noticeably lame. She gave him a couple of peppermints and slipped the halter onto him as he crunched blissfully. Luke wasn't in sight as she led the horse through the yard and across the field to his stable.

She tried to brush some of the mud off him, where he had rolled, but it was wet and sticky. She gave up and fetched him some hay and a fresh bucket of water. Then she leaned on the wall of the stable and watched him. There was something very relaxing about caring for animals, she thought. With the weather doing it's worst outside, here in this little oasis, there was peace and contentment and the rhythmic crunch, crunch, crunch of Jimmy working his way through the sweet smelling hay in his haynet.

Unfortunately, thinking of food concentrated her mind again and she looked at her watch, realising she should get back. There was food to prepare for the evening session, and Saturdays were usually quite busy. She wondered if Luke would be taking Mandy to the darts match? She must prime Alan to bring back a description of her. All Peggy would say, when asked about Mandy, was: 'Don't talk to me about that cow'. She hoped Peggy would be in a better mood this evening, as she was lending a hand while Alan was away.

Peggy was in a spectacularly good mood: laughing and joking with the customers and even grinning to herself as she prepared meals to carry through into the bar - to such an extent that in the end Heather had to comment.

'It's lovely to see you smiling again, Peggy.'

'Well, for once I've got something to smile about,' she said.

'What would that be?' Heather asked.

'You'll find out. Can't tell you just at this precise moment in time, but you'll find out, soon enough.'

'Now I am intrigued. Is it a man?'

'No!' Peggy scoffed. 'Not 'a man'… more like 'men'.'

'You've lost me,' said Heather.

'All will be revealed,' said Peggy, as she carried some starters past Heather and set them in front of a party of four holiday-makers, who had come in for supper.

Colin and Audrey came in and sat at the bar.

As Heather poured their drinks, she remembered Colin questioning Anne about his dog.

'Did you go to the vet about your dog, Colin?'

'Yes. Cor! Was he busy? He must be raking it in. His surgery was full of people and animals. There were dogs and cats and budgerigars and things in boxes. I had to wait ages to see him.'

'And what did he say?' Heather asked.

'He said I'd better bring the dog.'

Heather, who had been taking a sip from a mug of coffee she had under the bar, choked and hurriedly turned away to avoid spraying the bar with coffee. When she had finished coughing, she wiped the tears from her eyes.

'Really?' she asked.

'Daft, or what?' said Audrey.

'Well, I didn't know. Anne didn't say nothing about taking the dog. Now I've got to go up there again,' said Colin.

Halfway through the evening, Heather became vaguely aware of the sound of several cars passing through the village, but didn't fully register the increase in traffic until about an hour later, when Peggy grinned as she passed her in the kitchen and said: 'It's started.'

'What has?'

'You'll see.'

'Peggy, I'm fed up with you going all mysterious on me. *What* has started?'

'The rave.'

'Rave? What d'you mean, rave?...Like, loud pop music?...Drugs and so on?'

'Yes,' Peggy could hardly contain her glee.

'Where? Who around here would give permission for that sort of thing?'

'No-one,' said Peggy, laughing out loud. 'Especially Luke.'

'Oh my God! Peggy. He's not there. He's playing darts over at East Tegridge.'

'I know,' she said.

Heather opened the back door, and listened. The sound was masked by the wind, but she thought she could make out a rhythmic thumping coming from the direction of Hawkridge.

'My horse is down there. I got him in this afternoon,' said Heather, now really worried.

'Which stable is 'e in?' Peggy asked.

'The one across the field.'

''E'll be all right there. I told them to use the cart-shed.' Peggy was still smiling broadly.

'*You* told them?'

'Well, poor lads, they was stuck for somewhere to 'old it. They didn't know I wasn't livin' there any more. Nice one, eh, 'Eather?'

'Peggy, you are going to be in big trouble. I heard him threatening to murder you the other day after you put that brick....' Heather stopped, realising Peggy hadn't known she was there.

'Brick?' Peggy looked slightly shamefaced. ' 'Ow did you know about that?'

'I was there...in the stable. I saw someone across the field but I didn't realise it was you until I saw that tear in your anorak.'

'Well, 'e asked for it, that's all I can say,' said Peggy. She looked down at the tray she was carrying. 'I better get these coffees into the bar before they gets cold.'

Heather was left standing in the middle of the kitchen, frozen with indecision. As she gradually analysed the situation, she realised that the thing which worried her most was whether Jimmy was all right. Surely a bit of noise wouldn't upset him? After all, he had been to crowded racecourses. Should she ring the police? She shelved that idea for the moment, not wanting to get any more involved than she had to. She already felt like some kind of accessory now that Peggy had told her. She looked at her watch. Quarter to ten. There was just one couple left drinking coffee at their table in the bar, and Dave was still sitting at the counter. Colin and Audrey had gone. As soon as the couple went, she would close the pub and ask Dave to give her a lift down to Hawkridge. She went back into the bar.

Peggy looked up from where she was clearing plates from the table and put a finger across her lips, indicating that Heather should say nothing to Dave. No, Heather thought, I am not going to get drawn any further into this conspiracy; although she did decide not to say anything to Dave until nearer to closing time, in case he rushed off without her. She didn't fancy attending a rave on her own.

She would leave it until they got to the farm before phoning Alan and getting a message to Luke. Maybe by then someone else would have contacted him. Three more cars drove through the village.

'They wants their bill,' Peggy said, as she passed through on her way to the kitchen.   'I'll just wash this lot up and I'll be on my way 'ome. Not a word now. Our secret, eh?'

Heather toyed with the idea of opening a file marked 'Ashley - Top Secret' so that she would be able to remember which of the Ashley's had sworn her to what. Life was getting unnecessarily complicated.

Peggy called: 'Goodnight' from the kitchen, as she left. And the couple in the bar began to stand up and put their coats on.

'I'd better go, too,' Dave said.

Heather went across the bar, using the excuse of seeing the couple off to stand by the door. Then pretended to be listening to something, for Dave's benefit. Actually she didn't have to pretend. The wind had dropped slightly and the thumping bass was quite audible.

'Dave…I think there's something happening, down the hill. Come and listen.'

He joined her at the door.

'I can hear music,' he said. 'Loud music. All them 'blimmin' cars! It's one of those raves, that's what it is…sounds like my place…or maybe Luke's.' He put his head on one side to hear better. 'I'd better get down there.'

'Dave, wait a minute. Can I come with you? I got the horse in this evening. If it's Luke's place, he might be panicking. The horse I mean.'

'Luke's over at the darts match tonight. You got your mobile?'

'I'll get it.' She put on her jacket and grabbed the mobile phone and her keys, and, as an afterthought, picked up a small pencil torch off the dresser. She flicked it on and found the battery was almost dead, but put it in her pocket anyway.

As they got to the bridge, they could see cars lining the side of the road all the way up the hill. Dave didn't bother to stop at his farm. Apart from one car parked at the end, his track was clear. Luke's wasn't. There were cars parked right along the track and into the farm yard.

The noise, by the time they got there, was deafening; and it wasn't just the music. The pigs, behind the barn, seemed to have formed themselves into the Porcine Choral Society. While the cows were practising an aria in a slightly lower key, the whole punctuated by high pitched neighs from Jimmy, who still seemed to be across the field in his stable. Heather wondered what had happened to the pheasant and the hens. Luke's sheepdog was shivering inside the kennel to which he was chained, beside the back door of the farmhouse.

Dave took a piece of baler twine out of his pocket, tied it to the dog's collar and unclipped the chain.

'Here, take him with you. He's terrified,' he said. 'I'll come over and make sure the horse is all right. Can you ring Alan and get him to tell Luke to get back here.'

'Do you want me to ring the police?'

'They're no bloody good. They never turn up till everything's all over, and these kids are getting wise. If there's not more than a hundred of them, they gets away with it.'

Jimmy was sweating profusely and shivering; his ears almost meeting over his forehead as they pointed towards the cart-shed. He was pleased to see Heather, and calmed down a little. The collie crept into a corner and lay down in the straw.

'The little horse seems okay,' said Dave. ' I've had an

idea. Going to have a bit of fun with them. Teach them a lesson. You stay here and ring Alan.' He ran back across the field.

The rain, which had let up slightly, began to descend again in wind blown sheets, much to Heather's relief. They aren't going to be coming out of the cart-shed and roaming round the farm in this, she thought. There was just enough life left in the torch battery to see to dial Alan's mobile number. His phone rang twice, then she could hear the sound of a pub full of people enjoying themselves.

'Hello, love. Any problems?' Alan asked.

'Not with the pub, but is Luke still there?'

'Yes, why?'

'There's a rave going on at his farm. Dave and I are there now.'

'A rave? Did you say rave? Music, drugs and so on?'

'You've got it.'

'Luke didn't say anything about it.'

'Oh, come on, Alan…Luke doesn't know. Can you tell him to get back here…and it would be quite nice if you could come too. I don't want to have to walk home with all this going on.'

'Where, exactly, are you?'

'In the stable, with Jimmy. Dave's gone off somewhere. He said something about teaching them a lesson.'

'Have you rung the police?'

'Dave said it would be a waste of time. To be quite honest I'd rather not get in any deeper than I am now.'

'What d'you mean?'

'Oh, nothing. Tell Luke.'

'Luke! Luke! Come over here a moment.'

Heather could hear Alan telling Luke the news, then a roar from Luke.

'Okay, darling, we're on our way. Be there in about

twenty minutes. Crikey! Looks as if there will be a small army of us. See you in a minute.'

The rave music stopped, to be replaced by the sound of a generator which had been masked by the din. She realised this was how they had managed to flood the cart-shed with light, which spilled out through the wide doors into the yard. The sound of another engine filtered into the generator's clatter, and she could see tractor head-lights flickering through the hedge along the track. It seemed to be going very slowly; probably having difficulty squeezing past the parked cars.

A crowd of youngsters stood in the cart-shed doorway, laughing, and drinking from bottles. One of them tossed a cigarette out into the yard, sending sparks flying in the wind. Heather's stomach turned over at the thought that they might set fire to the farm. She mentally planned how she would have to set the pigs free from their sties, and check that there were no calves in their shed beside the milking parlour.

The tractor had now reached the entrance to the farm yard, and the music started up again. Heather, squinting through the rain, could just make out that the tractor was towing something. It drove slowly into the yard and manoeuvred the vehicle it was pulling, into position in front of the cart shed door. She realised what it was, just as Dave engaged the mechanism and began spraying the inside of the cart shed with a mixture of manure and slurry.

There was instant bedlam. Figures reeled and raced out of the shed, yelling. Two of them tried to climb onto the tractor, but Dave pushed them back. He then put the tractor in gear and drove round, and out of, the yard; still spraying anyone within reach. He trundled slowly away up the track, depositing the remains of the muck on the cars parked on the other side of the drive, and Heather understood why he had taken so long to come down to the yard. He had managed to cover all the cars, and their owners, in foul smelling muck. As his tractor turned out onto the road she could see the lights of three cars racing down towards the farm. She decided to wait in the stable until Alan came to fetch her.

The generator suddenly stopped and the lights in the cart-shed went out, to more screams and yells from it's filthy inhabitants. Heather saw a light come on in the farmhouse, then Luke appeared in the doorway, carrying something which looked like a shotgun. Alan was with him and seemed to be trying to persuade him to go back into the house. Luke shrugged him off and set off towards the cart-shed: but neither he, nor the gun, were needed. Dave's 'good idea' had been quite enough to dampen the youngsters' enthusiasm for the night. They were running off towards their cars and their second unpleasant surprise of the evening.

A figure coming across the field towards the stable, carrying a torch, proved to be Alan.

'Are you all right, darling?' he called.

'Yes. Am I glad to see you? I thought they were going to set the farm on fire.'

'You should have seen their cars! Dave - I suppose it was Dave - has managed to dump a load of muck all over them,' said Alan.

'Yes, and he sprayed it all over them in the cart-shed, as well.'

'No!...Good for Dave.'

'Have they all gone?'

'Not quite. Luke's got hold of one. I think I heard him insisting that they had permission to hold the rave on the farm.'

'They did. Don't say anything, but Peggy told me she'd

said they could, just before Dave and I came down here. Don't tell Luke…in fact don't tell anyone. I expect he'll find out - but not from us.'

'No. I think that's wise. We don't want a load of manure dropped in front of the pub. But what a good idea, eh? Good old Dave.'

The next morning Peggy was late for work.

'Sorry, 'Eather. 'Ad to get out of the window and do a bit of clearing up this morning. *Somebody*,' she said with huge emphasis, 'had dumped a load of muck on the doorstep. We couldn't get the front door open. It 'asn't done the paint-work much good, either.'

'Why did you have to get through the window? What was wrong with the back door?' asked Heather.

'The bugger had screwed a hook and staple to it. Probably used that battery screwdriver I gave 'im for Christmas.'

'I reckon you two are about quits, now, Peggy.'

'Quits! I 'aven't even started yet.'

'Did you hear what Dave did?' Heather asked.

'Yes, 'e rang Mum, this morning. 'E says 'e's always going to keep the muck spreader full in future, for emergencies. And 'e 'adn't 'ad so much fun in years.'

'What about the manure at your place?' Heather asked.

'Oh, I've barrowed it round the back. I needed some for the vegetable patch, anyway.'

Alan came into the kitchen.

'Morning, Peggy.' He wrinkled his nose slightly, and Heather realised there had been a lingering smell of dung in the air since Peggy had arrived.

'Darling, do you mind holding the fort for twenty minutes or so?' Heather asked him. 'I just want to go down and let Jimmy out, now that it has stopped raining.'

'No. Don't be long,' he went back into the bar.

Heather drove slowly down the track to Hawkridge, trying not to splash too much of the results of Dave's muck-spreading activities onto the car. She pulled into the yard. The rain had washed some of the muck off the barn wall, but the wind had been blowing from behind the farmhouse, and consequently the rain hadn't touched the thick coating which had spattered across the house wall and the kitchen window as Dave had turned out of the yard. Luke was attaching a hose to the outside tap.

'I'll get her for this,' he said to Heather, as she stepped out of the car.

'I thought you already had,' she said, thinking about Peggy's unsought dung delivery.

'Oh, you've heard about that, then.'

'Yes. Peggy's just arrived for work.' Heather looked round the yard. 'Were the chickens all right?'

Luke nodded to where they were scratching around by the barn.

'They seem okay. I haven't checked the egg situation yet this morning. They've probably gone off lay.'

'Where's the pheasant? Before I get attacked, I like to have some idea which direction it'll be coming from,' said Heather.

Luke gave a broad grin and nodded towards the gate post, at the foot of which sprawled the pheasant.

'Oh! he's not dead, is he?' Heather was surprised to find this idea upsetting.

'No...I saw him pecking at one of them 'spliffs' earlier, now look at him.'

Heather walked across the yard. The pheasant watched her coming with a benign expression. She would not have been in the least surprised if it had greeted her with 'Hi man,' and a languid wave of the wing. She roared with laughter as the bird closed his eyes and drifted off to sleep.

She wondered how the world appeared to a pheasant high on cannabis. It looked as if it was rather pleasant.

'Can't you get some and mix it in with his food, on a regular basis?' she suggested to Luke. He laughed.

Jimmy had heard her voice, and neighed.

'I'd better get on,' she said, unlatching the gate and stepping carefully round the slumbering pheasant.'

Luke waved as he turned on the hose and began to wash the muck off the kitchen window.

CHAPTER TWELVE

Heather and Alan were having breakfast, two days later, when she remembered she hadn't asked him what Mandy was like.

'Did you meet her, the other night...Mandy?'

'Yes. She's okay. Not a bit what I'd expected. Rather shy in fact. But...' he looked thoughtful, 'that could have been because Luke was there. He's very possessive. Couldn't keep his hands off her, as a matter of fact. But I did hear him telling someone that she wasn't much good with the cows yet.'

'Yet! Peggy would be even madder - if that were possible - if Mandy ever took her place to the extent of doing the milking. Those cows are almost 'family' to Peggy.'

'Shhh! She's coming,' said Alan, glancing through the window.

The back door opened and Peggy stuck her head round it.

'There's one of them French blokes in the square with a van full of onions and garlic. Do you need any?'

'Oh. Yes, please. Can you get me a string of each. Hang on. I'll get you some money.' Heather reached for her handbag.

'It's all right. Pay me in a minute.'

The door closed and Heather began to clear away their breakfast plates. Peggy was soon back, bumping her way in through the door, festooned with garlic and carrying two strings of onions.

'Expecting an invasion of vampires, Peg?' Alan laughed.

'What?'

'The   garlic   necklace,'   he   pointed.   'You

know…garlic…for warding off vampires?'

'Is 'e all right?' Peggy asked Heather.

'Don't mind him. Just his idea of a joke. My God! Peggy. I only wanted one string of garlic.'

'I only got you one; the rest are for me. I thought I'd practise some Italian cookin'.'

'Strewth!' said Alan, staring at the five strings Peggy was hanging next to her anorak on the back door. She'd mended the tear, Heather noted.

'I've got a good Italian cookery book you can borrow,' said Heather.

'No. It's all right. I'm goin' to invent me own recipes.' Peggy opened the cupboard door and began collecting the cleaning materials. She went through into the bar.

'Should somebody warn Mercy?' Alan grinned. 'This could wreck her love life.'

'We'd better find out how Dave feels about garlic, first,' Heather giggled.

'Garlic?' said Dave, later, sitting at the bar with his lunch-time pint. ' I don't mind it in moderation. Why?'

'Oh, it's just that Heather was planning the menu's…made me think of it,' said Alan.

'I like a nice hot curry,' Dave said.

'Did you hear that, Heather?' Alan asked.

'Yes. I'll see what I can do, Dave……shut up, Alan,' she hissed under her breath as she walked past him. Alan did shut up because his eyes were suddenly fixed on Jenny and Josie, who came in and sat at the bar.

'Two sweet sherry's, please,' said Jenny. Heather watched Alan's attempts to focus, with amusement, and wondered if these two always purposely arranged themselves so that their normal eyes paired in the middle, while the other two kept a lookout for possible danger from the side.

'We had to get out for a while,' said Josie.

'Yes. We seem to have 'neighbours from hell' today,' Jenny joked.

'Peggy and Mercy? What have they done?' Heather asked.

'Driven us out of our garden; and most of the people around. God knows what they're doing. The whole estate reeks of garlic. Unfortunately we are down-wind of them.'

'Peggy said she was going to start cooking Italian food,' said Heather.

'It smells as if she's started up her own factory,' said Josie.

'She should have borrowed my cookery book; I did offer it. It sounds as if she's using far too much,' said Heather.

Later that afternoon she went across to the village shop. As she was coming out she met Luke in the doorway. He looked quite presentable out of his working clothes.

'Just needed some 'fags',' he said.

Heather smiled and walked out of the door. Mandy, sitting in the driving seat of a small car, parked at the kerb, smiled at her. She wound down the window as Heather went across and bent down beside the car.

'Hello. I'm Heather,' she said. 'Alan's wife…at the pub.'

'Oh, yes. The lady with the horse. I've seen you across the field.' Mandy's hand was cool and firm. 'Come in for a coffee next time you are down. It gets a bit lonely on the farm, after Exeter. I could do with someone to talk to occasionally. I've just managed to persuade Luke to come into Exeter with me to get some clothes, that's if there's anywhere still open by the time we get there. He had to do the afternoon milking first. Actually it's a bit of an excuse for me to try out this car he's just bought me. I wasn't very good with the Land-Rover.'

'Hope you have a successful trip,' said Heather, as Luke

came out of the shop door.

'Don't forget. You're welcome any time for a coffee,' said Mandy.

'Thanks. 'Bye.'

Across the square, standing by the village hall, Peggy was watching the car intently as it drove away towards Exeter.

…………

Heather had started giving Jimmy a small meal in the evenings. Partly because the grass was being eaten by the sheep faster than it was growing, and partly because she enjoyed being with, and getting to know, the horse..

She pulled into Hawkridge farm yard, faintly relieved that, with Luke and Mandy in Exeter, she had the place to herself. Jimmy's food was stored in a rat-proof metal dustbin under the end of the barn, where Luke kept large bins of cattle cake. Mixing some bran and oats in a bucket, she added a handful of soaked sugar-beet pulp and dampened the mixture from the outside tap near the pig sties; keeping well away from the boar's pen. He had heard her coming and was standing up with his front feet hooked over the low sty wall, watching her. There was something sinister about the expression in those little eyes which followed her progress across the yard.

Jimmy came up across the field at her whistle, and followed her into the stable. He was walking better, she noticed, the limp had almost disappeared. She put his feed bucket down in the corner of the stable for him, and turned to gaze out over the door towards the farm buildings, just in time to see Peggy push her bike into the hedge on the drive, and climb through the gap she had used the day she'd thrown the brick through the Land-Rover windscreen. She knew it was Peggy. There was only one blue, hooded anorak like that in the village. She was carrying a bulging carrier bag.

Damn, thought Heather. If she left the stable now, Peggy would see her, and she didn't want to get involved in her war with Luke and Mandy. This meant that she was trapped in with Jimmy until Peggy left. She obviously hadn't seen Heather's car, which was parked on the other side of the barn. What on earth was she doing?

Heather watched her pull something out from beside the bins of cattle cake. It was the long galvanised iron feed trough that Luke used for the sheep. Peggy dragged this through the barbed wire fence and into the cows' field. Their heads had come up and they were already watching her, and some were beginning to move towards her. Having placed the trough, she went back to the feed bins.

Hooking the carrier bag onto her arm, she hefted a bag of cattle cake onto her shoulder and strode over to the trough, pouring in the cake as she walked along its length. Then she walked back, throwing handfuls of the contents of her carrier bag into the cake and mixing it in. By this time the cows were nosing into the far end of the trough and beginning to tuck into an extra ration of food, with gusto.

Heather chewed her bottom lip as she tried to decide what to do. What if Peggy was poisoning them? Should she call out to her, and make her presence known? Surely she wouldn't poison the cows? She loved them. Most of them she had reared as calves. Calling herself a coward - not for the first time - Heather stayed quietly where she was, and drew back into the darkened interior as Peggy glanced across at the stable. Jimmy was still tucking into his tea.

The cows soon finished the contents of the trough and wandered off again, some to the water trough where they queued patiently while their sisters drank. Then they moved up the field and lay down in the evening sun, belching occasionally, and chewing the cud with faraway expressions.

Peggy dragged the trough back through the fence and across to the tap by the boars pen. The boar had stood up and hooked its front feet over the wall again, and was watching her coming. Picking up a stick which was leaning against the wall, she hit the animal across the face, causing it to drop down into its pen with an angry squeal. She rinsed the trough under the tap, before dragging it back to its original resting place.

Then, stuffing the carrier bag into her anorak pocket, she walked back across the field, retrieved her bike and cycled away up the drive.

Heather gave her ten minutes to get up the hill and through the village, before letting Jimmy out and driving back to the pub.

'You've been a long time,' said Alan.

'Sorry, I…I mucked out the stable,' she lied. She had decided not to tell Alan what she'd seen at Hawkridge. Sometimes his attempts at subtle humour, while he was behind the bar, verged on the dangerous, and she wanted nothing to do with Peggy's vendetta.

She spent a sleepless night wondering if all Luke's cows were dying in agony, knowing she would never forgive herself if she found out that this was the case. In the morning, Peggy turned up for work as usual, a faint whiff of garlic hanging about her anorak. She apologised about this.

'Sorry. Me anorak pongs, a bit. It was 'angin' in the kitchen while I was cookin'. I'll give it a wash, this afternoon.'

'What did you cook, Peggy?' Heather asked.

'I done a sort of stew with some of that garlic, but I think I got it a bit strong. Mum didn't like it and made me throw the rest away. Say's she 'opes the smell is out of the 'ouse before Tuesday.'

'Dave says he likes a nice hot curry,' said Alan.

Heather threw him a look that said, 'be quiet'. He grinned and switched the kettle on.

'Coffee, Peggy?' he asked.

'Wouldn't mind.'

Dave came into the pub at lunch time, with Anne, who bought him a drink.

'Luke's good and mad this morning,' he was telling her. 'The tanker driver wouldn't take his milk...said it was contaminated. He's had to feed some of it to the pigs and chuck the rest away.'

'What was it contaminated with?' Anne asked.

'Garlic, the chap said. But the only wild garlic is that patch along the bank of the river, and Luke swears he hasn't let his cows down there. Mind you, you can't always believe what Luke says. They might have got out, state his fences are in, and I expect he took a chance on the milk being all right. Anyway, he's lost all today's milk, and probably tomorrow's, as well.'

'I didn't realise that the food affected the milk, like that,' said Anne. 'That's quite interesting, isn't it, Heather?'

Heather nodded.

'Good stuff, garlic,' said Dave. 'I feed it to my dogs. They never get fleas. It comes out through the skin and fleas don't like that.'

'You learn something new every day,' said Heather.

'I bet Peggy hasn't got fleas,' Alan said, in an aside to her.

'Alan, just shut up! You are treading on very dangerous ground,' she hissed under her breath.

'What's the matter?' he asked.

'Tell you later, but don't mention garlic again...trust me.'

CHAPTER THIRTEEN

Things seemed to quieten down in the village for a while after the garlic episode, and Heather began to relax, thinking that maybe Peggy had made her point and would now come to terms with life without Luke. That was until a couple of weeks later, when Luke came into the pub one evening, grim faced, and directed a pale Mandy to the table in the corner of the bar. She looked as if she had been crying.

'Pint and...what you having, Mand?'

'Whisky, please. Black Label,' she said.

'That's a pint and a whisky, please, Heather. And a menu...we've got no food left in the house,' Luke glared at her. 'That Peggy's not working here this evening, is she? We don't want our food poisoned. And I don't expect you'd be too pleased to have a murder done in your kitchen.'

Heather wasn't sure, from this remark about poisoning, whether he meant he knew about the garlic.

'To be quite honest, if you do have to murder Peggy, I would prefer you to do it somewhere else. I've just washed the kitchen floor,' she joked. He didn't smile. 'No,' she continued. 'She's not here tonight. She only helps out occasionally in the evenings.'

What did he mean about not having any food left in the house? Was he implying that Mandy's housekeeping skills left something to be desired? Best keep out of that one, she thought, pressing Mandy's glass up under the whisky optic.

'Make that a large one. She's had a shock,' said Luke.

'Oh, what's happened?' asked Alan.

'Well, we'd just been over to Crediton, and when we got back we found that somebody - and I think we can all guess who - had put the old boar into the house while we

94

were out,' said Luke.

'What old bore?' Alan asked, raising an eyebrow at Heather as if to say 'You never told me they had any family.'

'Mine, of course,' said Luke.

'Who would that be, then?' asked Alan.

'Who?…er,' Luke looked puzzled.

'Not bore, BOAR, Alan,' Heather spelled it out for him. 'His pig. Surely she wouldn't have done that, Luke?'

'You tell me who else would have thought of something like that?'

'Oh, my God!…A pig!…In the house? Has it done much damage?' Alan was truly aghast at the idea.

'It's wrecked the kitchen, emptied the fridge, and tipped over the freezer - I reckon she opened those for it. Anything breakable has been broken - in the kitchen and the sitting room. It's been all over the furniture. We're going to have to replace the carpet. Shit everywhere. The television was knocked over, and doesn't seem to be working now. Mandy was so upset we decided to come straight up here and have a meal and a drink before we start cleaning up. If we left it till after we'd straightened up a bit, you would have been closed. We'll be at it most of the night.'

'Have you told the police?' Alan asked.

'What good would that do? Apart from giving them a good laugh. 'Sides I can't prove it can I? Did you go down this afternoon, Heather? Did you see anything?'

'No, I didn't, Luke. Sorry.' Why was she apologising? It wasn't her job to police Peggy's movements.

Mandy came over and picked up her whisky glass with a hand that still shook slightly.

'It's not just that it was a pig in the kitchen,' she said. 'It was *that* pig. It's vicious, and I'd gone into the house by myself while Luke unloaded some more cattle cake. Bloody thing had me trapped in the larder for five minutes until Luke heard me shouting. It was snuffling along the bottom of the door and pushing against it.' She took a gulp of her whisky.

'How did she get it in there?' Heather asked.

'I forgot about the spare key; on the ledge in the barn. I've taken it away now,' said Luke.

'No. What I really meant was, how did she get the pig from the sty to the kitchen?' said Heather.

'She's helped me enough times at the shows to know how to drive him with a stick and a board…he's used to it. Mind you, he doesn't like her. Probably all she'd need to do is open the sty door and run. He'd have chased her into the kitchen.'

Heather remembered Peggy hitting the boar across the face with a stick, and could imagine him trying to get his own back.

'I've a good mind to take the boar up there tomorrow, and push it into *her* house,' said Luke, his face lighting up at the possibilities of this action.

'No, Luke. That's Mercy's house, as well. You can't do that,' said Heather.

'I'll get her…somehow I'll get her,' he promised.

Dave came into the bar, and Luke and Mandy began the story again for his benefit. Luke finishing up by warning Dave that he'd better be careful how he treated Mercy, as this kind of behaviour could run in families.

'Oh, Mercy's known me long enough to know what I'm like. We're just good friends,' said Dave.

'That's what you think,' Alan muttered to Heather.

'Shhh,' she said.

'Peggy and Mercy aren't likely to come in, are they?' Alan asked her, looking worried. 'We've got that other couple booked in for supper. I don't want a riot in here, upsetting our new customers.'

'No...there's a WI meeting tonight,' said Heather.

The more Heather thought about it, the more irritated she got with Peggy. If the boar hadn't gone where she had wanted it to, it could have been roaming the farm, terrorising Jimmy...and her. That was one animal she didn't want to meet without a wall between them. Peggy's antics were getting dangerous.

Peggy arrived with an ill concealed smirk, the next morning.

'Did you hear about the old boar?' she asked, as she hung up her anorak. Heather studied it for trotter prints. Play it cool, she thought.

'Boar?'

'Down 'Awkridge. It got out.'

'How did you know?' Heather asked.

'Er...Mum 'eard it down the village...in the shop.'

'Well, I don't understand how it managed to get into the house, and I'm not very happy about it escaping. Jimmy hates pigs. I may have to think about moving him to another farm.'

'Luke must've left the door open,' Peggy said.

'It's done a lot of damage. And Mandy nearly got attacked,' said Heather.

'Good! Maybe she'll go back to Exeter. She shouldn't even be there. It's me that put all the work in on that farm, then she comes along and benefits from all I did. Did you know 'e's even bought 'er a car? She won't stay there, you know. Eventually Luke will come to 'is senses. We was goin' to get married, after Rose is pronounced legally dead. I'll get 'im back.'

'I'm not too sure you're going the right way about it,' said Heather. As soon as she had spoken, she wished she'd kept quiet. She was treading on dangerous ground, and sensed that Peggy would welcome a conspirator.

'What do you mean? What d'you think I should do, then?' Peggy asked, pulling out a chair and sitting down at the kitchen table.

'Well, er…why not take up with somebody else. Maybe Luke will get jealous,' said Heather, thinking… and maybe all his pigs will suddenly challenge the Tornado jets for air space.

'Is anybody going to do any work around here today?' asked Alan, coming into the kitchen.

'Whoops! Boss on the warpath,' said Peggy, pushing back her chair.

'And what would your Lordship like *me* to be doing, today?' asked Heather with a relieved grin at being rescued.

'Well, it's the Best Kept Village judging on Saturday. Our tubs and baskets could do with a tidy. I'm going to sweep the fag ends off the cobbles out at the front. Might even give the bench a coat of preservative this afternoon.'

'I better do the windows as well, then,' said Peggy. 'They'm about due.'

The village was looking very attractive at the moment, Heather thought, as she nipped off a drooping petunia head. A lot of work had gone into preparing for the competition, starting way back in the spring, when Anne's first seedlings sprouted in the trays in her conservatory. Many of the busy lizzies, petunias and geraniums now filling the tubs and baskets around the square, had started life under her tender care, and she, and an army of waterers, had nurtured them into the peak of condition. Competition was really strong this year. They had come second to Pillerton Tracey, last year, and some secret spy runs out that way had confirmed that this rival display was 'not a patch on last year's.'

Several people in the village had had the same idea, and were tidying up their individual displays. Anne was across the square, dead-heading the flowers in the two long planters which stood on the pavement outside the church railings, and replacing any sickly plants with strong healthy ones from her greenhouse. Dave was mowing between the graves in the churchyard. Heather wondered where his thoughts were.

'What are you smiling about?' Alan asked.

'Was I? Nothing really. It's just so very pleasant and peaceful here, isn't it?'

The bar window was pushed up from the inside.

'D'you think I should 'ave my 'air restyled, 'Eather?' Peggy asked.

'Didn't realise it was already in a 'style',' Alan muttered under his breath, as he bent over a dustpan and brush, sweeping up his little pile of cigarette ends.

'Maybe, Peg. Yes, why not?' said Heather, dragging her mind away from Mercy's mower-wielding lover.

'Right. I'm goin' to do the outside, now. You 'aven't painted that bench or anything, Alan, 'ave you? I shall need it to stand on.'

'No. I'll just move it along a bit for you.'

Anne made 'coffee drinking' motions to Heather across the square, and pointed to her house. Heather nodded and raised a thumb.

'I'm just going over to Anne's for a quick coffee,' she told Alan.

'She's over there, by the churchyard,' he said.

'Yes, she's just asked me.'

'Oh! Into telepathy now, are we?'

'Something like that. Actually, I don't want to get involved in a discussion about hairstyles.'

'Neither do I. Hey! Come back!'

'Won't be long,' she called over her shoulder, joining Anne as she crossed the square.

'It's looking good, isn't it?' said Anne, sweeping her gaze round the square.

'It's gorgeous. Have you seen Pillerton Tracey's?'

'Yes…we're definitely better this year.'

They went into Anne's house, where Heather was greeted ecstatically by Rudi, who then pointedly ignored Anne by sitting with his back to her whenever she spoke to him.

'He's angry with me for going out without him,' she explained.

It seemed that Anne's main reason for inviting Heather over, was to get her opinion on Mandy, but as Heather had hardly spoken to her for long enough to form one, she was slightly disappointed. They spoke of horses, for a while, and when Anne mentioned shoeing costs, Heather suddenly realised that she hadn't given any thought to having Jimmy's feet attended to. They looked up blacksmiths in the yellow pages, and found a farrier with an East Tegridge address. Heather wrote down the number.

Later that day she had a good look at Jimmy's feet and saw that they were growing over his shoes, one of which was very loose, so she made an appointment with Barry Martin to meet her at Hawkridge, the following day.

Barry turned out to be a well preserved fifty-something, not unattractive, with a pleasant open face and a ready smile. Heather took to him immediately and, luckily, so did Jimmy. During the course of conversation she learned that he was a widower; his wife had died of cancer eighteen months before.

Barry took measurements of Jimmy's feet, and said he would be back on Monday with a new set of shoes for him.

As Heather was driving home, she decided to probe Barry, on Monday, to find out if he had a girl-friend...he could possibly be the man for Peggy. She wondered if he knew her? Half of her mind was telling her to keep out of this, but the other half was scared of what Peggy might cook up next in her war against Mandy and Luke. Apart from them, she and Jimmy could get injured if Peggy let the boar out again. It was almost her duty to try to distract her. Her mind was made up following an incident that night.

It was just after one o'clock in the morning, when Alan nudged her awake.

'Can you hear anything?' he asked.

'Burglars are your department,' said Heather, raising her head off the pillow to listen.

'Sort of scuffling,' Alan said.

She too could hear scuffling, and was just trying to work out what it was, when the precise clopping of iron-shod hooves joined the scuffling. Heather got out of bed and went to the landing window. Alan joined her. Lights were coming on in the cottages around the square - which was full of sheep. Some of them had wandered into the churchyard, and these were accompanied by a grey horse.

'It's Jimmy!' said Heather, dashing back to the bedroom, and dragging on trousers and a jersey over her silk pyjamas.

'It's not only Jimmy. It's about forty thousand sheep,' said Alan. 'And they're bloody wrecking our tubs.' He pulled on a dressing gown and raced downstairs to join other villagers, who were trying to drive the sheep off their floral displays. The sheep scattered, for once unwilling to come to a joint decision about which direction to take, with the result that several tubs and containers were overturned, and a very precious urn, loaned by the vicar to make a central focal point, was smashed. Heather telephoned

Luke, before snatching up Jimmy's halter and joining Alan outside.

She had just caught the horse and was trying to persuade him to walk back under the low arch of the lych gate, when Luke's Land-Rover roared up the hill into the square. He leapt out, whistling to his dog through the sound of six or seven villagers hurling abuse at him. Wound up by all the excitement, Jimmy began to emphasise his refusal to duck under the lych gate, by standing on his hind legs.

'Put a sack over his head,' said Luke, pushing past them with the dog to get the remaining sheep out of the churchyard.

'Sack?' said Heather stupidly, before realising he meant, cover his eyes so that he couldn't see the arch. 'Alan!' she called. He came over. 'Lend me your dressing gown. Jimmy won't go through the gate.'

'He went in through it.'

'Explain that to him. Can I have your dressing gown?' she repeated.

'Don't be silly. I've only got pyjamas on. You've got a jersey and trousers,' he said, pulling the cord tighter round his waist.

'It's not for me. I need something to cover his eyes, so he can't see the low beam. I can't get him out.'

'Here you are!' Luke flung her his jacket as he passed, driving five sheep out through the gate. His dog soon collected the rest of the flock and they set off down the hill.

Heather put Luke's jacket over Jimmy's head and held it there by the sleeves under his chin. With his eyes covered he calmed down immediately, and she was able to ease him through the gate arch.

'I'll take him straight back. Can you come down and fetch me?' she called to Alan.

'I'll just get dressed,' he said.

Heather led a prancing, over-excited Jimmy down the hill, with difficulty. By the time she got into the yard at Hawkridge, Luke had put the sheep back in the field and was standing by the gate waiting for her.

'I can't understand it,' he said. 'The bloody gate was wide open. Somebody must have done it on purpose. It had been lifted over that rut, which was keeping it open. The wind couldn't have done that.'

'There isn't any wind,' Heather pointed out, handing him his jacket.

Luke began scouring the ground with a powerful torch.

'Looking for footprints?' Heather asked.

'Yes…Peggy sized ones,' he said.

'Oh, no, Luke, she wouldn't have done that. Not wrecked the village just before the judging.'

'Not on purpose, maybe, but she knows that all the other times we've had sheep out, they've gone the other way, towards the moor. If she did do it, she probably thought they'd go that way again.'

'But Jimmy was turned out with them. Surely she wouldn't have let him out, as well?'

'Probably didn't think - or thought he would be in the stable,' said Luke.

Alan drove into the farm yard.

'Are you ready?' he called through the open car window.

Heather knew he hadn't got out of the car because he was worried about what he might say, or do, to Luke. The pub flower tubs seemed to have provided a particularly interesting supper for the sheep. She unbuckled Jimmy's halter, and let him go. He cantered away across the field, putting in a couple of bucks with the excitement of it all, and she hoped he didn't do that sort of thing when he had a rider on him.

'See you tomorrow, Luke,' she said.

'See if you can find out any more about this,' he said, meaningfully.

Oh dear! I seem to be running with the hare and hunting with the hounds now, she thought. Suddenly, her previous life in London seemed to have been remarkably uncomplicated.

They were halfway back up the hill before she remembered that Luke's Land-Rover was still parked in the square.

'Oh, Alan, we should have offered him a lift up.'

'He can bloody walk,' said Alan.

CHAPTER FOURTEEN

The following day, the nearest garden centre had almost the busiest day of the year. Bags of compost, and virtually any plants they had in bloom, were snapped up as fast as the till could ring: and the villagers worked until dark to repair the damage. But it all ended up looking slightly unbalanced.

Peggy had given nothing away, that morning. Could it have been her? Heather had watched her reactions carefully, but she seemed as outraged as the rest of the village, and had dropped dark hints to Heather about strippers and townies leaving gates open. It was not until some time later that Heather realised Peggy had been talking about the gate being left open, while the rest of the village were still under the impression that the sheep had broken out of a badly fenced boundary. And before she, herself, had mentioned the open gate to anybody except Alan.

The judges arrived the next day and walked round making notes, but giving nothing away. The pub was busy that evening with folks asking each other if they could tell anything from the judges' expressions. But everyone agreed that the display hadn't looked as good as it did before the sheep had rampaged through, and there was dark muttering about the possibility of lynching Luke for his lax attitude to confining his stock.

'I keep telling him his fences are no good,' said Dave.

'The gate was wide open,' said Heather.

'Was it?' said Dave, frowning.

The vet came in, a burly, cheerful individual wearing a Barbour jacket that had seen better days.

'I'll have a quick half,' he said. 'Just got time before surgery. On my way back from Hawkridge. He's got two or three sheep 'off colour'.'

'Probably petunia poisoning,' said Heather, handing him his glass. He laughed. Nobody else did.

On Monday, Heather walked down to Hawkridge to get Jimmy in for the farrier. It was a lovely afternoon - or would have been if Luke hadn't spent the morning spreading pig slurry on the ten acre field running alongside the road. The stench caught in the back of her throat and she hurried to get up-wind of it, arriving in the farm yard hot and breathless.

Mandy was crossing the yard, carrying a hunting crop with a long plaited leather thong attached. Several reasons for Mandy's possession of this implement ran through Heather's mind - all of them sexual. She felt slightly ashamed of these thoughts as she said hello to her. Mandy cast a glance around the yard before looping up the thong, and stopping to talk. She saw Heather's eyes on the crop.

'No. I'm not taking up hunting,' she said. Heather hadn't thought she was. 'It's that 'blimmin' pheasant.'

'Aahh!' said Heather, with relief.

'He doesn't like this.' Mandy released the thong and cracked the whip - very professionally, Heather thought. 'I think it reminds him of gunshots. Keeps him away from me, anyway. You look a bit warm. Would you like a cold beer or something? It's cool in the kitchen.'

'I'd love one, but I've got to get Jimmy in. Barry Martin's coming to put some new shoes on him, this afternoon.'

'Never mind. Give me a shout when you've finished, if you've got time. I wouldn't mind a natter.'

Barry turned up just as Heather was leading Jimmy into the stable. He parked his van by the field gate and walked across, carrying his box of tools and an iron tripod with a smoothly rounded top where the three legs joined.

'Nice afternoon,' he said. 'Hello, little fellow,' he ran a hand down Jimmy's neck and shoulder. 'Nice little horse,' he nodded to Heather.

'People are always calling him a 'little' horse. He's a full sixteen hands,' she said.

'It's the colour…greys always seem to look smaller. Pretty little fellow. More like an Arab than a thoroughbred. Right, let's have these shoes off, then.'

He ran his hand down Jimmy's neck again, but this time carried on down his shoulder and leg to the foot, which Jimmy obligingly lifted for him. In no time at all he had cut off the clinched ends of the nails and levered off the shoe. With all four shoes off, he pared back the overgrown horn with a sharp, curved knife. Then went back to his van.

He returned, after a few minutes, carrying a new shoe on the end of an iron spike, the point of which was embedded into one of the nail holes. Picking up Jimmy's foot, he held the shoe, which Heather could now see was glowing a dull red, against the horn. There was a sizzling sound and clouds of smoke arose around Barry's head, as he turned it this way and that to look at the foot. Heather and Jimmy were engulfed in the smell of burning feathers, but Jimmy didn't seem bothered about the fact that his foot was on fire.

When Barry removed the shoe, it had branded it's imprint into the hoof.

'That's fine,' he said. 'Can I drop it in here to cool?' he indicated the water bucket in the corner of the stable.

'Yes. Sure. Wasn't he good?' she said.

'Oh, he'll have had this done hundreds of times, being a racehorse. We change their exercise shoes for lightweight racing plates, every time they run. Was that what mucked his legs up? Racing, I mean?'

'Yes. Clever of you to notice he had a problem.'

'When you've run your hand down as many legs as I have, you notice every lump and bump out of the ordinary.'

Barry's iron tripod came into its own for the front feet. Having nailed on the shoe, he lifted the foot forward and settled it on the top of the tripod while he pulled the nails tightly through, with pliers, and cut them off, hammering the ends over and into the wall of the hoof, before rasping them smooth with a file. Then he rasped the horn above the shoe, level with the metal, and finished off the whole job by painting each foot with a nourishing hoof oil.

'There you go,' he said, lifting the last foot off the tripod. 'Those should last you for a bit; in fact they'll last you for quite a long time if you're not riding him. I'll just pare the feet back next time and put these shoes on again.'

'Thank you. He looks very smart now.'

She let Jimmy out of the stable and he wandered away towards the sheep, while she walked back to the van with Barry, and admired his gas fired forge. As she was paying him, she remembered her vague plans for matching him up with Peggy. She hadn't found out yet if he had a girl friend.

'I'd like to buy you a drink,' she said. 'We've got the pub in the village. Or supper maybe? Do you ever come out to North Tegridge, in the evenings? Bring a friend.'

'Don't have a lady friend at the moment, but I might pop in one evening. Does old Dave Fordesh still drink there?'

'Yes…most evenings, well…not Tuesdays…and Thursdays.'

'I know where he is on Thursdays; he's over our way seeing…oh, I can't remember her name…big woman. Lives down the end of the village.'

'Really?' said Heather, she hoped, non-commitally.

Mandy came out of the door of the farmhouse and put something in the dustbin. She saw them and waved.

'Who's that, then?' asked Barry, who'd done a double-take at the sight of Mandy's long blonde hair blowing in the light breeze.

'Mandy. Luke's new lady.'

'Jammy bugger! Oh! Sorry, madam.'

'Don't worry,' Heather laughed. 'And call me Heather.'

'What happened to that Peggy Ashley, then? I quite liked Peg. She found herself another man and run off?'

'Not as far as I know. She works for me up at the pub, now. Lives with her mother in the village.'

'Oh,' he said, looking thoughtful.

Heather punched the air with an imaginary fist and thought: Yesss! Now all she had to do was get Peggy interested in Barry. She waved goodbye to him, as he backed his van round and drove out of the yard. Mandy knocked on the kitchen window and held up a cup. Heather nodded and walked towards the house, wondering where Luke was?

'Glad you could come in. It gets a bit lonely out here. Piece of cake?' said Mandy, indicating a moist looking sponge stuffed with jam and cream.

'I definitely shouldn't, but yes, please. I'll have to walk extra fast back into the village to work some of that off.' She looked around the enormous kitchen. It seemed more or less as she remembered it from the first time, except that the dresser looked remarkably bare. 'You've cleared up well. No signs that you've had the boar in here,' she said.

'It's more a lack of signs…like there's no china on the dresser. He knocked it over. Pity the great heavy thing didn't fall on him. Everything was smashed. China that had belonged to Luke's mother - and grandmother, I don't doubt. He is seriously angry about it.'

'Where is he at the moment?' Heather asked.

'He's gone to buy some chains and padlocks for the field gates. He says anyone else wanting to let the stock out will have to turn up with bolt-croppers. He'll give you a key for the one to Jimmy's field, but keep it away from that bloody Peggy. Luke's almost certain it was her that let the sheep out the other night. She hasn't said anything, has she?'

'She wouldn't tell me,' said Heather, shaking her head and taking a bite of cake to hide her face.

'I don't know,' Mandy sighed. 'I thought my life had taken a turn for the better when Luke asked me to move in with him, but now I'm not so sure. I didn't know she felt like that about him. I mean, it's a bit obsessive, isn't it? To be quite honest, she frightens me. She did this you know.' She touched a red scar on her forehead.

'I know…er, I know what you mean. Yes. She does seem to be a slightly unhinged where Luke is concerned. How did she do that? Heather nodded towards the scar.'

'It was the day I arrived. She leapt out of the hedge and threw a brick through the windscreen at me when we turned into the drive. Luke said it was her. All I saw was a blue coat with a hood. More tea?'

Heather looked at the clock above the mantelpiece.

'Yes. I've got time for another one, thank you. Not that I am trying to interfere, but didn't you think about going to the police? You could have been seriously hurt.'

'That was my first reaction,' said Mandy. 'But Luke said he would speak to her, and tell her we would go to the police if anything like that happened again.' Mandy peered at her forehead in a small mirror on the kitchen window-ledge, as she lifted the kettle to pour more boiling water into the teapot. 'I reckon that *is* going to leave a scar…good job I don't have to rely on my looks as much as I used to.'

'Do you think you and Luke will get married? Oh, sorry, maybe I shouldn't have asked that. Just tell me if I'm being too nosy.'

'No, that's all right. We'd have to wait until Rose, his wife, is officially declared dead. She drowned herself you know, in the river; they never found the body.'

'Yes, I heard,' said Heather, visualising the sinister dark waters swirling under the bridge.

'She suffered from depression,' Mandy went on. 'I don't think Luke found it easy to live with her. Do you know they even suspected him of doing away with her, and hiding the body.'

'I heard about that, too,' Heather nodded, trying not to think of the bare earth of the grave in the copse behind her stable; where Luke said he buried animal casualties from the farm. An unpleasant smell from there had drifted into the stable one evening, and when she had investigated she'd found a hole where a dog, or a fox, had been digging into the mound. She'd kicked the soil back into the hole, terrified of suddenly finding a human hand, or worse, a head.

She finished her tea and stood up.

'Oh, Heather, can I give you my mobile phone number? Mandy said, suddenly. 'Just in case you might get the feeling Peggy is planning any more nasty surprises for us. You could let me know. Better on the mobile. Luke's liable to pick up the other phone and he gets a bit funny when Peggy's mentioned - thinks people are interfering.'

She wrote the number on a piece of paper and handed it to Heather.

'Okay. I'd better go. Alan will be wondering where I have got to.'

'He's nice, your husband. We had quite a long talk at the darts match,' said Mandy.

Luke's Land-Rover drew up in the yard, and he and Heather met in the doorway.

'Hello, Heather, don't leave on my account.'

'I wasn't,' she said. 'I have to get back.'

'Wait a minute,' he said, turning and going round to the back of the vehicle.

There was a clanking of chains, as he moved something, then he came over to her carrying a plastic bag containing a padlock, and two keys on a ring. He slid one of them off and handed it to her.

'This is the one to Jimmy's field. Keep it safe. And, whatever you do, keep it away from that Peggy.'

The pheasant walked round the front of the Land-Rover and attacked Luke's boot, receiving a kick, for it's pains, which sent it flying across the yard in a screech of ruffled feathers. It turned, obviously lining up for another attack, until Mandy and her whip came out of the back door. She unfurled the thong and snapped the leather into a loud report.

'I love it when she does that,' said Luke.

Heather looked at him and received a wicked grin, which unnerved her slightly. When she got home she gave Alan a big hug and a kiss.

'Thank you for being so normal,' she said. He held her away at arms length.

'What's that supposed to mean?' he asked.

'Nothing.'

'I don't know,' he looked thoughtful. 'For 'normal' I am reading 'boring'. Perhaps I should try to cultivate some hidden strange tendency.'

'Like what?'

'Don't know. I'll work on it. Meanwhile, how about a cup of tea and a piece of cake?'

CHAPTER FIFTEEN

The back door banged against the wall as Peggy entered carrying a large plastic bag, it was this which had knocked the door wide open as she struggled through. The wind spattered rain in across the mat and blew a newspaper off the kitchen table. Heather bent to pick it up as Peggy kicked the door shut and put the bag down on the floor. Then, turning towards Heather, she pushed back the hood of her dripping anorak.

'What d'you think?' she said.

Heather gasped. Peggy's long, rather wild, black hair had been tamed. It was now much shorter, and had been cut into a sort of layered effect with a spiky fringe which reached below her eyebrows, and caught on her eyelashes every time she blinked. This obviously irritated her, as she was unconsciously brushing it out of her eyes every few minutes. The new style didn't really suit her, Heather thought. But mostly it didn't suit her because the hair was now a daffodil yellow blonde.

'Well?' Peggy asked: rather pleased with the effect she had had on Heather, misinterpreting it as awed approval.

'It's... blonde,' said Heather, inanely.

'Full marks for observation,' said Peggy, going across to the mirror on the wall beside the door into the bar, and patting the shaggy ends back into place. 'But do you think it suits me?'

Alan came in from the bar, where he had been 'bottling up', and nearly collided with Peggy.

'Hello...who?...Dear God!...Peggy!'

'Good, isn't it?' said Peggy.

'It's...Wow!' said Alan, shaking his head in shocked disbelief; which Peggy interpreted as his being bowled over by her stunning beauty.

113

Although her rather sallow skin clashed horribly with the new colour, her black eyes and eyebrows stood out to remarkable effect behind the spiky yellow curtain of her fringe. She looked like a, possibly dangerous, wild animal lurking in a pile of straw. In a weird way the result was so startling as to be interesting, Heather thought.

'Do you know, Peggy,' she said slowly. 'I rather think I like it. It was a shock at first, but now I'm getting used to it, it's impressive. That's going to turn a few heads.'

'You think so?' Peggy looked pleased with this. 'Seems to have worked with Alan, doesn't it? Don't get me wrong, 'Eather. I'm not after your 'usband,' she laughed.

Alan looked relieved.

'What's in the bag?' Heather asked.

'Oh, I got a new coat while I was in Exeter getting me 'air done, only it's so wet today I didn't want to get it spoiled. I'll wear it 'ome, if it stops raining.' She pulled a 'hot pink' leather-look jacket out of the bag.

Alan suddenly turned and went back into the bar.

'Mum likes it...she says she's still making 'er mind up about the 'air,' she pulled on the jacket.

'It's very smart,' lied Heather, thinking that the new Peggy would not look out of place on the corner of one of the meaner streets of a large city - late at night. She could just see her bending down to speak through a car window to a prospective punter.

''As Alan got a cold?' Peggy asked.

'No, I don't think so,' said Heather. 'Why?'

'I thought I 'eard 'im coughin'...well, I'd better get on.' She took the jacket off and folded it carefully back into the bag. Then she collected the cleaning materials out of the cupboard and joined Alan in the bar.

Later that morning, Heather was in the bar, putting the new snack menus in their holders on the tables, when Alan opened the door for the lunch-time session.

'Hello, Dave,' he said, standing back to allow Dave in.

'Yes,' said Dave.

This rather odd response caused Heather to study Dave more closely. He walked across the room, deep in thought, hitched one hip up onto his usual stool at the bar, and paused for a second or two. Then he seemed to remember the other hip, and pushed himself properly onto the stool using his foot on the brass rail. He shook his head, then noticed Alan facing him across the counter, one eyebrow raised questioningly.

'What?' Dave asked.

'I said, your usual?' said Alan.

Heather joined Alan behind the bar.

'Are you all right, Dave?' she asked.

'Yes, yes, I'm fine - sorry. Just had a bit of a shock. God knows what Mercy thinks. I'm going up there for supper this evening.'

'Tuesday', Alan mouthed at Heather over Dave's bowed head. She pursed her lips to kill a smile.

'You've just met Peggy on her way home, haven't you?' said Alan. The rain had stopped and Peggy had left the pub in all her finery.

Dave shook his head again, in disbelief.

'What does she think she looks like? Only thing missing was the three inch high heels,' he said.

'I knew there was something,' said Alan.

'That hair!' said Dave. 'Reminded me of a ferret looking out of a hayrick.'

'Don't be unkind, you two,' said Heather, feeling horribly insincere as Dave had just repeated her own impression. 'If it makes Peggy feel better and more attractive, then good for her. Being thrown out by Luke, like that, really upset her.'

'Don't I know it,' said Dave. 'Cost me a whole spreader full of good muck.' He grinned. 'Mind you, I have to admit I've never had so much entertainment out of muck spreading before.'

More customers began to come into the pub, and soon Alan and Heather were busy satisfying their needs. Dave finished his pint and left, muttering something about 'worming the ewes'.

Just before closing time, Alan went into the kitchen where Heather was beginning to do the washing up.

'Luke and Mandy have just come in - you have to see this,' he said.

'I don't think I can stand much more excitement,' she said, drying her hands on a tea towel. 'What is it?'

'Come on,' he said, going back into the bar.

She followed him, said: 'Hello,' to Luke, and then did a double-take as she realised the woman standing next to him was Mandy.

Mandy was doing a remarkably good impression of the Queen, out for a day's shooting. Sensibly clad in a new waxed jacket, with her long blonde hair hidden by a head scarf, she looked far too 'county' for Luke. He had on his usual blue farm overalls, and *his* waxed jacket looked as if the pigs had borrowed it. Heather felt an insane desire to giggle.

'North Tegridge. North Tegridge. All change,' said Alan quietly, after the manner of a railway station announcer.

'Pardon?' said Luke, who hadn't quite heard.

'Barrel needs changing,' said Heather, quickly. 'Better go and do it, Alan.'

Alan dutifully pulled up the hatch in the bar floor and disappeared down the cellar steps with a wicked smile, saying quietly, in a very posh voice 'My husband and I.' Heather gave him a push with her foot, then nearly joined him as he grabbed her ankle.

'What are you two playing at?' said Luke, peering over the bar. 'Can anyone join in?'

'Nice jacket, Mandy,' said Heather.

'Yes, Luke thought it was about time I had something weatherproof now I'm going to start helping him with the milking.'

Oh God! Heather thought. Peggy will go mad at the thought of Mandy having anything to do with her precious cows. She hoped she wouldn't find out.

CHAPTER SIXTEEN

Heather met Anne in the village shop.

'You and Alan going to the fair on Saturday?' Anne asked.

'I heard someone talking about it in the bar. What is it exactly?' Heather put a jar of coffee into her basket.

'The East Tegridge Rural Fair. People come from miles around. It's really something. And it is exactly what it says…rural…not like your slick agricultural shows. It's a real fair run by enthusiastic amateurs. Things sometimes go wrong, which adds to the fun. A pig escaped last year and thoroughly upset the llamas.'

'Llamas?' queried Heather.

'Yes. I forget where they came from, but people go walking with them, apparently. I'd quite like to do that,' said Anne thoughtfully, then glanced through the glass shop door at Rudi who was tied up outside. 'If it wasn't for that little swine…he'd probably think llamas were a new exotic dish dreamed up by an enterprising Peruvian pet food manufacturer.'

Heather laughed. 'You love him, really.'

'I know. Sad isn't it?'

When Heather arrived back in the bar, she mentioned the fair to Alan.

'Dave said something about it, the other day. Yes, let's go. It sounds rather fun. I wonder who's doing the catering? Do you think we should start doing outside catering?'

'What, just the two of us?' asked Heather, realising better than Alan how much work this would entail.

'No, no, we'd have to take on extra casual staff, but it could be quite profitable. Peggy might help… and Mercy.

She's supposed to be a very good cook. I think I'll do a bit of research,' he said.

The day of the fair dawned wet and blustery. But by the afternoon, when Heather and Alan had closed the pub, the rain had stopped and patches of clear blue sky, with sunshine, were appearing more frequently. They drove the four miles to East Tegridge to find the small village packed with cars which had overflowed from the car park in a rather soggy ten acre field. They had to wait for five minutes before somebody left, to get a parking space.

'Goodness! Where did all these people come from?' said Heather, as they paid their entrance fee and walked into the fairground.

They stopped to chat to one of their customers, then Alan saw Dave, who was watching Barry Martin giving a display of wrought iron work. He had his forge going and was welding old horseshoes together to build an ornate garden gate. As Alan started to move towards Dave, Mercy and Peggy arrived through the entrance gate, and came over to them.

'You made it then,' said Peggy. Looking totally confident and insanely 'tarty' in her new jacket and a skirt which was much too short for a lady of her more mature years.

'Yes. We didn't realise how busy it would be,' said Heather.

'I wonder if Dave's here?' said Mercy, looking round.

At the same moment as Heather started to say 'yes', Alan said: 'No…we haven't seen him,' shaking his head frantically at her from behind Mercy and Peggy.

'Er, no,' said Heather, casting a sideways, surreptitious glance in the direction of Barry's stand, to see that Dave had been joined by an ambulant floral tent. The Big Woman from East Tegridge.

'Can I buy you two a drink?' Alan asked, steering them towards the beer tent which was in the opposite direction. He was at the tent entrance when he realised Heather wasn't with them. She was standing transfixed at the side of the central ring, where a girl in a flounced Spanish dress and sombrero, was giving a dressage display on a bright bay stallion with a flowing, black wavy mane and tail. Alan smiled and continued into the tent, with Peggy and Mercy.

'He's beautiful!' Heather breathed.

'Talking about me?' said a voice beside her.

'Luke! I didn't see you.'

'Shame. I thought my luck had changed for a minute.'

'Is Mandy here?' Heather asked.

'She's around somewhere. Who's the blonde your old man has just taken into the beer tent?'

'You mean you don't know?'

'Know what? He hasn't left you for somebody else has he? Nobody tells me anything, around here.'

Mandy joined them, her arms full of dried flowers she had just bought. Heather admired them, whilst frantically wondering what to do.

'Where did you get those?' she asked.

'Over there,' Mandy pointed to a stand the other side of the ring, and the other side of Dave and his tent.

'I think I'll get some, too,' said Heather. 'See you later.'

'Hey! What don't I know?' Luke called after her, but she pretended she hadn't heard him. As she glanced back she saw Luke and Mandy heading for the beer tent. She fumbled in her handbag for her mobile, and hurriedly dialled Alan's number.

'Hello. What's the matter? Are you lost?' he said.

'Don't say anything. Just get out of there fast. Leave Peggy and Mercy and get out. I'm by the dried flower stand.' She clicked the phone shut feeling like a character out of a spy movie, and stared across the central ring, dimly registering that the stallion had gone and the ring was now filling up with donkeys harnessed to racing sulkies. Heather's eyes were fixed on the crowded entrance to the beer tent.

She saw Alan's tall figure come out. He stopped for a second to speak to Luke and Mandy, who pointed across the ring to where Heather was standing. He slowed down as he walked up the side of the ring, and paused to watch four men setting out a race track around the perimeter, with eighteen inch high brushwood jumps at intervals along the course.

Mercy came out of the beer tent, and stared around. Was she looking for Alan, or Dave? Heather's eyes flicked round the stalls set out on the boundary of the field; then she spotted the floral dress, and Dave, who was almost hidden behind it. They were watching a sheep-shearing demonstration.

Mercy sat down at a table outside the tent in a small 'garden with picket fence' area, set between the guy ropes.

Four donkeys, drawing sulkies, were driven up to the starting gate. Alan reached her.

'Thanks,' he said. 'That was close - although it might have been fun to stay and watch. Not something I really wanted to get dragged into, though.' He looked across at the ring. 'Tell me - you seem to know more about these things than I do - how exactly do they propose to get those carts over the jumps?'

'It's been worrying me, as well,' said Heather.

They both stared in horrified fascination as the starting flag was dropped, and the donkeys were whipped into a reluctant canter by their enthusiastic drivers. The leading donkey flew over the brush fence, which then folded flat as the sulky wheels hit it. Alan looked disappointed.

Spectators on the other side of the ring, were turning and pointing towards the beer tent. Mercy was now standing up. One white donkey refused the third fence and began bucking furiously across the ring, to cheers from the onlookers, threatening to overturn the sulky and decant the driver.

'Luke didn't recognise Peggy,' Heather said. 'He asked me who your new blonde girl friend was.'

'That explains the wink and leer I got, as he and Mandy went into the tent.'

People were flooding out of the beer tent now; some standing in animated conversation, others drifting towards the joys of the main ring, stalls and side-shows. Heather sat down on a straw bale at the ringside.

'I hope nobody gets killed,' she said.

'They're not going that fast,' said Alan.

'No. Not the donkeys. In the beer tent.'

There was the sound of a police siren in the distance.

'Is that police, or ambulance?' asked Alan.

'Police, I think.'

'There go our outside catering plans,' said Alan. 'Peggy will probably be banned from every beer tent in the country. I wonder what's going on in there? Shall we go and look?'

'No, we'd only get involved.'

A police car drove into the field and parked by the beer tent.

'Oh no! She's really done it this time,' said Heather.

'Actually, we don't know that Peggy's done anything. She's probably just buying the drinks, and wondering why I had to make a sudden dash to the loo.'

'I have this very strong feeling that, whatever's happening in there, Peggy's in the thick of it. She hasn't come out. Mercy's still outside,' said Heather.

An ambulance raced along the road, turned in, and pulled up beside the police car. The paramedics followed the police into the tent.

'Dear God!' Heather exclaimed.

Dave and The Big Woman had started down the other side of the main ring, drawn by the drama at the far end of the show-ground, when he spotted Mercy outside the tent, talking to a policemen. He stopped and pretended deep interest in the harness and brasses of two heavy horses who were waiting their turn to parade in the ring.

'This is infuriating. Can't we just creep a bit nearer? I'm dying to know what's happened,' said Alan.

'I've a horrid feeling that we'll find out soon enough. No! Stay here, Alan,' she caught his arm and he sat down again beside her on the bale.

'Spoilsport,' he said.

The paramedics re-appeared, and walked towards their vehicle, one beside Mandy, who had her arm in a sling, and the other supporting Luke, who's head was bandaged. They were both helped into the ambulance, which then drove away.

Peggy, flanked by two policemen, came out of the tent and joined her mother at the table. The policemen had a word or two with her, before getting into their car and driving away.

'Now can we go and see?' Alan asked.

'All right,' said Heather, who was secretly dying to know if Peggy had inflicted all that damage by herself. And if she had, why she hadn't been taken away in the police car.

They reached the table just as Peggy and Mercy were getting up. They sat down again and indicated that Heather and Alan should join them. Peggy took out her purse.

'Alan, you couldn't get us all a drink, could you?' she said. 'Only I'm not allowed back in there.'

Alan and Heather exchanged glances over Peggy's head as she searched in her purse.

'What was all that about?' Heather asked.

'Bastard put 'is 'and up my skirt…well, almost. Said 'e didn't know it was me; not that that makes it any better. Said I was in 'is way and 'e wanted to get to the bar. So I 'it 'im with my glass. Waste of a pint. I didn't know 'e was going to fall on that silly bitch, did I? They can't blame me for that. All I know was that some bloke was touchin' me up, so I turned round and when I saw who it was, I 'it 'im.'

'But what about the police? Are you in trouble now?' Heather asked.

'Well, they asked 'im if 'e wanted to press charges, and I said if 'e did I would charge 'im with sexual 'arrassment. I said I acted in self defence.'

'Is Mandy's arm broken?' Alan asked.

'Dunno…'ope so. It's got to be x-rayed.'

'I'll go and get the drinks - don't bother about that, Peggy.' Alan nodded towards her purse. 'I'll pay for them.'

There was a burst of clapping from the main ring as the winner of the donkey race was presented with a prize.

'Have you seen Dave, at all?' Mercy asked.

'Er…no,' Heather lied. 'Oh, look at that! Aren't they magnificent?'

Two black shire horses, with white feathery fetlocks, were parading round the ring in full show turnout. Manes and tails plaited with straw and decorated with red, white and blue ribbons. Their black leather harness was polished, and brasses and buckles gleamed gold in the sunlight. After two circuits, they were led into the centre of the ring and spectators were invited closer, to inspect them. The two giants stood like statues while people rubbed their noses and patted their necks and small children wandered frighteningly close to their enormous hooves. One toddler walked right under one without seeming to realise what he had done. Heather stopped breathing for a few seconds, but nobody else seemed bothered.

Alan appeared with their drinks on a tray.

'Have I missed anything?' he asked.

'You didn't see Dave in there, did you?' Mercy asked.

'No, sorry. You'll be glad to know, Peggy, that the majority of the customers in the bar are on your side,' he said.

'So they should be,' was the uncompromising reply. 'Oh, look Mum! There's Dave.' Peggy pointed across to the far side of the ring. The cart-horses were just being led away, and Dave and another man were dragging what looked like miniature greyhound traps, into the ring. The floral tent was not in sight.

Alan nudged Heather under the table and nodded unobtrusively towards the show-ground entrance. The Big Woman and two other ladies were just leaving, carrying their day's purchases.

'It's the terrier racing,' said Mercy. 'Dave's little Gyp usually wins. Probably because he keeps the traps at his place, so she gets plenty of practice. He trains her with live rats. Little devil for rats, she is.'

'Shall we go over and watch?' said Heather, finishing her drink. Relieved now that she needn't try to keep Dave and Mercy apart any longer. 'Oh…they're not going to use live rats, are they?'

'Course not,' Mercy laughed. 'They winch a rabbit skin along on a rope and the dogs chase that. It's good fun. Anyone can enter their terriers.'

They walked across the, now empty, main ring to the straight track which had been set up along the far side, and joined the crowd lining the ropes. The man hand-winding the winch did a practice run with the 'hare', which bobbed jerkily along from beside the traps, up the track, across the finishing line, and then disappeared into a narrow gap between two straw bales.

The first three dogs to be pushed into the traps were Gyp, and the winch-man's two terriers. These three knew all about terrier racing, and were screaming with excitement and gnawing at the bars to get at the 'hare'. They came out of the traps like rockets. One of them grabbed the 'hare' halfway to the finishing line and began to shake it vigorously; while Gyp and the other one, who had bumped together as they came out of the traps, ignored the 'hare' in favour of a fight to the death.

Somebody threw a bucket of water over these two which, apart from making them wet, made no difference at all. Dave picked up both of them together, still locked onto each other's throats, and carried them across to the corner of the field where he dropped them into a water trough. Then casually lit a cigarette, whilst waiting for them to surface. This, to Heather, seemed to take for ever.

He came back with Gyp tucked under his arm. She was snarling down at the winch-man's terrier who was trotting beside them, jumping up every few strides, and snapping at Gyp's hanging back legs. Dave slipped a thin rope noose over Gyp's head and gave her to Mercy to hold.

The other two terriers were put back in the traps along with another entry for the second race, the vicar's 'westie', a rather portly white terrier who was looking totally bewildered, and promptly turned round to face the door by which he had been put into the trap. While the other two raged at the closed gates, he sat glumly with his back to the racecourse. The 'hare' was started, the traps flew open, and he continued to sit facing away from the resulting mayhem, patiently waiting for the vicar to let him out. This time the 'hare' made it to the straw bales and shot through the gap, so did the terriers with the result that the 'hare' ended up in two pieces.

As nobody else seemed inclined to pit their much-loved pets against the winch man's terriers - or Gyp - the ring was cleared again for an impressive falconry display which ended when the final act, a large white barn owl, flew up into the top branches of an oak tree on the field boundary and refused to come down. Heather and Alan couldn't stay to witness the end of this small drama, as they had to get back to open the pub. They offered Mercy and Peggy a lift home, but they had arranged to go back with Dave.

CHAPTER SEVENTEEN

Heather braced herself for another anti-Peggy tirade from Luke, as she turned into the farm the day after the fair. She got out of the car, and paused as she saw the pheasant limped across the farmyard towards her, his neck feathers raised, but he stopped when Mandy tapped on the kitchen window. He looked up at the window, then turned and limped back towards the cart-shed, flying the last few feet and landing on the handle of the wheelbarrow, just inside the doorway, where he hunched down looking very sorry for himself. Mandy came out into the yard, her left arm still in the sling.

'Hello, how are you both?' Heather asked. She nodded at the sling. 'Is it broken?'

'No, just a bad sprain, they said. It got bent backwards under me when I fell. I expect you heard what happened.'

'I got Peggy's side of it.'

'Paranoid bitch...I'm beginning to think she's really dangerous. She could have killed Luke, you know. She's stronger than she looks,' said Mandy.

'How is he?'

'He's just having a lie down before milking; he's got a terrible headache and he's a bit concussed. They didn't want to let him come home yesterday, but he insisted. Said he didn't want to leave me on my own with that mad woman about. Did you see what she's done to her hair? Oh, of course you have. Luke didn't recognise her - that was half the trouble. She said he molested her. He says he didn't. He just asked her to move over, so he could get to the bar.'

'Are you pressing any charges?' Heather asked.

'No...it was probably six of one and half a dozen of the other...not worth the hassle. Fortunately it's my left arm. I

128

just hope she'll give up now, and leave us alone.'

'What's wrong with the pheasant? Heather asked. 'He seems very lame.'

Mandy grinned. 'Unfortunate accident with my whip. The thong flicked round his leg and sprained his ankle...do pheasants have ankles?'

'I'm not sure,' Heather grinned. 'But he's the first I've seen with a whiplash injury.'

It was a blustery afternoon, but not raining, and she decided to take Jimmy out for a walk. She collected the halter from the stable and whistled to him. He was drinking from the stream at the bottom of the hill. All he needed was a single spiral horn, and he could have posed for a picture of a particularly beautiful unicorn, she thought, as he raised his head showering droplets of water from his muzzle. He came towards her up the field, walking sound except for the rutted areas where he crossed the tracks the sheep had trodden into the turf.

The wind swirled around, lifting his mane. High overhead the turbulence was tossing the rooks about the sky, until they looked like fragments of black bin liners. They seemed to be playing with the wind. Heather envied them that wild freedom - it looked like fun.

She led Jimmy through the farmyard, to no more than a bad tempered glance from the pheasant, and up the track to the road. As his feet hit the tarmac he began to jog sideways, excited by the change of scenery.

'Steady,' she said, beginning to feel nervous as she sensed the strength at the other end of the lead rope. She decided to go only as far as the village square, then back again. They went down the hill, over the bridge, and started up the other side towards the village. Every gust of wind made him bounce.

A vehicle was coming up the road behind them. She

pushed Jimmy onto the grass verge and made him stand, so that it could pass; but it pulled up beside them, and Barry Martin leaned across the passenger seat and wound down the window.

'Got the little horse out, I see. Good idea. Some light exercise will help to build up a bit of muscle.'

'Yes. He's a very twitchy, though. Maybe I shouldn't have chosen such a windy day for his first outing.'

'He'll be all right. I may be over your way tomorrow evening. I'll get that drink off you,' he said.

'Of course. We'll look forward to it.' Jimmy was fidgeting now, and Heather decided to take him back and try again in calmer weather.

As she walked, and Jimmy jogged sideways, back to the farm, she was plotting how she could get Peggy into the pub, the following evening, and push her and Barry together.

Luke came out of the farmhouse as they reached the yard. He looked pale and had a white gauze square bandaged to his head.

'Little horse looks lively,' he said.

'Bit too lively for me. We didn't go far. How's your head?'

'Painful, but I'll live; no thanks to that maniac. Maybe she'll lay off a bit now. The police warned her to behave. I didn't recognise her. She's smartened herself up a lot.'

Heather gave him a puzzled glance as he walked on across the yard, and decided he wasn't joking. He really did think that Peggy's new image was an improvement.

…………

Peggy seemed a bit subdued when she turned up for work on Monday morning. After half an hour of virtual silence, Heather felt bound to speak.

'Are you okay, Peg?'

Peggy's hand moved even more slowly over the bar table she was polishing, while she considered this question.

'I dunno … feel a bit down …I miss the farm…miss me cows.'

'Oh,' said Heather, running this idea round in her head, and deciding that she probably wouldn't miss cows. They seemed so characterless to her.

As if she had read Heather's thoughts, Peggy spoke again.

'They're such characters,' she sighed heavily, and stared vacantly out of the bar window into the square. Suddenly she seemed to come to life.

'There's Barry…Barry Martin…blacksmith from East Tegridge. Do you know 'im? Don't often see 'im in the village.'

'Well, yes, as a matter of fact I do. It was him I had to shoe Jimmy the other day. I think he's coming in this evening. I offered to buy him a drink.'

'Is 'e?' Peggy looked thoughtful. 'This won't do,' she said, suddenly coming alive and vigorously finishing off the table she had been slowly wearing away. 'Stick the kettle on, 'Eather. I'm nearly done in 'ere.'

'Thank you, God,' Heather whispered to herself.

Alan caught Peggy's last remark as he came into the bar.

'Who's the boss around here?' he said quietly, to Heather.

'Shh! I'm working on a cunning plan,' she said, pulling him into the kitchen.

'Oh dear…I don't want to know,' he said, then thought for a minute. 'Unless it's liable to involve us in any danger.'

'What do you mean?'

131

'Well, it's obviously to do with Peggy, and we've seen what she can do. How is Luke, by the way?'

'Bit concussed, but reckons he'll survive. He said he didn't recognise her.'

'Really? I bet he'll know her the next time they meet. I would say she's probably made a lasting impression on him.'

'Yes. There's a large white bandage covering it,' she smiled. 'Mandy's arm's not broken by the way, just sprained.'

Heather put some water into the kettle and switched it on, while Alan reached down three mugs from hooks on the dresser and took the lid off the coffee jar. A much happier-looking Peggy came through from the bar with an armful of dirty tea towels. She dumped these in the sink and turned on the hot tap.

'You need some more washing powder, 'Eather; this one's nearly empty,' she said, lifting a box from the cupboard under the sink and pouring an over-generous amount of the contents into the water. 'Oh, I forgot the dusters,' she went back into the bar.

'I suppose that means Mandy won't be able to help with the milking after all, then - well, not till her arm's....' Alan's voice tailed off at the frantic signals from Heather as she tried to alert him to the fact that Peggy was coming back into the kitchen.

Peggy's expression turned in a second from sunny, to dark and thunderous.

'What did you just say, Alan?' she asked, menacingly.

'I er...'

''As that bitch been messin' with my cows?'

'I er...' said Alan, again.

'Is that all you can say? I er,' said Peggy.

'I'm er, just going to the shop. I'll get some more washing powder,' said Alan, scuttling, crab-like out of the back door.

132

'What did 'e mean, 'Eather?'

'I er…'

'Is this a family thing, this 'I erring'? Tell me - you've been going down to 'Awkridge in the afternoons - is that bitch tryin' to do the milkin'?'

'I shouldn't think so. They were probably just joking.' The kettle boiled and switched itself off. Heather spooned coffee into the mugs.

'They?'

'Oh, Peggy, stop it. I don't want to get involved in this. By the way, that Barry Martin…'

'Yes?' Peggy interrupted.

'Well, I think he quite fancies you. He seemed very sorry you weren't at Hawkridge when he came to see Jimmy, the other day.' She poured water onto the coffee in the mugs.

'Was 'e?'

'Yes.'

'Oh,' Peggy looked thoughtful. 'I wonder if 'e'd recognise me? Luke didn't.'

'Why don't you come in for a drink this evening, and find out?' said Heather.

'Might do,' she sipped her coffee.

A hand slid through the back door and lifted Alan's cap off it's peg on the wall. The hand then tossed the cap into the room, and Alan looked round the door.

'Is it safe to come in again?' he asked. Heather nodded.

He was carrying a large box of washing powder and a packet of Peggy's favourite chocolate biscuits, which he placed on the table beside her.

'Frighten you, did I?' she grinned up at him, pulling open the plastic wrapper and offering him one.

'A bit,' he said, looking relieved that the impending storm seemed to have blown over.

133

CHAPTER EIGHTEEN

That evening, Barry came in early, still wearing his working clothes. Heather cursed quietly, as it looked as if he had only called in for a quick drink on his way home. Luke and Mandy arrived just behind him, which added to Heather's self imposed tension.

As she got them all a drink, she cast nervous glances at the door into the square and jumped when the wind rattled it.

'Are you all right?' Alan asked. 'You seem a bit twitchy.'

'I'm fine. I'm fine,' she dragged her eyes away from the door and handed Luke his pint.

Barry and Mandy seemed to be getting on well. Luke sipped his beer with one ear on their conversation as he asked Heather if she was expecting someone. He half turned so that he could face the bar door as well.

'No - not really,' she said.

'If it's Peggy you're bothered about, don't worry. If she comes in, we'll go. I don't want any more trouble at the moment. It upsets Mandy. We only popped in for a quick one, anyway. He turned away and joined in with Mandy and Barry's conversation. The door creaked and Dave came in, also in his working clothes.

'Saw your old van out there, Barry. Thought you might be in here.'

'What'll you have, Dave?' Barry asked.

'Me usual,' Dave nodded to Heather and Alan.

A flash of yellow bobbing along outside the bar window made Heather's heart skip a beat.

'What *is* the matter with you? You jumped, just then,' said Alan.

She nodded towards the door as Mercy and Peggy entered. Heather kept telling herself that this was what she'd planned for, and she should be pleased. Mercy headed straight for Dave. Peggy paused for a moment, torn between glaring at Mandy, and smiling seductively at Barry. The seductive smile won - though Heather found it almost more frightening than the glare. Barry smiled back, with a hint of a frown. He obviously didn't recognise the new Peggy.

She walked past Luke and Mandy, without acknowledging them further, and joined Mercy, by which time Barry had made the connection with Mercy and was standing up to offer Peggy his bar stool. Mandy caught the appreciative glance which Luke cast at the back view of the yellow hair and clashing pink jacket. She slid off her stool and lifted her handbag off the hook under the bar.

'Come on, Luke. Supper'll be ready,' she said.

He pulled his fascinated gaze away from Peggy's over-exposed legs, and finished his drink in one swallow.

''Night, Alan, Heather,' he said, replacing his glass on the bar. As he held the door open for Mandy, he looked back at Peggy. She and Mercy were just moving from the bar to a table, where they were joined by Dave and Barry.

Heather breathed a sigh of relief and pushed a glass up under the gin optic.

'You don't normally start this early,' said Alan, reaching for a bottle of tonic and taking the top off it before handing it to her.

'There. Isn't that a nice family picture?' said Heather, dropping a slice of lemon into her drink, and nodding towards the four, chatting animatedly at their table. She wondered whether Barry was *really* that funny. Peggy seemed to be laughing a lot.

'Family picture?' Alan smiled. 'I think there's somebody missing.'

'Who?'

'The Big Woman from East Tegridge,' he said.

'Behave! Or you'll be banished to the kitchen to make sandwiches. Don't mess this up, Alan. I've been trying to get Peggy and Barry together. If she can find another man to take her mind off Luke, maybe she'll stop doing disastrous things down at the farm. Jimmy could have got run over when she let the sheep out.'

'Was that her? You didn't tell me!'

'I think so…but don't say anything; it's all blown over now.'

'Stupid moo! Winning the Best Kept Village might have improved our takings from people who would have come out to visit North Tegridge.'

Barry came up to the bar and ordered four more drinks.

'I nearly didn't recognise Peggy,' he said to Heather. 'She's changed her hair. And her clothes, she looks…nice.' His voice tailed off a bit as he spoke, and Heather got the impression he didn't really mean what he'd just said. 'That Mandy seems nice,' he went on. Quite a different inflexion on the word 'nice', Heather noticed. 'Bit too good for Luke, if you ask me. He doesn't treat his women all that well…still, none of my business,' he said, picking up the tray of drinks and taking it back to the table.

After another twenty minutes, Dave swallowed the last of his beer and stood up.

'Gotta go. I only popped in to see if you were in here, Barry. See you tomorrow, Mercy.'

'I'd better be off, as well,' said Barry. 'Do you always come in on a Monday, Peggy?'

'Sometimes, it depends… depends on the company,' she gave him an arch smile through the yellow thatch.

'Might see you in here next Monday, then. I've got some hunters to see to over at Pillerton Tracey. I'll drop in on my way back.' He said goodbye to Heather and Alan, and left with Dave. They spoke for a moment on the steps of

136

the pub before getting into their respective vehicles and driving away.

Peggy came up to the bar.

'Can we 'ave two prawn sandwiches, please, 'Eather? Did you see 'er in that waxed jacket? Tryin' to look countryfied and posh...with 'er past! It's a good job they didn't stay. I might not 'ave been able to control myself. Did you 'ear 'er? Come along, Luke, your supper's ready, and off 'e trots like a good little boy. She can't 'ave seen the real Luke yet. I reckon they're scared of me. They certainly got out fast enough, didn't they?'

'How did you get on with Barry, then?' Alan asked, in a misguided attempt at re-directing the conversation. Heather kicked his ankle. 'Ouch!'

'What's the matter?' asked Peggy.

'A sudden pain,' he said, through gritted teeth.

'Want me to kiss it better,' Peggy joked.

'Er, no thanks,' he said, trying to rub the pain away, surreptitiously.

Peggy picked up the plates of sandwiches that Heather had placed on the bar, and carried them over to her table.

'What the hell was that for? It hurt...it still hurts,' Alan said.

'You idiot! Peggy doesn't know she's supposed to be getting on well with Barry,' Heather hissed.

'I don't understand.'

'No. You're right. You don't understand. Just leave it, and for God's sake be discreet.'

'Oh, I give up. It's all too complicated for a simple bloke like me...and dangerous.' He rolled his sock down and inspected his ankle for bruising.

'I'm sorry. It wasn't meant to be that hard, but you moved,' Heather said.

'Clumsy of me,' he said.

The bar door rattled open and Jenny and Josie came in.

'You serve them,' Alan said. 'They get my eyes in a muddle. I'm going to put something on my ankle to stop it swelling.'

'Wimp!' said Heather after him, as he went into the kitchen.

Mercy saw the two sisters come in, and came across to the bar.

'Let me buy you both a drink,' she said. 'Bit of an apology for stinking you out with that garlic, the other day. Two sherries, Heather, please.'

'Thanks,' said Jenny. 'But it was probably no worse than that pig muck Dad used to spread on the garden. You had to put up with that often enough.'

'Good old boy, your dad,' said Mercy. 'He loved his garden, didn't he? Grew some wonderful vegetables. You know, I've often wondered why he never used that greenhouse?'

'Funny, that,' said Josie.

'What's funny?' asked Alan, catching the tail end of the conversation as he came back into the bar.

'The greenhouse. Dad's greenhouse,' said Jenny.

'What was funny about it?' Heather asked, placing two sherry glasses on the counter and reaching for the bottle.

The sisters looked at each other - or past each other, depending on where you were standing. Some secret communication seemed to establish that it was Josie who should tell the story.

'Well,' she began. 'Our parents were quite strict - not unkind - but you didn't take liberties with their rules, and one of those was that we were never allowed in their bedroom. So we never did go in, ever. Not even after Mum died. It wasn't until Dad died, a few years ago, that either of us had ever set foot in that room. Felt strange going in

138

there, didn't it, Jen?'

'Yes. I kept expecting one of them to shout at us.'

'Anyway, that's when we found it.' Josie paused for effect.

Two customers, sitting at one of the tables, had stopped talking and were listening. Heather was standing with the sherry bottle poised above the first glass. Mercy and Peggy were listening with rapt attention, as if the story was new to them.

'I can't bear the suspense. Found what?' said Alan.

'The greenhouse, of course!'

Alan looked blank.

'He had a greenhouse in there!' Josie explained.

Heather and Alan looked at each other and Heather began to feel the hysteria, which North Tegridge's inhabitants engendered more and more often in her, rising to the back of her throat.

'In the bedroom?' Alan struggled with the idea. 'It must be quite a large bedroom,' he said seriously.

Heather knew it was not. Jenny and Josie's semi-detached house was a mirror image of Mercy and Peggy's, next door.

'Oh, no! It wasn't *up*,' Josie said, giving Alan a pitying look. 'It was stacked under the bed.'

'Of course!' said Alan, entering into the spirit of things.

'We had quite a struggle getting it out,' said Jenny. 'But d'you know, they'd had the two of us children, and never even cracked a pane of glass.'

The rising hysteria overwhelmed Heather, and Alan rescued the bottle of sherry as she collapsed on the counter in helpless giggles, and the rest of the pub erupted with laughter. The sisters looked pleasantly surprised at the reception of their tale.

'I love it down here,' Alan said quietly to Heather, as he poured the sherries.

CHAPTER NINETEEN

Luke's Land-Rover and trailer pulled out of the farm track just as Heather indicated to turn in. He waved, as she slowed down to let him out, but didn't stop. She parked in the farmyard and glanced across at the kitchen window, in case Mandy was there, but there was no sign of her. As she unlocked the gate to Jimmy's field, she noticed the last of the cows wandering into the parlour for afternoon milking. If Luke was out who was doing the milking, she wondered? There was a crash of metal striking concrete, followed by a wail from Mandy.

Heather looped the halter she was carrying, over the gate post, and went across to the milking parlour.

'Mandy?' she called. 'Are you all right?'

'No, I'm bloody well not. Luke's gone off and left me with this lot to milk.'

'Where's he gone?'

'Barnstaple. He's got to pick up some pigs. He was going to do it tomorrow morning, but the chap's had a car accident and gone to hospital. His wife was in a state and said would Luke collect the pigs today. I've only helped him with this twice. Oh, this is a nightmare!'

'Give me something to do. I've got a bit of spare time. I'll give you a hand.'

'Would you, Heather? I'd be ever so grateful. Watch you don't get kicked...no, perhaps it would be better if you went round the other side and put some food into their trough.'

Mandy had managed to attach the milking machine clusters to the teats of two of the cows. The machine was pumping away rhythmically, but not very much milk was flowing along the pipes.

'They don't like me. They won't let their milk down,' she complained.

'Can they do that…control the flow?' Heather was fascinated.

'Luke says so. If it just trickles out like that it's going to take hours to milk all of them.'

'Music!' said Heather. 'I read somewhere that they like music. It relaxes them. Have you got a radio?'

'Good idea. I've got a little tape recorder. I'll fetch that, and a selection of tapes. What d'you think they'd like?'

'I haven't the faintest idea,' Heather laughed. 'Have you got 'Old Macdonald had a Farm?''

'Er, no…that may be a little too lively; something soothing I think. They're a bit fidgety.'

As if to emphasise this, one of the cows kicked at the cluster, dislodging it from a teat. Then kicked at Mandy as she replaced it.

'Bit dangerous, this milking,' said Heather. 'Rather you than me.' She poured scoops of cattle cake into their trough, while Mandy went to fetch the tape recorder..

She came back and placed it on the grimy, cobweb festooned window ledge, putting in an old Sinatra tape. But the cows didn't seem interested in 'flying to the moon and playing among the stars'.

'Let's have a look?' Heather thumbed through the tapes in the carrying case, and smiled suddenly. 'What about this one?' she said.

The irrepressible beat of 'The Stripper' thumped out, echoing through the parlour. Mandy and Heather both began to giggle. The cows' ears flipped back as they listened, then they started to tuck into their food. The beat of the music was exquisitely timed to the regular pulse of the milking machine, and soon the milk began to flow along the pipes towards the cooler in the dairy.

141

'Cracked it!' said Mandy, as she shimmied sideways along the row of cows' bottoms, seductively removing her waxed jacket. 'Ouch!' She stopped and pulled the jacket back onto her shoulder.

'You all right?' asked Heather.

'Yes…I forgot my wrist. It's all right as long as I don't bend it the wrong way.'

'I'll just go and give Jimmy his tea and I'll come back,' said Heather.

Mandy was just turning out the last of the cows an hour and a half later when Luke pulled up in the yard with a trailer full of young, noisy pigs. He got out of the Land-Rover.

'Shut that bloody row!' he yelled, banging the side of the metal trailer as he walked past, and causing the pigs to squeal even louder.

Heather was at the far end of the milking parlour, beginning to hose down the floor. The strains of 'The Stripper' were still ringing through the shed, and she wondered how many times you could play a tape before it wore out?

This tape didn't get a chance to find out.

Luke roared into the parlour with a face like thunder. He didn't see Heather. Snatching the tape recorder off the window ledge, he dashed it to the floor and stamped his boot on it. There was a second of silence. Heather's stomach turned over, and Mandy went pale, as she glanced at Heather.

'I told you you're done with all that,' Luke shouted at Mandy. 'What the bloody hell were you playing that for? Missing it are you? Eh?' He towered over Mandy.

Heather turned off the hose, which was making a lake round her feet. The movement made Luke spin round.

'What the hell d'you think you're doing?' he asked.

142

'Luke, it was my fault,' Heather said. In a detached way she was interested to find that she was shaking inside - violence in real life was far more terrifying than the nightly airing of it on television.

'What was your fault? What are you doing in here?'

One of the cows had turned back to see what was going on.

'Goo on! Get out of here!' he yelled, whacking a broom down with vicious force across the poor beast's hindquarters. She galloped to the door, sliding on the damp concrete floor.

'I was just helping Mandy. She still has a sore wrist.'

'Leave it, Luke,' said Mandy. 'Heather came to give me a hand. The cows wouldn't let down the milk.

'The tape recorder was my idea,' said Heather, bravely, her eyes flicking to the crushed pile of plastic on the floor at Luke's feet.

'Oh! 'Taking the mick', were you? Think it's funny what Mandy used to do, do you? I expect you all have a good laugh about it. I bet that bitch Peggy lost no time in spreading the word.'

Heather's unfortunate sense of humour tried to lighten the atmosphere.

'The cows didn't like Frank Sinatra.'

Mandy was shaking her head at her behind Luke's back.

'Didn't they? Right!' Luke took the carrying case of tapes off the window ledge, dropped it onto the dirty floor and twisted his boot into it. 'Now they won't have to listen to him, will they?'

'Luke - don't!' Mandy said, but it was too late.

'I'll see you later. I've got pigs to unload,' he snarled at her. 'And I don't need *you* interfering in my life!' he shot at Heather, as he went out through the door.

'You'd better go. I'm sorry, Heather - here, give me that

- I'll finish washing the milking parlour,' said Mandy, taking the hose from her.

'Will you be all right?'

'Yes, he'll calm down in a while. I'll keep out of his way for a bit, and give him a good supper. He's just jealous.'

'Shall I ring you later?'

'No, that would make things worse. Just leave it; and thanks for all your help. He'll be all right when he sees how much milk is in the cooler.'

'Okay…if you're sure?'

Mandy nodded and turned away to pick up a broom. As Heather walked across the yard to her car she could hear the swish of the bristles on the concrete floor as Mandy swept the lake of water into the gully which lead to the drain. Luke wasn't in sight, but there was a cacophony of squealing and swearing coming from the direction of the pig sties.

Heather shut the car door, muffling some of the noise. As she turned the key to start the engine she noticed her hand was shaking on the steering wheel. She took a deep breath, which felt like the first one for some time, and drove slowly back to the village; to nice, safe predictable Alan. He was down in the cellar when she arrived.

'Is that you?' he called.

'No. Do you want a cup of tea?' she asked.

'You're late. What've you been doing?'

'Helping Mandy with the milking.'

'You?'

'Do you want that tea?'

'Yes,' he said, appearing in the kitchen doorway. He frowned at her. 'Something's the matter. What is it?'

'I've got Mandy into deep trouble. Luke's boiling mad, and I'm frightened he's going to take it out on her. I saw the other side of him today. The one Peggy's always

144

talking about. He smashed Mandy's tape recorder.' She suddenly realised that water was spilling out of the top of the kettle, and turned the tap off.

'Hang on, hang on.' Alan took the kettle from her, emptied out some of the water, and plugged it in. 'Now, let me try and unravel this. You were helping Mandy. How did that upset Luke? And what's a tape recorder got to do with it?'

'The cows wouldn't let down and....'

Alan interrupted.

'Wouldn't let down what?'

'The milk, of course.'

'Oh, sorry...I'm still getting used to these farming terms. Go on.'

'So we played some music to them, to help them relax.'

'That sounds like one of your ideas,' he smiled. 'What sort of music do cows 'let down' to?'

'The Stripper.'

'You mean da da da - de - da da da?' Alan sidled across the kitchen moving his hips in what he considered was a sexy wiggle, and began to laugh. 'And Luke heard it, I suppose?'

'He came back in the middle of it,' said Heather, trying not to smile.

'No wonder he got mad. Don't you realise how sensitive he would be about Mandy's previous occupation.'

'I do now,' Heather said. 'I didn't think. It just seemed like a joke. Mandy and I were both laughing.'

'I worry about your sense of humour, sometimes.'

'I'll watch it in future. Luke can be pretty scary,' she poured some boiling water into the teapot. I think I may ask Dave if he has anywhere I could keep Jimmy at Small Profits. Luke will probably throw us out now.'

She mentioned this idea, quietly, to Mandy, the next

morning when she met her in the shop.

'Oh, no, don't worry. He won't do that,' she said. 'He's calmed down now. And I like you coming down to the farm. It's someone to talk to. Just carry on as if nothing had happened. That's what he'll do. He's even going to buy me a new tape recorder. Said he was just in a bad mood about having to rush over to get the pigs. It's all forgotten now.'

It seemed that she was right. The next time Heather met Luke, it was as if nothing had ever happened, and she began to wonder whether she had made too much of it. Somehow, the rules of accepted civilised behaviour seemed to be different, out here in the country. People didn't wander round muttering and brooding about their problems; they just had huge rows, and got over them very quickly.

Except Peggy, she thought. But even Peggy was mellowing slightly.

When *she* bounced into the kitchen, on Monday morning, she was positively sparkling; which threw Heather slightly, until she remembered Peggy was meeting Barry that evening.

'You're happy today, Peg,' Alan said, looking up from the newspaper which was spread out on the kitchen table beside his toast and marmalade.

'Well, it's a beautiful day, isn't it?' she said, giving him an arch look as she flicked her fringe out of her eyes. Heather itched to cut half an inch off it. Just watching how it irritated Peggy made her want to rub her own eyes.

Collecting the cleaning materials, Peggy disappeared into the bar from where she could be heard humming. Alan poured himself another cup of coffee and went back to the paper. It *was* a beautiful day, Heather thought, scratching an eyebrow. There was a hint of autumn about the bright, crisp morning.

'Nearly out of polish,' Peggy shouted from the bar.

'Okay,' Heather called back. 'Just going to the shop, Alan. D'you want anything?'

'No. Yes! Some chocolate biscuits - a large packet. Peggy keeps eating them.'

Heather smiled and pulled on her jacket, stuffing her purse into the pocket.

While she was in the shop being served, Luke came in. He pointed to a packet of cigarettes on the shelf behind the till, and the young girl behind the counter reached them down for him while his eyes wandered over her body. Heather sighed. Luke seemed to be one of those men who never give up gauging the availability of the local talent.

'Oh, Heather. Can I have a word?' he asked.

'Yes. I'll wait for you outside.'

The bell on the shop door rang as he joined her.

'It's about Peggy,' he said. 'Is she going out with Barry, now?'

'Yes. I think she's meeting him this evening, in the pub.' Heather felt a perverse satisfaction at imparting this news.

'I might pop in then. I want to ask her something.'

'I don't think that this evening would be a good idea, Luke.'

'No? No - maybe not.' He looked at his watch. 'Is she over there now? Could I have a quick word?'

'I suppose so,' Heather said grudgingly. 'But I don't want any trouble, Luke.'

'Trouble? You won't get any trouble from me.'

'I'll let you in through the bar door. Peggy's in there,' she said.

She went into the kitchen and handed the packet of biscuits to Alan.

'Stay out of the bar for a moment. Luke's outside and

wants to speak to Peggy. I said I'd let him in,' she said.

'Oh God! I hope nothing gets broken,' said Alan, opening the biscuits and offering her one.

'No, thanks,' Heather shook her head as she went into the bar. 'Peggy! Luke's outside. He wants a word with you.'

'Does 'e?' Peggy straightened up from the table she'd been polishing and hitched up her shoulders. If she'd been wearing a revolver her hand would have been poised, claw-like over the holster.

Heather stifled an hysterical giggle and crossed the bar, to open the door for Luke. Then went back into the kitchen and left them to it. There was a murmur of voices from the bar, then a sudden shout from Peggy.

'Milk the cows! You want me to milk your cows?'

Alan got up and eased the door open, slightly.

'Just don't want the place wrecked,' he whispered to Heather.

'I'll pay you,' Luke said. 'It's just that they don't seem to like Mandy. They won't let down for her and I ain't got time to do both lots of milking.'

'You let that bitch near my cows?' Peggy screamed.

'They're my cows, Peg,' he started to say, but she butted in.

'After what you done! You think I'll come back and work for you down there…with 'er?'

'I thought things might be better between us now that you are going out with Barry,' said Luke.

'Who told you that?'

'Well, aren't you?'

'None of your business, you bastard. Now go on, 'push-off' and leave me to get on with my work.'

'Okay, okay…just thought I'd ask.' Luke turned and went out of the bar door which Peggy slammed behind him with quite unnecessary force, ramming home the bolts with the heel of her hand. She came bursting into the kitchen, scarlet with fury, her face clashing horribly with her hair.

'Bastard! Did you 'ear that? Only wanted me to milk 'is bloody cows. Apparently she's been tryin' to do it.'

'Excuse me. Work to do,' said Alan, dashing into the bar before the laugh he was stifling, burst through.

Peggy snatched a mug off the dresser and spooned coffee into it.

'It's time 'e 'ad another reminder that it's not a good idea to mess with me,' she said, through clenched teeth.

The kitchen suddenly seemed to grow dark, until Heather realised there was a bank of cloud building up outside. Nevertheless, Peggy's remark had struck a chill into the air.

'What are you planning, Peggy?' Heather asked.

Alan came back in from the bar and caught Heather's last remark.

'We don't want to know,' he said. 'I think we'd better stay out of your vendetta, Peg. We've got the pub to run. We have to stay impartial.'

'I'm worried in case anything happens to Jimmy, Alan,' Heather said.

'Why should anything happen to Jimmy?' Peggy asked. She poured hot water onto the coffee in her mug and spooned in three generous portions of sugar.

'No reason…I hope,' said Heather, backing down. She felt she had made her point.

'Time I got on. I'll take this into the bar with me,' said Peggy, picking up her coffee. 'Oh, by the way, 'Eather, we won't be in this evening, after all. Barry's taking me into Exeter. We're goin' clubbin'.' She went back into the bar.

'Clubbin'?…I mean clubbing?' said Alan. 'Do people their age go clubbing?'

'Don't ask me,' said Heather. 'Now leave me alone so I can worry about what Peggy's going to do next to upset Luke and Mandy. I don't mind about Luke, but I'm getting quite fond of Mandy.'

'Nice girl. Why don't you ask her up here, sometime?' said Alan.

'Because they come as a pair. Luke's too jealous to let her out on her own.'

Heather picked up her coffee mug and stared out of the kitchen window into the deserted village square, watching the bank of dark cloud billowing up from the west.

CHAPTER TWENTY

By the afternoon, the storm cloud had dropped most of its rain and blown over, and Heather decided to walk to Hawkridge to check on Jimmy. She picked up the binoculars on the way out. Luke had moved Jimmy and the sheep into the field which ran between the wood and the main road and he'd told her that there were badgers in there. Although dimly aware that badgers were nocturnal, she decided to look for them in daylight: she wasn't prepared to go and sit beside that spooky wood, Luke's burial ground, at night, in the hope of seeing one.

The day before, she had found their sett dug into the bank. No mistaking this for a fox's earth; the hole was actually shaped to fit a badger's body, being narrow at paw level and broadening out to accommodate the girth of it's owner.

The sun was warm on her back as she passed Dave's apple orchard, which ran alongside the road. The branches were heavy with fruit waiting to be turned into Dave's golden nectar. An apple had fallen onto the grass verge and she picked it carefully out of the stinging nettles, then rubbed it on her jacket, before taking a bite from it - which she instantly spat out. The apple was so sour that it made her teeth grow fur.

Reaching the farm she leaned on the field gate, and watched Jimmy grazing. Peace fell around her shoulders like a blanket. The ground was still damp after the shower and everything smelled fresh. Even Jimmy was clean and gleaming, as he had forgotten to roll in the mud after the rain had washed off his usual coating of dried red earth.

An eerie cry made her look up to where two buzzards were wheeling lazily overhead, riding the thermals in interlinking olympic circles, calling alternately to each other. She trained the binoculars on them for a while, until they made her feel dizzy. Lowering the glasses, she rubbed her eyes. Then focussed them on the entrance to the badger sett. But nothing was happening there.

From her position she could see over most of Hawkridge farm; and sweeping the binoculars around the area she picked up Luke and Mandy coming out of the farmhouse. She watched them get into the Land-Rover and drive away.

Turning back she caught a movement in the farm yard and, with a sinking feeling, recognised Peggy's blue anorak. After a moment's hesitation she decided to make her presence known and, hopefully, prevent whatever devilry Peggy had planned.

She climbed onto the gate and waved, but Peggy didn't see her. She was busy unlocking the door into the farmhouse kitchen. Luke had said he'd removed the spare key, so Peggy must have had one cut for herself. She disappeared into the house, carrying a plastic bag, and Heather stepped down off the gate. She was too far away. By the time she got down to the house, Peggy would have done whatever it was she had planned. She must have been watching for Luke and Mandy to go out. Heather decided she would only intervene if there was any letting out of farm animals involved in Peggy's latest scheme.

The back door opened and she raised the binoculars again, watching Peggy as she came out carrying a large casserole dish. She was using oven gloves, so it must have been hot. Casting a surreptitious glance around the yard and up the track, Peggy flung the contents of the dish in the general direction of the chickens, who came running from all around the farm yard. She went back inside, then re-appeared a few minutes later. Locking the door carefully behind her, she mounted her bicycle and pedalled furiously away up the track to the road.

Well, if all she had done was feed Luke and Mandy's dinner to the chickens, that wasn't so bad, thought Heather, wondering if Peggy was mellowing - or losing her touch? She set off across the field towards Jimmy, who saw her coming and walked up to meet her. He was hardly lame at all now. A fact that made her slightly nervous. One day she was going to have to sit on that smooth silver back, and trust him to take care of her.

Her mind flicked back to Peggy again. Was that really all she had done? Thrown their dinner away? Poisoning it would have been more her style.

She found out what had gone on in the farmhouse kitchen, sooner than expected, when Luke and Mandy came into the pub, just after opening time, that evening.

'Usual please,' said Luke, glaring at Heather. 'Were you down at the farm, this afternoon?'

'Er, yes. I walked down as far as Jimmy's field.'

'Did you see anybody? When I say anybody, I mean did you see Peggy Ashley down there?'

It was easier to lie, and Heather did. She hadn't even told Alan she'd seen Peggy.

'That crazy cow's got a key from somewhere,' Luke fumed. 'I'm going to have to change the lock on the back door.

'Disgusting bitch!' said Mandy, wrinkling up her nose, and shuddering.

Heather's mind went off at a tangent, wondering why, when people wished to denigrate another human, they were usually compared with fairly innocuous animals, like dogs and cows. She pulled herself back. She really did want to hear an explanation of what she had witnessed that afternoon.

'Why? What's happened?' asked Alan, placing a whisky in front of Mandy and pulling a pint for Luke.

'You tell 'em, Mandy. I'm too angry. Give us a menu, Heather.' He took his drink over to a table and sat down, studying the menu as if it had done him a personal injury.

Mandy glanced at him and turned back to Heather and Alan, lowering her voice.

'I've had a terrible job stopping him from going up to her house. I don't know what he'd have done. Actually, at the moment, I don't really care what he does to her, but I don't want to have to spend the next few years visiting him in prison. And also I quite like Mercy. I wouldn't want him to frighten her.'

Frighten Mercy! Heather thought. A woman who had driven a hay-rake over her husband. Then murdered him. *Then* danced and made love on his grave. Don't even begin to go down that road, she told herself, firmly.

'So what *has* Peggy done?' Alan asked.

'Well, I'd made this lamb casserole and put it in the oven, while we popped out to South Molton. We came back expecting to be greeted by an appetising smell. Only it wasn't - appetising, I mean. I've never smelt anything like it in my life,' she shuddered again and almost gagged.

'What was it?' chorused Heather and Alan. Revolting recipe ideas, like 'cooked rat, served in its fur', were running through Heather's mind. She wouldn't put anything past Peggy.

'Shit!' said Luke, suddenly. Heather thought there was something wrong with the menu he was studying.

'Exactly,' said Mandy.

'You mean…' said Alan, turning pale.

'Cow-shit,' Mandy explained. She'd filled my casserole up with cow-shit. Have you ever smelt cooking cow-shit?'

Alan's eyes locked with Heather's, but before they could

154

answer this question, Mandy continued.

'No, of course you haven't. The stink has got everywhere. We've had to open all the windows and get out for a bit. That bloody woman's insane.'

Luke's chair scraped back on the wooden floor and he came over to the bar.

'We'll have steak and kidney pie,' he said, putting the menu back in its holder. He didn't consult Mandy about his choice, and she didn't seem to notice. He went back to the table and sat glowering into his pint.

'I can't take much more of this,' Mandy muttered quietly to Heather, as Alan went across the bar to close the windows. The evenings were beginning to have an autumnal feel about them.

'I'm not surprised,' said Heather, with feeling. She was wondering how she could get rid of Peggy from the pub. She knew Alan would ask her to, now. She watched him as he commiserated with Luke, then she turned back to Mandy.

'Can't Luke get some sort of restraining order on her?' she asked. 'Something to stop her visiting the farm.'

Mandy bit her bottom lip and sighed.

'I've asked him to. I asked him again this evening; but he's still saying no. Says he'll settle it his way. I'm beginning to think that in some weird sort of way he enjoys fighting with her. Well, I don't want to live like this.' She half emptied her glass in one long swallow.

Alan came back behind the bar, and Mandy took her whisky over to join Luke. The bar door rattled as the three youths who'd been involved in the rave, came in. They saw Luke, turned as one, and went out again. Heather smiled to herself and went out to the kitchen to start cooking. Alan stuck his head round the kitchen door. From there he could watch the bar and talk to her.

'We're going to have to get rid of her,' he said.

'I knew you were going to say that,' she said, sweeping some thinly sliced carrots off the board into boiling water.

'Well, I'm right, aren't I?'

'Yes…but what if she starts on us? She's very vindictive. What reason could we give her? There's nothing wrong with her work here. None of the stuff she's done down at Hawkridge has been proved. She could deny it all; and then what could we say?' As she spoke, she was desperately trying to erase from her mind the picture of Peggy flinging the contents of the casserole dish at the chickens.

'Why on earth is she still doing these things? I thought she'd got over Luke and was going out with Barry.'

'She's furious because Mandy's been doing the milking, and you know how Peggy feels about the cows.'

'Well, yes. But I have difficulty getting my mind round that concept. Are cows more interesting than I had previously thought?'

'No,' said Heather.

'Surely what she's doing is criminal,' he said.

Some more customers came into the bar, and Alan went to serve them before Heather could reply. These four customers ordered a meal which kept her busy until about nine o'clock, when she took them their coffee.

Mandy and Luke were still sitting at their table. They had both sent most of their steak and kidney pie back to the kitchen, whilst assuring Alan there was nothing wrong with it. And Luke, at least, had embarked on some serious drinking, though Mandy was trying to persuade him to take her home.

'Don't keep nagging, woman. We'll go when I'm ready. Alan, two more scotch's here,' Luke thumped a fist on the table, rattling the empty glasses.

'Not for me,' Mandy shook her head at Alan.

They were still there at ten thirty, when Peggy and Barry came in. Peggy looked flushed and excited. She didn't immediately see Luke, who had his back to her. Mandy had just gone to the 'Ladies'.

''Ello, 'Eather, Alan. Thought we'd finish off 'ere. Just been to darts over at Pillerton Tracey. Barry's team from 'The Bull' was playing them.'

'How did you get on?' asked Heather, watching two visitors to the village who were just standing up and putting on their coats. She willed them to hurry up and get out before Luke turned round.

'We won,' said Barry. 'A pint, and a half, please, Alan.'

'*You* won you mean. It was all down to you,' Peggy clutched at his arm and gave him a brilliant scarlet-lipped smile.

The visitors smiled and waved goodnight as they went out of the door.

Mandy came back into the bar, saw Peggy, and stopped. At the same moment Peggy noticed her and looking round the room, saw Luke.

'Oh oh,' she said. 'Maybe we won't stop, after all. Perhaps you'd better take me 'ome, Barry.'

Alan paused, one hand on the pump handle and a glass held under the nozzle.

'Why?' asked Barry, turning round and catching sight of Mandy. He nodded to her and managed a half smile before Peggy pulled him away by the arm.

Luke looked up from the whisky he was studying, saw Mandy, and turned in his chair to see what she was staring at. It took him a couple of seconds to focus. Then he roared and staggered to his feet, tipping his chair over with a clatter.

'Come on, Barry. I'll explain later,' said Peggy, as she dragged him, puzzled and protesting, out of the door.

As Luke lurched towards them he caught his foot in the overturned chair and fell over with a crash. He lay there for a moment, too drunk to work out what had happened.

Alan pushed up the bar flap and went to help Mandy get him to his feet. Then between them they half carried him, mumbling curses, towards the door.

'I'll just see them home,' Alan called over his shoulder to Heather. 'Won't be long.'

Heather picked up the chair and cleared the glasses and a full ash tray off the table, thankful that there weren't any other customers in the bar to apologise to. The bar clock showed a quarter to eleven and she decided to close early, pushing home the top and bottom bolts on the door with a sigh of relief. It could have been worse.

She had washed up, tidied the kitchen and was sitting at the kitchen table with a glass of wine, trying to unwind, when Alan came back - over an hour later.

'What took you so long?' she asked.

'Don't ask,' he flopped down onto a chair opposite her and took a swig of wine out of the bottle. Heather got up and fetched him a glass.

'God, their house stinks,' he said. 'Luke passed out in the car. We had a hell of a job getting him to bed. Then Mandy made a coffee. She was so depressed I felt I had to stay and talk for a little while…try and cheer her up a bit.'

Heather felt a mild twinge of jealousy. No, she thought, I will not turn into another Peggy.

CHAPTER TWENTY-ONE

Peggy arrived for work looking very pleased with herself. She grinned at Heather as she hung her anorak on the back of the kitchen door.

'Close thing, last night. Didn't think Luke would be in the pub. I thought it was probably better not to risk a row in front of Barry. Don't want to put 'im off. D'you like 'im?'

Heather switched the kettle on. 'You speak to her, she's got to go,' Alan had said before he left to go to the local farm shop for some vegetables. Heather wasn't happy about this, but thought maybe it would come better from her. After all, she was armed with knowledge about Peggy's antics that Alan didn't have. She reached down two mugs from the hooks on the dresser.

'Barry? Yes, he's very nice. You ought to hang onto him,' she said.

'That's what Mum says,' Peggy looked pensive for a moment; then pursed her lips and sighed. She watched Heather spooning coffee into the mugs, and glanced at the kitchen clock. 'Bit early for coffee?' she said.

'I wanted a word with you, Peg - while Alan's out.'

'Sounds ominous. What's the problem?'

'Sit down, Peggy,' Heather indicated a chair. 'Well, the immediate problem is the lamb casserole.'

'The what?' Peggy was suddenly on the defensive. 'Don't know what you're talking about.'

'I saw you. I was at the farm yesterday.'

'Oh...oh...well, they asked for it. 'E shouldn't 'ave let 'er near my cows. Did you tell 'im it was me?'

'No. Nobody else knows I saw you. Peggy that was a disgusting thing to do. Of course they knew it was you, and you have really upset Alan, as well. What on earth were you thinking about?'

'Well, I 'adn't really planned to do that. It just sort of came to me when I smelt the stew. I was going to put it in their bed.'

'Oh, that would have been all right, would it?' Heather asked sarcastically.

Peggy smiled.

''E dumped too much of it on my doorstep, after the rave. Didn't need all of it for the garden, so I thought I'd let 'im 'ave some of it back.'

'We serve food in here, Peggy. And you help out in the kitchen, sometimes. What do you think this will do to our trade, when it gets out? To be honest, Alan is not happy about you working here any more.'

'Are you saying you want to sack me?' Peggy's expression had hardened.

'I'm saying…'

'Because if you are,' Peggy interrupted, ' you'd better 'ave a good reason; and one you can prove. You've 'eard of unfair dismissal. There's nothin' wrong with my work 'ere.'

'Don't threaten me, Peggy,' Heather could feel her blood pressure rising and was beginning to wish she hadn't decided to take Peggy on alone.

Peggy looked at the steaming mug of coffee in front of her.

'I don't want this. It's too early for me,' she got up and flung the contents of the mug down the sink. Then turned on the tap, rinsed the mug, and dumped it down on the draining board. She turned back to Heather. 'So what are you saying, then…I'm fired?' Peggy's black eyes were boring into Heather's, and she had the irrelevant thought that this was probably how Peggy controlled the cows - by sheer will power; as against Luke's practice of bludgeoning them into obedience with a broom.

'No. I'm not saying you're fired.' Heather backed down, suddenly aware of the damage that could be done if she, Alan, and the pub, became the focus of Peggy's malevolent attention. 'I'm just asking you to stop this war with Luke and Mandy because it's beginning to involve us; and we're not happy about it.'

'Don't see as 'ow you're involved?'

'I am. And I find I'm having to watch what I say to Alan...and I don't like it.'

'Oh, all right, then,' Peggy suddenly lowered her mesmerising stare. 'Tell you what. You don't sack me - and I'll lay off them. But you can tell Luke, I won't 'ave 'er messing with the cows.'

'Tell him yourself. I just said, I'm not getting involved.'

'Right. So, I still work 'ere, do I?'

'Yes.'

'Best get on, then.' Peggy went into the bar and Heather could hear her putting chairs up onto the tables, ready for cleaning the floor.

Alan's car pulled up in the yard and she went to help him unload the vegetables. He put a box of broccoli down on the kitchen table and glanced towards the door to the bar.

'Did you speak to her? What's she doing? Working out a week's notice?'

'To answer your questions in order. Yes, cleaning, and no.'

'You didn't sack her?'

'I sort of compromised,' said Heather.

'I knew I should have done it myself,' he said, running his fingers through his hair.

'How can you say that? You asked me to get rid of her, and ran away.'

161

'We needed some more veg. I can't be everywhere at once!' his voice was raised.

'This is silly. Now she's got us arguing.'

'Sorry, darling,' he came across and gave her a hug. 'All right. She can stay for now; but she's on probation.'

Anne came in for a drink at lunch time. She was grinning as she pulled herself up onto a bar stool.

'You look happy,' said Heather.

'I've just met Jenny and Josie…and their new friend.'

'Friend?' asked Heather.

'They've got themselves a dog. Totally unsuitable for them. It's an enormous shaggy Airdale terrier. It's towing them round the village as I speak. But, here's the best bit…it's only got one eye. It's a rescue dog; been badly treated, or something.'

'Who's only got one eye?' asked Alan, coming in on the end of the conversation.

'Jenny and Josie's new dog,' said Anne.

Alan groaned. 'It's not in the middle of its forehead, is it? Do they walk with it in between them?'

'Shut-up, idiot,' said Heather.

Anne took a sip of the gin and tonic that Heather had just placed on the bar in front of her. 'Oh, that's good,' she said. 'I just met that Mandy, in the shop. She seems quite nice. I can't think what she's doing with Luke. She doesn't look too happy to me. Is he up to his usual bullying tricks, I wonder?'

'Don't know,' said Heather, shrugging her shoulders in what she hoped was a non-committal way.

'I wouldn't say she's really his type,' said Alan.

'No,' Anne said thoughtfully. 'In fact, if only he realised it, Peggy is his type; but try telling him that.'

'I wouldn't, if I were you; not just at the moment,' said Alan.

'Is he still angry about the rave?' asked Anne.

'Something like that,' Alan said, picking up on the hard look Heather was giving him, as she willed him to shut up.

Peggy had left her purse on the dresser when she'd gone home before lunch; a small sign that she was actually preoccupied about their conversation that morning, Heather thought. She put it in her coat pocket as she left to go to the farm to see Jimmy, and drove round the village to the estate where Peggy lived, to drop it off.

As she walked up the path to the front door, a movement from the next door garden caught her eye. There was somebody in the greenhouse. That must be *the* famous greenhouse, she thought. Jenny and Josie had now had it erected in the corner of their vegetable garden.

She couldn't see which one of them was in there as the figure was semi-disguised by the tin colander she was wearing on her head. Heather was rapidly learning not to be surprised by anything which happened in the village, but this had to be a first. She waved, and Josie, for it was she, waved back and came across to the fence to talk to her.

'Hello, Heather…oops! Sorry! Forgot I had this on,' she removed the colander and shook her hair, flicking it lightly with her fingers, as if to remove something.

'I heard you had a new dog,' said Heather.

'Not any more. That's why I'm wearing this.'

'A local form of mourning?' asked Heather, suddenly unable to control her tongue.

'Mourning?…No. He's not dead; though he could well have been, silly bugger. No, he was too strong for us, really. We want a smaller dog. Something like one of them little dash-hounds, like Anne's got. Jenny's taken him back to the rescue home.'

'What did he do? Did he have an accident?'

'He did it on purpose, really. Well, perhaps it *was* an

163

accident, in a way. I mean, he didn't know, I suppose. He did strike me as being a bit thick,' said Josie thoughtfully, as she considered the intelligence quotient of Airdale terriers. She seemed to come to a conclusion. 'Yes. I think maybe he *was* just a stupid dog.'

'I can't bear it,' said Heather. 'What did he do?'

'Well, I was working in the greenhouse. Dad's greenhouse. That's the one I was telling you about, you remember? Under the bed?' Josie pointed across the garden.

'Yes, yes,' said Heather, trying to move the story on.

'And he was in there with me; lying down so quiet I thought he was asleep. I never even saw him stand up, you know, but he must have done. He couldn't have done that from lying down.' She considered the picture in her mind.

'And?' Heather prompted.

'Well, then…Oh, it did give me a shock…I could have been injured, too; not that he was. I'll never know how he escaped without a mark on him. They've got very thick wiry coats, you know, them Airdales - must have protected him.'

'Josie…I can't take any more suspense. What happened?'

'Oh, sorry. I'll get to the point, shall I?'

'Yes, please,' said Heather.

'Well, it was this pigeon,' Josie stopped, and studied the sky, as if for more pigeons.

'Yes, yes…a pigeon,' said Heather.

'Well, stupid great thing, it landed on the greenhouse roof, didn't it. And that bloody dog went straight up in the air after it - like one of them exocet missiles. Put his head through the roof. Glass everywhere. That's why I'm wearing this,' she waved the colander at Heather. 'Stops the bits of glass falling on my head while I'm clearing it up.'

'That's really very practical,' said Heather, when she'd finished laughing. 'Shame about your dad's greenhouse after it staying intact for all those years.'

'Yes. I think that's what made Jenny take the dog straight back, really. She was that angry. Well, I'd better get it cleared up. I think Peggy's out, but Mercy's there.'

Heather walked on up the path and knocked on the door, which Mercy opened.

'Peggy left this,' she said, handing over the purse.

'Oh, thank you. You shouldn't have bothered. Peg knew where she'd left it. She's gone into Exeter with Barry. Says she needs some new clothes to go to these clubs in. I don't know... she seems to be getting into her second childhood since she met Barry. Still, why not, if she's enjoying herself. I just hope she doesn't start on them drugs.'

'I don't think that'll happen, Mercy. Even if Peggy felt tempted - which I'm sure she wouldn't - I don't think drugs are really Barry's scene.'

'If you ask me, I don't think clubs are really Barry's scene, either. But he's that taken with Peggy, he gives in to her.'

'Well, so long as they're happy,' said Heather, beginning to turn away. She didn't want to talk about Peggy, and she wasn't sure that Barry *was* happy. She suspected he was more of a pubs and darts sort of person than a strobe lighting and deafening music afficionado.

She drove into the yard at Hawkridge just in time to see the pheasant chasing the animal feed representative from the local granary, back into his car. The man slammed the door shut an inch away from the raking talons, and sat gripping the steering wheel for a couple of seconds, before starting the engine. Luke stood by the back door, laughing. The man wound down his window as he drew level with Heather.

'I'm seriously thinking about not calling on this customer, any more,' he said.

'You'll be all right if you bring some cannabis with you,' she answered.

He looked at her as if she was as mad as the pheasant, and drove off, ducking over the steering wheel as a Tornado jet roared over at tree-top height. Heather ducked as well, heart thumping and adrenaline pumping as the timeless instinct to flee from danger kicked in. Luke was now laughing at both of them. The pheasant was back on his beam in the cart shed, screeching an alarm call after the distant roar of the aircraft.

Heather got out of the car.

'How long does it take to get used to that noise?' she asked Luke.

'Some people never do,' he said comfortingly. He turned back, screwdriver in hand, to where he was fitting a new lock on the back door. 'She won't get through this,' he said, his smile disappearing as he forced a screw into the solid oak.

'Is it all right if I take a couple of bales of straw, Luke? I'm keeping a count of how many I've had. I want to bed the stable down really well. I may have to bring Jimmy in if the nights get much colder.'

'Yes. The barrow's in the cart-shed.'

'So's the pheasant.'

'Here,' he reached round the door to the hook on the inside, and handed her Mandy's whip. 'Show 'im this,' he said.

Heather felt uncomfortable about actually cracking the whip, so she just waved it at the bird, who glared but didn't get off his perch. She loaded the bales, wheeled them across the field to the stable and tipped them inside, then felt along the ledge under the roof for her kitchen knife.

She cut the strings, and the bale of tightly packed golden straw fell open in sections. Fetching the fork, which she kept tucked round at the back of the stable, she spread the straw evenly around the floor.

'Finished with the barrow, then?' Luke's voice made her jump.

'Yes…yes, take it. Oh, and here's the whip. Thanks,' she furled up the plaited leather thong and handed the whip to him.

'I'll have to give you some lessons in how to crack that properly,' he said.

Not bloody likely, Heather thought. You'd enjoy it too much.

'Some other time,' she said. 'Where's Mandy?'

'Gone shopping.' Thinking about Mandy seemed to divert him. 'I'd better get on,' he said, picking up the handles of the barrow and pushing it away across the field.

A short while later she heard the tractor start up and drive along the track towards the road.

When she had finished the stable, she went back to the yard and stood by the car for a few minutes before getting in, absorbing the gentle country sounds; and smells, she suddenly realised. Steam was rising from the dung heap where the quietly crooning chickens were busily raking the noxious pile of dirty straw across the yard, searching for kernels of grain which had escaped the combine harvester.

She turned her back on them and watched two cows, in the field beside the farmhouse, as they siphoned up vast quantities of water from their trough. She could hear the water hissing through the valve in the box at the end, as it struggled to keep up with their thirst and refill the trough.

Her gaze wandered past the farmhouse, with it's mellow stone walls lit to a pink glow by the afternoon sun, and down across the fields to the river, dark where it passed between the trees at the bottom of the valley. Was that the last view Rose had seen before committing suicide? A chill touched the back of her neck. She got into the car and turned the key in the ignition, trying to push away unpleasant thoughts and suspicions.

CHAPTER TWENTY-TWO

Heather was sitting at the kitchen table, studying a recipe book and concentrating on planning a change of menu. Alan was bottling-up. And Peggy had just switched on the floor polisher in the bar; when suddenly the village was full of the sound of high-powered cars and police sirens. The cars swept through the square and turned towards Riverview Close, a neat estate of private bungalows which had almost doubled the size of the village twenty years previously.

Heather went into the bar and across to the window.

'What's going on?' asked Alan, joining her.

A police car pulled up outside and Alan went to open the bar door.

'Have you got any customers in there, sir?' asked the policeman.

'No - we're not open yet.'

Peggy switched off the rattling polisher and came over to them.

'What's goin' on?' she asked.

'I'm afraid we're going to have to ask everyone to stay indoors and keep away from the windows,' said the policeman.

A canvas covered army lorry full of soldiers raced across the square towards the estate.

'We've found a UXB, er, sorry, an unexploded bomb, sir. We're evacuating everyone from Riverview Close, and taking them up to the church hall. You should be all right here. We'll let you know when it's been dealt with.' He turned and went across the square to the shop.

'You haven't been making bombs, have you, Peggy?' Alan asked.

'Ha ha, very funny. Anyway, it's not our estate they're

evacuatin'.'

'I suppose we'd better do as he says and stay away from the windows, in case it does go off,' said Heather.

'What sort of a bomb? Is there a secret IRA cell in the village?' asked Alan, of no-one in particular.

'There's no Irish people here. I wonder how you make a bomb?' said Peggy thoughtfully. 'I think I heard it was fertilizer and sugar.'

These two ingredients were too readily available for comfort, Heather thought.

Then Peggy shook her head. 'No...no, it would frighten the cows. Oh my goodness. If that one goes off they could stampede and hurt themselves; and they're on their own. Luke'll be at market today. I'll 'ave to get down there. Can I 'ave some time off, Alan?' She had taken his permission for granted, as she was already unplugging the polisher.

'Er, yes. I suppose so. No, don't put that away. I'll finish the floor,' he said.

'Should you be going out?' Heather asked her. 'The policeman said to stay under cover.'

'Let them try and stop me,' Peggy was pulling on her blue anorak.

'Can you keep an eye on Jimmy for me, as well?' asked Heather. 'Here, take my mobile. Ring us if there are any problems.'

As Peggy left through the front door, Colin and Audrey came in, half supporting a thick-set man with close-cropped, gingery hair.

'Can we wait in here, Alan?' asked Colin. Audrey was looking very pale, and clutching a handkerchief.

'Of course. What on earth's happening down your way? The police didn't really tell us anything.' said Alan.

'Oh, Colin, we're going to lose our home. Our lovely bungalow. All our things,' said Audrey, beginning to cry.

170

'It's a bomb,' said Colin.

'Who's been making bombs?' asked Alan.

'The Germans made this one,' said Colin. 'Hundred pounder, the bomb disposal man said.'

'What?' said Heather.

'It's an unexploded World War Two bomb. It arrived in a load of topsoil I ordered for the back garden. This is Angus, by the way. It was him who brought it,' said Colin.

Angus had climbed onto a bar stool and was staring at the optics with unfocussed eyes.

'Bliddy hell. Bliddy, bliddy hell,' he said. 'Aa've jist driven that bliddy thing a' the way frae Plymouth... bouncing alang the roads.'

'Give him a brandy will you, Alan?' said Colin.

Angus pulled himself together for long enough to change the order to whisky. He emptied the glass Alan handed him, in one swallow.

'Do you have any chocolate or anything? I need something wi' sugar...for the shock,' Angus said.

Heather indicated the sweet cabinet at the end of the bar.

'What would you like? On the house.'

'Eh...a Mars bar, large one, please.'

As Heather went to the cabinet, she whispered to Alan.

'The Scots like them deep fried in batter, don't they? D'you think I should....'

'No,' said Alan, making a face.

'Give us one of those, would you, Heather? D'you want one, Aud?' asked Colin.

'Let's all have one,' said Heather, dealing them out. There was a definite feeling of comradeship in the face of adversity, building up in the bar.

The bar door banged as Jenny and Josie scuttled in.

'We were in the shop,' said Jenny. 'But Josie suggested it might be a bit more fun to wait in the pub.'

Angus glanced at them, then did a double take, before turning his head away and making the same eye stretching facial movements that Heather had noticed Alan doing after exposure to the sisters.

'You should have worn your tin hat, Josie,' Heather said.

Josie laughed, but the joke was lost on the rest of the gathering. Alan lifted the bar flap and went over to the polisher, looping up the cord, and dragging it back with him behind the counter.

'Too many in, now. We'll leave it today,' he said to Heather.

Anne came in.

'I'm a member of the Devon Emergency Volunteers,' she said. 'In times of war or crisis I'm supposed to make cups of tea for the village. Anyone want one?'

'No thanks,' Heather laughed. 'Have a gin and tonic.'

'Better not. I have to get to the village hall and put the tea urn on. Exciting isn't it!' she left.

'It's not exciting for them as have a bomb in their garden,' said Audrey, sniffing again.

The phone was ringing in the kitchen and Heather went to answer it. It was Peggy.

''Ere; you tell 'im, 'Eather. 'E don't believe me about the bomb.'

'Luke's come back, has he?' Heather asked.

'Yes, and 'e's threatening me. 'E's...oy!'

The phone was obviously snatched away from her, as Luke suddenly came on.

'Heather, what's this lunatic talking about now?'

'There really is a bomb, Luke.' She related the morning's events.

'Bugger me!' he said slowly. There was a pause while he took it all in. 'Have you seen Mandy up there?' he asked.

'No. She could be in the shop, or the village hall. The

172

police are trying to keep everyone under cover in case it goes off.'

'How did Peggy get down here, then?'

'Take more than the police, a squad of soldiers and a mere bomb to come between Peggy and those cows.'

'I found the bitch prodding the boar with a pitch-fork. Right, well, she can get back the way she came; after I've dealt with her over that business the other day.'

'Let go my arm…' It was Peggy's voice.

'Luke, don't do anything silly…' Heather started, but the phone went dead.

She stopped talking and stared at Alan, who had walked into the kitchen in time to hear her last remark.

'What's wrong?' he asked.

'Luke's come home and found Peggy down at Hawkridge. He says he's going to deal with her over the casserole incident.'

'Where's Mandy?'

'I don't know. She's not there, because Luke asked me the same thing.'

Alan went back into the bar where talk was turning to everyone's war experiences.

'Has anyone seen Mandy, this morning?…Luke's Mandy. Was she in the shop when this started?' He looked at Jenny and Josie, who both turned towards him. Heather, who had followed him, smiled as he hurriedly looked away, screwing his eyes up in what was becoming the rather odd nervous twitch which affected him whenever the sisters appeared. It seemed that no-one had seen Mandy, that morning.

'Why are you so worried about her?' Heather asked.

'I'm not. I just wondered,' he said.

'Well, I'm worried about what Luke may be doing to Peggy,' said Heather quietly.

'I'm not. Can you fetch that tray of sandwiches through? This lot may be here for a while.' He reached across the bar to take the pint glass Colin was holding out for a re-fill, and Heather went back into the kitchen.

She had arranged the sandwiches on the tray earlier, ready to slide it into the refrigerated display cabinet on the bar, and was just garnishing them with quartered tomatoes and sprigs of parsley when there was a clatter outside, as Peggy leaned her bike against the yard wall.

The back door was opened by a policeman, who ushered Peggy through.

'Could you look after this lady,' he said? 'She fell off her bicycle. I understand she works here. I don't think she's badly hurt but she'd better stay here until the 'all clear'.'

'I can speak for myself,' said Peggy.

The policeman smiled at Heather, and left.

'Didn't fall off my bike,' Peggy muttered. 'Can I borrow your bathroom, 'Eather?' She put Heather's phone down on the kitchen table.

'I think you'd better. The shampoo's in the bathroom cabinet and the hairdryer is on my dressing table.'

It was immediately obvious how Luke had taken his revenge. Peggy's yellow thatch had been energetically combined with a large handful of the dung heap. Her efforts to remove this had been largely unsuccessful, resulting in some un-edifying smears across her face.

'Get up there before Alan sees you,' said Heather, pushing her towards the hall and the stairs.

'Who was that? Thought I heard voices,' said Alan, coming into the kitchen.

'Peggy's come back. She fell off her bike. She's just gone upstairs to repair the damage.'

'Oh. Is this ready to take through?' he indicated the tray on the kitchen table.

'Yes.'

Alan picked up the sandwiches and shouldered his way through the door.

Heather followed him back into the bar where a jolly atmosphere was beginning to grow; mainly to mask the gathered villagers' individual worries, she suspected. Audrey was still looking pale and shaky.

Angus had now got some colour back into his cheeks, quite a lot of colour, she noticed. In fact it was pretty obvious that he was no longer capable of driving his tipper lorry back to Plymouth. Colin was in full flow with war reminiscences from the blitz of London's East End.

'Went all through the war without a scratch, and bloody Hitler's still trying to get me,' he said. 'We lived sixty yards from Woolwich Arsenal, but my mum wouldn't let us be evacuees. Said she wasn't going to let bloody Hitler drive her out.'

He went on to describe the night an incendiary bomb fell through the roof of their house into the attic.

'Bugger was burning away up there. We couldn't put it out. Kept bringing buckets of sand up until there was such a pile up there the weight of it broke through the ceiling and it fell into the bedroom, and it was still burning. There was relays of us up and down the stairs with more sand but we couldn't stop the flames. Burned right through the bedroom floor and dropped into the sitting room. Bloody thing was in the basement before we managed to put it out.'

'Funny time of day for a party,' said Dave, coming in to the laughter which followed Colin's story.

'How did you get past the police?' Heather asked.

'I didn't. I've just come in from East Tegridge, and they won't let me go on down the road to the farm. They've got it cordoned off. There's a television van just arrived. I decided to wait in here till it's all over. Pint please, Alan.'

Peggy stuck her, now clean, head round the bar door.

'I'm off 'ome, now, 'Eather. See if Mum's all right. I'll do extra tomorrow to make up.' She nodded to Dave, and left.

'Peggy's working late,' he said.

'Not really. She hadn't been here long before she decided to go and save Luke's cows from the bomb. I gather there was no-one at the farm to look after them,' said Alan.

'No, Luke will have gone to market; and I saw Mandy's car in East Tegridge.'

'Oh, what was she doing there?' Alan asked.

'Dunno, only saw the car. She used to live there when she was a kid. I expect she knows people there,' said Dave, only half his attention on Alan, as Angus was trying to say something to him and Dave hadn't yet had time to get his ear attuned to the whisky enhanced Glaswegian accent.

It wasn't long before the television team decided that the best place to interview residents of the village, was in the pub. Here they struck gold when they found the driver of the lorry, and the couple in whose garden the bomb was currently residing. Well, they *almost* struck gold. Audrey was too tearful to give an interview without breaking down every few seconds, and Angus's accent was by now so well oiled as to be practically unintelligible to a southerner. Colin rose to the occasion manfully and told them all about the war, and helpfully translated, as best he could, some of Angus's more horrified utterances. Colin had the advantage of having heard Angus's side of the story several times, before he had descended into his present pixilated state.

'Best lunch time, for business, we've had in a long time,' said Alan to Heather, ducking to avoid a fluffy grey microphone which was swung over his head as the television team turned to interview Jenny and Josie. There

176

was a momentary pause as the interviewer re-focussed, but the man was a professional, and the sisters were both eager to have their say; though what they could possibly contribute, Heather couldn't guess.

Half an hour later, Anne came in with Rudi.

'They're all full of tea at the village hall,' she said. 'So I thought I'd rescue Rudi from his lonely state at home, and come over here where all the action seems to be.'

She actually brought some of the action with her, as Rudi suddenly caught sight of the fluffy grey cover over the microphone and became convinced it was one of those - admittedly rare - flying rabbits. The sound recordist was not a dog lover, in fact he had a phobia about dogs, with the result that he leapt straight onto one of the bench seats, breaking a light bulb with his microphone. Rudi made a valiant attempt to follow the rabbit up to the ceiling, but his legs were too short to even get him as far as the sound recordist's place of safety.

'Maybe we'll go and sit over there, in the corner,' said Anne, dragging Rudi away.

'I'll bring your drink over, in a minute,' said Heather, fetching a dustpan and brush to sweep up the broken bulb.

There was a loud explosion from somewhere outside, and Audrey fainted.

The bar erupted into action as everyone made for the door, except Colin, Anne and Heather, who were attempting to lift Audrey onto a chair.

'Put your head between your knees, dear,' said Anne helpfully, as Audrey regained some of her senses. When she regained all of them she became hysterical.

'We've lost everything. We've lost everything,' she screamed repeatedly.

'Shall I slap her?' Colin asked reluctantly.

'I wouldn't. She'll be all right in a minute. Go and see

what's happened,' said Heather.

Colin and Alan came back a few minutes later.

'It's all right,' Colin said. 'Audrey, it's all right. Nothing's damaged. That wasn't the bomb. They've made it safe. That was the detonator we heard…they took it out and blew it up in one of Luke's fields.'

In a few seconds everyone, except Alan and Heather, had left the pub and gone to see the hole in Luke's field.

'It was about the size of my dining room table,' Anne said later. She seemed a little disappointed that such a loud bang should have produced so small a crater.

Alan and Heather sat down in the kitchen to a late lunch.

'Was Peggy all right after her bike accident?' Alan asked.

'She didn't fall off her bike. That was what she told the policeman.' Heather told him what Luke had done to Peggy. He laughed.

'Well, you can't say she didn't ask for it. Dung seems to be the main weapon of war down here. Maybe world leaders should be informed of it's efficacy. Can't see riots lasting long if they let Dave and his muck-spreader loose on the rioters. Maybe he should diversify his farm into a military training ground for this purpose.'

'Are you feeling all right, darling?' Heather joked, putting her hand on his forehead. 'Maybe you should lie down for a while…or get out more.'

'Good idea,' he said. 'Tell you what: I need to go to the builders merchants and get some cement to patch that hole in the yard. Want to come?'

'No, I think I can live without a trip to the builders merchants. I'll just pop down and make sure Jimmy's all right.' She put her plate in the sink, and pulled on her jacket and wellingtons.

CHAPTER TWENTY-THREE

It took longer than usual to get to the farm as most of the villagers seemed to be out and about discussing the bomb, and all of them wanted Heather's version of Colin and Audrey's reaction in the pub.

Viewed from the road, the hole in Luke's field seemed undramatically small. Luke already had his digger out and was beginning to fill it in, watched by two policemen whose car was parked at the roadside.

Heather waved to the digger driver and, as he waved back, she realised it was Dave, not Luke. She walked on and turned into the track to Hawkridge. The ewe with the cauliflower ear and her lamb, who was now almost big enough to go to market, were grazing along the side of the track. She gave them a wide berth, walking awkwardly with one foot on the verge and the other on the rise of the bank, but they ignored her.

Turning the last bend in the track, she saw that Mandy's car was back in the farmyard. As she began to cross the yard she could hear raised voices coming from the farmhouse, and suddenly the back door flew open and crashed against the wall. Mandy got halfway across the yard before Luke caught up with her. He grabbed her shoulder and spun her round.

'Let go, you bastard!' Mandy yelled, as she struggled.

Heather decided that she had been a wimp for too much of her life. Instead of backing away up the track, hoping they hadn't seen her, she walked on towards them, thinking, he can't beat up both of us - can he? This thought had to be quickly pushed away before she lost her nerve.

They saw her coming and froze for a second, before Mandy struggled free from Luke's grip. In the back of her mind Heather held the picture of the two policemen, just up the road. She felt in her pocket to check that she had her mobile phone with her: it still smelt slightly of the farmyard from it's last trip to Hawkridge, with Peggy.

'Keep out of this, Heather. Go and see to your horse,' Luke said, through gritted teeth.

'No. Are you all right, Mandy?'

'It's none of your business. Bloody women!' he snarled, and walked off towards the pig sties with his fists clenched rigidly at his sides. The pheasant, excited by the air of menace and violence hanging over the farmyard, hurtled out of the cart shed at Luke, then hurtled back again propelled by Luke's boot.

'Goal!' Heather muttered, as the bird passed between the door posts.

Mandy came over to her: 'Thanks, Heather. I can't explain now. It'll only make him worse if he sees me talking to you. I'll give you a ring later, if I get a chance.'

'I don't like leaving you alone with him in this mood. There are a couple of policemen down the road…he was assaulting you, you know?'

'Not really. He'll be all right now - now he knows you've seen us. Go on. Go and see to Jimmy. I'm okay. I'll phone you.'

'If you're sure, then. Be careful.'

'Yes. Go on, before he comes back.'

'Okay.'

Heather walked away towards the field gate, passing the cart shed on the way. There was no sign of the pheasant. She pictured him lying injured inside but lacked the nerve to go into the dark interior to check. 'There is a limit to my bravery,' she muttered.

It was a relief to walk across the field and put her arms round Jimmy's neck. He put up with being hugged because he knew the reward would be peppermints - his lips were nuzzling her pocket as she pressed her face into his mane.

'You're not complicated are you, my love?' she said. Moving her hand down and scratching him gently at the base of his mane. This inspired him into raising his head and scratching her shoulder but, as he was using his teeth, she put an end to the reciprocal horse equivalent of a hug by giving him a handful of peppermints to crunch.

She looked back towards the farm. Luke was standing by the pig sties, staring across the field at her. The hair on the back of her neck prickled slightly and she decided to walk home across country, rather than re-trace her steps through the farmyard.

Mandy rang just before opening time, that evening. Alan answered the phone in the kitchen, ignorant of the drama Heather had interrupted that afternoon. She was beginning to hold back controversial news from him until she had properly digested it. Alan had a habit of blurting things out without thinking in the convivial atmosphere of the bar.

'We were worried about you.' She heard him say, through the open door to the living room. There was a pause as the caller spoke to him.

'Um - no - when they were disarming the bomb. No-one seemed to know where you were. What are *you* talking about? Oh, well, all right. I'll get her for you. Heather…it's Mandy, for you,' he called. He put his hand over the mouthpiece as Heather came into the kitchen.

'I think something's happened at the farm, but she say's no. Do you know something you haven't told me?' he asked.

'I'll speak to her,' said Heather, taking the phone from him and ignoring his question.

She stared at him as he hovered in the doorway to the living room, until he gave up and went back to his chair in front of the television.

'Hello, Mandy.'

'Heather, I just wanted to apologise about this afternoon. I've got a few minutes. Luke's out on the tractor.'

'Is he being all right to you, now?'

'Yes, he was just angry because I had been out without telling him. I didn't realise he'd be back so soon. He's been in a foul mood until about half an hour ago, when some bloke rang and booked two sows in to be served by that bloody boar. Suddenly now he's as pleased as if someone had booked two nubile young blondes in to him for service. Anyway, it's all blown over.'

'Well, that's a relief. I've been really worried. Jealousy like that must be very hard to live with,' said Heather.

'Yes, it's…well… we'll see. Thanks for worrying, anyway. Better go now.'

What had Mandy been going to say? Heather wondered just how capable of real physical violence Luke was? Once again she found her mind wandering to the enigma of Luke's missing wife, Rose.

'Why were you worried about Mandy?' It was Alan, standing in the doorway again.

'It's rude to listen to other people's phone calls,' she said.

'Come on, Heather. What's happened?'

She told him about Luke's reaction that afternoon. 'He seems to think he has a right to control her every move.'

'That bloke's an animal,' said Alan.

'Animals don't behave like that. They're altogether nicer than people… except pheasants … and occasional sheep,' said Heather, remembering the ewe with the cauliflower ear charging at the car on their first meeting.

'What?'

'Never mind. Isn't it about time we opened?'

CHAPTER TWENTY-FOUR

Heather winced and blinked as Peggy came through the back door wearing a new, acid green, anorak with an orange flower motif. It was impossible not to comment on it as she hung it on the hook behind the door.

'New coat, Peggy?' Heather asked, adjusting her eyes to the luminous aura surrounding the garment.

'I 'ad to, didn't I? 'E ruined my other one with all that muck, and 'e tore it as well. Mum said, throw it away and get a new one. She said 'e ought to pay for it.'

'I think it would be pushing your luck to ask him,' said Heather.

'Nasty piece of work. I was only tryin' to 'elp 'im. Would 'e listen?'

'He said you were teasing the boar with a pitch-fork.'

'Did 'e? Luke idolises that bloody thing...always starin' at its 'you know whats', and boastin' about the litters it's sired.'

'I gather there were two sows booked into it yesterday. That cheered him up a bit.'

'Pity!' Peggy snorted.

'What are you two talking about?' Alan walked into the kitchen, and winced as the sunlight fell on Peggy's coat. 'My God! You're not likely to get run over wearing that!'

'We were talking about sex,' said Heather.

'Oh...I'll be in the yard if anyone wants me,' he beat a hurried retreat without waiting for a rejoinder from Peggy after his remark about her coat. He didn't come back indoors until Peggy was nearly ready to go, and just finishing her coffee.

'Met Luke and Mandy in the shop,' he said. 'They're on their way to Exeter to do some shopping. Well, I think it's Mandy who wants to do the shopping; Luke didn't look all that keen.'

''E never took me shopping in Exeter,' Peggy sniffed.

'Barry takes you to Exeter, doesn't he?' Alan asked.

'Yes. I suppose 'e does.' She shrugged her arm into the new anorak. 'Did you say they was on their way to Exeter now?' she asked Alan.

'Yes,' he replied absently, as he looked at his watch and compared it with the kitchen clock. 'Crikey! We should have been open five minutes ago.' Somebody was knocking on the bar door. 'Have you put the sandwiches out?' he asked Heather, as he went into the bar.

'Of course,' she said.

When she turned round, Peggy was already going out of the back door. If Heather had wanted to quiz her about her interest in Luke's activities, she was too late.

She started to prepare the vegetables for the evening meals - they had two tables of four booked. She peeled potatoes and placed them on a board ready to slice up for chips. So far she had shunned buying ready-made frozen packs, and regular customers said they preferred 'proper' chips. She reached toward the block for a larger knife, but that slot was empty.

'Bother you, Alan,' she muttered. He was very bad at putting things back in their place. She had to use an even bigger knife which wasn't so comfortable to handle.

The lunch-time session was so quiet that Heather decided to leave early to check on Jimmy. That would give her plenty of time to concentrate on preparing the evening meals.

As she turned the car out of the pub yard into the square she saw Mandy's car, with Luke driving, going through the village towards Hawkridge. That was a short shopping expedition, Heather thought; imagining that Luke would not be the ideal tolerant bloke to take round department

184

stores. She set off after them, but quickly lost them as they roared over the bridge and up the road on the other side; the entrance to Hawkridge was just over the brow of the hill. She dawdled slightly, hoping to give them time to get into the house before she arrived, not wanting to get involved in any more possible domestic disturbances.

She was halfway up the hill when, suddenly, an acid green anorak leapt out of the hedge bordering one of Luke's fields. Heather slammed on the brakes, heart thumping, as Peggy rushed out in front of the car, frantically waving her arms. Leaning a hand on the bonnet she levered her way round the car as Heather skidded into the verge. Then, wrenching open the door, Peggy dived into the passenger seat.

'Quick, 'Eather! Get me 'ome!' She slid down in the seat, trying to get out of sight.

She had left a hand-shaped mark on the bonnet; and when Heather got a proper look at Peggy, she realised she was covered in mud and blood. She stared at the mess, mind momentarily blank. Had Luke run her over in the drive? No. There hadn't been time for that to have happened and for Peggy to have reached the road.

'Drive, 'Eather! Drive! Get me 'ome.'

'I'll take you to the surgery. What on earth's happened? Where are you hurt? Blast I haven't brought my phone,' she scrabbled in her pockets.

'I'm not 'urt. Turn round, quick.'

A wide lorry came down the hill from the village and Heather had to pull further onto the verge to let it pass. Then she did as Peggy wanted and, using a muddy field gateway, did an ungainly three-point turn in the narrow road and started back towards the village.

'Where's all that blood coming from, Peggy? There are some tissues in there,' she pointed towards the glove compartment. 'Is it just your hand? What's happened? What have you been doing? Please let me take you to the surgery.'

'Stop askin' questions, and get me 'ome. I'll be all right. I'll fetch me bike later.'

Heather visualised damage done at Hawkridge, probably a window smashed as Peggy broke in.

'Did you cut yourself on glass? You've got to stop all this. You can't get away with this vendetta of yours for ever, you know.' Heather glanced over at Peggy as they crossed the bridge.

Peggy moved up in her seat slightly, and stared speculatively at her.

'It's getting to be that you know a bit too much,' she said slowly.

'For God's sake, Peggy, don't look at me like that.' The theme from 'The Godfather' began to play through her head. 'This is North Tegridge...not bloody Sicily.'

Peggy gave a grim smile. 'Sorry, 'Eather. 'E nearly caught me. If I 'adn't 'eard the car comin' back...above all that row...you're right. I think I may 'ave gone a bit too far this time. Not that 'e didn't deserve it. Look what the bugger done to me, last year.' She pulled up her bloodstained trouser-leg and Heather took her eyes off the road for long enough to register a livid and ragged scar on Peggy's calf.

'Luke did that?'

'No - not Luke, the bloody boar.'

'The boar! You haven't put it back in the house?'

'No. It's in the crush.'

'Crush?'

'The cattle crush.'

'Peggy, is that pig's blood?'

'Yes,' she slid down in the seat again as they passed

186

through the village square.

'Have you killed the boar? What have you done?'

'Look out! You're going past,' Peggy said.

Heather braked hard and turned into the estate, then pulled up in front of Peggy's house.

'No, I 'aven't killed it; leastways, I don't think so.' She opened the car door. 'I've got to get in and get cleaned up before Mum gets back from the village 'all. She's puttin' out jumble.' Peggy climbed out of the car.

'What about the pig?'

'Luke'll 'ave found it by now. It was making enough noise. Not a word, now, 'Eather.'

'We'll have to have a proper talk tomorrow morning,' Heather said. 'While Alan's out. He's going to Exeter'

'See you tomorrow,' said Peggy. 'Oh, and thanks,' she called from the front door.

Heather sat in the car for a few moments with the engine running. The hand print on the bonnet still glistened. It must be blood, she thought, wondering how she could get rid of it before going back to the farm. She turned off the engine and found an empty can of coke in the car rubbish bag. Pouring the dregs out of it onto a tissue she got out of the car and began to rub at the stain. The tissue quickly disintegrated; but several more, which she spat onto, seemed to disguise the shape of the mark. She crumpled up the, now pink, tissues and squashed them into an empty crisp packet before putting them back into the rubbish bag.

Then she got back behind the wheel and studied the passenger seat. That was going to need more serious cleaning, but she could do that at home. She put her coat over the seat, to hide the stains, and set off back to the farm.

Heather took deep breaths as she drove slowly down the hill, trying to calm the fluttering feeling in her stomach. A

187

car horn behind her made her pull over and a black Range-Rover passed her and roared up the hill. She recognised the vet from the practice in the village.

She nearly turned round and went back to Alan, and sanity. Then pictured the scene as she told him what had happened. There would be a row over the mess in the car. He would ring Luke. There would probably, at the very least, be an RSPCA cruelty case over whatever it was that Peggy had done to the boar. She herself would be called as a witness, and maybe prosecuted as an accessory after the fact.

'I drove the getaway car,' she moaned.

She and Alan would, most likely, become objects of Peggy's insane venom. She remembered the chilling look Peggy had given her in the car. Or, she thought, I could do nothing and drive down to the farm as normal - just be Heather going to visit Jimmy. She would have to act her surprise at whatever she found there.

She didn't have to act. The surprise and disgust she felt at what Peggy had done came completely naturally.

Mandy came over to meet her as she parked beside the vet's Range-Rover.

'Pity you didn't get down here earlier, Heather. They might have heard you and run off.'

'Who?…What's happened? I saw the vet. He just passed me.'

'Somebody's tried to castrate the boar. The vet's just going to give him an anaesthetic, so he can examine him and see how bad it is. Luke's in shock.'

'Bloody Hell!' Heather said, putting her hand over her mouth to stop anything more incriminating escaping her lips. 'Who would do a thing like that?' She had to know if they suspected Peggy. It seemed they didn't - well, not yet, anyway.

'I don't know. Luke says there's one or two that wouldn't mind his boar being put out of action. Apparently, Luke had a fight last year, at the County show, with the chap from Lower Litten who came second. There's always been bad feeling between them. And then maybe some of those ravers are getting their own back at their cars and equipment being messed up. I don't know.' She shook her head and sighed. 'I thought it would be lovely and peaceful living out here in the country. D'you want a cup of tea? I'm just going to make one for the men.'

'No thanks, Mandy. I'll just check that Jimmy's okay, and get off. I don't want to be in the way. I hope the boar will recover all right.'

'We'll see. It's lost a lot of blood.' Mandy turned and went over to the farmhouse.

'I know. Half of it is in my car,' Heather muttered, walking across to the field gate where Jimmy was waiting for her. She gazed round the farm yard, wondering where Peggy had hidden her bike. If they found that, it would be an open and shut case. Why was she thinking in police terms?

As if on cue the sound of a distant police siren drifted in on the wind. The white car, with its blue light flashing, pulled up in the yard a minute later. She waited until Mandy had escorted them round to the back of the barn, gave Jimmy two more peppermints, and got back to her car as quickly as she could. Making my escape, she thought, trying not to look at the smudge on the bonnet.

As she drove back into the village, she saw Peggy and Mercy coming out of the village hall with two other ladies.

'Establishing an alibi,' she said, out loud.

Another police car drove fast through the village towards Hawkridge. They can't be very busy today, Heather thought. Peggy turned and watched it go, then looked straight across at her as she turned into the pub yard - it was not a pleasant look. A wave of anger swept over her at the position Peggy had put her in. She wrenched the car into its parking space, turned off the engine and sat there for a minute. She suddenly wanted to turn the whole problem over to Alan, but, as her anger receded, she realised that this would promote endless difficulties for them both. Alan was always saying they should keep out of village feuds and politics, but for her this was becoming increasingly difficult. She would have to say something, though. The attack on the boar would be all over the village by tomorrow, if not that evening. It would look odd if she had been down to the farm and noticed nothing.

Her immediate problem was how to clean the car without Alan noticing what she was doing. He was in the sitting room, watching television. She stood in the doorway for a second or two, taking in the peaceful room with its low ceiling and central beam, which Alan now automatically ducked under. The late afternoon sun was flooding through the window, fading the furniture covers, but she had never been able to draw curtains and shut out the daylight, especially sunshine. Alan was completely relaxed in his chair, shoes off and feet on a footstool, engrossed in a cricket match.

'Hi,' he said, noticing her. 'Wouldn't mind a cup of tea if you're making some. You going to join me?'

There was nothing she would have liked more than to stay in that cosy, safe room, even if it did mean having to watch cricket, but she had to clean the mess out of the car while Alan was otherwise occupied. The Test Match was a gift. She knew if she sat in there with him she would end up telling him everything about her part in the afternoon's happenings. Going over to his chair she bent and kissed the top of his head.

'Love you,' she said.

His hand reached back and patted her face.

'What brought that on?' he asked, his eyes never leaving the television, and his hand suddenly clenching into a fist and punching the air beside her head as the batsman hit a four. 'Yess!' he exclaimed.

Heather backed out of range.

'I'll get some tea,' she said, as the bowler started his next run-up and Alan leaned forward in his armchair with total concentration on the screen.

She put the kettle on, and while it boiled she fetched the front seat covers in from the car and put them in some cold water to soak. The water immediately turned pink. She had to empty and refill the sink twice more before the water was clear; then she put the covers into the washing machine and crossed her fingers.

She took Alan his cup of tea and placed it on the small table beside his chair.

'Bit of drama down at the farm, this afternoon,' she said.

'What's he done to her, now?' Alan asked.

'No, not them. Somebody has attacked Luke's boar.'

'Who? Not Peggy, again?'

It was a good job Alan was still looking at the television when he said this.

Heather turned away to hide her face. 'Some rival breeder, Mandy thinks. They had to get the vet.'

'Never a dull moment out here in the country, is there? Oh, well played!'

Heather heaved a small sigh of relief and left him to the cricket. She filled a bucket with cold water and carried it out to the car. Fortunately most of the damage had been done to the covers, and the rest of the mud and blood was on the rubber floor mats. Destroying incriminating evidence, she thought, as she wiped surfaces and dunked the mats up and down in the bucket. There was still the mark on the bonnet, but when she tried to wipe it off with a wet sponge, it didn't disappear. She fetched warm water and some washing-up liquid, sponged it again, and dried the patch off. The mark was still there.

'Damn,' she muttered. Maybe the coke wasn't such a clever idea. It seemed to have damaged the paint-work. She fetched some spray polish and a duster, but that didn't make a great deal of difference. She gave up and hoped Alan wouldn't notice.

Back indoors she took the seat covers out of the washing machine, and inspected them before placing them in the dryer. The stains seemed to have gone. Heather flopped onto a chair at the kitchen table and began to breath normally again - she felt exhausted. Alan came into the kitchen.

'Oh, here you are,' he said. 'What's wrong? You look tired.'

'I am, a bit,' she said. Nothing like getting involved in a good 'pig mutilating' session for draining one's nervous energy, she thought, suppressing a wild, and inappropriate desire to giggle.

'Why don't you go into the sitting room and put your feet up for a while. We've got a busy evening coming up. Two more people booked for dinner while you were out. I'm not so sure this horse business is such a good idea, darling. You're spending so much time down at the farm you're not getting a proper rest in the afternoons.'

'Two more people, or two more tables? If business keeps growing, we'll have to get a waitress.'

'Mercy said she'd help out, if we needed her,' he said.

'No!'

'Why, no? What's wrong with Mercy? Worried she'll

192

strip off and dance on the tables?'

'With Dave…' Heather began to giggle, but stopped herself as she caught it slipping into hysteria. 'I'll think about it. But for now I'll do as you suggested and put my feet up. You can bring *me* a cup of tea.'

CHAPTER TWENTY-FIVE

Heather spent most of that night dreaming up, and discarding, ways of trying to tell Peggy she didn't want her to work at the pub any more; but now that Alan had discussed how busy they were, with Mercy, none of them rang true.

She finally fell into a doze around half past four, and come groggily awake with the alarm at seven-thirty. Three mugs of black coffee had pushed her into some semblance of normality by the time Peggy arrived for work. Alan was just leaving as she came through the door.

'I'll be back in time to open up,' he said. 'Morning, Peggy.'

'Mornin'.'

Heather noticed that she'd managed to get the bloodstains out of her new anorak. Forensic would probably still be able to pick up traces of pig DNA, she thought. Perhaps it wouldn't hurt to give the car another thorough clean, when Alan wasn't around.

Peggy went to the cupboard where the cleaning materials were kept, and Alan came back into the kitchen.

'Where are the car seat covers?' he asked.

'Oh, sorry - I washed them, yesterday.' Heather opened the dryer door.

Peggy dropped the cleaning box on the floor and swore. Alan picked up a tin of polish which was rolling towards him and handed it back to her. Peggy muttered her thanks and shot Heather one of her 'looks', behind Alan's back, as she went through the bar door.

'I'll help you put them on,' Heather said, pulling the crumpled fabric out of the dryer. As she tried to smooth the creases out, on the car seat, she remembered her missing chip cutting knife.

'Oh, where did you leave my big chip knife, Alan?'

'I haven't had it,' he said.

'Are you sure? Only it wasn't there yesterday when...,' her voice tailed off as realisation dawned. 'Doesn't matter,' she said. 'Have a good trip.'

'I'm only going to Cash and Carry - you make it sound like a holiday.'

'A holiday would be nice,' she said.

She returned to the kitchen, her stomach knotted with fear as she imagined her bloodstained kitchen knife lying on the ground beside Luke's cattle crush. It will have my fingerprints on it, she thought, her mind descending into slow motion. She stood by the sink, certain now that she would have to go to the police and tell them everything, before they came for her. Don't be stupid, she thought, no-one would think it was me.

'You used *my* knife, Peggy. You absolute bitch,' she said quietly to herself, and stared across at the knife block - trying to decide what to do. It only dawned on her slowly, that all the knives were in place, except the one she herself had taken down to the stable. She stretched out her hand and pulled out the chip knife, turning it over and inspecting it thoroughly.

'It's all right. I gave it a good wash,' came the voice from the doorway, making her jump.

Heather turned and stared at Peggy; suddenly so angry that all the things she wanted to say became blocked inside her. This is what it is like to be speechless with rage, she thought. Her look of fury, and the fist clenched round the knife handle, seemed to get through to Peggy, who lowered her gaze and shifted uncomfortably in the doorway.

'I'm sorry,' she said. 'But I 'ad to seize the opportunity - it wasn't planned.'

'That makes it all right, does it? For somebody who professes love for animals that was a cruel and wicked thing to do. You crazy idiot! Now you've involved me in your insane war with Luke. What the hell good do you think all this is doing? You're upsetting everyone around you - and now the police are involved. How do you think you're going to get away with it?'

'No-one knows it was me - except you. Everyone knows I was 'elpin' Mum at the village 'all, yesterday afternoon. I went back and fetched me bike after dark.'

'You've probably killed that poor pig.'

'I didn't mean to kill it; just cut its balls off. I 'ope Luke was good and upset.'

'You are unbelievable!'

'You're not from the country. You don't understand country people.'

'I understand cruelty; and there are laws in England which affect the countryside as well as towns. Why am I getting into this argument with you? I think you'd better go home. I don't want you around here this morning. I'm too angry.'

'Are you firin' me?'

'I don't know what I'm doing. Just go home.'

'What'll I tell Mum?'

'I don't know,' Heather's voice was rising with fury. 'Tell her you've got a headache.'

'I don't get 'eadaches.'

Heather pointed at the back door with the knife.

'Out! Get out now…and leave me some space to think.'

'All right, all right, keep your 'air on. I'm goin'.'

She pulled on the green anorak; there was a slight stain on the sleeve, Heather noticed.

Peggy opened the back door and turned to face her.

'Don't forget. You 'elped me,' she said.

'Just go,' said Heather, through clenched teeth. She slammed the back door behind Peggy, and stared for a moment at her white knuckles clutched round the knife. Taking a deep breath she put it back in the block with the others, then immediately took it out again and put it in the sink with the dirty breakfast things. After a moment of indecision, she went into the bar and let off steam by cleaning and polishing the room in half the time it normally took Peggy. Then she bottled up for Alan, tidied the kitchen, and washed the floor. Having thoroughly washed the knife, she left it to soak in disinfectant. After all this activity she sat at the kitchen table with her hands clasped round a mug of coffee, and tried to decide what to do.

The car pulled up in the yard, and Alan came into the kitchen carrying boxes of crisps.

'Hi,' he said. 'I got a good deal on these, and the cans of soft drinks were on special offer. Looks nice in here. Have you been having a purge?'

'Yes.' She stood up and put her arms round him. 'You're so nice, Alan. Most men don't notice things like that.'

He gave her a hug. 'Now put me down. I have to unload the car,' he grinned down at her.

The lunch-time customers were full of the story of what had happened to Luke's boar.

'I reckon it was Peggy,' Dave laughed. 'Showing Luke what she'd like to do to him.'

Heather's blood ran cold. As the rest of the customers laughed, she managed to screw her face into something resembling a smile.

'What d'you think, Heather?' Dave asked.

'Leave me out of this,' she said, turning away to push a glass up under the gin optic, for Anne.

'I don't think Peggy would hurt one of the farm animals,' Anne said.

'It couldn't be her,' said Audrey. 'Yesterday afternoon she was over at the village hall helping to put out jumble with Mercy. I spoke to her when I took some up.'

'Oh well, I reckon the police will find out who it was,' said Colin.

'Our lot? I doubt it,' said Dave.

Heather's eyes flicked nervously back and forth between the speakers. Had Dave thought his remark was just a joke? She couldn't tell. If it was it was in pretty poor taste.

'Is the boar dead?' Anne asked Dave.

'No. It's in a bit of a mess and lost a lot of blood, but the vet thinks it'll recover. They're not sure yet whether it will still be able to sire litters. Vet says the knife should have been sharper to do a proper job.'

All the men in the bar winced. Heather could feel the handle of the knife as she had gripped it so fiercely that morning. She looked down at her empty hand and rubbed her palms together.

'Have you got any of those tarragon chicken sandwiches?' Anne asked Heather.

'Yes, I'll make you some.' She was glad to get out of the bar.

By the time she returned and placed the sandwiches in front of Anne, the conversation had become more general.

As they were tidying up after closing time, Alan said: 'Poor bloody pig. Who would do a thing like that?

'No idea. Can we go into Exeter, this afternoon? I've decided to try riding Jimmy soon, and I'll need a saddle and bridle. I think there's a shop that sells second-hand saddles.'

This, as she had hoped, distracted Alan.

'Isn't it a bit soon? I'm not sure I want you riding him, anyway. A racehorse is a bit high-powered. If you must ride, why don't you sell him and get something slower and safer.'

'Don't try to put me off, Alan. I must admit I am a bit nervous, but it's becoming a question of proving I can do it. I've told too many people I'm going to to back out of it now.'

'That's not a good reason, at all.'

'I promise I'll be careful. He's very gentle, and he's used to me.'

'Well, I'm coming down the day you try riding him. Just in case.'

Heather didn't argue about this as she found the idea rather comforting. Also it would stop any, possibly disquieting, comments from Luke on her lack of ability.

CHAPTER TWENTY-SIX

An uneasy truce developed between Heather and Peggy. There was no friendship between them; just an unspoken understanding that silence on the subject of pigs was to the advantage of both. Heather tried to put the whole episode out of her mind.

That afternoon she met Barry, at Hawkridge. One of Jimmy's shoes had worked loose and Barry had managed to fit in a visit to her between larger jobs. They chatted about horses for a while and, as she was taking advantage of Barry's expertise by asking him to choose between the two saddles she had brought home on approval, he asked her about Luke's latest upset.

'How's the old boar, then?'

'Oh, the news has reached East Tegridge, has it?'

'Yes. It's the talk of the pub over there. Funny - I saw Peg yesterday evening and she never mentioned it.'

'How are you two getting on, then? Could you be considered an 'item', as they say?' Heather was frantically trying drag the subject away from failed castration attempts.

'Don't know, really. She's good company. Likes a laugh,' he looked thoughtful. 'She's not quite the Peggy I thought I knew, though. All this clubbing, and that. She used to be a quiet country girl, but now she seems to be trying to make up for a lost youth. To be honest I'm not sure I can keep up. Still, we'll see.' He moved the second saddle slightly on Jimmy's back. 'That's the better one of the two. Not ideal though. It would be better if you could get the saddler to have a look at him and fit him properly. He might be able to alter this one if he re-arranges the stuffing, a bit.' He lifted the saddle off and placed it with the other one on the stable door. 'Right, finished with you, son,' he patted Jimmy on the shoulder.

'Thank you very much for the advice,' said Heather.

'That's all right. Saw old Dave over our way, the other day, visiting his lady-friend,' he said.

'Really? He's a bit of a lad is Dave,' said Heather.

'Still, don't do any harm as long as he sticks to widows, and them as aren't married,' said Barry.

'Oh, she's a widow, too? The big woman I saw him with at the fair?'

'Yes, her old man died a few years back. I don't think she misses him much. Drunk by closing time most nights, Alf was. That's what killed him,' said Barry.

'The drink?'

'Well, in a roundabout sort of a way. She'd had enough of it. And one night when he didn't come home for his supper, she got so mad she locked him out and went to bed. Middle of winter, and wickedly cold it was. So he started banging on the door and shouting; and d'you know what she did?'

'No,' said Heather.

'She leaned out of the bedroom window and poured a bucket of water over him - then went back to bed. When she unlocked the door in the morning, he sort of toppled in from where he'd been sitting on the doorstep. Frozen solid he was. Like he'd been set in an ice cube. She didn't half get a shock.'

'You mean...he was dead? Heather was picturing the scene only too vividly.

'Oh, yes. Froze to death - what with the water and the alcohol.'

'Didn't she get into trouble?'

'No. Accidental death, they said. He'd thawed a bit by the time she'd pulled him into the kitchen and got the doctor. The bit about the bucket of water never came out.

People were sorry for her. Well, it *was* an accident, really. She never meant to kill him, did she?' He looked at his watch. 'I better be on my way.' He started to pick up his tools.

Heather paid him and watched him walk across the field to his van. Then she leaned on one of the saddles resting on the stable door, inhaling the faint smell of saddle soap and letting her gaze wander over the rolling countryside spread out before her, trying to reconcile the placid view with the undercurrent of violence and death which seemed to pervade the area.

'Dave won't be after *me*, then,' she said to Jimmy. 'He specialises in murderesses.'

A sudden shiver flicked over her as she remembered the vision of her bloodstained hands, outside the pub, when they had first arrived in the village. Had that been something to do with her knife being used on the boar?

Jimmy snorted a stray oat out of his nose, tipped over his empty bucket and moved across to his haynet for a few mouthfuls, before joining her at the door. He sniffed at the smell of other horses on the saddles, then raised his nose in the air and curled up his top lip.

'Did that belong to a sexy mare then, boy?' said Heather.

He started to push at the saddles and was in danger of tipping them off the door.

'There's not room for both of us here. Get back,' she pushed at his chest so that she could open the door and let him out into the field. Then, picking up the saddles, she walked back towards the car. Mandy was in the yard, feeding the hens, and although Heather would have preferred to avoid the subject altogether, she felt she ought to ask after the boar. But Mandy spoke first.

'You going to start riding him, then?' she asked, nodding towards the saddles.

'Not just yet. Neither of these fit properly. How's the boar coming along?'

'Vet thinks he'll get over it, all right. Whoever did it only managed half the job. Luke's over there with him now if you want to see him.'

'No, I must get back. I'm glad he's going to recover. You all right?'

'Yes, I'm fine,' said Mandy, but she didn't look too happy.

Neither did the pheasant, who was hobbling across the yard towards her, but then seemed to think better of it and stopped. After glaring at her with his ruff raised for a second, he turned and went back to the hens who were scratching frantically after the corn Mandy had just thrown out. Must have been that kick from Luke, the other day, Heather thought. She wondered why the bird chose to live there with all the violence and drugs it had to contend with. It had only just got over the limp that Mandy had inflicted with the whip, when Luke had booted it into misery again.

CHAPTER TWENTY-SEVEN

'There was a police car parked outside Peggy's house when I came past this afternoon,' said Alan, turning on the lights in the bar. 'D'you know what it could be about?'

'Apart from her hitting Mandy on the head with a brick: releasing stock onto the main road: poisoning peoples' casseroles - and their cows. No, I've no idea. Perhaps they think Josiah's death was suspicious and it's Mercy they want.

'You don't really think Mercy did that.'

'No, of course not,' she said, but she couldn't forget the sly look Mercy had given her over Josiah's grave.

The door rattled as Peggy and Mercy came into the bar. Peggy shot Heather a very strange look while she was hanging up their coats. Then she spent a few minutes with Mercy, deciding where they should sit, and buying drinks for them both. When Mercy was settled, Peggy came up to the bar.

'Can I 'ave a word?' she said to Heather.

'Of course.'

'Not 'ere - in private.'

Heather's heart sank. Now what? They went through to the sitting room. She didn't invite Peggy to sit down.

'What's the problem?' Heather asked.

''Ave you said something to the police?'

'Of course I haven't. Why?'

'They was round interviewing me, earlier. Wanted to know where I was that afternoon.'

'You were at the village hall sorting out the jumble.'

'Yes, they wanted to know times.'

'And?'

'Mum said I was there all afternoon, with 'er. I 'ad to tell 'er the truth. I never told 'er you brought me 'ome, but she knows the rest and she said she'd stand by me. She knows 'ow rotten Luke can be, and she's always been angry with the boar for scarring my leg like that...did I show you?' she began to bend down.

'Yes, you did,' said Heather hurriedly.

'Oh...Well, I just wondered why the police came, in the first place.'

'Well, I didn't send them. I'd be mad to mention any of it considering how you managed to implicate me.'

'I suppose so. I bet it was that bitch 'es livin' with.'

'Look, Peggy, I really have had enough of your war. D'you think we could stop discussing it, altogether. Luke and Mandy are customers, just as you and Mercy are. I refuse to take sides. Just keep me out of it.' Heather took a step towards the door but Peggy didn't move.

'Mum says I'd better stop.'

'Mercy's right. You'd do well to listen to her.'

'It's all right for 'er; she's got Dave.'

'And you've got Barry...he's nice.'

'Yes, I suppose so. 'E used to be a bit more of a goer. I sometimes think 'es not very...well, you know...excitin'.'

'There's been far too much excitement around here, lately. Why don't you settle for 'nice', for a while. Now, if you'll excuse me, I've really got to get back to the bar.'

'What was that about?' Alan asked, as Peggy walked back to sit with Mercy.

'Nothing - just women's stuff.'

Luke came in and walked towards the bar. Her stomach lurched.

'Yes, Luke, what can I get you?' she asked, raising her voice. She was trying to deflect his gaze and warn Peggy of his presence at the same time; but Luke noticed Mercy and Peggy turned to look at him.

'Shit!' said Heather, under her breath; but Alan heard her.

'Pardon! Not like you to swear. What's the matter?...Oh!' He saw where she was looking.

Luke and Peggy had locked eyes, and for a tense moment nobody in the bar spoke. Thank goodness they're not wearing revolvers, Heather thought.

'That's a pint, then, is it Luke?' She tried to break the spell.

He turned slowly towards the bar, wearing an odd, thoughtful expression.

'Pint please, Heather,' he said.

'How's the old boar, then, Luke?' It was one of a couple of old boys who came in most evenings for a game of dominoes.

Once more the air was electric. Peggy fixed her black eyes on Heather, giving her the uncomfortable feeling of being drawn into a spider's web. She finished pulling the pint for Luke and placed it on the bar. He fumbled in his pocket for some change as he answered.

'Not too bad, Albert. Vet thinks he'll come through, okay. More'n the bloke who did it will when I get my hands on him.'

Him, Heather thought. Good sign.

'How's Mandy?' Alan asked.

'She's all right. Why are you so interested?'

'I er...just making conversation. Yes, Mercy. What would you like?' Alan moved quickly to the other end of the bar.

Mercy ordered some sandwiches, and Heather left the bar to make them. She wondered vaguely about Mandy. It was the first time for ages that Luke had come into the pub on his own.

She trimmed the outside leaves off a lettuce and took them to the bin under the sink. It was full, so she carried it outside to empty into the dustbin. The air was fresh and tinged with frost and the village was silent and dark, the sliver of new moon giving no light. She still couldn't get used to the lack of traffic sounds. Somewhere behind the church a sheep coughed; a sound so human that if she'd been walking alone in the dark it would have scared her. In the wood across the valley a tawny owl called and was answered by a much fainter call. She leaned her elbows on the wall and felt the recent tension in her shoulders drain away.

Alan stood in the kitchen doorway.

'What are you doing? Mercy wants her sandwich. They want to get back to watch something on telly.'

'Just coming, sorry.'

'What's so riveting about the dustbin?' Alan asked.

'Nothing. Tell her I'll bring it through in a moment.'

'The dustbin?'

'Not even remotely amusing, Alan - get back in the bar.'

'Don't be long. Luke's making me nervous,' he said.

'Luke makes everyone nervous.'

'Except Peggy,' said Alan. 'Did you see the look she gave him?'

'Yes, chilling. Peggy has a way with 'looks'.'

Peggy and Mercy finished their sandwiches quickly, and left to catch their television programme. Heather watched them go out of the door. It's probably 'Crimewatch', she thought. Her mind wandered off, imagining the police crime re-construction of the boar castration. She'd just got to the bit where a Peggy look-alike policewoman, in a fierce yellow wig, leaps out of the hedge and flags down a passing car driven by someone looking remarkably like herself, when she noticed Luke staring at her. Her stomach tightened, was he reading her mind?

'Heather - wake up! Two more prawn sandwiches, please,' said Alan.

'Right,' she quickly wiped up a small pool of spilt beer on the bar with the cloth she had in her hand. As she turned to go, Luke asked her for some cheese and onion crisps. She reached into the box under the bar and handed him the packet, turning over the extended hand to receive the money he was offering. He cupped her hand with his free one and dropped the coins slowly into her palm; his look challenging as he watched her expression.

'What's his game?' asked Alan quietly, as she passed him on her way to the kitchen.

'I don't know - ignore it.' The last thing she wanted was any confrontation between him and Luke. She wished Luke would go home, but he seemed determined to get morbidly drunk and had now gone on to ordering whisky 'chasers' with each pint.

About half an hour before closing time, Dave came in. Luke had moved from his rather unsteady perch on a bar stool, to a table in the corner, under Rose's sampler, though he didn't appear to have noticed it.

'What's the matter with him?' Dave inclined his head in Luke's direction.

'Don't know,' said Alan. 'He's taken on quite a skinful. I'm not looking forward to having to get him home, again.'

'Don't worry - I'll take him back,' said Dave. 'Let him drink himself past the point where he could be nasty to Mandy. She doesn't deserve him, you know. He was always a bully.'

By closing time it was all Luke could do to get to his feet, but Dave seemed to have a soothing effect on him. Instead of the violence which Heather had expected, Luke was verging on the maudlin. It seemed nobody loved him - a fact which Heather found quite understandable. But as they lurched out of the door, Dave was assuring him that Mandy did love him, and telling him he would feel better

208

after a good night's sleep. Dave raised his eyes heavenwards as he spoke these words, and grinned at Alan and Heather who had come to the door to see them off.

'Phew... glad that passed off peacefully. Lets leave the clearing up till the morning, and have an early night,' said Alan.

CHAPTER TWENTY-EIGHT

Heather came out of the shop and paused to watch Dave and his tractor turn out of the housing estate where Peggy lived, and come down towards the square. At first Heather thought he had been visiting Mercy, but then she noticed he was towing a long trailer, and, as he drove down the side of the square, she could see that the trailer was full of children. She did a quick head count. There were eight of them of various ages and sexes. Anne joined her on the pavement.

'Morning, Anne. Tell me, why has Dave abducted all the village children? And where is he taking them?'

'Oh, he does it every year,' said Anne.

'Does he bring them back?'

'Most of them - some escape and walk back.'

'Now you're making me nervous. Stop messing about. Where is he taking them?'

'It's apple-picking time. They go out to Luke's other farm, at East Tegridge. There's about two acres of orchard there. He lets Dave have the apples. The children pick up windfalls for the cider-making and Dave pays them so much a sack. They start off full of enthusiasm, and then the numbers dwindle as their backs start to ache and they get stung by wasps. He's usually down to around three by the time the orchard is cleared.'

'I didn't know Luke had two farms.'

'Yes, he lets the other one. Hawkridge was where he was born, and after his father died, he came back.'

That afternoon, Dave's tractor and trailer passed her as she was just turning into Hawkridge to go and feed Jimmy. She'd counted the children out, and now she found herself counting them back again, and was relieved to find there were still eight.

As she arrived in the yard, the cows were just leaving the milking parlour and wandering slowly back to their field. She wondered if cows ever hurried? The only other thing she had seen them do, apart from strolling along in that aimless fashion, was to lie down. What did Peggy see in them which inspired such passion?

She parked beside Mandy's car and cast a surreptitious glance at the kitchen window, and around the yard, but there was no sign of the car's owner. As she got out of her car, there was a clatter as something was dropped in the milking parlour, followed by a stream of bad language from Luke. She didn't want to slam the door and draw his attention to her presence, so she pushed the car door gently to, until it clicked half onto the latch, and walked quickly round the barn to the feed bins. Here she measured out and mixed Jimmy's feed as quietly as she could, not wanting any kind of confrontation with Luke. He sounded in a foul mood. She replaced the galvanised lid gently back on the bin, picked up the bucket and turned round to find Luke standing right behind her.

'Luke! You made me jump. I didn't hear you coming.'

'You weren't supposed to.' He stood, almost blocking her way. She could smell the alcohol on him, probably from the night before. He looked hung-over and rough.

'Erm...I haven't got time to chat now. Alan's expecting me back in a minute - busy evening, you know.' She circled awkwardly past him and set off fast across the field to the stable. When she looked round he was walking across the yard towards the house. She put the bucket down in the corner of the stable, and Jimmy, who'd followed her in, dropped his nose into it.

Heather leaned back against the stable wall, realising that her heart was thumping uncomfortably. She took deep breaths, trying to slow it down. Damn the man. Why did he make her so nervous? She didn't want to stay and groom Jimmy, as she usually did. As soon as he'd finished his feed, she turned him out again and hurried back to the pub.

'How's the boar?' Alan asked.

'I forgot to ask. I only saw Luke, and he didn't look at all well after last night's session.'

'I met Dave in the shop, buying sweets for several hundred noisy children he was carting about in his trailer,' said Alan.

'Eight,' said Heather.

'What?'

'There were only eight. I counted them.'

'Why?' asked Alan.

'I don't know why, it's just one of those things you do, subconsciously,' said Heather.

'I always knew you were a bit odd, but this place seems to accentuate it,' said Alan.

'Don't be horrid. What were you doing in the shop?'

'Re-stocking with chocolate biscuits. I've never known anyone get through them like Peggy.'

'It's probably stress; it affects some people like that,' said Heather.

'Word in the shop is that the police don't have any leads to follow up about the boar. The chap Luke thought had done it was on holiday in Spain,' said Alan. 'Oh, and I bought some cake; would you like a slice?'

'Yes, please,' Heather was trying to think how she could change the subject. Then Alan did it for her.

'Mandy all right?'

'I don't know. I didn't see her. Why do you ask?'

'I just wondered. It's unusual for them not to come in together, and Luke was pretty depressed last night.' Alan handed her a plate with a large slice of fruit cake on it. 'There's some tea in the pot. I've just got to change a couple of bottles on the optics.'

He went through to the bar, leaving Heather wondering how the police could *not* suspect Peggy of the savage, blatantly sexual, attack on the boar's, and Luke's, pride and joy. She tried to stand back from it all and see what had happened as if she hadn't been involved. But she was unsuccessful. She would never lose that mental image of blood-soaked Peggy leaping out in front of her car.

....

The next day, Dave's amoral double-dealings began to catch up with him, when Mercy overheard one of the children who'd been apple-picking, telling her mother that Mr. Fordesh had been kissing a 'huge fat lady' in a shed in the orchard. There weren't many huge fat ladies in East Tegridge.

According to Peggy, her mother had come home and had 'a good cry', then begun to get angry and, it seemed, angry in the calculated, vengeful plotting sort of way which obviously ran in the family.

'I'm not sure I want to hear this,' Heather said, as Peggy described what Mercy would like to do to the big woman - and then to Dave.

'Oh, that's just Mum lettin' off steam. I don't think she'd really do anythin' violent. That Marion Ede's a lot bigger than 'er.'

'Marion Ede? Oh, the big woman.' Heather found she was slightly disappointed to have a name to put to the Big Woman from East Tegridge. It was a bit like calling the Beast of Exmoor, a puma. 'Do you think Dave will stop seeing her? Does this Marion know about Mercy?'

'I don't think so,' said Peggy.

'It's amazing, isn't it? The whole village has known

about it for ages, but not those two,' said Heather.

'Well, that Marion will know soon; since that little nosey-parker Sharon followed them into the shed. She always was a sneak, that child. Never 'appy unless she's stirrin' up trouble.'

'Lot of gossiping going on in here - any chance of some work today?' said Alan, coming into the kitchen from the bar.

Peggy went back to work.

'What's the latest, then?' asked Alan.

'Dave's dastardly secret has been exposed.'

'Not the Big Woman from East Tegridge?'

'Her name's Marion Ede,' said Heather.

'I prefer the Big Woman. You mean Mercy's found out?'

'Yes.'

'Oh my God! Poor Dave. D'you think a Mercy spurned is likely to be as dangerous as a Peggy spurned?' asked Alan.

'She's her mother, isn't she?'

And you don't really know just how dangerous Peggy is, she thought.

'Should I warn Dave?' asked Alan.

'I think we'll keep well out of this one,' said Heather, remembering she was already the keeper of one of Mercy's 'little secrets.' She didn't want to hear any of her future plans for Dave, or his paramour.

CHAPTER TWENTY-NINE

Although Heather didn't want to know about the growing saga of Dave and Mercy's love-life, it was proving impossible to avoid, as Peggy was bringing her daily reports. In some way it was a relief to realise that Mercy's problems had deflected Peggy from her war with Luke and Mandy. This could only be a good thing.

Apparently Mercy's first move had been to write to Marion Ede, telling her to 'back off'. This letter had contained a veiled threat about mentioning the bucket of water to the police. Pot calling the kettle black, thought Heather. As yet there had been no reply from the Big Woman.

Dave broke with tradition on Tuesday evening, and came into the pub, obviously at a loose end with his routine Tuesday visit to Mercy having been denied him. His unusual presence on that day, aroused some rude, and somewhat unsympathetic comments from other customers who were conversant with his normal peregrinations. After one pint he said he'd 'had enough of this,' and left.

'Hey, you lot. Stop losing me customers,' Alan said.

'Don't know how he's got away with it for so long,' said one of the elderly domino players.

'You're only jealous,' said his opponent, pushing a tile across the table and leaning back in his chair.

Dave was in again on Thursday - his usual evening for visiting Marion. He seemed to have stirred up a hornet's nest of rejection, and was looking rather fetchingly woebegone, Heather thought. There wasn't so much banter this time as people were beginning to feel sorry for him. In a quiet way there was a lot of affection for Dave in the village.

Colin and Audrey came in.

'How's things, Dave?' asked Colin.

'Not too good,' Dave said quietly. 'Mercy says I've got to choose between the two of them. I don't really want to be bothered with all that, at my age. To my mind it feels a bit too much like making a commitment. I could wring that bloody little Sharon's neck. I used to get a good home-cooked supper Tuesdays and Thursdays, and now I have to get me own.' He looked up at Heather. 'Toasted bacon sandwich, please.'

'Now he's got me feeling sorry for him,' she said to Alan, as she made for the kitchen.

Anne, who was sitting at a table with a friend who was visiting her from London, heard Dave's last remark, and called across to him.

'Why don't you come and have lunch with us on Sunday, Dave? I promise to keep Rudi under control. I don't like to think of you living on bacon sandwiches.'

Dave seemed momentarily taken aback, but then his stomach got the better of him - Anne's cooking was renowned for its excellence - and looking somewhat bemused, he accepted.

'How does he do it?' asked Alan, as he followed Heather into the kitchen to fetch a lemon for Anne's next gin and tonic.

'Do what?' She turned on the grill and took a packet of bacon out of the fridge.

'Play that 'look at poor unloved and starving me' line, and get people like Anne to invite him for a meal.

'You're just jealous. If you like, I'll throw you out on Saturday night and maybe Anne would take pity on you, as well.'

'Ha ha,' he said.

'I wonder if Anne has considered the potential danger she may be placing herself in?' mused Heather aloud.

'What - from Dave?'

'No, Mercy,' said Heather.

'Don't be silly. She's got that friend staying with her. It's not as if they will be unchaperoned.'

'I still think it could draw Mercy's attention to her. You know Anne's always had a soft spot for Dave. The banter between them shows that,' said Heather.

'Banter! As I remember it, he was threatening to shoot her dog, not so long ago.'

'Oh, he didn't mean it.'

'No? Could've fooled me,' said Alan, taking two lemons out of the fruit bowl and going back into the bar.

....

The next day hardly dawned at all. The fog around the village was so thick that it was difficult to see across the square. Rather than crawl to the farm in the car, Heather decided to walk, regretting this decision slightly as she picked her way through the damp, eerie stillness. All the usual animals and birds seemed to have been silenced by their lack of vision; and even the river water flowing under the bridge had a muffled sound.

'Mists and mellow fruitfulness,' she muttered, as she side-stepped to avoid a pile of squashed and rotting apples, which must have fallen off Dave's trailer as he swung into Small Profits. She proceeded cautiously along the track to Hawkridge, in case the ewe with the cauliflower ear was lurking down there. In the fog she would never have seen it coming if it had decided to charge at her. She wished she had brought a stick to repel any possible attack from the dysfunctional livestock which seemed to wander at will on Luke's farm.

Whilst picking her way carefully across the farm yard, she almost collided with Mandy.

'Heather! I didn't see you coming. You gave me a fright.

Isn't this fog awful.' She seemed to be keeping her head turned away as she spoke.

'You startled me, too. It's been so quiet all the way down. Creepy isn't it.' Heather laughed, relieved to see that Mandy was still at the farm, and seemed to be all right. 'Haven't seen you for a while,' she said.

'No, I've…oh I can't hide it from you,' she turned to face Heather, who could now see that both of Mandy's eyes were severely bruised and she had a cut across the bridge of her nose. 'That's why I have been keeping out of sight for a while, but it's fading now. I'll soon be able to cover it with some make-up,' she said.

'Luke?' Heather asked quietly - for all she knew he could have been standing a few feet away from them in the murk

'I don't know what's the matter with him. He's morose and bad tempered. I can't do anything right. He says I've changed, but I don't think I have. *He* certainly has. I offered to leave the other day, and he said, if I did, he'd kill me.'

Heather felt a chill at the back of her neck, as she visualised freshly turned earth in the copse behind Jimmy's stable.

'Of course, he wouldn't,' Mandy went on. 'But I really don't know what he wants.'

'You shouldn't have to put up with threats like that,' said Heather, rather at a loss as to how to advise Mandy.

'I don't think I will. Not for much longer. Whatever he says,' she looked away from Heather.

There was the sound of the Land-Rover coming slowly along the track, its fog lights carving two white beams behind the hedge. Mandy started to move towards the house.

'I'd better not be seen talking to you, in this state,' she said.

'Hope things get better for you soon, Mandy. You know where I am if you want to talk.'

'Thanks,' said Mandy, shutting the back door.

218

Heather slipped quietly round behind the barn as the headlights turned into the yard, barely illuminating the ghostly surroundings. Jimmy found her with no difficulty at all, though, as she crossed the field with his feed bucket. He loomed out of the fog with a welcoming 'whicker' through fluttery nostrils.

'Hello, boy,' she stroked her hand down his neck as he walked beside her to the stable.

When he'd finished his feed, she turned him out again and made her way, stumbling over the ruts, back across the field; she hadn't realised just how much he had guided her to the stable. She could see nothing and when she came up against a hedge, instead of the expected gate, she realised she had been walking in a right handed circle. At least she'd thought it to be a right handed circle until she sought to correct this geographical error by turning left and found herself following the hedge uphill, when her memory insisted that the farm was downhill from the stable. Turning again, she followed the hedge back round the field until she came to the gate. It was a relief to get back to the pub.

'If we're going to get many more fogs like this, I'm going to need a compass,' she said to Alan. He laughed. 'No. I'm serious,' she said. 'There's something very unnerving about getting lost in a place you know perfectly well.'

'You do seem to have a lot of adventures, down here,' he said.

She smiled. You don't know the half of it, she thought.

'Oh, by the way, I met Mandy at the farm. She's still with him, in spite of the rumours.'

'Oh, good...well, not good, really, that she's still with Luke...but, well, it was worrying wasn't it?'

'Mmm,' said Heather. ' I reckon we're going to be very quiet this evening, with all this fog.'

219

CHAPTER THIRTY

'I'm on the scrounge for jumble again,' said Anne as she came through the back door. 'It's for the Methodist Chapel roof repair fund this time - sale's on Saturday. We've had so many in the village, lately, we're running out of stock. I'll take anything; books, whatever you can find.'

'I'll have a look,' said Heather. 'I think there's a box of books we haven't even unpacked yet. How did your Sunday lunch with Dave go?'

'Oh, it was enjoyable. He can be quite amusing. And he brought me some stuff for the jumble sale.' She looked thoughtful. 'But I'm beginning to wonder if asking him was such a good idea. Mercy cut me dead in the shop, this morning, and I think he's under the impression that I may be thinking in terms of making this a regular Sunday occurrence.'

'Oh dear!' Something yellow caught the corner of Heather's vision and she turned to see the mobile library van parking in the square. 'Talking of books, I need to take my library book back. Jim's just arrived.'

'Has he? So do I. I'll call back on Wednesday morning to collect anything you can find for the jumble,' said Anne.

Heather climbed the steps into the van and smiled at Jim, the driver cum librarian.

'I'm looking for something about keeping horses, or riding,' she said.

They both scoured the shelves, but the best Jim could come up with was a small book from the children's section called 'Care of your Pony'.

'I'll take it,' she said. That would have to do until she could get into Exeter and find something to unravel the more technical aspects of which kind of bit to put into the mouth of an ex-racehorse.

'Makes a change from the usual borrowed books,' Jim said. 'Murder mysteries are usually big in North Tegridge.'

'Now why doesn't that surprise me?' Heather said. Jim looked questioningly at her. 'Doesn't matter,' she said, shaking her head.

Mercy came up the steps.

'Hello, Jim...Oh hello, Heather.'

Heather tried to turn the title of 'Care of your Pony' away from Mercy's sharp eyes, but she wasn't quite quick enough.

'You thinking of getting a pony, then? What's that for? Keep the old horse company?'

'No, it's just that I'm not very knowledgeable about horses. I need all the help I can get.'

'Why don't you ask Dave? His father used to work the farm with cart horses.'

Mercy moved down the van and reached a copy of 'Lives of the Great Poisoners' off the shelf. Heather's blood ran cold. Was she thinking of inviting Dave back for a meal? Mercy turned back to her. 'You want to ask Dave if you can go mushrooming in his field down by the river; it's coming up that time of year.' She looked past Heather. 'Jim, have you got any books on mushrooms and toadstools? You need to be so careful with them.'

Jim handed her a small book with a magnificent Fly Agaric depicted on the cover.

'Now I do know that one's not very good for you,' she said. 'Look nice with a gnome sitting on it though, wouldn't it? Them red ones with white spots always look exciting, don't they?'

'I've got a feeling they are,' said Heather, dredging her memory. 'I think those are the ones that people in Lapland eat when they want to go on hallucinogenic trips - and their reindeer eat them too, and get intoxicated.'

221

'Really? I never knew that,' said Mercy.

And I wish I hadn't told you, thought Heather. Who was Mercy planning to 'do away with' next. Marion Ede? Or Anne? Or Dave?…or all three…while Peggy got rid of Mandy and Luke. Pull yourself together, woman, she told herself severely.

'Who are you planning to 'do away with', then, Mrs Ashley?' asked Jim.

Heather had a moment of panic that people really could read her thoughts.

'I haven't quite decided yet,' Mercy laughed.

Anne arrived with the books she wanted to exchange. Mercy glared at her, and Anne's eyes dropped to the titles of the books she was holding, then she looked up at Mercy's face.

'For heavens sake, Mercy! I only invited him for lunch. I have no designs on Dave, and I'm too young to die.'

Heather began to giggle, and Mercy lost her angry glare, and laughed.

'Sorry, Anne. It's just that…well I expect you've heard about that 'blubber mountain' from East Tegridge. I'm a bit upset with Dave, at the moment.'

'You're not planning to poison Marion Ede, I hope?' said Anne.

'No, of course not.' She returned 'Lives of the Great Poisoners' to the shelf. 'Just don't want to make any mistakes with mushrooms, and such. I used to ask Rose what you could eat, she knew all about things like that. She had that 'second sight', you know. She used to say she thought it was the gypsies had left her.'

'Left her?' Heather asked.

'Oh, no, I suppose you wouldn't know, would you? She was a foundling. Somebody dumped her in a flower bed at a hospital in Plymouth. That's why the nurses called her

Rose. I don't think she had much of a life, really. She was in a children's home until she was ten, then she was fostered by a couple in the village; but they'd both died by the time she was eighteen. Then she married Luke, and found she couldn't have children, which was what she really wanted. It's no wonder she got depressed... but none of us realised she was suicidal. Shame.' She looked at her watch. 'I've got to go. See you at the jumble sale, Anne.'

'I'm glad we're back on speaking terms again,' Anne said, as Mercy walked away across the square.

'Yes...I'd better get back. See you later,' said Heather.

....

Saturday lunch time was quite busy. A jumble sale at the village hall always seemed to push up the trade. Luke and Mandy called in. If Heather hadn't already seen the bruises, she wouldn't have known about them. Mandy had done a good job with the make-up. But she and Luke didn't seem comfortable as a couple any more, and Heather got the impression that Luke had persuaded her to come out just to put paid to the rumours, which had been rife in the village, that she may have left him; people had gradually realised that no-one had seen Mandy for days. She left after one drink, saying she was just going to pop over to the jumble sale.

'I'll wait here, then. Jumble sales aren't my scene,' said Luke.

She hadn't been gone long, when Jenny and Josie burst into the bar, both talking at once to the assembled company in general.

'It's chaos! They're fighting,' said Jenny.

'Stuff going everywhere,' said Josie.

Luke leapt off his stool.

'That bloody Peggy!' he said, and stormed out of the pub.

'Has Peggy attacked Mandy?' Alan asked the sisters, whilst trying not to look directly at them.

'Peggy?' they chorused, as Luke returned to the bar with Mandy.

'World War three has broken out over there,' Mandy was grinning. 'I got out. You can never tell how these things may spread.'

'We'll have another drink, Heather,' said Luke.

The rest of the customers were either surrounding Jenny and Josie, clamouring to know what had happened, or leaving the pub to find out for themselves. There hadn't been this much excitement in North Tegridge since the bomb.

'Who's fighting, then?' Heather asked Mandy, as she placed a drink in front of her.

'I'm not sure, there was such a scrum and several tables had gone over. The vicar seemed to be involved, though I think he was trying to sort it out. Nobody seemed to be listening to him.'

'What's new?' said Luke.

Jenny and Josie, having now virtually cleared the pub of customers, left in order to join this new spectator sport.

'I think we should find out what's going on. Go and have a look, darling,' said Alan.

'That's just typical of you. Anything remotely dangerous and you send me. If you're not careful I'll tell Mandy how you hid under the bedclothes when that bat came into the bedroom. Yelling at me to get rid of it, he was - in a muffled sort of way.' She grinned at Mandy.

'Well, they carry rabies, don't they?' Alan said. 'I knew you'd be all right because you're mad, already,' he ducked as she flung a tea-towel at him.

Actually her curiosity *was* getting the better of her. She pushed up the bar flap and walked across to the pub door. From there she could see across the square to the village hall. Anne was heading in that direction, so she joined her. Shouting and screaming, accompanied by bangs and thumps, was issuing from the open windows of the hall. A sudden unmusical crash silenced the crowd standing round the door.

'The piano!' somebody said.

'It's just been tuned,' said someone else. 'That's expensive, you know - having pianos tuned.'

'I bet it's not half as expensive as having them put back together again,' said Anne.

'Who's fighting who?' Heather asked Anne, and the lady standing next to her answered.

'It's Mercy Ashley and Marion Ede. You know, that big woman from over East Tegridge. They got in an argument over something on the men's stall. Next thing, all hell broke out. I thought I'd better get the children out. Here Freddie, if I lift you up you can see through the window and tell us what's going on.' She hoisted a child up onto her shoulders, and he peered through the high windows.

'Can't see nothing. It's dark in there,' said Freddie, trying to shade his eyes. 'I think it's stopped. The piano's fallen off the stage.'

'That's where the men's stall was,' said his mother.

'Can you see Mrs. Ashley? Is she all right?' asked Heather. She had a picture of Marion Ede in her mind which didn't allow Mercy much chance of surviving a hostile close encounter.

'She's talking to the vicar.'

'What about the other woman; the big one?' asked his mother.

'She's sitting on the stage steps.'

'You'll have to get down, now. You're too heavy,' his mother bent forward, and Heather helped Freddie down.

People began to trickle back into the hall, and Anne went with them to start clearing up the mess and get the sale back on track. Heather turned away to go back to the pub, just as Peggy turned up.

'What's goin' on? The vicar's just rung me to come and fetch Mum. He says she's hurt her arm.'

'I think she and Marion Ede have had a bit of an argument,' said Heather. 'I've got to get back to the pub.'

'That Dave's got a lot to answer for. Men!' Peggy raised her eyes skyward and followed the crowd into the hall.

Luke and Mandy had gone by the time Heather got back, and the pub was empty. Alan was just collecting glasses and wiping tables. She gave him a report on the unseemly events at the jumble sale - as far as she knew them.

'What were they fighting about?' asked Alan.

'Something to do with Dave, I expect.'

'They're a very physical lot, down here, aren't they? Has the vicar remained unscathed?'

'I think so. But the piano doesn't look very well.'

That evening Peggy and Mercy came into the bar early.

'Mum says she needs a brandy to settle 'er nerves; we 'aven't got any at 'ome. I'll 'ave a pint,' said Peggy.

Mercy adjusted the sling on her left arm.

'Good job I'm right-handed,' she said, reaching for the brandy glass which Alan had placed in front of her.

'Dare I ask what happened?' he said.

'Well,' Mercy settled herself on the stool. 'You know I had a bit of trouble with that woman…with Dave and that?' Alan nodded. 'Well, it were just that I suddenly saw it… on the men's stall. Didn't see her. Mind you, how I could miss her I don't know?' she paused.

'Saw what?' said Heather and Alan together.

'The pullover - the one I give Dave, two Christmases ago. I thought, what's that doing here? Then I thought that I'd get it as a memento of Dave.'

She's going to hang it over the fireplace with Josiah's stick, thought Heather. She giggled, and hurriedly turned it into a cough. Alan frowned at her.

'So did you?' Alan asked Mercy.

'Did I hell as like! I'd just got my hand on it, when 'blubber mountain' grabbed hold of it. 'I give him that - let go of it,' I said to her. 'No you didn't,' she said. She said she give it to him. Lying bitch. Anyway, she pulled and I pulled, and the table went over when she pulled me into it.'

'Gives a whole new meaning to the word pullover,' said Heather, beginning to giggle again. Mercy ignored her, and carried on with her story.

'Let it go,' I says. 'Tes mine.' 'Never,' she says, and the vicar's dancing about saying, 'Ladies, Ladies.' Blubber mountain stood on his foot and he fell against the piano, and it went off the stage. Only just been tuned, you know; it's very expensive having a piano tuned.'

'So who got the pullover?' Alan asked, struggling to keep up.

'I let her have it. Wasn't much good with only one sleeve, and she's a bloody sight stronger than me. Can I have another one of these?' she held out her glass to Alan.

A movement caught Heather's eye and she looked up to see Dave peering through the bar window. When he saw Mercy, he shook his head at Heather, and waved goodbye.

Heather had thought this was the end of the drama that came to be known as the 'Rumble' sale, until the full story came out, the following day.

CHAPTER THIRTY-ONE

Dave's tractor and trailer clattered across the square. Heather, standing by the landing window, watched him go and counted only seven children bouncing about on the piles of empty sacks in the trailer. Was the missing child 'Sharon the Sneak'?

'We must take Dave up on his offer to go and see how the cider's made,' she said to Alan later.

'Yes, but don't forget how strong it is. Very deceptive, Dave's cider.'

'I don't want to drink it - well, I do - but I'd like to see it made,' she said. 'Are we going to buy some for the pub?'

'Yes, definitely. We should support local enterprise, where we can.'

'Especially when it's Dave's cider,' she smiled.

'Presactly!'

Anne came in at lunch-time.

'Gin and tonic please, Heather.' She hitched herself up onto a bar stool, and sighed. 'I've just been assessing the damage at the hall, and I'm afraid the piano is beyond repair. Such a shame. It had only just been tuned and …'

'… it's very expensive having a piano tuned!' chorused Heather and Alan.

Anne looked momentarily startled, then she laughed.

'Yes. Everyone seems to be quoting the vicar. He's very upset - seems to think it was his fault, and he wants to buy a new one, but I don't think he realises how much a decent piano would cost.'

'That's a shame. He was only trying to help, wasn't he?' said Heather.

'Yes. I think we are going to have to have another sale to raise money for a new piano,' said Anne.

'Better make sure you bar Mercy and the Big Woman

from East Tegridge,' said Alan.

'Marion Ede,' said Anne.

'There's no romance in 'Marion Ede',' said Alan.

'Pardon?' said Anne.

'Never mind him. D'you want ice in this,' said Heather, indicating the glass in her hand.

'No, it's a bit chilly, today - just lemon. I'm still not sure what started that row, yesterday; but it ended up with one of Dave's old pullovers in two pieces.'

'Lucky he wasn't wearing it,' said Alan. 'Do you think it will go down in history as The Battle of Dave's Pullover?'

'You are getting sillier. Ignore him, Anne,' said Heather.

The pub began to fill up as the church services ended. Most of the parishioners who attended the morning service were traditionally Methodists, who went to the small chapel on the edge of the village; whilst newcomers, and those from the holiday homes, attended the square towered flight navigation point in the centre of the village, otherwise known as the church of Saint Lawrence. Some of the Saint Lawrence's congregation hadn't been to church for years, but the relaxed pace of village life rekindled old values. They tended to arrive in the pub after church, eulogising about life in a village where everyone knew their neighbours and were mutually kind, tolerant and helpful.

For the sake of good business, Heather agreed with them over the bar, while at least two of the horsemen of the apocalypse cantered about in the back of her mind. She was ever conscious of the fact that the police were continuing their search for the boar mutilator, but they still seemed to be looking for a man, somehow unable to conceive that a woman could do such a dastardly deed. She supposed that the crime didn't warrant bringing in a criminal psychologist, who would - almost instantly in her mind - point the finger at Peggy's metaphorical attempt to castrate Luke. Dave had been the only one clear-thinking enough to glimpse the possibility, but he hadn't pursued it.

Dave himself came in that evening, having peered through the bar window first. He had the crisp, sharp smell of crushed apples about him. Heather inhaled, unobtrusively, every time she passed him. That is, she thought she'd been unobtrusive until Alan followed her out into the kitchen.

'Why do you keep sniffing at Dave? He's going to notice in a minute.'

'Sorry. He smells gorgeous. I think he's been crushing cider apples.'

'Well stop it. You're beginning to look like a pet dog.'

'How are you getting on with the cider-making, Dave?' Heather asked, as she placed the sandwich he had ordered, on the bar in front of him.

'Not bad. I've only just started, really. We'll get on better when Colin comes to help me. It's hard work winding down the press single-handed. He's had a bit of a cold.'

'Could Alan and I come down and see how it's done, some time?'

'Of course. You could lend a hand, if you like.'

'What are you letting me in for?' Alan asked.

'Just a bit of press-winding,' said Heather.

Anne came in and said hello to Dave; then did a double-take.

'How did you do that?' she asked, staring at his chest.

He looked down at himself, then back at Anne, in puzzlement.

'Do what? What's the matter with me?' He brushed a hand down the front of his pullover.

'I threw it away. How did you get it?'

By now everyone in the bar was staring at Dave and his purple pullover, edged at the neck with green.

'And the arm was off,' Anne continued.

Dave was now looking at Anne as if she had become completely unhinged. One questioning eyebrow raised, he turned to Heather for enlightenment. She shook her head and shrugged, although a dim light was beginning to dawn. Was Anne implying that Dave had managed to retrieve, and mend, the pullover which had precipitated the jumble sale battle. If so, he had done a remarkably good job.

'You *have* heard about the fight at the village hall, yesterday?' Anne asked him.

'Yes, of course - daft mares!'

'You do know what they were fighting over?' said Anne.

'Well, me I suppose - since that damn child dumped me in it,' Dave looked a bit sheepish as he said this.

'No. It was that pullover,' said Anne, pointing at his chest. 'Well I suppose it *was* you, in a way; but that pullover got torn apart and I threw it out. How did you get it?'

'Oh! That's what it was, was it?' Dave said.

'Yes, they both said they'd given it to you, and both wanted it back.'

'Two years ago,' Dave laughed, and shook his head. 'Two years ago, they both gave me the same present for Christmas. I didn't want to hurt anyone's feelings. Made it easy really, could keep both of them happy, even when one pullover was in the wash. Well, I don't need two the same any more, now, do I? So I gave you one for the jumble.'

'So they both thought the other was lying. No wonder they got so mad. Each one was adamant that they had given it to you,' said Anne.

Dave turned back to Heather.

'I'll be glad when all this simmers down and people stop

staring at me,' he said. 'Had Mercy on the phone, today. She says I've got to choose between them. And Marion's not speaking to me.'

'Oh dear.' Heather's reply was as non-commital as she could make it. She was not getting involved. She found violent women almost more frightening than violent men.

A few days later Dave was back in the pub with a smiling Mercy. She went and sat at a table in the corner and Dave came up to the bar for their drinks.

'This looks good, Dave. Have you two patched things up?' asked Alan.

'Yes. I've had to agree to go up to Mercy's Tuesday's *and* Thursday's and give up seeing Marion. I had to get it sorted out. I'm just too busy with the farm and the cider at the moment to be concentrating on all this nonsense.'

'How's Marion taking it?' asked Heather.

'Well, not too bad, as it happens. She's taken up with the postman. Apparently he's been stopping off there for breakfast for the last six months - the bastard!'

Heather and Alan both began to laugh at the outraged expression on Dave's face.

'Well...I know...still, it's all sorted out now. I can get back to normal. Give us two packets of crisps.'

'Your usual cheese and onion?' said Alan bending down to the box under the bar.

'No, better make it plain...I could get lucky, tonight.'

CHAPTER THIRTY-TWO

It was one of those quiet golden autumn afternoons, with a hint of bonfire smoke in the air, when Heather decided to lead Jimmy out again. As she walked him to the end of the Hawkridge track and onto the road, she decided to turn away from the village. A trip through the square would involve too many stops, as people would want to talk to her about the horse, and she knew he would get fidgety and impatient.

She set off along the road towards East Tegridge with Jimmy striding out beside her, ears pricked at the novelty of being out of his field. He was no longer limping and she knew, with a mixture of fear and excitement, that she would soon be able to ride him out, quietly.

After about half a mile his head went up even higher, and he seemed to be listening to something. Then he neighed, and in the distance Heather could hear the sound of another horses hooves on the tarmac. Jimmy quickened his pace and began to jog sideways on the end of his lead rope, putting in a little half-rear as a horse and rider came into view round the bend ahead of them. She shortened the rope, pulling him into the side of the road, and tried to hold him back.

As the bay horse drew closer she could see that it looked tired, and both it, and the rider, were spattered with mud. The man pulled up beside her and touched the peak of his cap with his whip.

'Hello,' he said. 'Haven't seen you two around, before. Are you new here?'

'Fairly,' Heather smiled up into a lean, slightly weather-beaten face with a streak of mud down one cheek. 'We've got the Shepherd and Dog pub in North Tegridge.'

'Really! I heard there was a new landlord. I must come

in, sometime,' he pulled off his glove and reached down a hand to her. 'Keith Field. I live in Pillerton Tracey.'

'Heather Pearce. You're a long way from home.'

'Not too far, really. The Meet was at East Tegridge, today, and we ran east, away from the village - west would have been better for us, wouldn't it, boy?' He leaned forward and patted the muddy bay neck. His horse seemed content to stand, resting a hind foot. 'Do you ride him?' he asked, nodding towards Jimmy who was fidgeting and trying to touch noses with the bay.

'I'm thinking about it. He's recovering from a tendon injury,' she said.

'Do you hunt?'

'No. I'm not even sure I can remember how to ride. It's been a long time since I was on a horse…the last one was a Shetland pony.'

He laughed, and nodded at Jimmy. 'Well, that's quite a step up. May see you around when you get going. If you need any help, I'm in the book. Give me a ring.'

'Thanks. Whoa! Jimmy,' she dragged him back as he lunged towards the other horse.

'You've got quite a handful there,' said Keith, as he shortened the reins and nudged his weary horse with his heels. He waved as they walked away up the road.

Jimmy seemed determined to live up to his newly bestowed reputation of 'a handful' by trying to go with them. Not wanting to appear totally incompetent, Heather forced him to walk towards East Tegridge until the bay and his rider had clopped out of sight, then she allowed him to drag her round and head back for home.

Arriving back at the farm, she found Luke leaning on the field gate.

'Oh, I was wondering where he was. I didn't see you go out,' he said.

'He seems all right with traffic,' Heather said, wondering if Luke was going to stop leaning on the gate and let them through. She stroked Jimmy's neck, he still had one ear back listening for sounds of the other horse.

'Haven't seen Peggy, lately,' Luke said. You should be thankful for that, Heather thought. 'Is she still going out with Barry Martin?' he continued.

'I think so. She's getting to be quite a 'gad-about' is Peggy.' She pulled Jimmy closer to the gate.

'She never used to be like that,' Luke said gloomily.

'Um. Luke, do you mind? Only I've got to get Jimmy's feed and get back to the pub.'

'Oh, sorry,' he stepped back and opened the gate for them.

Mandy came out of the back door and put something in the dustbin. She raised a hand to Heather and went back indoors. Luke watched the house for a moment, then went off towards the pig sties. When Heather went across to fill the feed bucket, he was leaning over the wall of the boars pen, scratching the beast's back and gazing into the middle distance.

She drove back into the village, exploring her feelings about the afternoon encounters with Keith and Luke. The former had given her a glimpse of life outside the village; whilst dealing with Luke, and his growing depression, had made her feel claustrophobic. She decided she needed to get right out of North Tegridge for a few hours, to restore her equilibrium.

When she got back she checked the diary and found that they had no bookings for meals on Wednesday night. She made a phone call to Mercy. Alan came in from the yard, where he had been stacking the empty beer kegs ready for the brewery to collect.

'Hello, darling,' Heather said. 'Is it all right with you if I go up to Ormskirk and see Mum and Dad on Wednesday? I'd come back on Thursday. There's nobody booked.'

'Yes, okay. I'd rather not have Peggy to help in the bar, though.'

'I took a chance on you saying yes, and I've already asked Mercy. Peggy's going out with Barry on Wednesday.'

'That sounds all right, then,' he said.

…………

Heather fed Jimmy on her way to Ormskirk on the Wednesday morning, but didn't see anyone at Hawkridge. Mandy's car wasn't there.

She called in again on her way home on Thursday evening, to do his feed. It was a relief to be out in the open air after the long drive. She stretched her arms and back and leaned on the stable door, as she waited for Jimmy to finish crunching his supper in the gloom behind her.

It was dusk, almost dark, and tawny owls were calling to each other. One from the wood behind her was being answered from across the river, on the other side of the valley.

She breathed deeply, freeing her brain from visions of motor-ways, fumes, rushing traffic and oncoming headlights. Jimmy finished his feed and tipped over his bucket, and she let him out.

As she walked back into the farmyard, Luke was standing beside her car.

'You're late, this evening,' he said.

'Yes. I'm just on my way back from Lancashire. I've been to see my parents.'

'When did you leave, then?'

'What, here, or my parents?' Heather frowned at the odd question.

'Here.'

'Yesterday morning… why?' she asked.

'Right!' he said abruptly, and turned and strode off towards the house.

Now what? Heather thought, getting into the car: the mild euphoria of the quiet evening, shattered by the aggression emanating from Luke.

'I don't want to know. I really *don't* want to know,' she muttered as she started the engine.

She opened the back door into the kitchen to the appetising smell of cooking, and realised she was hungry.

'Hello, darling,' said Alan, giving her a hug.

'Careful,' said Heather, as he got tangled up with her overnight case and handbag which she hadn't had time to put down. 'You've obviously missed me. Have you been busy?'

'So much for romance,' said Alan. 'I've made you some supper.'

'*You* have?'

'Well, Mercy made it actually - yesterday. But I've heated it up. How were your parents?'

'Fine. They seem quite happy. They were fascinated by the photo's I had taken of the pub and Jimmy. Dad's a bit worried about me riding him. Oh, that looks good!' Alan was taking a steak and kidney pie out of the oven.

'Yes. Doesn't it? I'll have some later. I can see why Dave was so upset at the thought that he may have lost out on his Tuesday suppers.' Alan glanced at the clock. 'Can you dish up your own vegetables? I should open up.'

'Yes. I'll join you in a while. Any bookings?'

'No, not yet, but Mercy's prepared chips and some vegetables in case.' He gave her another hug and kiss. 'It's nice to have you back,' he said.

'It's nice to be back…I think. I've just fed Jimmy, and

met Luke. He turned very peculiar when I said I'd been away. I don't understand it,' she said.

'Really? If you ask me Luke's always peculiar. Okay. Enjoy your supper. I'll see you in a minute.'

As she was eating, she pondered over the sudden change in Luke's behaviour as she was leaving the farm, and found she was beginning to worry about Mandy. He had obviously stormed off to have something out with her - but how could it possibly be connected with her trip to Ormskirk? She reminded herself that she didn't want to get any more involved with that dysfunctional relationship. She leaned back in her chair, stretching and massaging her stiff shoulders, and reflected that the folk in Ormskirk seemed relatively straightforward compared with those in North Tegridge.

Alan came in from the bar with a glass of red wine. The rich ruby glow of the liquid in the glass struck up an immediate rapport with her taste buds.

'How did you know that was just what I needed. A little something to help me unwind.'

Two glasses later, she was feeling pleasantly mellow, and had just decided to put in an appearance in the bar when she heard raised voices coming from that direction. One of them sounded like Luke. She got up, crossed the kitchen quietly and peered round the door into the bar. It *was* Luke. And he appeared to be having some kind of argument with Alan.

'So what were you two talking about?' Luke's voice was raised, and people were staring at him.

'I don't know what *you're* talking about,' said Alan. 'Keep it down, Luke, you're upsetting the customers.'

'Frightened your missus might hear, more like.'

Hear what? thought Heather.

'I saw her through the kitchen window,' said Luke. 'She

was on that phone for twenty minutes. I pressed re-dial and got the pub answer-phone and naturally thought she'd been talking to Heather. Then I find out Heather wasn't here. So what were you and Mandy getting so cosy about?'

Yes, what? thought Heather.

'Luke, you're being ridiculous. We were just chatting - nothing in particular,' said Alan.

'Ridiculous am I? D'you want to come round this side of the bar and say that?'

'Not a lot,' said Alan. 'And if you don't calm down, I may have to ring the police.'

Luke began to laugh, a bitter, uncomfortable sound.

'The police! What bloody good do you think they'd be? They wouldn't get here till next Wednesday, by which time you'd have been in hospital a week.'

Heather thought it was about time she tried to calm the situation. She pushed the door open and walked through.

'Bit noisy in here, this evening. What's the problem?' she asked.

'You ask him,' said Luke, pointing at Alan. 'Ask him what he was doing last night while you were away.'

'I can't imagine, apart from running the bar. Oh, and taking a call from Mandy. I must ring her back,' said Heather.

'You can't ring her tonight; she doesn't feel very well. She's gone to bed,' said Luke quickly. 'They were talking for twenty minutes, last night,' he glared at Alan.

'So what? What's the problem?' said Heather calmly. Why doesn't she feel very well? she was thinking. What have you done to her, you bastard? She stared at Luke.

'Well...well, if you're not worried...Oh bugger it!' Luke turned and stormed out of the pub, banging the door.

'Whew!' said Alan, looking a bit pale, and topping up his glass of red wine. 'Thank you, darling. I thought he was going to hit me. Is that man jealous, or is that man jealous?'

'He is, and you already knew that. You shouldn't push your luck. And you never know, I might be jealous as well. Just what *were* you two talking about for twenty minutes?' Heather asked quietly. The other customers in the bar had stopped enjoying the show and gone back to their own conversations.

'Nothing, really. Just life, and relationships in general, you, and the horse. I think she's really lonely stuck out there with Luke spying on her every move.'

'I'll give her a ring in the morning,' Heather said. 'I think I'll go into the sitting room for a while. I feel exhausted, all of a sudden. Shouldn't have had that second glass of wine.'

CHAPTER THIRTY-THREE

When Heather rang Mandy, there was no reply. She dialled her mobile number and Luke answered.

'She can't come to the phone at the moment,' he said. A cow moo-ed next to the phone and it was switched off. What was Luke doing with Mandy's mobile out on the farm? Or had he just snatched the instrument from her and answered it?

'Damn!' said Heather quietly. Now she was going to have to worry about Mandy until she could get down to Hawkridge in the afternoon. She called out: 'Coffee!' to Peggy and Alan, who were working in the bar.

Peggy put two spoons of sugar into her mug and stirred it noisily. Alan winced, and to stop the clatter he pushed the plate of chocolate biscuits towards her. She took three and balanced them on her saucer, where the chocolate began to melt in the heat from the mug.

'Mum said she enjoyed working 'ere on Wednesday night,' she said.

'I certainly enjoyed the steak and kidney pie she made,' said Heather. 'It was just what I needed after that long journey. I'll give her a ring and thank her, later. How was your evening? You and Barry were going out, weren't you?'

'It was all right. We went to Pillerton Tracey...'ad a meal in the pub there. Barry annoyed me a bit, though. 'E spent most of the evenin' talkin' to one of his customers about 'orses and 'untin'.'

'Oh, who was that, then?' Heather tried to ask this question in an off-hand way.

'Oh, I don't know...Mr. Field I think Barry called 'im...tall, thin bloke, solicitor or somethin'. Anyway it was a bit borin'. I'm not really interested in 'orses. I'd rather talk about cows.'

Heather was quiet for a minute or two as she tried to analyse why she wasn't owning to having already met Keith Field, and why she hadn't mentioned meeting him to Alan. It wasn't really that important, she decided... except that he may come into the pub one day and it would look very odd if he knew her and she hadn't said anything, now.

'I think that must have been the man I met riding home from hunting, the other day - his name was Field. He stopped to admire Jimmy when I was leading him out for a walk,' she said.

'You didn't tell me,' Alan said.

'I didn't think about it. I was trying to organise my trip to Ormskirk.'

'You go down to the farm every afternoon, now, 'Eather. Do the cows look all right?' Peggy asked.

'How would I know? Cows always seem to look the same. They're either facing the milking parlour, ready to come in, or facing the other way because they've just been turned out. Yes, I suppose they look all right...and the pigs seem okay as well,' she said, in an attempt to stop Peggy from launching into a tirade about Mandy and Luke.

Peggy gave her a mild version of one of her black-eyed 'looks', from under the yellow fringe, and picked up a biscuit, 'tutting' at the sticky mess of melted chocolate which transferred itself onto her fingers. She got up and went over to the sink where she rinsed her fingers under the tap, unable to resist giving a sidelong glance at the wooden knife block with its array of sharp steel.

Alan stood up, rinsed his mug, and went back into the bar to finish bottling-up. Heather picked up the phone and made an appointment with the saddler to come out and fit Jimmy for a saddle. She was going to stop dithering, and start riding.

That afternoon, she braced herself for a confrontation with Luke, but the Land-Rover wasn't there. Mandy's car was, though. Heather parked beside it and, after a few seconds thought, decided to knock on the door. She could always say she just wondered why Mandy had called her while she was away. She turned off the engine, and flinched as a colourful bundle of feathers shot past her window.

The pheasant had watched her come into the yard, and was now attacking her car with vigor - making up for the lost time when, due to boot induced bruises, he had gone through a lack-lustre phase of indifference to yard trespassers. The cows were massing by their field gate. It occurred to Heather that they were facing the wrong way. Milking had usually finished by this time of day.

She climbed out of the car, swinging her jacket at the pheasant, which confused him sufficiently for her to get across the yard to the kitchen door. She knocked and waited a moment, then knocked again. When there was still no sound from inside, she moved along and, shading her eyes, peered through the kitchen window. The kitchen was silent and neat. Maybe they had both gone out in the Land-Rover, but it wasn't like Luke to neglect his animals. She studied the cows more closely as she filled Jimmy's feed bucket and, judging by their swollen udders, it was quite obvious that they hadn't been milked.

As she stood in the stable waiting for Jimmy to finish his meal, she was relieved to see the Land-Rover coming down the track, and then to see Luke open the gate to allow the uncomfortable cows to stream into the milking parlour.

Jimmy nudged her in the back, asking to be let out, just as she realised that when Luke parked the Land-Rover, next to the cows field, he had been the only person to get out of it. So where *was* Mandy? Heather certainly wasn't going to ask Luke this; not after the previous night's display of temper. Oh, the hell with it. It's not my problem, she thought, turning Jimmy loose with a pat, and walking back to the car. She didn't try to avoid Luke, but he didn't appear.

Anne came in just after they opened, that evening, and gave a tired sigh as she eased herself onto a stool at the bar.

'Just thought I'd unwind with a quick one before I go home,' she said.

'You look as if you've had an exhausting day,' said Heather, wondering how old Anne was. She gave such an impression of health and competence one tended to overlook the fact that she'd probably been drawing her pension for at least ten years.

'I've just been into Exeter. You know Margery Townsend?'

'No, I don't think so,' said Heather.

'Well she's in hospital there - thought I'd better visit the poor old thing. Her family live up country,' she took a sip of her gin and tonic. 'Hey, you'll never guess who I saw as I went into the ward.'

'Tell me,' said Heather.

'That Mandy, with Luke sitting beside her bed. She didn't look too good, very pale, and her head was bandaged.'

Heather felt her stomach muscles shrink. 'Do you know what happened to her?'

'No,' said Anne, shaking her head.

'What happened to who?' said Alan, coming into the bar with a tray of clean glasses from the dishwasher.

'Mandy, Luke's partner - she's in hospital,' said Anne.

Alan set the tray down carefully on the bar.

'That bastard! What's he done to her?'

'Alan,' Heather put a restraining hand on his arm. 'We don't know why she's in there. Don't jump to conclusions.'

'What's wrong with her?' he asked.

'We don't know yet, but you can bet it won't be long before somebody tells us,' said Heather. Nothing much in the way of village gossip escaped an airing in the pub.

As it happened, none of the customers that evening did seem to know of this latest twist in the Hawkridge saga, and Heather and Alan had agreed that they shouldn't be the first to bring it up.

After breakfast, the next morning, Alan seemed to come to a decision. He glanced at the kitchen clock.

'Heather, just a minute, before Peggy gets here. Do you think you ought to pop into Exeter and visit Mandy?'

'Me?'

'Well, you two get on all right, and she did try to ring you. And I feel a bit guilty about the fact that I seem to have caused trouble by speaking to her the other night.'

'I don't really know her that well, Alan; only in a chatting over the fence sort of way at the farm, and I've already been warned off by Luke after the milking episode. If he did put her in there - and we don't know that he did - it's going to put me in a very difficult position if I poke my nose in. I still have to go to the farm every day.'

Alan thought for a minute, still with one eye on the clock.

'Well, you could ring her, then. Say Anne saw her there and you were worried.'

'*I'm* worried, am I?' There was an edge in her voice which Alan picked up from the window, where he was watching for Peggy.

He crossed the kitchen to where Heather was unloading the dishwasher and put his arms round her.

'I'm sorry…it's just that there's something very vulnerable about her.'

'She was a stripper, for God's sake, Alan!'

'Yes, but why was she? She always seems to have been exploited by men. Now that bastard is knocking her about, and don't say he isn't. I know he is.' He let her go as Peggy's bike banged against the stone wall outside the back door.

'All right. I'll ring Mandy, okay?' Heather said. 'Just because that would be a natural thing to do, as Anne saw her there.'

The back door opened and Peggy came in.

'Blimmin 'orrible out there,' she said, hanging her anorak on the back door, where it dripped steadily onto the floor.

'I know, and I've got the saddler coming to fit Jimmy this afternoon. I think I'll ring him and ask if he could bring out a waterproof rug for him, as well,' said Heather.

'I'll pay for it,' said Alan.

Heather's lip twitched, as she realised she had got through to him.

'Huh! It's all right for some,' said Peggy, dragging the vacuum cleaner out of the cupboard.

'Thank you, darling,' said Heather, trying to keep any hint of sarcasm out of her voice.

She waited until Peggy was well into her morning cleaning routine, then went upstairs to use the telephone in the bedroom. Getting through to Mandy in the hospital was remarkably easy.

'Mandy? It's Heather. Anne told me you were in there. Whatever's happened to you?'

'Hello, Heather,' Mandy's voice was rather feeble, followed by a quick in-drawing of breath and a rustle of bedclothes against the receiver as she pulled herself upright in bed. 'Ouch! I… was attacked by a cow.'

Heather knew she was lying.

'What's the damage? Anne said your head was bandaged.'

'Yes, I cut it as I fell, and I have a broken rib. That's the worst bit really, trying to breathe carefully round the pain.'

'How did it happen?' Heather had no alternative but to go along with Mandy's story.

'Luke told me not to go near this cow and her calf, he said she was dangerous...' her voice tailed off as if she realised that this story was wasted on Heather. 'I'm okay, Heather, they're just keeping me in for observation because of the bang on my head. Luke's taking me home tomorrow.'

'Is there anywhere else you could go?'

'Why would I want to do that?' asked Mandy defiantly.

Heather backed off, remembering that she had to play along with Mandy's version of events.

'Sorry, I just thought you didn't sound well enough to go home tomorrow.'

'I'm all right. I can rest when I get back. There's plenty of food in the freezer, and Luke's not totally incapable. He's been quite worried about me. Even put visiting me before the milking, yesterday.' She started to laugh and then thought better of it. 'Oof! I must remember not to do that.'

Heather wondered what it was about Luke that inspired such misplaced loyalty. Mandy's story was impossible to believe. What would she have been doing getting into the pen with a dangerous cow and its calf, in the dark. This must have happened after Luke had shouted at Alan and stormed out of the pub.

Alan came up the stairs and into the bedroom. He mouthed a silent 'Mandy'? to her. She nodded.

'Oh, all right, then, Mandy, but you take care of yourself.

And if there's anything you want brought down from the village, just say so.'

'Thanks, Heather.' There was a rattle of a cup on a saucer, and Mandy said: 'Thank you' to somebody. 'But there's nothing I need at the moment. 'Bye now, see you back at the farm.'

''Bye. Take care,' said Heather, replacing the phone thoughtfully.

'Well?' Alan asked.

'She says she was attacked by a cow.'

'D'you believe her?'

'No. But if that's the way she wants to play it, there's nothing we can do - and I mean that Alan. Don't interfere. It's none of our business, and you could only make things worse for her.'

'The bastard!' said Alan quietly. He sighed. 'Oh well, I suppose you're right, you usually are.'

When Heather met the saddler at Hawkridge, that afternoon, she was relieved to see the uncomfortable cows waiting to be milked. That was two days running that Luke had put Mandy before the herd. Maybe he was turning over a new leaf.

CHAPTER THIRTY-FOUR

Heather deliberately left her next visit to Jimmy until late in the afternoon, hoping to avoid Luke and Mandy. Hopefully he would have fetched her from the hospital, finished the milking and be indoors. Both vehicles were in the yard and there was a light on in the kitchen, to combat the approaching dusk, but she didn't see either of them.

She fed the horse and set off back to the village, enjoying the cool silent evening after what had been quite a warm autumn day. The sun had set and a huge white moon was rising above the hill behind Small Profits, stirring the owls into life. Their quavering calls drifted across the light mist which rose from the river and crept up the sides of the valley.

As she drew level with the entrance to Small Profits, Dave drove up the track towards the road. He stopped and wound down the window.

'D'you want a lift, Heather?'

'No thanks, Dave. I'm not in a hurry and I'm enjoying this lovely evening.'

'If you've got time, then, why don't you go down and pick some mushrooms? They're bursting out of the ground as we speak. Go and help yourself. Here...,' he reached behind him in the car and came up with a carrier bag, which he passed to her. 'Use this. It's the field that goes from the house down to the river.'

'That's very kind of you, Dave. Thanks.'

'See you,' he said, and drove out onto the main road.

The sound of his engine faded into the distance as she walked along the track and climbed over the gate into the field Dave had indicated. The mushrooms were not hard to find, in the gathering dusk they glowed with an almost phosphorescent brilliance as the moonlight picked them out against grass, which had faded to grey in the gloaming.

She began to gather them, remembering what Mercy had said about Rose's knowledge of country lore, and about Dave's having once said he was sweet on Rose. The ripple of the water running over rocks in the river impinged onto her consciousness, and she wished her thoughts had not strayed in that direction.

A shadow moving along the river path made her jump and hurriedly refocus her eyes from the mushroom she had stretched out a hand to pick. It was only a fox, grey in the half light, just the tip of its brush glowing white as it saw her and bolted across the corner of the field and into the hedge. A minute later the hoarse squeals of a captured rabbit spoiled, even further, the idyll of her evening. She kept still, willing a quick death for the rabbit. Mercifully the squeals stopped.

She picked two more handfuls of the smooth, perfect mushrooms and made her way down to the river path, where she walked quickly along beside the black swirling water and climbed the stile onto the road. She almost ran up the hill to the square, a sudden primitive fear of the dark dogging her footsteps.

Alan was reading a newspaper in the kitchen, as she walked in.

'It's creepy out there, tonight,' she said, putting the mushrooms down on the table. He stretched out a hand to the bag.

'What's this, then? Oh. Mushrooms, real mushrooms. Who gave you these?'

'I picked them. Down at Small Profits.'

'In the dark?'

'It's not quite dark. Dave says this is the best time. I could have got more but it got a bit spooky down by the river. And when nature started doing its 'red in tooth and claw' bit, I decided to come home.'

'Nature?'

'A fox killed a rabbit in the next field.'

'Oh. See anyone down at Hawkridge?'

'No, but I think they were there. The light was on.'

For the next few days Heather got the impression that Mandy was avoiding her when she went down to the farm. She wasn't really worried, she was far too busy trying to pluck up the courage needed to ride Jimmy. She had been leading him out for a walk, wearing his new saddle and bridle, for a couple of days, but was getting embarrassed by the number of people who seemed to think she had been thrown off and needed assistance to re-mount. By the time the third car had pulled up alongside, its concerned driver asking if she was all right, she had made the decision.

'Will you come down and help me when I get up on Jimmy, tomorrow afternoon?' she asked Alan.

'Yes. As long as Luke doesn't hit me.'

'If we time it right, he'll be busy with the milking.'

'Do you want me to lead Jimmy while you are riding him?' asked Alan.

'That might be wise.'

'Only, I've never led a horse before. Is it difficult?'

Heather looked at him for a moment, thinking he was joking, then realised he wasn't.

'Oh, we'll muddle through,' she said, wondering if she should have asked somebody else - like Keith Field, perhaps? No, she thought, it was only the uniform thing she found attractive, handsome man in full hunting kit, tan topped boots and powerful thoroughbred horse. Stop it! she told herself. Alan would look just as good in the same circumstances ...but that was never likely to happen. She sighed.

'What's the matter?' Alan asked.

'Nothing, why?'

'That was a big sigh.'

The next day they got Jimmy tacked up in the stable, and Heather led him out into the field and tried to put her foot in the stirrup to mount him.

'He's a bit high. Can you give me a leg up?' she asked.

'What? Like they do with the jockeys?'

'Yes.' Heather gathered up the reins and lifted and bent her left leg.

'Okay.' Alan put his cupped hands under her knee.

It would probably have worked quite well if Heather hadn't pushed off with the other foot as he lifted. As it was, she had a fleeting glimpse of the saddle and Jimmy's mane, as she flew over them and landed with a breath-expelling thump on the damp grass. Jimmy turned his head and gazed down at her with a puzzled expression.

Alan rushed round the horse, and pulled her to her feet.

'You prat!' Heather said, rubbing a bruised shoulder.

'I didn't know you were going to jump at the same time. Are you all right. I told you I thought riding was dangerous,' he said.

'I think that to ride, you actually have to be *on* the horse - not vaulting it!' She looked across the field to the farm. 'D'you think anyone saw that?'

'No, there's no-one there. D'you want to go on with this?'

'Yes, of course. Come on. But gently, this time.'

Jimmy was amazingly tolerant, if not slightly bemused by the ineptitude of his new owners. He allowed Alan to lead him round the field as Heather got used to being back in the saddle, after years of not even thinking about horses.

'Right. Let go, Alan. I can manage.'

'Are you sure?'

'Yes.' She was. She felt completely in tune with the little

horse and knew he was with her. She walked a circuit of the field by herself while Alan leaned on the stable door and watched. She even nudged Jimmy into a bumpy little trot for the last few yards.

'Was he limping, at all?' she asked.

'I didn't notice.'

'Well, it didn't feel as if he was. I think that will do for a first time.'

'Shall I help you down?' Alan asked.

'No, thanks. I think I can manage. You've already helped me down once today,' she grinned at him.

'Well, I'm impressed,' said Alan, giving Jimmy a pat. 'I was expecting some kind of fireworks and was braced to phone for an ambulance.'

'The nearest I came to needing one was when you tried to launch me into outer space.' Heather led Jimmy into the stable and removed his saddle and bridle.

'Yess!' she said, doing a milder version of Alan's air punching when runs were scored. 'I've done it!'

'Were *you* worried as well?' asked Alan.

'Terrified. But not any more. I feel great.'

Heather gave Jimmy his feed bucket and they leant on the stable wall, waiting for him to finish.

'It's very quiet down here, isn't it?' said Alan.

'Yes, when they're not having raves.'

'And pig murderings,' said Alan. 'They still haven't got anyone for that yet, have they?'

'No,' she wished he hadn't brought it up. She had begun to think that she was pushing the memory of that afternoon out of her mind.

Jimmy finished his tea and knocked over his bucket, which Alan retrieved.

'Right!' he said. 'I think this calls for champagne. Come on.'

CHAPTER THIRTY-FIVE

After her initial success, Heather was keen to take Jimmy for another trip round the field by herself, the following afternoon, but lost her nerve when she saw how lively he was. The weather was blustery. Rooks and jackdaws were tossing about in the sky, playing with the wind; and Jimmy was doing much the same on the ground. His tail was up and streaming like a banner behind him as he pretended to be scared by a plastic fertiliser bag, which was blowing about in the field.

When it settled he would creep up to it. Then as the wind lifted it again, he would take off at full speed towards the corner of the field, skid to a halt in front of the fence and turn, snorting his excitement through flared nostrils.

She watched him playing for a while, her fingers crossed that all the sliding to a stop wasn't putting too much strain on his tendons.

'Don't go lame again now, boy. Not when I've just started to ride you,' she muttered.

She went to the bin to mix his feed, halving his ration of flaked maize in case this was what was contributing to this sudden explosion of energy. Fun though it looked, she wasn't in a hurry to sit on top of it.

While Jimmy was eating, she went down to the farmhouse to pay for that month's keep. The Land-Rover was out, so she was hoping that Luke wasn't there. He wasn't; and Mandy asked her in for a cup of tea.

'How are you?' Heather asked, noting the fading bruises under Mandy's eyes.

'I'm okay. The rib's still a bit sore. I can't lift anything and I have to be a bit careful how I move. Sit down,' she indicated a chair at the long kitchen table and reached down two mugs from the dresser. The kettle was steaming away on the Aga, and the room felt warm and comfortable without Luke in it.

'Was it really a cow?' Heather asked bluntly, unwilling to go along with the pretence when they both knew it was Luke who had put her in hospital.

Mandy looked up at her, as she poured water into the teapot, then back at the kettle. She replaced it on the hob, and sighed.

'No. Of course not. It was Luke. He'd got it into his head that…and it isn't so, Heather, I promise you…he thought that I fancied your Alan. I think he had had an argument with him about it.'

Heather nodded.

'Well, I'd like to apologise for that. Will you tell Alan?'

'Yes, of course. Don't worry about it.'

'I think Luke feels insecure, though goodness knows why. I feel sorry for him in a way,' said Mandy.

Heather tried to feel sorry for Luke, but didn't manage it.

'Anyway,' Mandy continued. 'He's being very kind and loving now. That hospital business scared him. We were arguing and he pushed me. I fell and caught my head on the corner of the table and was knocked out. He had to get the ambulance. By the time we got to the hospital he was crying.'

Heather tried to imagine Luke crying - but she couldn't manage this either.

'He's asked me to marry him, when he's free,' said Mandy.

'Are you going to?' Heather asked.

'Yes. He's really changed, Heather. There hasn't been one cross word since I came out of hospital.'

He's scared, thought Heather. Men can't get away with knocking their partners about, nowadays. He probably thinks the hospital may have their suspicions. Especially if

255

the ambulance men picked her up in the kitchen, rather than the cow shed. She nearly asked Mandy about this, then decided against it. It didn't really matter, as long as Luke stopped hitting her. None of my business, she thought, and wondered how often she had said this to herself since coming to North Tegridge, whilst finding herself sucked deeper and deeper into the drama surrounding the inhabitants of Hawkridge Farm. She changed the subject.

'Did you see Jimmy playing with that plastic bag, just now?'

'Yes. He's full of beans, isn't he? Yet he was so quiet when you rode him yesterday,' said Mandy.

'You saw?'

'Yes.'

'How much did you see?'

'Everything. How are the bruises?'

They both burst out laughing, and were still laughing as Luke opened the back door, though Mandy had one hand on her sore rib, and was trying to stop.

'Having a party?' Luke asked.

'Hello, Luke. I just came in with your money,' said Heather.

It was difficult to gauge his mood. He looked at Mandy, then pulled his face into a smile.

'It's good to hear you laugh,' he said.

'I'd better get back to Jimmy. He'll have finished his tea, by now.' Heather got up and rinsed out her mug under the tap and placed it upside-down on the draining board, while Luke counted the money she had handed him.

'Thanks,' he said, stuffing it into his wallet.

Alan was out in the yard when she arrived home.

'Did you ride him?' he asked, taking the saddle from her and carrying it into the kitchen.

'No. It was too windy.'

'Windy?'

'You should have seen him, Alan. He was practically turning cartwheels.'

'He was all right yesterday.'

'Different weather. This kind is, apparently, very exciting. Oh, by the way, I saw Mandy. She apologised for Luke's behaviour up here the other evening.'

'She all right?'

'Seems to be. Says they're going to get married, when Luke's free to do so.'

'She's mad,' he said, balancing the saddle on the back of a kitchen chair, then quickly catching it as the chair started to topple over under the weight.

'I tend to agree with you. Put that on the banister in the hall; I'll put it away in a moment. I just need to ring Barry; one of Jimmy's shoes is loose after all that twisting and turning in the field.' She dialled the number and arranged to meet Barry at the farm the following afternoon.

Peggy was humming as she came through the back door, the next morning.

'You sound happy, Peg,' said Alan.

'Why shouldn't I be? The sun's shinin', and I've got a date with Barry, tonight. 'E's takin' me to that posh Indian place in Exeter,' she paused and studied them for a second or two, then seemed to come to a decision. 'I'll let you two into a secret - don't tell anyone, mind,' she paused again while they both agreed not to, and were conscious of deliberately not looking at each other. 'I think 'es goin' to ask me to marry 'im.'

'Oh, that's lovely,' said Alan. 'Happy endings all round.'

'What d'you mean?' asked Peggy.

Heather tried to stop him, but Alan wasn't looking at her. 'Well, Luke and Mandy and you and Barry getting married,' he said.

Peggy's face changed.

''E can't marry 'er. 'E's still married to Rose. 'As 'e asked 'er to marry 'im?'

Alan was beginning to realise he had put his foot in it, again. This was confirmed when he turned towards Heather and found her with both hands over her face.

'Er, I sort of assumed...er...I don't know. Don't listen to me, Peggy. I'm always getting the wrong end of the stick.'

'Well, either 'e 'as, or 'e 'asn't... 'Eather?'

'Don't involve me in this,' said Heather, turning away from them and taking some smoked salmon out of the deep freeze to make sandwiches for the lunch-time customers.

''E 'as. I can tell. The bastard! She's not right for 'im. She'm useless around the farm. 'E'll regret it. Oh yes, 'e'll regret it, all right.' Peggy was practically grinding her teeth with rage. She dragged the vacuum cleaner out of the cupboard with maximum force, knocking a large chip out of the wooden door frame.

'Hey! Careful Peggy! That's an expensive cleaner,' said Alan, wilting slightly under the glare with which she answered this remark. She stormed into the bar.

Alan looked at Heather.

'What did I say? If she's marrying Barry, why shouldn't Luke marry Mandy?'

'I really don't want to go into that, Alan,' she said, shaking her head. 'Maybe you have to be 'a woman spurned' to understand.'

'Oh God, what've I done? You don't think she'll go and do anything silly, do you?' asked Alan, running the fingers of both hands through his hair, and clutching the back of his head.

'Yes. But I'm not going to worry about it. What would

you like for lunch? I want to prepare it early because I have to meet Barry at the farm, just after closing time.'

'Are you going to tell him?'

'Tell him what?' Heather queried.

'I don't know. I'm confused. I think I'll go and buy a newspaper. Maybe there's a nice major war going on somewhere that I can read up on for a little light relief.'

Heather arrived at the farm to find Barry had got there ahead of her. He was standing in the yard, deep in conversation with Mandy. The Land-Rover was there, but the tractor was out, and she could hear the engine and clatter of the machinery as Luke harrowed the meadow where they'd blown up the bomb detonator. Barry saw her and picked up his box of tools. Heather didn't miss the light touch on Mandy's arm as he said goodbye to her, or the way she watched him as he walked towards the gate to Jimmy's field.

Don't even think about it, Barry, she thought. The idea of nice, gentle Barry taking on both Peggy and Luke was like watching him teetering on the crater's edge of a particularly nasty volcano. She was worried. Apart from liking him, farriers were hard to come by.

CHAPTER THIRTY-SIX

Heather's hope that Barry might deflect Peggy from her war with Luke, faded when she turned up for work two days later with a large piece of sticking plaster on her leg. Heather looked at it.

'What have you done?' she asked.

'Bloody phea…er, I scratched it on a bramble, blackberrying,' she said, with a glance under her fringe to see if Heather, the 'townie', had swallowed this.

Very weak excuse, Peggy, thought Heather. Even I know blackberries are over by this time of year. She'd been down to Hawkridge again, unless there were other 'leg shredding' pheasants in the area. What had she done this time? There didn't appear to be any blood on the anorak hanging on the hook on the back door. Ignore it, she told herself. Change the subject.

'How did your Indian meal with Barry go? I forgot to ask,' she said.

'All right,' said Peggy, shortly.

Ah! So no proposal of marriage, then, Heather interpreted, throwing Alan a look which shot him out of the kitchen into the bar.

'Just going to clean the pipes,' he said.

She heard him pulling up the flap in the bar floor and descending the steps into the cellar. The phrase 'gone to ground' slid through her mind. Peggy suddenly giggled. The sound was so unusual, and unexpected, that it made Heather jump.

'You know I've been down there, don't you?' Peggy said with a sly smile.

'I guessed. But as long as Jimmy's all right, I don't want to know what you've been doing.'

'You should…it was you put the idea into my 'ead. 'Ead,

that's a good one,' she giggled again.

A chill crept up Heather's back. It was happening again. She was getting drawn into the insane nightmare of Peggy's jealousy.

'I'm sure I have put no ideas into your head, Peggy. All I have ever wanted was for you to stop this nonsense.'

'Nonsense, is it? How would you feel if someone took Alan away?'

Heather had never really considered the idea; but now that she did, she found the thought of life without Alan, pretty devastating. But the result of that short mental exercise, she suddenly realised, was pushing her towards more of a fellow feeling with Peggy than she was prepared to entertain.

'I would be very unhappy. But that's not likely to happen,' she said firmly. 'And I refuse to believe that I have given you any unpleasant ideas to incorporate into your vendetta with Luke.'

'Don't you want to know what I've done?' Peggy was obviously dying to tell her.

'No,' said Heather, turning away and taking a packet of prawns out of the freezer. How on earth could she have inspired whatever devilry had now occurred at Hawkridge.

'You know what you were sayin', about North Tegridge not being Sicily?' said Peggy.

'Vaguely…I'm trying to forget that afternoon. What are you getting at?'

'The Mafia, and that,' said Peggy. 'I saw that film, too.'

'Is anybody dead?' Heather could feel the blood draining away from her face. The woman standing in front of her was probably dangerously insane. She wondered how fast Alan could get up the cellar steps if she screamed.

Peggy laughed - not a pleasant sound.

'Of course not. But I am goin' to get that bloody

pheasant, one day,' she glanced down at the sticking plaster on her leg.

An appalling thought struck Heather. Horse's head!

'Is Jimmy all right? What have you done?'

Peggy laughed again.

'You are funny, 'Eather; you're catching on, though,' Peggy could hardly contain her glee.

Heather didn't know if she wanted Alan to walk in and put a stop to this, or stay well away until she had found out what Peggy had done.

'They'll 'ave 'ad a nasty shock when they went to bed, last night.'

Heather just stared at her, feeling slightly sick. The memory of Luke changing the lock on the back door came to her.

'How did you get in?' she asked.

'You forget, that was my 'ome. 'E's changed the lock on the back door, but I knows the windows that don't shut properly. And I knows they always goes shoppin', Wednesday afternoons.' She giggled again. 'Oh, it did look funny. You should 'ave seen it.'

'What?' Heather groaned, the tips of her fingers covering her lips.

'I put a pig's 'ead in their bed - instead of an 'orse's, like the film - because it's the pigs that Luke likes best. Couldn't get an 'orses, anyway, what with you being so touchy about yours,' she looked at Heather's stunned expression. 'Joke, 'Eather...it was a joke.'

'You've killed one of the pigs!' Heather's eyes turned inadvertently towards the knife block, but the only one that was missing was the one she used to cut string on the bales at the farm, and yesterday that had been on the ledge under the stable roof.

'Course I 'aven't! I got it at the butchers. But 'e

262

wouldn't know that until 'e'd checked the sties. Good eh? And all your idea.'

Heather sat down on a kitchen chair and willed Alan to come up from the cellar and restore some sanity to the morning. It seemed to work. She heard his feet on the wooden steps as he climbed back into the bar.

'You don't tell 'im,' Peggy raised a finger in front of her mouth as she spoke. 'Our secret - remember it was you give me the idea.'

Alan came into the kitchen carrying a bucket, his eyes flicking nervously between the two silent women.

'Just want to get some hot water,' he said. He looked more closely at Heather, and frowned. 'Are you all right? You look pale.'

She got up and, taking a bowl from the cupboard, she opened the packet of prawns and poured the tinkling frozen mass into it.

'I'm fine,' she said. 'I haven't put any make-up on, yet.'

Peggy smiled, and went into the bar to start work.

When Heather had the kitchen to herself again she stopped what she was doing, and stared unseeingly out of the window into the yard, wondering how she could get rid of Peggy's presence in the pub. Why had she ever taken her on? It hadn't felt like a good idea from the beginning.

'Not thinking of trying to get rid of me, are you?' Peggy was right behind her.

'Don't do that!' Heather snapped. 'Tell Alan I've gone to the shop.' She took her purse out of her handbag and left the kitchen without looking at Peggy, though she could feel the black eyes fixed on her as she went.

Anne was in the shop, buying a newspaper, and Rudi was tied up outside, keeping guard in case the shop was suddenly invaded by marauding cats.

'Got time for a coffee?' Anne asked.

'Yes,' said Heather, unwilling to return to the unpleasant atmosphere that Peggy had created.

They walked across the square to Anne's cottage.

'Heard the latest, 'Anne asked, as she opened the door.

'No - what now? Doesn't life ever run smoothly in this village?' said Heather.

'How did you know it wasn't running smoothly?' asked Anne, with a smile.

'It would probably be a first if it did. I suppose I just assumed it from the way you said it. So what *is* the latest then?'

'Hawkridge again...this one has the hand of Peggy all over it, she never liked the pigs.'

'What's she done?' The words came automatically as the ones she should have spoken.

'Only gone and put a pig's head in Luke and Mandy's bed. Did you ever see that film, 'The Godfather'?'

How had Anne found out so quickly?

'She's definitely unbalanced. Who told you?' Heather asked.

'I heard it in the shop. Luke was up there, earlier. He's hopping mad. He had the police up at the farm last night, apparently,' said Anne, handing her a cup of black coffee.

'I think I need this,' said Heather. Maybe her problem would be solved. Perhaps they would take Peggy away and put her in prison. She took a long drink of her coffee as she embraced this happy thought.

'For a while Luke thought it was one of *his* pigs, until he managed to calm Mandy down and go out and check. I don't know where she got it.'

'Butcher's,' said Heather, still allowing her mind to picture Peggy in a cell, behind a slamming steel door.

'How do you know?' asked Anne.

'Er, seems logical,' said Heather, dragging her mind

away from the satisfying mental image.

'I suppose so. Do you want another one of those?' Anne nodded towards Heather's cup and reached out a hand to the coffee pot.

'No, I'd better get back. I told Alan I was only going to the shop. Thanks.'

Alan was unlocking the bar door as she arrived. He had the phone in his hand.

'I was just going to ring Anne. I didn't know where you'd gone. You left your mobile here.'

'I had a coffee with Anne. Why did you want me?'

'The police have just been and taken Peggy away.'

Yeesss! Clang went the steel door, and rattle went the keys as they turned in the lock.

'Police?' she said.

'I don't know what's going on. I thought at first something may have happened to Mercy, but it looked as if they were arresting her. They said something about pigs. Peggy just took her coat and left. She didn't say anything. D'you know what this is all about?'

'Yes, I think so. Anne's just told me. It's probably all round the village by now. Peggy's pushed Luke too far this time with her tasteless attempts at breaking up his and Mandy's relationship.'

'Please get to the point. What's she done?'

'The full 'Godfather' bit…she put a severed pig's head in Luke and Mandy's bed.'

'How the hell did Peggy decapitate a pig? Not that poor old boar?' said Alan, his face stretched in a grimace of horror.

'No. Not this time. She got it from the butcher.'

'The woman's sick. D'you think getting taken in by the police will stop this crazy vendetta of hers?' asked Alan.

'I hope they lock her up. I don't want her here, any more. She worries me.'

'I don't think they'll lock her up for playing practical jokes,' he said.

'Practical jokes!'

Alan stared thoughtfully at her.

'What did you mean ' not this time'?' he asked.

'What?' she'd never been any good at subterfuge, especially with Alan. Her mind went into overdrive. Could she swear him to secrecy? He wouldn't want her involved. She was probably an accessory after the fact...she should have spoken up. She'd been sheltering a criminal.

'You heard me,' he said.

She made the decision.

'Please, Alan, you're not to say anything about this to anyone else, or I'll probably end up in the cell next to Peggy... It was Peggy who did that to the boar.'

'PEGGY!'

'And afterwards she flagged me down on the road and I took her home. There was all this blood, and I thought she'd hurt herself.'

'Shit!' said Alan, who very rarely swore.

'That probably makes me an accessory; so please don't say anything.'

'Why didn't you tell me?' he asked, shaking his head at her.

'Two reasons, really. Peggy can be quite intimidating and...I'm sorry...but you're not always the soul of discretion.' She chewed her thumbnail as she waited for his reaction.

He took a deep breath and let it out slowly.

'None of this really matters to us, though, does it?' he said. 'Let's pretend it never happened. We're just here to serve drinks and food, not get involved in local wars. Come here.' He put his arms round her.

'There - that's nice!' said Dave, walking into the bar and

smiling at them. 'Nice to see people getting on. Heard the latest?'

'Yes,' they chorused.

'Oh. All right then. I won't bore you with it. Bacon sandwich please, Heather.'

'Do you want mushrooms with it...no extra charge, they're yours. In fact no charge at all. Those are absolutely superb mushrooms, Dave. Thank you,' Heather said.

....

There was no-one at Hawkridge when Heather went down there, that afternoon. Both vehicles were out. Probably at the police station putting together a case against Peggy ...involving me, she thought, trying to push the idea away. It was a warm sunny afternoon. The kind of afternoon that the farm animals could enjoy, as the irritating flies which had plagued them through the summer seemed to have disappeared with the first few frosts. The pigs were snoozing quietly, with just the occasional satisfied grunt. And the cows were grazing at the top of the field. Luke seemed to have done the milking early.

Jimmy was lying flat on his side halfway across the field doing a good imitation of a dead horse, apart from one ear which twitched occasionally. Heather didn't want to disturb him and was trying to sneak his bucket of food across the field, prepared to wait for him to wake up for his tea, when she tripped in an unexpected rut and rattled the bucket.

Jimmy's head came up. He saw her, stretched out his front legs and pushed himself up onto his feet, then stretched one back leg out, thought about doing the other one, but shook himself instead. Having got his moving parts into satisfactory working order, he set off towards her on a track which would intercept her, just before the stable.

The rut, which she had tripped in, was one of a pair which she now noticed crossing the field into the wood behind the stable, and amongst the trees she could see the yellow shape of Luke's digger parked there. Surely he wouldn't have taken the digger just to bury a pig's head, she thought, and wished she hadn't.

'Come on, Jimmy,' she opened the stable door and put the bucket down in the corner for him.

....

Heather and Alan spent most of that evening trying to think of ways to terminate Peggy's employment at the pub; ways that wouldn't somehow rebound on them. The words 'unfair dismissal' hovered over them in the background, competing with the phrase 'accessory after the fact'.

'It's no good. We're stuck with her,' said Heather tiredly, tipping the last dregs of the wine, with which they were consoling themselves, into her glass. It was past closing time, and they were sitting at the kitchen table.

'Maybe this latest escapade has concentrated the minds of the police, and they have now worked out that it was Peggy who injured the boar. If she tries to implicate you we would definitely have a reason to sack her.'

'It doesn't alter the fact that I should have told them what I knew - we're going round in circles, Alan.'

'Don't worry. It's not the end of the world if they do find out. And…it's Peggy's word against yours…we can always lie. Who's going to believe her?' he said.

'We're not making much sense. Come on, lets go to bed,' said Heather.

'Best idea you've had all evening,' said Alan, pushing back his chair.

CHAPTER THIRTY-SEVEN

A very subdued Peggy turned up for work, and Alan tackled her as soon as she'd got her jacket off.

'What was all that about, yesterday, Peggy?'

'Didn't 'Eather tell you?' She sneaked a look at Heather.

'We've heard the story - it's all round the village,' said Alan.

'It was just a bit of a joke,' she gave a nervous giggle. 'But Luke didn't think it was funny. Anyway, it's all sorted out, now...I never thought he'd take it as far as going to the police. That was 'er doin', I reckon. Luke said 'e wouldn't press charges if I apologised... to 'er! And 'e said I wasn't to trespass on 'is farm, no more. That was my 'ome for years.'

'So that's the end of it, then, is it?' asked Alan, glancing at Heather.

'Yes.'

Heather quietly breathed a sigh of relief. It seemed that Peggy had got away with the far worse crime of mutilating the boar.

'So that's it,' said Peggy. 'I've got to stay away from 'Awkridge. That's no great 'ardship, I wasn't intendin' to go down there again, anyway. I've got over what Luke done to me. I'm going to concentrate on Barry and get on with the rest of my life. Mum agrees with me. She never liked Luke.'

'Well, that's good, then, Peggy,' Alan said. 'We'll say no more about it, except that I want you to appreciate that it's not good for pub customer relations to have the police turning up on the doorstep. So no more trouble, or we will have to consider letting you go.'

Heather was impressed. He had prepared the ground

beautifully for getting rid of Peggy if she gave them any more grief. Peggy was trying to catch her eye, but Heather consciously avoided her by leaving the kitchen.

'I'm just going to tidy upstairs,' she said.

Peggy kept her head down and got on with her work, she didn't even stop for a coffee.

'I've got to make up for leaving early, yesterday,' she said.

That afternoon, Alan had arranged to go down to Small Profits and give Dave a hand with the cider-making. The day was quiet, the sun was shining and Heather felt inspired to have another go at riding Jimmy. She didn't tell Alan she had planned this, as she intended to ride the short distance between Hawkridge and Small Profits and surprise him.

Jimmy was in a relaxed mood as she tacked him up and led him down the field into the farmyard. Beside the milking parlour there was an old, stone built, churn stand which Luke had said she could use as a mounting block. She glanced at the kitchen window to see if Mandy was watching her, but there was no-one there. Then she realised Mandy's car was gone - she must be out. Heather knew where Luke was because she could hear the tractor in the river meadow. The pheasant walked past them, but seemed unable to separate her two legs from Jimmy's four, to make an acceptable target, and after pausing for a moment, it wandered on towards the field.

She climbed onto the churn stand and pulled Jimmy alongside, then stepped astride him and lowered herself gently into the saddle. He jiggled sideways a bit while she tried to hook her toes into the stirrups, then she gathered up the reins and pushed him on up the track to the road. He walked out smartly, keeping a wary eye out for any tigers which might be lurking in the hedge, ready to jump on him, and dived sideways when a piece of torn polythene, hooked onto some barbed wire, rustled in the light breeze. But nothing he did felt as if it was going to unseat her, and she began to relax.

They travelled the short distance along the main road and turned into the track to Small Profits. As they came closer she could hear the noisy two-stroke petrol engine that drove the apple crusher, and the clattering of the apples as they rolled down the chute. She rode up to the door of the barn. Jimmy seemed unafraid of all the noise and action going on inside.

Alan and Dave were winding down the huge screw of the old cider press, using a long iron pole poked through holes in the head of the screw. This was pressing down on a board placed on the pile of pulp filled sacking which was stacked in a metal tray. From the lip in the tray a steady stream of juice trickled into a half barrel below.

So unfazed was Jimmy by all this activity that, as Heather pushed him forward to attract Alan's attention, he walked on into the barn before she could stop him, and slurped up a mouthful of freshly pressed apple juice.

'Hey!' Dave shouted, as she jumped off the horse and pulled him back out of the barn.

'I'm sorry, Dave. I'd no idea he was going to do that. Will it be spoilt?'

Jimmy was rattling his bit as he tried to lick the last drops of juice from around his mouth.

'No. It won't hurt the cider. All the impurities work out of it, once it's in the barrel.'

'You didn't tell me you were going to ride him,' said Alan, joining Dave at the barn entrance.

'I wanted to surprise you.'

'Little horse seems very quiet, doesn't he?' said Dave, giving Jimmy a pat.

'Dave!' It was Mercy, calling from the back door of the farmhouse. She held up a teapot.

'Just coming. D'you want a cup of tea, Heather? Mercy's just made us one,' Dave said.

Jimmy was beginning to fidget. If he wasn't allowed to help with the cider making he wanted to get moving again.

'No thanks, Dave. This was just a short, confidence building trip. I think I'll take him back again, now.' She looked around the yard. Is there anything I can stand on to get back onto him?'

'Here, give us your leg,' said Dave, and lifted her lightly into the saddle.

She looked at Alan, trying to suppress a smile.

'That's the way to do it,' she said, giving them both a wave as Jimmy bounced a couple of strides, eager to be off.

She allowed him to jog up the track to the road. So! Mercy had made her way into Dave's house. She wondered if this was a permanent arrangement. Peggy hadn't said anything, but then her mind had been on other things.

Alan came home just before opening time, and handed her a bag of mushrooms.

'Mercy picked these for you,' he said.

A picture of Mercy in the library van clutching 'Lives of the Great Poisoners', flitted through her head.

'Thank you. That was nice of her. Has she moved in with Dave?'

'No, I think she'd like to. Looks to me as if she's slowly working her way in with a bit of housework here, and a bit of cooking there. I don't think it's what Dave wants. To a degree, I think he's still lusting after the Big Woman…but he says Mercy is a better cook. Did you see Mandy today? Did she say anything about the pig's head?'

'She was out. And Luke was on the tractor at the other

end of the farm,' said Heather.

Luke came into the pub alone that evening.

'See you had the horse out, again, today,' he said to Heather.

'How did you know? You were right down by the river.'

'Ah! But you left hoof-prints across the yard,' he said.

'Of course!' she nodded.

Colin and Audrey came in and walked up to the bar.

'Hello, Luke,' Audrey said. 'Nasty, that business with the pig's head. Must have been a terrible shock.'

'If you ask me, that Peggy wants locking up,' said Colin.

'Well, you'd know all about being locked up, wouldn't you,' said Luke nastily.

This observation may have been correct, but Heather thought it a little uncalled for. She wondered if Colin still had any connections from his London underworld days who would be prepared to avenge unkind remarks like that. It seemed he did.

'That's quite enough of that from you, young Luke,' snapped Audrey. 'We were only making a civil enquiry.'

'Sorry,' said Luke. 'Here, what'll you two have to drink?'

They both ordered 'shorts', and Heather smiled as she turned away, a glass in each hand, and pushed one up under the whisky optic and the other under the gin.

'No Mandy this evening, then?' asked Audrey, tipping a little more tonic from the bottle into her glass.

'She's gone away for a few days - to stay with her sister in Exeter,' said Luke.   'Cheers!' He lifted his glass slightly and moved away from them to the other end of the bar, where Alan and Dave were talking about cider. The three of them began discussing the apple crop from Luke's orchard on his East Tegridge farm.

Luke drank steadily throughout the evening, and by

closing time it was clear that he wasn't fit to drive home.

'I'll give you a lift,' said Dave.

'I can bloody drive myself. I'm not drunk,' said Luke, grabbing one of the handbag hooks under the bar to steady himself as he stood up.

Dave quickly palmed Luke's Land-Rover keys from where they were lying on the bar.

'Where's my bloody keys?' Luke mumbled, as he felt in his pockets. 'Sod it! Must have left them in the Land-Rover. 'Night all,' he waved a vague hand round the bar as he staggered across to the door.

'Thanks for your help this afternoon, Alan,' said Dave, as he followed Luke out.

'What was that Luke was saying about Mandy? He didn't seem very happy,' said Alan, as they were clearing up.

'She's gone away for a few days. She's got a sister in Exeter.'

'Wouldn't surprise me if she'd left for good,' said Alan.

'Why do you say that? They're planning to get married, eventually.' Heather hoped what Luke had said *was* true, because she'd suddenly remembered Mandy saying once, that Luke had said he'd kill her if she tried to leave.

'I could ring her,' she said slowly. 'No, she's only just gone away. I'm sure it's nothing sinister.'

'Why would her leaving be sinister?' asked Alan, frowning at her. 'Do you know something I don't? I don't think Luke could afford to have too many disappearing wives, or partners. Mandy's in Exeter, having a break from Peggy. Something we could all do with, darling. These are not our problems.'

CHAPTER THIRTY-EIGHT

Not our problems, Alan had said. Nevertheless, Heather found herself subconsciously counting the days that Mandy's car was not parked at the farm. When it got to eight, she mentioned it to Alan.

'Do you think that eight days is more than 'a few days', Alan?'

'I wish you wouldn't do that,' he said.

'What?'

'Ask me questions that need in-depth disentangling before I can formulate a reply. What exactly are we talking about?'

'Mandy, she's been gone for eight days, now - I think.'

'You think.'

'Well, I haven't seen her car at the farm for eight days,' said Heather.

'I told you. She's run away. Good for her.'

'D'you think I should ring her?' Heather asked.

'No. I thought we had decided to settle for a quiet life and not involve ourselves with the customers' private lives.'

You've changed your tune a bit, she thought, remembering how worried he'd been when Mandy went missing on the day of the bomb. Still, she was relieved to see that he didn't seem particularly bothered about her now. Luke's threat to put him in hospital seemed to have struck home. Alan was not an aggressive person and he found Luke's low boiling point rather intimidating.

That afternoon, as she pulled up at Hawkridge, she found two cows making their way into the yard through the open gate of their field. Luke didn't seem to be around, so she drove them back in and latched the gate. The chain and padlock were missing. There was a nearly empty whisky bottle on the churn stand, and as she walked round behind the barn to the feed bins, she found Luke slumped across some straw bales beside the pig sties, snoring. Just the other side of the low wall a huge sow was also sound asleep, snoring alternate snores with Luke.

'You're in the right place - almost,' she said quietly, looking down at him, dirty, unshaven and wearing filthy blue overalls. She raised her voice, 'Luke!'

There was no reply.

'Luke! The cows were out.'

The sow twitched an ear and snorted, but the rhythm of Luke's breathing didn't change.

'Oh, stay there and sleep it off, then,' said Heather, and got on with mixing Jimmy's feed.

As she was fishing in her pocket for the key to the gate padlock, she realised Luke had removed this one, as well. Perhaps he thought that Peggy had now given up her reign of terror.

A bank of navy blue cloud was moving in from the west as she led the horse into the stable and, by the time he'd finished his meal, the waving sheets of rain she had watched drifting across the countryside, finally reached the farm. Heavy single drops on the tin roof gradually changed to one long rattle of sound, and water poured down the grooves in the galvanised sheets, overflowing into a curtain across the stable door.

That should sort Luke out, she thought, as she waited with Jimmy until the worst of the squall was over. A sudden brief appearance of the sun, fashioned a magnificent rainbow against the black cloud as it swept on towards Exmoor. Jimmy nudged her, indicating that it was now safe to go out.

As she crossed the field, she saw Luke, now completely

drenched, stumble across the yard and in through the back door of the farmhouse.

'Nice one, God,' she muttered.

Walking past the cart shed, she exchanged glares with the pheasant, whose intended attack had been thwarted by a rippling puddle in front of the shed which was turning into a mini-torrent, fed by water running off the field.

She drove home wondering whether Luke had always been a heavy drinker, or if this was something new. And, if so, what had caused it?

He came into the bar that evening. Even a wash and change of clothes didn't disguise the fact that he looked rough.

'Whisky, Heather. I think I've got a cold coming.'

Heather had great difficulty fixing an acceptable expression on her face as she filled his glass.

'I'd better have a bottle as well. We seem to have run out at home. You need whisky for a cold, don't you?'

She noted the 'we' and couldn't stop herself.

'Mandy back from Exeter, then?'

'She will be. Soon as she's sure bloody Peggy has stopped all her nonsense.'

'Yes. That was a bit much,' said Heather, non-committally.

'You have to hand it to her, though. Got a sense of humour, Peg has,' said Luke, with a hint of a smile.

Alan caught this remark and raised one eyebrow at her from the other end of the bar.

Luke sneezed and searched for a non-existent handkerchief. Heather handed him a paper napkin, glad of the diversion because she couldn't come up with an acceptable answer to Luke's idea of humour, and Peggy's portrayal of it.

'Thanks,' he said. 'Here, can you sell me a lemon. I think

this is going to need hot lemon and whisky treatment. Oh, and some aspirin.'

Heather got him these items, revelling in the fact that she didn't feel in the least sorry for him. He was obviously fishing for some female sympathy.

'I think you ought to have an early night, Luke,' she said.

'You offering to tuck me in?' he leered, and burst into a fit of coughing.

'Serve you right,' said Heather quietly, as he spluttered.

'What?'

'It's a dirty night,' she said, glancing at the rain gusting against the bar window.

'Maybe I will go home. I think I'm getting a temperature,' he said, putting the lemon and aspirins into his pocket and picking up the whisky bottle. ''Night all.'

''Night,' said Alan. He looked at Heather. 'He didn't stay long. What are you grinning about?'

Heather described how she had found Luke that afternoon, and his subsequent soaking.

'Serve the silly bugger right,' said Alan. 'Dave - did Luke always drink like this, or is it something new?'

Dave looked up from a farm sale catalogue he was studying at the end of the bar.

'He drank quite a bit after Rose died, I seem to recall. Why?'

'Oh, no reason. He just seems to be drinking more than usual; still I suppose it's all good for business,' said Alan.

The words 'after Rose died' stayed in Heather's mind. After Rose died. After Mandy died? The digger parked in the wood behind the stable? It was no good; she had to ring Mandy's mobile number. But what if Luke answered, again? Well, he wouldn't would he? Not if he was trying to cover up the fact that he'd killed her, she reasoned with herself.

'Heather!' Alan waved his hand across her face. 'Wake up. I've got a sandwich order for you.' Two people sitting at a table in the bar were smiling at Alan's attempts to attract her attention.

'Sorry - sorry,' she said, trying to smile apologetically back at the people.

'You were miles away,' Alan said.

'Yes. When I've done this order, I'm just going to take quarter of an hour off. There's something I need to do.'

Alan didn't have time to ask what.

'Another one in there, Alan, please,' Dave pushed his pint mug across the bar.

Heather made the sandwiches and took them through to the customers, then went into the sitting room. She sat for a few moments with her phone book open in front of her, then began to dial Mandy's number; halfway through she depressed the button and cut herself off, then dialled one four one before re-dialling the number. If Luke answered, she didn't want him tracing the call.

The phone was ringing. Her heart was racing.

'Hello.' It was a woman's voice.

Heather had so convinced herself that something awful had happened to Mandy, that it took her a few seconds to recognise the voice.

'Hello? Who's there?' asked Mandy. 'Is that you, Luke?'

'No…no…it's me, Heather. I…'

'Heather! Hello. How are you?'

'That's what I was going to ask you. I'm sorry if I'm interfering; only I hadn't seen you for a while and I…well…I just wondered…I was a bit worried.'

'I did think about ringing you,' said Mandy.

'Luke said you're staying with your sister, for a few days.'

'Did he?'

279

'Yes.'

'Well, that'll do for the moment. I have some big decisions to make. How is he? I mean, I know how he tells me he is - but how is he?'

'Well…it's none of my business, really, Mandy. I just wanted to find out if you were all right. I'm glad you are. I'd better go now, we're a bit busy.'

'All right. Nice to talk to you…and thanks, Heather.'

''Bye. Take care.' Heather replaced the phone.

You stupid idiot, she said to herself. You read too many murder mysteries. Her mind strayed to the farm, the digger, the dark little wood. This place is getting to me, she thought.

Alan stood in the doorway.

'What are you doing? It's getting busy out there,' he said.

'I'm just coming. Tell me I'm an idiot.'

'You're an idiot. Why are you an idiot? Never mind, tell me later…I've put some orders on the kitchen table.' He went back into the bar.

'Whew! That was a good evening,' said Alan pushing home the noisy top and bottom bolts on the door. He collected the dirty ash trays off the tables on his way back to the bar, where Heather was washing up the last of the glasses.

'All right, idiot,' he said. 'Why are you an idiot?'

'I thought Luke had done something awful to Mandy.'

Alan just looked questioningly at her and waited for her to go on.

'So I rang her,' she finished quickly.

'I thought we'd agreed to mind our own business,' he said.

'Yes - sorry. You were right, and she's all right, and I feel stupid,' said Heather, putting the tea-towel down on a

280

pile waiting to be washed.

'Never mind. Things seem to be calming down, anyway. Mandy has escaped from Luke's malign influence. Peggy's involved with Barry, who seems very nice, and Mercy has destroyed all opposition and is back with Dave, it looks...'

'Mandy's still thinking about Luke,' Heather butted in.

'Well, she's daft if she is. The man's a brute. How did you get rid of him so quickly this evening?'

'He was fishing for sympathy because he's got a cold, and it wasn't forthcoming,' she said.

'He was a bit ambitious wasn't he? Even I don't get sympathy for a cold.'

'I'll smother you with sympathy and cold remedies next time,' Heather promised.

Alan frowned slightly before smiling back.

CHAPTER THIRTY-NINE

As the days shortened towards winter, the weather turned much colder. Instead of lingering in the square and chatting as they shopped, people were turning up their coat collars and heading for home. The always peaceful village seemed to change to a depressingly silent and almost empty place. The summer visitors and day trippers disappeared, and with them a fair proportion of the Shepherd and Dog's custom.

To Heather, the dark days became increasingly claustrophobic. Alan was worried about the downturn in business. Peggy seemed to have gone into mental hibernation and spoke only in monosyllables, and then only when spoken to. Heather was extremely glad that she had Jimmy to take her out of the pub for a change of scenery every day. She was spending more time at Hawkridge now, as she was keeping him in the stable at night. This meant she could escape much of Peggy's gloom by going down first thing every morning to turn him out and muck out the stable.

Mandy still wasn't back at the farm. She'd now been away for three weeks; and as Luke waited for her return, his farming became ever more haphazard. He frequently left behind him a strong trail of stale alcohol fumes when Heather passed him in the yard; and often the cows only got milked when the decibel level of their complaints about full udders was impossible to ignore. When he was not actually working, Luke seemed disposed to follow Heather around the farm and lean on the stable door to talk to her as she groomed Jimmy, or mucked him out. He still insisted that Mandy was coming back. She just needed a rest, and wanted to be sure that Peggy had stopped pestering them.

Heather wasn't happy about having to put up with so

much of Luke's company, but he was her landlord, it was his farm, and there wasn't much she could do about it. He was also one of their better customers, as he now spent most evenings at the pub, and it didn't do to upset the 'bread and butter' winter trade.

'It's a bit quiet here in the winter, isn't it?' said Alan, after a particularly silent morning session with Peggy. 'Do you think we did the right thing in moving down here? I'm in danger of becoming bored.'

'Why don't we get another horse? Then you could ride with me,' said Heather.

'Me! On a horse!'

'Go on, you'd look ever so handsome in breeches and boots.'

'You always did have a 'thing' about uniforms, didn't you? You'll have me in full hunting kit, next. You didn't warn me you had a kinky side, when we married,' he said.

'That's got nothing to do with it. I'm just after someone else to help with the mucking out.' With the added advantage, she thought, that if Alan appeared at the farm from time to time maybe Luke wouldn't hang around her quite so much.

She finished the flower arrangement she had made to brighten up the bar, and handed it to Alan to take in while she cleared up the snipped off ends of the stalks. He and Peggy passed in the doorway and she didn't even comment on the flowers.

'How's Barry?' Heather asked her, any conversation would be better than this heavy silence, and she realised that Peggy hadn't mentioned him for about a fortnight.

''E's borin',' was all she said, as she put the cleaning things away in the cupboard. 'No sense of 'umour.'

'Oh?' said Heather.

''E didn't think the pig's 'ead thing was amusin', and 'e

didn't seem too pleased about the police bein' involved. That was embarrassin', bein' took off like that by the police. Kids down the estate are still makin' police car noises when they see me.'

Peggy seemed so depressed that Heather tried to cheer her up a bit. She obviously thought the whole world was against her.

'I think that, in spite of him being angry about the effect it had on Mandy, there was a part of Luke which found your little Mafia joke amusing. Not that he would admit it,' said Heather.

'Really?' Peggy brightened up a little. 'What did 'e say, then?'

'Just that you've got a good sense of humour.'

'See! I knew it was a joke. There was no need to get the police onto me, like that. That was 'er doin'. I suppose the only good thing is that nobody seems to suspect about the 'other',' she laid heavy emphasis on this last word.

'Don't even begin to mention it, Peggy. That never happened, okay?'

'Right.'

'How's Mercy?'

'Oh, she's fine. Spendin' a lot of time down at Small Profits now, what with Dave bein' so busy with the cider-makin', as well as the farm. She's doin' 'is meals, an' that.'

'Lucky Dave. She's a good cook, your mum.'

'Yes, and she's really fond of Dave; be nice if they could get together, permanent like.'

'Who's getting together?' asked Alan, coming into the kitchen.

'Mum and Dave. I'd better go now. I said I'd go to the farm shop with 'er. Don't want to miss the bus.'

After Peggy had pulled on the acid green anorak and departed, Alan glanced at his watch.

'Just time for a coffee, before we open. I wonder if anyone's told Dave that he and Mercy are likely to 'get together'?' he said.

'I don't know. Dave's nice, but he doesn't give much away, does he?' said Heather.

Peggy's coat passed the kitchen window as she wheeled her bike out of the yard. Alan winced, and grinned at Heather, who smiled.

'I'm beginning to like it,' she said. 'It's a welcome splash of colour on these dull winter days.' She looked out of the window. 'I think I may take Jimmy out for a ride this afternoon, the rain seems to be clearing.'

The sky to the west was definitely brightening. She gazed at the distant blue patches which must be hovering above Dartmoor, and wished they lived nearer to the moor so that she could ride Jimmy there, amongst the wild ponies.

'Why don't we sell this place and buy a pub up on Dartmoor?' she said.

'Because they're more expensive,' said Alan, taking his coffee into the bar and un-bolting the door onto the empty square.

'Right,' said Heather, turning to stir the large pan of comfortingly thick, home-made ham and vegetable soup which was bubbling gently on the cooker.

That afternoon the patches of blue sky had reached North Tegridge, and dramatic shafts of sunlight were striking through the clouds, illuminating alternate areas of fields and woods like a wandering spotlight. Heather decided to ride Jimmy away from the village and onto a bridleway which led to the top of the hill behind Hawkridge. From there she would have a view across miles of countryside to the distant purple heights of Dartmoor.

'You taking him out for a ride, then?' asked Luke, who had appeared from the milking parlour as she led Jimmy, fully saddled and bridled, through the gate into the yard.

No, I'm going to take him into the cart-shed and teach him how to knit, she thought.

'Yes,' she said.

Luke shut the field gate for her and followed her across the yard to the churn stand.

'Here. I'll hold him for you,' he said, grasping the reins near Jimmy's bit.

'It's all right, thanks, Luke. Jimmy knows the drill - I can manage.'

Luke didn't release his hold on the reins, and Jimmy began to fidget in an effort to free his head from too firm a grip.

'Come on,' Luke said.

Heather decided that the best thing she could do was to mount quickly and regain control of her horse. In her haste to do this, her foot slipped on some damp moss growing on the stone block and she fell awkwardly, landing between the horse and the churn stand. Luke let go of the reins and reached down to pull her to her feet.

'Are you all right?' he asked.

'Yes,' said Heather trying to free her hands from the clasp of his rough fingers, and turning her head away from the whisky fumes which mingled with the stale smell of unwashed clothes.

'I'm okay, thanks, Luke.'

Jimmy had wandered across the yard and was grazing on a patch of grass beside her parked car, in danger of stepping on the reins which were trailing on the ground.

'I'm all right, Luke,' she repeated. 'Let me catch Jimmy before he takes off up the lane.'

His hands tightened and he pulled her roughly towards him.

'You're beautiful,' he said, and clamped his foul smelling

mouth over hers.

Heather freed a hand and smacked at his face as she struggled to get away. He pulled his head back as her thumbnail caught the corner of his eye.

'Let go, you bastard! What the hell d'you think you're doing?' she shouted.

He seemed to come to his senses and let her go, rubbing the corner of his eye, which was now watering freely.

'Gets lonely, up here,' he said, wandering away towards the milking parlour. At the doorway he stooped to pick up a bottle of whisky from the step, and disappeared inside, unscrewing the cap.

Heather walked fast across the yard, and picked up Jimmy's reins with shaking hands. As she went to lead him away up the track towards the road, he snatched a last mouthful of long grass, growing strong and green from its close contact with the dung heap. She pulled her own handful of wet grass from the verge, further away, and wiped her face and lips with it. Jimmy stretched out his nose towards this tasty morsel, but she flung it away.

'You wouldn't like that, my love,' she said.

Halfway up the lane, she found a jutting section of the hedge bank which she could use as a mounting block, and climbed into the saddle. Only then did she begin to calm down. She had noticed before, that close contact with Jimmy had this effect on her. Though still nervous about the idea of riding, once she was in the saddle all tensions drained away and she felt completely in tune with the horse. She nudged him with her heels and he walked smartly on up the track, one ear flicking back to listen to her as she told him what a wonderful horse he was for not running away when he had the chance.

She turned out of the Hawkridge track and listened to the soothing, regular cadence of Jimmy's shoes as they struck the metal road surface. It wasn't long before she managed to put the memory of Luke's amorous advance in its rightful place, as the 'one off' action of a lonely drunk, and reduce it to complete unimportance in her mind.

They reached the turning onto the grassy ride which led up to the top of the hill. The sun had now come out properly and the air smelled fresh and sweet after the rain. Jimmy snorted and bounced at the feel of the soft turf under his feet. As a final act to rid her mind of thoughts of Luke, Heather relaxed her tension on the reins slightly, and allowed Jimmy to move straight into a smooth, gentle canter. She knew this wasn't a sensible action with his newly healed legs, but the urge was too strong to resist.

Jimmy strode out up the hill, snorting his pleasure at every stride. The fresh wind swept past her face and Heather could feel the power for real speed underneath her, only held in check by her firm hold on the reins. After a few hundred yards, common sense prevailed and she pulled him back to a walk, stroking an ecstatic hand down his neck.

At the top of the hill, she halted beside a huge beech tree, now almost completely stripped of is autumn leaves, and drank in the view she had promised herself. The air was very clear, after the rain, and she could see for miles across the patchwork of fields and hedges. Small areas of woodland hugged the banks of the river where it wound its way along the bottom the valley; turbulent where it carved a passage over shallow boulders, and smoothly rippled over the deep stretches.

The sound of a hunting horn drifted to her on the breeze, and over to the right she could see two riders, wearing hunting pink, standing at the corner of a wood. A group of hounds were sitting or lying around the horse of the Master, who was blowing his horn to collect up the stragglers of the pack before heading for home. Heather watched two hounds, which were out of his sight, heading round the edge of the wood towards him. As soon as they arrived, the pack and the two riders moved off across country towards the road.

'One day, Jimmy… perhaps… when you get fit, and I get brave,' she said quietly.

As she pulled him round to go home, her eye was caught by something on the smooth trunk of the beech tree. She eased the horse closer, holding him up slightly as he stumbled on a root.

'Sorry, lad,' she said, and leaned forward in the saddle to try to make out a carving in the bark. It was old, and overgrown where the edge of the bark had rolled in as it healed, but she could make out DXXR. Jimmy neighed suddenly and turned away from the tree, and Heather saw Keith Field, on his hunter, following the track over the brow of the hill behind her.

'Hello!' he said, bringing his horse to a halt alongside her. 'So you're actually riding him, now. How's he going?'

'He's perfect,' she said, as Jimmy demonstrated how perfect he wasn't, by bouncing up and down with excitement at the arrival of another horse.

A large tri-colour foxhound trotted wearily round the corner behind Keith's horse and sat down beside it. Heather pointed.

'You seem to have acquired a friend,' she said.

Keith looked down and laughed.

'That's Donovan. He's always getting lost. Get away on!' he said, cracking his whip in the direction of the hound, who flinched away, then heard the horn and loped back the way he'd come. 'Which way are you headed?' Keith asked.

'I'm going back now. We're only doing very short

outings, at the moment.'

'I'll ride with you,' he said, patting his horse. 'This lad's tired. I'm thinking of retiring the old boy, soon. He loves his hunting but he's not really up to a full day any more.'

'That's a shame.' A sudden thought struck her. 'What will you do with him?'

'Oh, find him a home somewhere with somebody who just wants a bit of light hacking. Unfortunately I can't afford to keep two.'

'Obviously I would need to discuss this with my husband, but would you consider giving me first refusal when you do decide to part with him? I want to try to persuade Alan to ride with me. Is he quiet?' She looked at the handsome bay. 'I've only seen him after a tiring day's hunting.'

'Yes, completely bomb-proof,' he said.

'A necessary attribute in North Tegridge,' Heather said, smiling.

'What? Oh yes. I remember. You had a bomb, didn't you?'

They turned onto the road and rode side by side towards the Hawkridge turning.

'Well, regarding Mallard, here, I'll let you know when I do decide it's time to part with him. He has slight shoeing problems. Who's your blacksmith?' he said.

'Barry Martin.'

'Oh, that's all right, then. He's been looking after his feet for years. He's a good farrier, Barry. Nice bloke, as well. Losing his wife was a terrible blow, but this new girl friend seems just right for him.'

Heather stared at him for a moment. How could any sane person think Peggy was just right for anyone?

They had arrived at the Hawkridge track.

'Anyway, nice to have met you again,' he said. 'I'll be in touch.' He waved a hand and roused Mallard into a trot towards the village.

Jimmy didn't want to leave his new friend, and tried to go too.

'I wouldn't put too many oats into that little lad,' Keith called back over his shoulder, as Jimmy half reared in his attempts to follow them.

'Good advice,' she shouted after him.

He waved a hand in reply, and Jimmy finally consented to put all four feet on the ground and walk along the track to the farm. Why don't I think before I speak? Heather wondered. What had seemed like such a good idea five minutes ago, now seemed crazy. Alan didn't want a horse. He was even afraid of leading one, let alone getting on top of Mallard.

'It's been a very odd day, James,' she said, stroking his neck. Her stomach lurched slightly as she wondered where Luke was.

There was no sign of him at the farm. She fed the horse and hung up his haynet as quickly as possible, heaving a sigh of relief as she got into the car and set off back to the village, without seeing Luke.

CHAPTER FORTY

Dave and Barry came into the pub together, just before lunch time closing. They were discussing the farm sale they had attended, that morning.

'Two pints, please, Heather,' Dave said.

'How's the little horse? I hear you've been riding him,' said Barry.

'He's fine. Word does travel fast in this area, doesn't it?' she said.

'Oh, I was talking to Keith Field, last night. He said he met you on Telegraph Hill, yesterday,' said Barry.

'Telegraph Hill, eh? Used to do me courting up there when I was a lad,' said Dave. 'There's a big old beech tree right up on the top. Good for sheltering under when it rained.'

DXXR, Heather thought.

'Did you have a girl friend whose name began with R,' she asked.

Dave grinned and glanced round the bar, checking its other occupants.

'Yes, I did. But don't shout it about. It was a very long time ago. It was Rose; but she was a bit younger than me, and in the end she preferred Luke,' he suddenly frowned. 'Why did you ask that? You're not psychic, are you?'

'Did you ever leave your mark on that beech tree?' Heather smiled.

'My goodness! Is that still there? I'd have thought it would have all grown over by now. I was nineteen when I carved that.'

'Carved what?' Barry asked.

'Oh, the usual; D kiss kiss R,' said Dave.

'Young love, eh?' said Barry.

Heather wondered how Barry's more mature love life was going.

'Keith Field was very complimentary about Peggy, yesterday. He said she was just right for you,' she said.

Barry frowned and glanced at Dave who, after grinning at this remark, turned away to tell Alan what he had bought at the farm sale. Barry inclined his head towards the other end of the bar.

'Can I have a quick word?' he said.

Heather collected some dirty glasses and took them along the bar to the sink.

'Did Keith actually say 'Peggy', by name, like?' he asked, in a low voice.

'Erm, no. He said your new girl friend…isn't that Peggy?'

'No, but please don't say anything to Peggy. I haven't told her yet,' he said.

'Oh my God! She's gloomy enough at the moment without finding out that you're dumping her.'

'I know. If you want the truth, I'm having difficulty getting up the nerve to say I want to break off our relationship. After some of the things she's done to Luke and Mandy, I sometimes wonder if she's quite sane. On the other hand, she has been telling me I'm not exciting enough - that doesn't do much for a bloke's self esteem.'

'Perhaps, if you wait a bit longer, she will finish with you,' Heather said, seeing this as the best solution all round.

'That's rather what I was hoping. I'm concentrating on being deeply unexciting at the moment,' Barry smiled.

'I expect it will work out all right,' said Heather, hoping that Barry wasn't going to ask for her help. He didn't - but dived in with a nerve jangling change of subject.

'I hear you're thinking of buying old Mallard,' he said.

'Sshh!' Heather hissed, casting a frantic glance along the bar to where Alan and Dave were leaning over the sale

293

catalogue, studying an entry. 'I haven't said anything to Alan, yet. In fact it seemed like a rather silly idea almost as soon as I had mentioned it to Keith.'

'Oh, okay - but if you do decide to, you could do a lot worse.'

'What are you two plotting, over there?' called Alan.

'Nothing. Just horse talk,' said Heather.

Next morning, Peggy waited until she and Heather were alone in the kitchen.

'You been down to the farm, then?' said Peggy. It was more of a statement than a question.

'Yes.'

'She back there yet?'

'I haven't seen her, if you mean Mandy. But that doesn't mean that she's not there. Why?' Heather asked.

'Just wondered. What do you think of Barry?'

'Barry? I er...well...he's all right, he's nice,' said Heather carefully, not sure where this conversation was leading.

'D'you think I should stick with 'im?' asked Peggy, running her hand backwards and forwards along the back of a kitchen chair, and not looking at Heather.

'Peggy, I don't know. That's a decision for you to make.'

Peggy sighed and stared unseeingly at the hand she'd been rubbing on the wooden rail.

'It was good at the beginnin'. But now 'e doesn't seem to want to go out any more. Say's 'es tired after work. Just wants us to sit and watch videos. 'E likes war films.'

'Ugh!' said Heather.

'I know. 'E says clubbin' gives 'im an 'eadache.'

'I sympathise with him there; all that noise and flashing lights,' said Heather.

'That's the bit I like. I think I missed out on that in my youth.'

Alan came into the kitchen, and Peggy suddenly nodded vigorously.

'Yes,' she said. 'You've made my mind up. Thanks, 'Eather.' She went back into the bar and switched on the polisher.

'What have you made up her mind about?' asked Alan.

'I don't know,' Heather ran both hands through her hair and massaged the back of her neck. 'This pub business is a lot more complicated than one thinks. It's not just a question of serving food and drink. One has to become accomplished in the art of sitting on the fence.'

Unfortunately Barry seemed to have come to a conclusion at roughly the same time as Peggy, because the next day she arrived in a filthy temper. Heather got back from turning Jimmy out, to find Alan in the kitchen making toast.

'More breakfast?' she asked.

'I had to get out of the bar,' he said. 'It's not safe in there.'

There was a crash as one of the chairs, which Peggy had stacked on the tables while she polished the floor, slipped off as the polisher collided with a table leg.

'Bloody stupid chair!' Peggy's raised voice sounded barely under control.

'What've you said to her?' Heather asked.

'Me? Nothing! She turned up in that mood. I'm going to the shop. D'you want anything?'

There was another crash from the bar.

'I'd better go and talk to her while we've still got some furniture left,' said Heather.

She went through the door into the bar.

'Morning, Peggy.'

'It's not a good morning, thanks to you,' said Peggy.

'Me? What've I done,' said Heather, shocked by the

295

venom in Peggy's voice.

'Only interfered in my life,' she banged a chair back down on the floor.

'Peggy, I don't know what you're talking about.'

'Dave said you and Barry were talkin' about me, in the pub.'

'Pardon?' Heather's mind was working frantically. All Dave could have heard was her initial remark about Keith liking Barry's new girl friend. She repeated this to Peggy.

'No, there must 'ave been more than that. The bugger dumped me last night, and it's all your fault. I reckon you warned him off me.'

'Hang on. Of course I didn't. This has got nothing to do with me - and anyway, I thought you'd had enough of him?'

'I 'adn't quite made up my mind, till you interfered.'

'I've had enough of this conversation, Peggy. Perhaps you'd better go home and cool down. I'll finish off in here.'

Peggy flung down the duster she was holding.

'You can do the lot from now on - I can't work for people that don't show me no loyalty. And keep your trap shut about the boar, or it'll be the worse for you.'

Heather was about to tell Peggy not to threaten her, when she suddenly realised that Peggy was actually going to leave them. She stood back as the angry woman pushed past her into the kitchen and snatched her coat off the hook. Heather kept silent under the final glare directed at her, as the back door was wrenched open. It didn't matter how Peggy went, as long as she went. She and Alan had both had enough of her.

Alan came in through the same door, a few minutes later, and glanced towards the bar.

'It's quiet in there?'

'Wonderful news, darling,' said Heather.

'What?' he looked puzzled. 'Have we won the lottery?'

'Better than that. We've lost Peggy.'

'Lost?'

'She's just walked out.'

'Hells bells! Who's going to do the cleaning?'

'I thought you wanted to get rid of her. We'll do it between us until we find someone else.'

'What triggered this?' he asked.

Heather felt uncomfortable. Somehow she had managed to get involved in Peggy's life, again. She felt her hands distractedly rubbing the back of the same kitchen chair as Peggy had been, the day before, and snatched them away quickly.

'I think Dave implied that I was discussing her with Barry.'

'And were you?'

'Actually, I was trying not to. I told you, sitting on the fence is a very difficult art, which I seem unable to master. Peggy's unbalanced, anyway. I'm glad she's gone.'

'Damn!' Alan stood gazing out of the window, chewing his bottom lip.

'I'm sorry, Alan.' Why was she apologising? Peggy had been nothing but trouble.

'We'll give her a couple of days to see if she calms down,' he said. 'And if she doesn't, I'll put an advert for a cleaner, in the shop window. I hope she doesn't manage to damage our village trade.'

'I doubt she'll do that - they all know about the pig's head, and being arrested,' said Heather.

'Don't be too sure. That sort of thing can sometimes turn a person into a local hero, especially in a small community...they do tend to hang together against outsiders.'

Heather didn't answer this. She was trying to shake off a nasty feeling that all this could turn out to be her fault, although she couldn't quite see how.

'I brought you a magazine,' Alan said, taking the newspaper from under his arm and sliding a copy of Horse and Hound from its folds. There was a picture of a horse just like Mallard on its front cover.

'Thanks...I'd better finish the polishing,' she said, placing the magazine, face down, on the dresser.

CHAPTER FORTY-ONE

It was a relief to get out of the pub and away from the aura of Peggy's anger, which was still pervading the atmosphere there. Heather had considered taking Jimmy out for a ride, but the sky was heavy with cloud and it would not have been a good idea to get him wet before he had to face a chilly night.

She walked across the bridge and started up the road the other side, moving onto the verge to avoid a van coming towards her, and stumbling slightly in the deep ruts where countless winter rains had worn away the edge of the tarmac. As the vehicle came closer, she recognised it as Dave's. He pulled up alongside and wound down the window.

'I think I might have got you into a bit of trouble,' he said.

'Just a bit, if you mean Peggy.'

'I only told her I'd heard you saying someone said he liked Barry's new girl friend. I don't know why she went off the deep end at me. She stormed out saying she was going to 'have it out' with you. I don't know what's the matter with her. Now Mercy tells me Peggy's given up her job at the pub.'

'That's right. If she doesn't change her mind, we are going to have to find someone else to help us. If you hear of anyone who might be interested, let me know,' said Heather.

'Well...I didn't say this, all right?' he waited for her to agree that he hadn't said it - whatever it was.

'Right,' she said.

'Could be, Mercy might be interested. But she said she'll wait for a bit in case Peggy changes her mind.'

Heather thought for a moment. Having Mercy to work

for them would be an asset because she was such a good cook; and she herself wouldn't mind sharing the cleaning in exchange for having some of Mercy's dishes on the menu.

'All right. You didn't tell me that. But if you decide to, I could be interested.'

'Okay,' he tapped the side of his nose, wound up the window and drove on.

Near the top of the hill she turned into the Hawkridge track, skirting the ewe with the cauliflower ear, and her adolescent lamb, who had managed to avoid the butcher by living away from home with it's wandering mother. They were busy mowing the grass verge and took no notice of her. When she reached the entrance to the farmyard, she saw that the space where Mandy used to park her car was now taken up by the muck-spreader. So, she was still away.

Luke was there, though. He was standing at the entrance to the cows field, empty now, as the cows had been moved to the river meadow the day before. He didn't see her coming towards him, as he was contemplating how best to disentangle the tractor and harrow from a fence post and ten feet of barbed wire fencing, which he'd managed to wind round the harrow. When she spoke it made him jump.

'Hello, Luke. Problem?'

'No - I always harrow the field towing a fence post and some barbed wire. It's an old Devon custom.'

Heather didn't know whether to take this as sarcasm, or if Luke was making a joke; in which case she should try to laugh. A laugh would have come easily at the scene before her, but he staggered slightly as he took hold of the wire and she could see he wasn't entirely sober. She wondered if it was an offence to be drunk in charge of a tractor on your own land. Luke being somewhat unpredictable, she decided against the laugh and settled for a non-committal 'Oh,' instead. Then walked on into the farm yard, keeping a wary eye open for the pheasant.

She was searching at ground level, and consequently missed the sight of him launching himself off the cart shed roof at her. If he had done it silently he may well have scored a hit, but his screeching battle cry gave her just enough time to duck, and as he hadn't planned his attack any further than hitting the target, he over-flew and crashed into the end of the barn. He flapped, raggedly down the wall, accompanied by some detached feathers, to stand slightly stunned at the bottom. Heather made her escape through the field gate before he had time to recover.

As she fed Jimmy she heard the tractor start up again, and the rattle of the harrow as Luke resumed work.

....

After three days, Peggy still hadn't appeared for work, or contacted Heather and Alan. Then they learned that she had got a part-time job as a cleaner at the village school. The headmaster, who'd known Peggy for years, had decided to overlook her recent police record. This information had come from Mercy, when she came to offer her services in Peggy's place.

'She's a bit old,' Alan had said, as he and Heather discussed it, after telling Mercy they'd let her know.

'She's a wonderful cook,' said Heather.

Alan's eyes lit up. 'She is that. Maybe we could go on sharing the cleaning and get Mercy to cook?'

'Excellent idea,' said Heather, foreseeing that this would allow her more time in the mornings to look after Jimmy.

Mercy started work at the pub the following Monday, and they all relaxed into a comfortable routine. She was a gossipy soul, but she didn't seem to suffer from Peggy's moodiness. Occasionally Heather would look at her and have a mental image of her pushing Josiah down the stairs, and wonder if they were employing a murderess - maybe even a nymphomaniacal murderess. Had Mercy ever told Dave that Heather had seen them that night, in the churchyard? Probably not. Dave had never seemed in the least embarrassed with her.

Heather began to relax. With Peggy out of the way she felt more distanced from the goings on at Hawkridge, until one pleasant Friday evening session in the bar, suddenly became charged with menace.

Luke was in, sitting on his usual stool at the bar and chatting quietly to Dave. Two tables were occupied by people having meals, and Alan was leaning on the bar, with a half pint of Dave's cider, talking to Anne. Heather had just finished serving coffee to the diners and was having a sip of Alan's cider, when Keith Field and Barry came in.

Barry glanced at Luke, who acknowledged him from the other end of the bar with a slight nod, to which Barry replied with a nod and a tentative grimace, lost before it could become a smile. Luke continued to chat with Dave.

Heather moved along the bar to take Keith's order.

'Hello,' he said. 'That's a whisky for me...and, what are you having Barry?' he turned back to Heather. 'Barry just came out especially, to tighten up a loose shoe on Mallard, before the meet tomorrow.'

'Yes, I don't normally reckon to work this late in the evening...think I might join you in a whisky,' said Barry, still with a wary eye on Luke.

'That's two whiskies, then, Heather. And whatever you're having,' said Keith.

'Thank you,' she said. 'I think I might have a glass of cider.'

She got them their drinks, and pushed the water jug along the bar towards them.

'Oh, by the way,' Keith went on. 'I've decided not to part with Mallard until the end of the season.'

'Sshh!,' said Heather, glancing along the bar to see if Alan had heard this remark. It seemed he hadn't, he was still deep in conversation with Anne.

'Secret, eh?' asked Keith.

'Yes…not a word. Well, not until the spring, anyway.'

Heather reached under the bar for a half pint glass and was just about to move to the cider pump, when Keith asked Barry how Mandy was. Heather's eyes shot towards Luke - who was still talking to Dave - and then to Barry, whose drink went down the wrong way and precipitated a fit of coughing. Keith rescued the glass of whisky from his hand, and slapped him on the back.

By the time Barry had regained his composure, Keith had forgotten what he'd asked him, but Barry leaned towards him and whispered something. Keith looked quickly at Luke and then nodded, mouthing, 'sorry'.

So that was where Mandy had got to! Heather remembered the cosy chat Mandy and Barry had been having in the farmyard at Hawkridge. Well, good for her. And good for Barry, she thought. But possibly not so good for Barry when Luke found out. And even worse for Barry, when Peggy found out that she had lost two men to Mandy.

It wasn't long before Keith and Barry finished their drinks, and left. Heather heaved a sigh of relief and moved along the bar to talk to Alan and Anne, just in time to hear Dave ask Luke when Mandy was coming back.

'Next week, I hope. I'm going to ring her and tell her we haven't had any more trouble from Peggy. Looks as if she's learnt her lesson.' Luke shifted on his stool and his eyes caught Alan's, which *he* took to be a request for confirmation of this fact.

'Yes,' Alan said. 'I think she knows, now, that you can't go round mutilating peoples' pigs.'

As Heather realised exactly what Alan had just said, her stomach tightened itself into a knot; but Luke only nodded and turned back to Dave. After a minute, she let out the breath she had been holding...too soon.

Luke suddenly frowned, and looked back at Alan.

'What did you say about mutilating? She got that head from the butcher's. He told me that she...' He stopped speaking, and Heather watched his face with awful fascination, as light began to dawn, and he realised they were talking about two different pigs.

He turned on his stool so that he was directly facing Alan, who had gone pale, as the implication of what he'd just said began to sink in. Alan flashed a look at Heather who saw it coming, and turned away to pick up a tea towel.

'What did you mean, just then?' Luke asked. 'D'you know something I don't? Has Peggy told you something?' He looked at Heather, who was pretending to be busy. He turned back to Alan. 'The boar - did *she* do that? Come on, tell me.' He stood up and leaned threateningly across the bar. Dave put a restraining hand on his arm.

'No - no - I *was* talking about the pig's head. It did come from the butcher - yes - I was getting mixed up with that Mafia film where they put the horse's head in the bed.' Alan was speaking fast, and Heather could see beads of perspiration breaking out on his top lip.

'Of course Peggy didn't do that to the boar,' said Anne. 'A woman couldn't have done that.'

'Peggy could,' Luke spat at her.

Anne looked towards Heather for confirmation that the

frailer sex would not be capable of such an act. Heather just shook her head, noticing that, apart from physically restraining Luke, Dave was saying nothing. His eyes locked with hers for a second; the corner of one of his eyebrows flicked up and she realised that he'd suspected Peggy right from the start. She picked up some dirty glasses and began to run warm water into the small sink under the bar.

'Heather?' Luke was looking directly at her.

'Yes?' she squeezed washing-up liquid into the sink and turned off the water, glad that there were other people around and that there was a solid wooden bar counter between her and Luke.

'What do you know about this?' he asked.

'Only what everyone else does,' was her careful reply. 'Peggy put a pig's head in your bed.'

'She never talked to you?' he said.

'No,' she lied.

He turned back to Dave, who removed his hand from Luke's sleeve.

'I don't know - she bloody could of, you know. I thought it was that bugger from Lower Litten, but he was away.' He looked thoughtful for a moment, then tipped up his glass and drained it, setting it down on the bar with a bang. 'I'm going up there to have it out with her,' he said.

Dave looked up at the bar clock, which showed ten forty-five. 'Leave it, Luke. You can't go up there now. It's too late.'

Luke looked at his watch, while Heather quietly blessed the fact that he didn't seem to be as intoxicated as usual; and Alan regained some of his wits and offered Anne, Dave and Luke, 'one for the road'.

As they tidied the bar, after closing time, Alan asked Heather if she thought they should warn Peggy of Luke's suspicions.

'No!' she said vehemently. 'Keep out of it.' She would have liked to add 'you've done enough damage,' but Alan already knew this. She decided to keep the revelation about Mandy to herself. As long as Dave's tongue-loosening cider was around, Alan was not to be trusted. And, anyway, Dave would probably have a word with Mercy about Luke's suspicions. *She* would warn Peggy that Luke now suspected her of the bungled boar castration.

CHAPTER FORTY-TWO

Heather wasn't looking forward to going to Hawkridge again, in case Peggy and Luke had already clashed and, somehow, Peggy had managed to drag her into more trouble. But when she reached the farm, Luke's Land-Rover wasn't there.

She quickly fed Jimmy and turned him out into a sun-drenched morning. The air was crisp from an overnight frost, which was fast dissolving into steam, and rising off the grass and hedgerows where the sun touched them. It was impossible to feel gloomy on a morning such as this; somehow the weather had been far less noticeable in London. Two sparrows were twittering to each other on a roof truss inside the stable; waiting for her to finish mucking out so that they could investigate the corner where Jimmy's feed bucket stood, in case he had missed the odd oat.

She bedded the stable down with deep fresh straw, rolling it up the side of the box into a bank until it looked so cosy she could have slept there herself. Then, as Luke still wasn't back, she filled the haynet and water bucket, ready for the night, and walked across the field to give Jimmy a hug and a few peppermints. She promised herself another short ride to the top of the hill that afternoon, if the weather held.

In no hurry to get back into the low-ceilinged pub, which would seem dark after all this sunlight, she drove slowly back into the village.

'Any problems?' Alan asked.

'Luke wasn't there.'

'He's probably up at the council estate, killing Peggy,' he said.

'That's not funny, Alan,' she looked round. 'Where's Mercy?'

'She rang. She's got a headache.'

'That's what she says…I hope Luke *isn't* killing Peggy.'

Luke wasn't killing Peggy, because he had more important things on his mind. They heard later that he was out looking for Barry that morning, after a phone call from Mandy to say that she wasn't coming back…and why. Luke had wasted most of the morning driving around to those of Barry's customers that he knew, searching for him. He didn't find him because Mandy had phoned Luke from the airport, before she switched off her mobile and boarded a plane, with Barry, for a holiday in Florida.

Luke had arrived back at the farm, frustrated and furious.

That afternoon, when Heather pulled up in the farmyard, he was just setting off to go down to the cows' field with a large round bale of silage on the front forks of the tractor, and he didn't see her.

By the time she heard the tractor starting back up the hill, she had Jimmy saddled up and was leading him through the gate into the yard. As she went to shut the gate, the wooden latch snapped off. There was no stock in the field, so she left the gate open, intending to tie it shut with some twine when she returned. Luke drove the tractor into the yard just as she had mounted from the churn stand. He shouted something after her as she trotted away up the track, but she pretended not to hear.

She slowed Jimmy down as they reached the road and let him walk quietly along, relaxing into the rhythm of his stride. There was no urge for speed, today. She just wanted a quiet period away from the complications of other people's lives.

They turned off the road, and Jimmy plodded up the grassy track to the top of the hill on a loose rein, glancing sideways at the wandering ewe and her lamb as if he knew them well. They just moved a few steps out of his way. A robin was singing its sad little winter song from the hawthorn hedge on her right, a piping solo that always reminded her of holly trees and Christmas.

She gently tightened the reins and came to a halt under the bare branches of the beech tree, letting her eyes rest on the patchwork view spread out before her. With the winter sun so low, and the hedge-banks so high, every field still had a triangle of frost across its corner where the sun had been unable to reach it. Any stock in the fields was avoiding these patches, and soaking up the last of the day's warmth, before the promised frosty night. She could already smell the chill in the air as the huge red ball of the sinking sun touched the highest tors on Dartmoor.

She watched it setting for a few minutes, until Jimmy began to fidget. Then turned him round and walked back towards Hawkridge, trying to ignore the nervous twitch which was growing in the pit of her stomach as she faced the possibility of a confrontation with Luke.

The tractor was back in the yard; and the squeals and grunts coming from the sties behind the barn, indicated that Luke was round there feeding the pigs. Judging from the swearing that was accompanying the pig chorus, he was in a foul mood. And, from the angle at which he had parked the tractor, probably drunk as well. If she was quick, and quiet, she might just manage to get across the field to the stable, unnoticed.

The field gate, which she had left open, was now closed; and as she slid out of the saddle she found that Luke had tied it up so tight, with baler twine, that the knots were impossible to undo. After struggling with it for a few minutes, cursing under her breath at the delay, she finally gave up and, tying Jimmy to the top rail by his reins, climbed the gate and ran across the field to fetch her knife from the ledge in the stable.

She ran back as fast as she could, worried that Jimmy may try to free himself and break his reins - bridles were expensive. But he was still standing quietly waiting for her. She climbed over the gate and gave him a peppermint before turning her attention to cutting through the string.

'You knew, didn't you?' the snarl came from directly behind her - she froze. 'You knew about Mandy and Barry Martin, didn't you?'

The wave of alcohol fumes made her catch her breath, as Luke grabbed her shoulder and turned her to face him.

'No, I…'

'Don't lie, you bitch! You've known all along. And you knew about Peggy cutting the boar.'

'Let me go, Luke! I…'

'Don't bother lying - I've spoken to her. I'll deal with her when I've sorted the rest of you out, starting with you, as you're here. You stuck-up bitch.'

His hand moved down her arm, and he tried to drag her towards the pig sties. Heather struggled, hitting out at him with her other hand, half mindful of the sharpness of the knife it was holding, but unwilling to drop the only weapon she had. Luke stumbled against Jimmy, as they struggled, and the horse reared, snapping a long piece of the rotten top rail of the gate as the reins lifted it.

Luke hit out at the horse, who swung round and cantered away through the yard and out onto the track, the piece of wood banging against his legs as it was dragged along by the reins.

'Jimmy, whoa!' Heather shouted. 'Luke, let go of me! What d'you think you're doing? Let go!'

'Bitch!' was all he said, as he tried to grab her other, flailing arm.

She felt the knife go through his jacket, and into something more solid as it slipped up under his arm.

Almost immediately, she felt a warm wetness as blood poured out over her hand.

'You've cut me, you stupid bitch!' He let go of her and clasped his hand up under his arm.

Heather could see his sleeve turning black with blood. He staggered back a step or two, looking shocked. Freed from his grasp, she ran away along the back of the barn, past the pig sties, intending to cut across the corner of the field and, hopefully, reach Jimmy before he got out onto the main road.

The boar reared up, hooking its front legs onto the wall as she passed. Luke was following her and shouting, but his drunken staggerings were no match for her fear induced burst of speed. She looked back at him as she ducked between the two strands of the barbed wire fence round the field. He'd stopped chasing her and was leaning on the wall of the boar's pen, a hand pressed to his wound.

'Serve you right, you mad bastard,' she sobbed, as she ran on across the field and climbed through the fence onto the track, to find that Jimmy was still ahead of her.

Suddenly conscious of the knife in her hand, she flung it into the hedge. As it left her hand it nicked her finger which began to bleed, and she struggled to find a handkerchief in her pocket as she ran. She couldn't see Jimmy now, but heard his hooves hitting the tarmac of the main road ahead of her.

'Oh, no,' she groaned. 'Please don't let there be any traffic. Jimmy!' she shouted, then listened again.

Faintly to the right the clatter of hooves was suddenly silenced. He's turned into Small Profits, she thought. Well that was better than the main road. She ran on, her lungs beginning to hurt as she forced more air into them to cope with the unaccustomed exercise. The running became easier as she reached the main road, and started downhill towards the Small Profits entrance. Just as she was turning into the track, a flash of acid green in the half light, drew her attention to a bicycle in the distance. Oh, no. I don't need Peggy as well, now, she thought, as she ran on, hoping she hadn't been seen. She dropped to a walk to try and get some air back into her lungs. She couldn't hear Jimmy's hooves drumming on the track, any more. Then, as she walked round the last corner, she almost bumped into him. His flight had been halted by the closed gate into Dave's yard.

'Oh, good boy,' she said with relief, as he 'whickered' a greeting at her.

She untied the reins from the piece of wood, and inspected his legs as best she good in the gathering darkness. As far as she could see there were no cuts. Then she put both arms round his neck and rested her face against his mane for a moment, as she tried to think what to do. There were no lights on in Dave's house, and his van wasn't in the yard. She'd left her car at Hawkridge - but there was no way she was going back there.

The small field where she had picked the mushrooms was empty of stock, and she was sure Dave wouldn't mind if she used it - just for the night. She removed his saddle and led Jimmy through the gate. When she slipped the bridle off over his ears he took a few steps, then lay down and rolled the feel of the saddle off his back before getting to his feet, having a shake, and wandering off to inspect his new premises. He was walking sound, and it didn't look as if he had come to any harm from his recent experience.

Heather closed the gate. In the distance she thought she heard a scream, but it could have been a vixen on the prowl, calling for a mate. She took a few more deep breaths to calm herself; then picked up the saddle and set off down the field to the footpath along the river bank.

This way was a slightly shorter route to the main road at the bridge than going back along the farm track.

Reaching the shingle beach, trodden out by the cattle and sheep, she lowered the saddle and bridle onto the grass and crunched across the stones, until she could reach a hand into the water. It was very cold, but that was an advantage as it quickly and efficiently rinsed the blood off her hands and the right cuff of her shirt. She soaked her handkerchief and wound it round her cut finger.

Picking up the saddle and bridle, with semi-frozen hands, she climbed over the stile back onto the road, and walked briskly across the bridge. In ten minutes she had reached the village. The pub kitchen was warm and welcoming.

Alan, who was sitting at the table with a cup of coffee and the newspaper, looked up.

'Hello, darling. I didn't hear the car.' He studied her face. 'Are you all right?' he asked, then noticed the damp, and bloodied, handkerchief. 'You're bleeding. Have you fallen off?' He took the saddle from her as Heather sat down heavily on a kitchen chair.

'No, I'm not hurt. Just shocked. Can I have a brandy? Some of that will do,' she nodded towards a bottle on the dresser.

'What's happened?' he asked, pouring some cooking brandy into a mug, and glancing out of the window into the yard as he brought it to her. 'Have you had an accident? Where's the car?'

'It's still at the farm. Oh, Alan…' her lip quivered, and then she pulled herself together again. 'Luke was drunk, and he attacked me, and Jimmy got loose and ran away.'

Alan suddenly looked more angry than Heather had ever seen him.

'Luke attacked you! Why? Are you hurt? Was it something to do with this boar business? Where's Jimmy, now?'

'It was the boar and Peggy and Mandy and Barry, all rolled into one. He's found out about Mandy and Barry, and seems to think it was all my fault...I think he's gone mad. I've left Jimmy at Small Profits. Dave wasn't there.'

'Mandy and Barry?' He looked puzzled, then shook his head. 'Never mind about them. What did the bastard do to you? Are you hurt - apart from your hand?'

'No. I got away from him.' For some reason she decided not to mention the knife. If Luke told people she'd cut him, she would face up to it then, but she reckoned that when he'd sobered up he would be too embarrassed to admit how he'd got hurt.

Alan was pulling on his jacket and putting the car keys and his mobile phone into his pocket.

'Where are you going?' Heather got up from the table and stretched out a hand to him. He put his arms round her and held her tight for a moment.

'I'm going to fetch the car, and sort bloody Luke out, once and for all.'

'No Alan! He's dangerous....'

'Don't try to stop me,' he butted in. 'I'm not frightened of that bully. It's time someone stood up to him. If I'm not back in half an hour - phone the police.'

'No, Alan, don't, it's...' But it was too late. He'd gone; slamming the door behind him.

She realised she had forgotten to tell him that Peggy was probably at Hawkridge, as well.

Quarter of an hour ticked by, while she sat at the table staring unseeingly at the newspaper. Then she went upstairs and changed out of her riding clothes. Alan's specified half hour hadn't quite passed when she decided to try and ring him before getting the police. She went back into the kitchen. But just as she stretched out her hand to the phone, it rang, making her jump. It was Alan.

314

'Serious problems down here...,' he said. Heather was facing the window and missed his next words as an ambulance raced across the square, its siren drowning out his voice. It disappeared down the hill towards the river.

'I'm sorry. What was that? I couldn't hear you,' she said.

'There's been an accident here. I'm just waiting for the ambulance. Oh, I think I can hear it coming. It's not me. I'm okay, don't worry. Tell you when I get home.'

Over the phone she heard the siren, and Alan shout: 'Over here', then the phone was cut off.

Now what? She poured herself another brandy and tried to work out what could have happened. Had Alan had a serious enough fight with Luke to put him in hospital? She discarded this idea almost immediately. Alan had never had a fist fight with anyone, as far as she knew. It was more likely that Luke had done something awful to Peggy; she remembered the scream she had heard while she was at Small Profits, and thought was a fox. That made more sense. She swallowed a mouthful of brandy, and sat down at the kitchen table again.

The room seemed suddenly darker and her mind filled with a vision of a crumpled and bloodstained acid green anorak...so much blood. She got up quickly, walking across the room to shake away the picture - which went almost as fast as it had come. The darkness seemed to lift out of the room, and she remembered the similar feeling she'd had outside the pub when they'd first arrived in the village. She looked down at her hands. That premonition had come true...the knife...the blood. The hairs rose on the back of her neck.

Turning on the tap over the sink, she washed her hands again, with washing-up liquid; only she used too much and the sink filled up with froth which refused to rinse away. Why this should make her cry she didn't know, but she let

315

it happen and felt better afterwards.

The phone rang...Alan...she grabbed it with soapy fingers.

'Heather? It's Dave. I seem to have got your little horse in my field.'

'Oh, Dave, I'm sorry. He ran away and I caught up with him at Small Profits. Something's happened at Hawkridge. Is it all right if I leave him with you for a while? I'm not sure what's going on at the moment.'

'I thought I heard an ambulance, just now. Has that gone to Luke's? What's happened?'

'I don't know. Alan's there.'

' I'd better get over there and find out what's up.' He replaced the phone just as she was about to try to explain further.

'I'll take that as a 'yes', then,' she muttered, looking at her watch and willing Alan to come home - it was nearly opening time, and she didn't feel like having to face customers and make small talk.

She sat down at the table again, and stared blankly through the window across the dark square towards Hawkridge. She should have waited on the road and warned Peggy not to go up there. The phone rang again, and she snatched it up.

'Alan?'

'Yes. Look, darling, can you hold the fort for a bit. The police have just turned up and I've got to make a statement.'

'Alan, what's happened? Are you all right?'

'I'm fine. Don't worry. It's the other two who are hurt. Peggy was here. Oh God, what a mess...they want me now. I'll be back as quickly as I can. 'Bye.'

Police! If there was going to be some sort of a court case, Alan had now become mixed up in all this. They'd both been sucked into the crazy war between Peggy and Luke.

'Jimmy, it's all your fault,' she muttered. If she hadn't bought him they would never have got involved with Hawkridge. She inspected the bruises on her arm, where Luke had tried to drag her towards the pig sties, and felt sick as she wondered what fate she had escaped; and whether it had now overtaken Peggy.

She heard the siren again and watched the ambulance, lights flashing, race through the square and disappear along the Exeter road. Ten minutes later, Alan drove into the yard.

He came in through the back door, his face white and drawn, and his clothes soiled with mud and blood. As Heather rushed towards him, he held her off with one hand.

'No, don't! I'm filthy. I'm all right,' he said, pulling out a kitchen chair and sitting down heavily at the table. 'Get me a whisky, darling.'

Heather dashed into the bar and came back with two glasses and a bottle of Glenfiddich. She sat down opposite him and poured them both a generous measure, taking in the state of him, and feeling her face go pale as she realised just how much of the mess on his jacket was actually blood.

'Are you hurt?' she whispered, then found her voice and repeated the question.

'No,' he shook his head and sipped the whisky, before straightening slightly and leaning back in the chair. 'Oh, Heather, I don't ever want to see anything like that again. It was like something out of an old first world war film, except of course it was in gory technicolour. The mud and the blood, and his injuries. Oh, God!' he shook his head again as if to try and remove the picture. 'I don't know if he'll survive. He was unconscious and they said he'd lost an awful lot of blood.'

'LUKE?' She'd been so sure it was Peggy who'd been hurt by Luke. What on earth had Peggy done to him?

'Both of them - Peggy's not so bad. She'd been trying to get him out...well, she did, eventually.'

'Out of what? Out of where? For God's sake, Alan! Did Peggy start a fire?' No, it couldn't have been that. She'd have seen the fire engine.

'No fire - sorry, didn't I tell you? No, of course, the ambulance turned up at that point.
Luke's been attacked by the boar - the one Peggy was always saying was dangerous.'

She recalled her last sight of Luke, as she'd climbed through the barbed wire fence. He'd been leaning on the wall of the boar's sty, his hand clutched up under his arm where she had stabbed him. No! Not stabbed! It was an accident!

'You look as white as I feel, darling.' Alan stretched a muddy hand across the table towards her, saw the mess it was in, and withdrew it. 'Peggy managed to pull him out of the sty. She was attacked, as well,' he glanced towards the kitchen clock. 'I need a shower. Can you open up? I'll tell you all about this when I come down. Dave's gone to take Mercy to the hospital. Peggy's got some nasty bites and slashes on her legs and arms, and she's very shocked. Kept saying, over and over again, that she wanted to tell Luke she was sorry.

'Sorry?'

'If I understood it right, she'd gone down there to apologise for trying to castrate the boar. Pity the damn thing didn't die then. Oh God! Heather. Me and my big mouth. D'you think I precipitated all this with what I said last night in the bar?'

'It would have all come out eventually, I expect,' she said.

He pushed back his chair and stood up, finishing the last of his whisky as he did so.

'Dave said he'd ring from the hospital and let us know what's happening,' he took off his jacket, screwed up his face at the mess it was in, and dropped it on the floor beside the back door. 'I'll sort that out later,' he said.

Alan went upstairs, and Heather sat on for a few minutes. All the energy seemed to have drained out of her. She wasn't even sure she could stand up. She could see it all now. The knife must have severed an artery - there had been an awful lot of blood. She imagined Luke passing out as he leant against the wall, and falling into the boar's pen. Or maybe it had dragged him in. She saw again the evil little eyes, and the razor sharp tusks, and pictured the scene as the animal rooted at the wet patch under Luke's arm, excited by the smell of blood.

'No!' she said aloud, her hands gripping into fists.

As she tried to push this picture out of her head, another thought struck her. If Luke died - would that make her a murderer?

'Par for the course in this village,' she muttered, frantically trying to decide whether to tell Alan, and possibly the police, about the knife.

Her instinct for self-preservation, kicked in. She would wait and see. All this might not have had anything to do with the knife wound. Luke may have gone into the boar's pen and been careless. She didn't really believe this. If Luke died, she would speak up, she decided. Of course, if he didn't, then he would tell the police about the knife...or would he? That would be an admission that he had attacked her.

She looked at her watch. It was almost opening time. She got up and walked into the bar. As she switched on the lights she began to compose a story for Dave, to explain why she hadn't taken Jimmy back to Hawkridge. She decided on the truth. Dave was fairly circumspect, and he knew what Luke was like. She'd just say that he'd been drunk, had tried it on with her, and frightened the horse, and she hadn't wanted to go back until he'd sobered up.

She drew back the bolts on the door. There was nobody waiting to come in. The mixture of brandy and whisky she had drunk were beginning to make her head swim, and she went back into the kitchen for a mug of strong, black coffee. This was no time to be struggling with a fuddled head.

CHAPTER FORTY-THREE

It wasn't long before people began filtering into the bar. The unaccustomed sound of the police and emergency services tearing through the village had aroused the villagers' interest. Anne was the first.

'D'you know what's going on, Heather?'

'There's been an accident at Luke's farm.'

Alan came into the bar, his hair damp. He smelled of the expensive after-shave Heather had given him for his birthday, and she fell in love with him all over again.

'Why are you looking at me like that?' he asked, smiling.

'You smell nice,' she said, surprised at the strength of feeling for him which had suddenly swept over her.

'Thank goodness,' he said. 'I think I'm going to have to throw all those clothes away.'

'Clothes? We're having a jumble sale to raise money towards a new piano for the village hall,' said Anne.

Colin and Audrey came in.

'You wouldn't want these,' Alan said, as he drew a pint for Colin, while Heather got Audrey's drink.

'What's going on with all the police, and that?' Audrey asked.

'Something's happened at Hawkridge,' Anne told her, then looked enquiringly at Heather. 'There was an ambulance. Who was hurt?'

'Peggy and Luke,' said Alan. 'They're both in hospital. Luke's very bad, I'm afraid. It's going to be 'touch and go' for him.'

'What on earth's happened?' asked Anne. They were all staring at Alan, nobody had touched their drinks. 'Have they had a fight? Has Peggy gone too far with one of her pranks? What was she doing down there? I thought Luke and the police had banned her from the farm. Whatever has she done this time?'

'Possibly saved his life,' said Alan.

'I think you probably did that,' said Heather. 'Wasn't it you who called the ambulance? Or had Peggy already rung them?'

'It was me. I found Peggy crawling across the yard, when I arrived. She was trying to get to the phone. Luke was lying outside the boar's pen. He was unconscious.'

'Where's the boar?' asked Heather, imagining the vicious thing on the loose out in the dark, somewhere.

'It's still in the pen. Peggy managed to shut the gate after she'd dragged Luke out.'

'He was attacked by the pig? The one they had to call the vet out to?' Audrey asked.

'Didn't know pigs attacked people,' said Colin. 'Well, not the four-legged kind anyway.'

'Careful, Colin,' said Audrey.

'It happens,' said Anne. 'But you'd think Luke would have been more careful. He's had pigs all his life. How did Peggy get hurt?'

'The boar attacked her as she was pulling him out,' said Alan.

'I wonder what she was doing down there?' said Anne thoughtfully. 'Well, lucky for Luke she was there, I suppose.'

Neither Heather nor Alan answered her.

It was nearly nine o'clock before Dave rang. Heather answered the phone.

'I told Alan I'd let him know what's going on,' he said. 'Well, they think Luke may recover, though he 'crashed' twice in the accident and emergency. He's still unconscious and in intensive care, now. He's been in the operating theatre for the last hour and a half. They're not sure whether he'll lose his left arm, or not - it's terribly

322

damaged. That damn boar was trying to eat him alive.'

Heather gagged.

'Are you all right, Heather?'

'Yes, sorry, Dave…felt sick.'

'Nobody seems to know how he managed to get attacked, like that. What was it that frightened your horse?' Dave asked.

'Keep this to yourself, Dave, please.' Her heart was pounding as she told him her prepared story about Luke's drunken advances.

'Oh, right…sounds like him. Probably least said about that, the better. Where was he when you last saw him?'

'Standing by the pig sties,' she said.

'Right. Well, Peggy's okay now. They've stitched up her wounds, and she's under sedation. She's very shocked, and terrified that Luke might die. Mercy and I have been to see her but she's not making a lot of sense. I'm taking Mercy home now. If Luke recovers, I reckon you can tell Alan that him being there probably saved his life. Oh, and you can leave the little horse at my place. If you want to move him there permanently, I've got a stable you can use.'

'Dave, you're a saint,' said Heather with relief. She didn't care if she never saw Hawkridge again.

'Talk to you about that tomorrow. Mercy's waiting for me. 'Bye.'

''Bye, Dave… and thanks,' she hung up and went back to the bar to give them the news.

'Poor old Luke,' said Colin. 'Was he right or left-handed?'

There was a quiet moment while they all tried to visualise Luke lifting a pint of beer.

'Right, I think,' said Anne.

'Well, that's one small blessing,' said Audrey. 'Come on, Colin. Time we were off.'

By ten thirty the pub was empty. Alan stood in the doorway and looked out onto the silent square; shivering slightly in the frosty air.

'It doesn't look as if we're going to get anyone else in, tonight...I think I'll close early,' he said.

'Good idea. Are you hungry?' Heather asked.

'No, not really. There are a couple of prawn sandwiches left. I'll have one of those. How about you?'

'I'm just going to have a hot, milky drink and go to bed. Let's clear up in the morning. It's been a rather horrid day. Oh, by the way, Dave says I can keep Jimmy at Small Profits, from now on.'

'Excellent! I like Dave, he's sexy but sensible,' said Alan.

Heather smiled.

CHAPTER FORTY-FOUR

Mercy arrived for work looking tired, but full of praise for her daughter's bravery.

Heather told her to go home, but she said she would rather be busy.

'I've just rung the hospital,' she said. 'Peg says she's all right. They're giving her painkillers. She's not really bothered about herself. Luke's still hanging on - just about. He hasn't come round yet; and now they've discovered he's got a broken skull, along with all the other injuries.'

Had they found the knife wound? Heather felt sick.

Mercy prattled on, but nothing incriminating arose out of what she was saying.

Around mid-morning there was a phone call for her, from the hospital. Heather handed her the phone.

'Hello,' Mercy said. 'Right…Hello, Peg. What's happened?' she listened for a long time.

Heather hovered in the doorway, unwilling to leave the kitchen, horrified by the conviction that Peggy was telling her mother that Luke had died.

'When are they interviewing you?' Mercy asked.

Interviewing Peggy! The police? What could she tell them? Nothing, she thought. Peggy knew nothing about the stabbing…accident. Unless Luke had managed to tell her! Was he still conscious when she dragged him out? She gave up trying to be discreet and walked into the kitchen, and sat down at the table. I'm a murderer, she thought; and found her mind had got stuck - she couldn't think beyond this thought which filled her head.

Mercy said goodbye, and replaced the phone.

'They're coming to see Peggy. She's going to be on television!' she said.

'What?' said Heather stupidly.

325

'She'll be on television, this evening. The hospital have arranged for a hairdresser to come in.'

'Hairdresser?' said Heather.

'Are you all right?' Mercy asked, peering at her.

'She'll need her hair done…yes,' said Heather slowly, trying to drag herself back to normal.

'Yes. And Luke's come round.'

Heather felt as if an ice cold knife had pierced her stomach. I can't cope with much more of this, she thought.

'Come round? Conscious, you mean? Will he be all right? He's not going to die?'

'Seems not. Peggy says he recognised her, but he can't remember anything about last night. He seemed to think he'd had an accident with the tractor. Doesn't remember about the boar. Probably just as well.'

You never spoke a truer word, Heather thought.

Halfway through the lunch-time session, the television people rang to ask if they could interview Alan. He surprised Heather by saying no.

'Why not?' she asked. 'It could be good for business, perhaps.'

'You know what I'm like,' he said. 'I'd have to invent a plausible reason why I was down at Hawkridge; and I'm no good at that sort of thing. I don't think we'll tell the whole truth, not with Luke lying there half dead. I'll have a quiet word with him about attacking you, when he's recovered.'

'No, don't. I think it would be best just to forget it, darling. What did you tell the police at the farm?'

'Oh something vague about the horse running away and I'd come down to fetch the car; nobody was really bothered about that.'

When they had closed the pub, after lunch, Heather went down to Small Profits to make a proper arrangement with Dave about keeping Jimmy at livery there. The stable he

326

was offering was actually in the farmyard, not far from the house, and was stone built with a nice tiled roof - altogether more in keeping with Jimmy's status as a thoroughbred, she thought.

They discussed Luke's return to consciousness, and Heather said that maybe Luke wouldn't even remember she had been there, just before his accident.

'Oh, by the way,' Dave said. 'I never mentioned to anybody what you said about Luke being drunk and trying it on with you. Like I said, that's best forgotten, I reckon, as things have turned out. We'll just tell him you've moved Jimmy here while he's in hospital, so's I can keep an eye on him for you.'

'Thank you, Dave. I agree. In view of what's happened, I think it is best forgotten.' She looked round the peaceful yard. 'Luke's mad pheasant doesn't get down this way, does he?'

'No,' Dave laughed. 'Most I can provide in the way of dangerous livestock is that old ewe from Moor Farm, and she's only grumpy when she's got a new lamb.'

Mercy tapped on the kitchen window, and waved. Heather waved back.

'I'm taking her to the hospital, in a minute,' said Dave.

'Might see you on TV, as well, then.'

'Not if I can help it,' he said.

'Tell Peggy we'll come and visit her tomorrow afternoon...I don't expect Luke's allowed visitors yet?'

'Only family, at the moment, but he's only got a brother; lives up country somewhere. Peggy said she'd try to get in touch with him. I think the police said they would try, as well.'

'Right,' said Heather. 'I'm just going round to Hawkridge now, to collect some of Jimmy's food. Who's doing the milking up there at the moment?'

'I've got a relief bloke in. I'm looking after the sheep and the pigs.'

'What's going to happen to the boar? Will it be destroyed?' Heather asked.

'No, I don't think so. We'll have to see. It probably wasn't the boar's fault.'

No, it was mine, Heather thought. Why should the boar die?

That evening they watched Peggy being interviewed about her daring rescue of Luke. She was loving the attention, until the interviewer asked her why she thought the boar had become so dangerous to humans. Alan looked at Heather and raised an eyebrow. Heather tried to smile but she was too busy trying to listen to Peggy's answer, which was just something along the lines that all farm animals could be dangerous.

'I'll go along with that,' said Alan. 'Though castration without anaesthetic could possibly have stuck in his little piggy mind.'

Heather and Alan arrived at the hospital, the following afternoon, carrying two bunches of flowers. A nurse directed them to Peggy's ward, but her bed was empty, and enquiries drew the information that she was probably in the intensive care ward.

They made their way there and, through the glass door, were treated to the sight of Peggy, wearing a brilliant orange dressing gown and scarlet lipstick, sitting beside Luke's bed and holding his hand. His head, on the pillow, was turned towards her.

'D'you think we should go in?' Alan asked.

'We're probably not allowed to. We're not family. No. Let's go back to Peggy's ward and send a message by somebody, to say we're here.' Heather was suddenly afraid that her presence may stir up memories, in Luke, which should stay forever buried.

Peggy joined them for long enough to thank Alan, again, for getting help out to the farm, but she was obviously dying to get back to Luke, so they didn't stay long.

'Would you take these to Luke,' Heather said, giving her one of the bunches of flowers. 'The others are for you, Peggy. I'm so glad to see that you at least are up and about.'

Peggy looked at her bandaged arms and legs, and grimaced. 'Oh, I'll be all right. I'm tougher than I look.'

That must make you pretty tough, Heather thought.

'Will Luke recover completely?' she asked.

'Well, 'e'll always feel the effects, and they still think that he may lose his left arm. It's terribly damaged. 'E's goin' to need all the 'elp 'e can get when 'e comes 'ome. But I'll be there for 'im. There's not much on the farm that I can't do. Anyway, thank you for coming...I'd better get back to 'im now.'

As they left the hospital and walked over to the car, Heather began to feel hopeful about the future. She hadn't become an inadvertent member of the local band of murderers; and nobody had mentioned a knife wound.

'Those two were looking a bit cosy. Do you think the war between them might really be over?' Alan asked.

'Oh, I do hope so,' said Heather, with feeling. 'I thought we came to Devon for some peace and quiet.'

'I think you've lost weight, darling,' said Alan.

'I'm not surprised. Come on, lets go and find us a cream tea, and put some of it back.'

CHAPTER FORTY-FIVE

Peggy was discharged from hospital after four days, and limped up the garden path to a hero's welcome from the neighbours, who had hung banners over the door and arranged a bit of a party at Mercy's house. Heather and Alan went up there with some drinks for the assembled neighbours and friends.

Peggy accepted the acclaim with less enthusiasm than Heather would have expected, but that was partly due to the fact that Luke had lost the battle to keep his arm, which had been amputated. The evidence of the stabbing had gone into an incinerator somewhere. Heather was just beginning to relax about this when she remembered the knife she had thrown away.

She spent a fruitless hour searching for it, later that afternoon, but it had been nearly dark when she had got rid of it and she couldn't remember how far up the track she had been when she had hurled it into the hedge. The search was interrupted by Dave driving back up the track after feeding the pigs, and she had to pretend she was just going up to Hawkidge to collect a bucket for Jimmy. She had to go past the pig sties to carry through this subterfuge, and the boar was still there. He reared his front feet up onto the wall as she passed, sniffing the air. She noticed, with a crawling sensation of fear, that there was a dark stain running down the outside of the wall, below his trotters. The blood should have all been on the inside. This must have come from the stab wound, as Luke leaned against the wall.

Heather spent the next twenty minutes carrying buckets of cold water, and casting nervous glances behind her as she scrubbed at the wall with a yard broom. Finally the stain had almost disappeared, trickling to the base of the wall in a pink stream. She flung the remains of the bucket at the wall and set off back to Small Profits, wondering if she would ever be free of the ramifications of that one small self-defensive act.

…………

It didn't take long for Peggy to demonstrate the 'toughness' she had boasted about in the hospital, by moving back into Hawkridge and taking on most of the farm duties, with some assistance provided by Dave and the relief cowman. It would be a while before Luke joined her, but his condition was continuing to improve.

Peggy was now enjoying her status as a local celebrity, and magnanimously forgave Heather and Alan for what she still reckoned was their 'disloyalty'. Heather swallowed all the comments she could have made, and shook hands with Peggy, for the sake of peace. Relieved of having to nurse Peggy's secrets, she could now concentrate on trying to wipe the memory of her own out of her mind, and devote her time to Alan, the pub, and Jimmy.

Mercy was spending more and more time at Small Profits. She had made new curtains for the sitting room at the farm - after a long discussion in the pub kitchen, with Heather, over a choice of materials. This had all been pretty pointless as Heather had gone for a very tasteful green and yellow ivy design, which had had the immediate effect of hardening Mercy's conviction that the pink and blue floral print would be perfect.

'What does Dave say?' Heather asked.

'Him? He doesn't care. Tomorrow I'll bring in the tiles I'm looking at for the bathroom and you can help me choose.'

'I'll look forward to it,' Heather smiled.

Alan grinned as he watched Mercy laying out a selection of tiles on the kitchen table, the next morning.

After the lunch time session, while he and Heather were having a snack in the kitchen, he mentioned the tiles; wondering whether Dave preferred dolphins to roses?

'Probably dolphins,' said Heather. 'But I bet he gets roses.'

'Has Mercy actually moved in there, yet?' Alan asked.

'Not quite. I think she's plucking up the courage to finally give up her council house. It's a big decision. I don't think it's too easy to get back on the council list once you've made a move like that...also, I don't think Dave has actually asked her, yet.'

'D'you think he will?'

'She may wear him down. He plays his cards very close to his chest, does Dave. He doesn't give much away.'

. . . .

Mercy had already left, the following morning, having decided on tiling Dave's bathroom with pink roses. Heather was placing clean ashtrays on the tables on her way across the bar to open the door for the lunch-time session. There were a couple of minutes to go, and she idly watched through the window as the bus from Exeter drew up in the square. Only one passenger got off, and it wasn't anyone she recognised. The woman took the suitcase the driver was handing down to her, and placed it on the ground. It looked heavy. The bus pulled away, heading for Barnstaple.

The woman, who was probably in her mid-fifties, was smartly dressed in a fawn overcoat with a silk scarf tucked casually into the neck. She pushed dark brown hair back from her forehead and gazed around the empty square.

The church clock began to chime, and Heather pulled back the bolts on the door into the square. As the door opened, the woman seemed to come to a conclusion and, picking up the case, she crossed the square to the pub. She left the case by the door and went up to the bar and ordered a drink from Alan. It was a dreary day and Heather had gone to the far end of the bar to switch on the wall lights.

As they came on, the woman turned, and saw her for the first time. Heather smiled at her, but the woman just gave her a penetrating stare before taking the drink to a table in the corner. From there she seemed to be keeping watch on the door.

Anne came in, glowing from just being dragged round the village on a cat hunt, by Rudi.

'I've left the little bugger at home,' she said, in answer to Heather's query at Rudi's absence. 'He's got the wind under his tail this morning... after anything that moves.' She glanced round the bar. 'New face. Who's that?' she whispered. The woman was staring out of the window, and across the square.

'Don't know,' Heather whispered. 'She just got off the Exeter bus.'

'Usual,' Anne said to Alan, who was already waving a glass under the gin optic.

There was the sound of boots stamping mud off on the cobbles outside, and Dave came into the bar. The woman half rose, then sat down again and took a sip of her beer, her dark eyes fixed on him.

'Morning,' said Dave. 'Pint please.'

As he heaved himself onto his usual stool at the bar, he glanced round the room. Then froze, half onto the stool, one foot on the brass rail, and the other on the floor. 'Bloody hell!' he breathed.

333

The woman beckoned him urgently over to join her in the corner. Dave went as if in a trance, forgetting the pint which Alan had just pulled for him.

'Oh dear! Has Dave got himself another woman? That'll cause trouble,' said Anne.

'She's brought a suitcase,' said Heather. 'Do you think she's planning to stay with him? Maybe she has a husband who's thrown her out.'

'Who is that?' asked Alan, realising there was a small drama playing out at the other end of the room.

'Shhhh!' said Heather and Anne together. They were trying to hear what was being said between the two.

The woman and Dave were deep in conversation. As they spoke, he reached for his pint on the table, before realising he had left it on the bar. Heather carried it over to him, catching the end of the woman's last sentence: '...so I thought I'd come and get what's rightly mine. We're still married.' Dave nodded abstractedly at Heather as she placed the glass on the table, and both he and the woman waited for her to leave before continuing their conversation.

'Is Dave still married? That's not her is it?' Heather asked Anne.

'No. Unless there's another one we don't know about. Always been a dark horse, that Dave. Why do you ask?'

'She just said they were still married.'

'What's that doing here?' The woman's voice was raised. She was pointing at the sampler hanging on the wall behind Dave's head. He turned round to look.

'I don't know. Don't recall seeing it before. Why?'

'Nothing. Never mind.' The woman dragged her eyes away from the sampler and lowered her voice again. Then she and Dave rose. He carried their empty glasses to the bar.

'Can you save us a table for lunch,' he said. 'I'll just go

and get cleaned up.'

Picking up the woman's suitcase, he held the door open for her and they walked across the square to where he had parked his pick-up. Heather and Anne watched through the bar window as the car drove slowly away down the hill towards Small Profits.

'Well! A mystery!' said Anne.

'What's a mystery?' asked Peggy, as she and Mercy came into the bar. 'That's a pint, and what you 'avin', Mum?' She turned to Heather. 'Mum says she made jugged hare for you today. I fancied some of that for lunch. I think I've done enough already today to qualify for a bit of a treat. Did all the milkin' myself, this mornin'.' Peggy still had bandages on both legs and one arm, but seemed to be managing well.

'What's this mystery, then?' Peggy asked Anne.

'Oh, nothing important,' said Anne.

'We'll sit over there, then,' said Peggy, and she and Mercy took their drinks over to a table.

Anne was chatting to Alan, and they were laughing about Rudi's latest exploits, when the door opened and Dave and the woman came back in - this time without the suitcase.

Dave looked round the bar, saw Peggy and Mercy, and pointed them out to the woman. At that moment Peggy looked up, half rose, turned paper white, and sat down again heavily. Mercy turned to see what had so affected her daughter.

'My God! It can't be! You'm dead!' Mercy gasped.

'We thought you was drowned,' Peggy whispered, hoarsely.

'You were meant to,' Rose Butler said grimly. 'I didn't want that bugger following me. I had to get right away from him - for good. He threatened to kill me when I said I wanted to leave him. I was really scared. I though the best

335

thing I could do was to pretend I was dead, so I left that bottle by the river, where I used to sit.'

Mercy and Peggy rose and came across to the bar.

'That fooled everyone,' said Mercy. 'All these years I've been feeling bad about not realising how depressed you were.'

'I'm sorry, Mercy. But you can see how I couldn't say anything. After I left the bottle, I went back to the house for some money I'd hidden in the wardrobe. Couldn't take any clothes or anything. Couldn't even take my handbag. I ran out of the side door just as he drove the tractor into the yard.'

'But you don't drive. How...? Rose interrupted her.

' I was telling Dave,' she glanced at him. 'I went across the fields and through the wood and caught the Exeter bus on the main road. Luckily, I didn't see a soul I knew.'

'How have you managed? It's been nearly four years. Where did you go?' asked Mercy.

'Down to Plymouth. Got a live-in job cleaning at a guest house. They never asked too many questions. I just told them the truth. Battered wife, escaped from husband without being able to collect handbag and any papers. They didn't bother as long as I did a good job.'

'But what about that stuff on the television news, about you vanishin'? Didn't anyone down Plymouth recognise you? Peggy asked.

'I gave them a different name, so they didn't connect me with that. I enjoyed it down there. Nice clean job in the dry. No tramping around a muddy farm in all weathers. Made some friends. Then I saw what had happened to Luke, and you,' she nodded at Peggy, 'on the telly. Since it looked as if you two were a bit of an item, I thought I might as well come back and get a divorce. After all, half of those two farms is legally mine, and I could do with the money. I know Luke's still in hospital, so I was going back to Hawkridge, but Dave said you were living there, Peggy.'

'I...' Peggy couldn't go on. She just shook her head at Rose.

'Are you all right, Peggy?' Anne asked. 'Get her a brandy, will you, Alan. On me.'

'Sorry to hear about Josiah, Mercy,' said Rose.

'Yes. It were very sudden. I was next door with Jenny and Josie, and we heard this crash, and bumping. We ran in, but he was dead. Gone from top to bottom of the stairs by the look of it.'

Heather's head was spinning. So, Mercy hadn't killed Josiah. She had an alibi. And Luke hadn't killed Rose. She clutched her arms across her chest; the only near murderer in this room was her.

'What's the matter, darling? Cold? Shall I turn the heating up?' asked Alan.

'No. I'll go and get a cardigan.'

She went upstairs, trying to work out the ramifications of this latest turn of events. First of all, it looked as if there was nothing, now, to stop Luke and Peggy getting married - once a divorce had gone through. That would be a good thing.

Where had Dave taken Rose's suitcase? Had that ended up at Hawkridge? Or Small Profits?... DXXR...A vision of a bathroom tiled with roses by an expectant Mercy. She groaned and hoped Rose had found herself a new man in Plymouth.

Heather stood in the bedroom, trying to remember why she had come upstairs. Cardigan! Yes.

Back in the bar she saw that Rose and Dave, had joined Mercy and Peggy at their table. Mercy was staring at Rose like a hypnotised snake.

'What's Mercy looking at her like that for? I thought she and Rose had been friends,' said Anne quietly.

'She's just found out that Dave took Rose's suitcase to Small Profits,' said Alan.

'Oh dear!' said Heather. 'I'd better get Peggy and Mercy's lunch - do they want starters, Alan?'

'No, just the main course, the jugged…'

'Yes, I know,' said Heather.

Peggy and Mercy stood up and began to put their coats back on.

'Hold the lunch,' said Alan.

'I've got to go and see Luke,' said Peggy, easing her bandaged arm carefully into her pink jacket. 'I'll explain it to him, Rose. If you walked in there 'e might die of shock. 'E's not very strong at the moment. Come on, Mum. We've just got time to catch the bus.'

'I'll be down this evening, Dave,' Mercy said pointedly, as Peggy dragged her towards the door. 'Oh, and sorry about the lunch, Heather.'

'Come on, Mum, quick.' The Exeter bus was just pulling up in the square.

Dave watched them go. It was the first time Heather had ever seen him look worried. He turned back to Rose, and took her hand across the table. She smiled at him.

'Oh! oh!' said Alan and Anne together.

When all the lunch time customers had left, Heather was just clearing the tables and emptying ash trays when she glanced up at the sampler, wondering if Rose would like it back. Then realised what she was reading.

'That's me!' she whispered. 'Twixt wielded steel and razor tooth, be only one who knows the truth.' I'm the only one who knows the truth. How much could Rose, with her second sight, see?

'What, darling?' said Alan.

'Nothing.'

'Oh, I thought you said something.'

'No. I think I'll give this to the next jumble sale.' She took the sampler down off the wall and went to the kitchen

338

where she wrapped it in newspaper. She very nearly put it in the dustbin, but Rose had seen it and might ask for it. She would keep it out of sight for a while: then destroy it if no-one else mentioned it.

. . . .

The next morning, Mercy came in through the back door doing a very good imitation of one of Peggy's more dramatic entrances. Alan stuck his head round the door from the bar.

'That sounded like Peggy,' he said.

Heather, who'd seen Mercy's face, shook her head at him. Mercy stared at him.

'Two-timing bastard,' she said grimly.

'Me? What've I done?' asked Alan, eyes open wide.

'Not you. That bloody Dave!' Mercy wrenched open the cupboard door, and knocked another chip out of the door frame with the vacuum cleaner.

Alan cast a frantic, questioning glance at Heather over Mercy's head, as she bent to pick up the box of polish and dusters. Heather raised her shoulders in an elaborate shrug.

'What's the matter, Mercy?' she asked.

'He's only told me we're finished! Says he's always been in love with Rose! Well, we'll see about that. He can't lead me on like that and then dump me, after all I've done for him; getting the house nice and everything. I'll get him back - you see if I don't.' She pushed past Alan in the doorway, and began to bang the chairs up onto the tables in the bar. There was a crash of broken glass as an ash tray slid across a table top and onto the floor.

Heather and Alan stared at each other across the kitchen.

'Déjà vu,' they chorused, despairingly.

THE END

339